P9-DYZ-824

Apart at the Seams

Center Point
Large Print

Also by Marie Bostwick and available from
Center Point Large Print:

Between Heaven and Texas
Ties That Bind

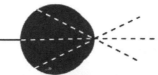

**This Large Print Book carries the
Seal of Approval of N.A.V.H.**

Apart at the Seams

MARIE BOSTWICK

CENTER POINT LARGE PRINT
THORNDIKE, MAINE

This Center Point Large Print edition is published in the year 2014 by arrangement with Kensington Publishing Corp.

Copyright © 2014 by Marie Bostwick.

All rights reserved.

The text of this Large Print edition is unabridged.
In other aspects, this book may vary
from the original edition.
Printed in the United States of America
on permanent paper.
Set in 16-point Times New Roman type.

ISBN: 978-1-62899-143-7

Library of Congress Cataloging-in-Publication Data

Bostwick, Marie.
Apart at the seams : a Cobbled Court Quilts novel / Marie Bostwick. —
   Center Point Large Print Edition.
   pages cm. — (A Cobbled Court Quilts novel)
   Summary: "When her marriage of twenty-six years seems to be coming
apart at the seams, Gayla flees to New Bern, Connecticut, to see if she
can overcome the feelings of betrayal, forgive her husband, and create a
new future"—Provided by publisher.
   ISBN 978-1-62899-143-7 (library binding : alk. paper)
   1. Female friendship—Fiction. 2. Quilting—Fiction.
   3. Connecticut—Fiction. 4. Large type books. I. Title.
PS3602.O838A83 2014
813'.6—dc23
                                                    2014011822

With thanks . . .

To Anne Dranginis for her expert and insightful advice on legal matters, and for her friendship, which I value so very much.

To Betty and John Walsh, Lisa Sundell Olsen, and Jamie Van Kirk, my first-round readers, for helping search out all those missing words and misplaced commas. Without you, I'd be lost and my poor readers would be confused.

To Audrey LaFehr, my editor, and Liza Dawson, my agent, for being so generous with their advice, encouragement, and patience during a project that turned out to be a lot more challenging than any of us realized. Thank you for hanging in there with me, ladies.

To Brad, who makes me happy.

❧ Prologue ❧

Gayla Oliver

Have you ever thrown a pity party?

It's easy and requires no advance planning whatsoever. For pity parties, spur of the moment is the norm. Start with a life crisis, a betrayal, a major disappointment, or a smattering of all three, add a carton of cigarettes, two boxes of Kleenex, and a bottle of whatever alcohol you have on hand (scotch works well and, as an added benefit, will clear your sinuses), and you're good to go. No need to call a caterer or send out invitations; pity parties generally have a guest list of one. And if conditions are right, they can last for days. Or even weeks.

Mine did.

Because the thing is, even though Brian wrote that . . . What was it he wrote? I'll have to go back and look at the exact wording. Ah, yes. Here it is.

> Gayla, I'm sure it will come as no surprise when I tell you I am unhappy in our marriage. It's obvious that you are as well and have been for some time.

But I *was* surprised. Shocked! Gobsmacked! As Brian would say. And no matter what he said, I *was* happy with our marriage, or happy enough. But not *un*happy—definitely not.

I am forty-five years old. Brian is forty-seven. We have been married for twenty-six years. In that time, I've seen a lot of my friends get married and divorced, sometimes more than once. Lanie is on her third husband. These things happen.

When they do, and word gets out, and the gossip mill starts churning, somebody always says, "Well, she *must* have known. Down deep, she had to have at least *suspected*. I mean, really. They've been growing apart. Anyone with eyes in their head could see what was going on."

Sometimes the person who says it has been me.

Maybe it's true, at least some of the time. But now I think this is one of those statements we toss out, not because we necessarily believe it but because we *need* to believe it. Why? Because if those women, those *other* women, knew deep down what was happening and chose to look the other way, then it means that the fault was at least partially their own. And that means that the rest of us are safe.

Maybe some women do know. I wasn't one of them. Until I stumbled across that memo, the possibility that Brian and I would not stay married for the rest of our lives never crossed my mind.

Brian wrote the memo last July. And as of May,

8

when I found it, he hadn't sent it. Obviously, I wasn't supposed to know about it. But I did know. And now that I did, what was I supposed to do? I couldn't quite wrap my head around it. How could this be happening?

Brian and I are the solid couple, the ones who've made it. The people who other people point to when looking for proof that marriages really *can* last if you stick with it.

Okay. Sure. Things aren't as exciting as they were early on, but what did he expect? We couldn't spend the rest of our lives just floating around Italy on a barge. Yes, in the early days we had been content living on love and ramen noodles, but that was before we had kids and jobs and a mortgage. Two mortgages, thanks to him! And now, out of the blue, after all we've been through together, after the years and the work and the beating of the odds, he says he's unhappy and wants to divorce?

And the thing that really shocks me is that he assumes his announcement will come as no surprise. But I never saw it coming. Until two weeks ago, on a Friday in May that was as cold as February, I thought he was happy. I thought we both were.

1

Gayla

A cold, sleety rain was falling that day. Everyone in Manhattan, including me, was trying to flag down a cab. I stepped off the curb and into the street as far as was possible without getting run over. After five minutes of frantic waving, a black SUV sped past, spattering me with muddy water. Not an auspicious beginning to the day.

I decided to walk, which made me late for the dentist and every other appointment I'd scheduled that morning. Skipping lunch helped make up some of the lost time but did nothing to improve my spirits. As I was heading back to the apartment for my two o'clock phone conference, I decided to take a detour down West Twenty-fifth Street so I could walk past The City Quilter, thinking that might cheer me up.

If you want to buy silk, organza, or charmeuse, you can find yards upon yards of it in shops that cater to the wholesale design and garment trade. But plain old fabric, the kind people use to make quilts, is hard to find in Manhattan. I don't know of another shop in the city that sells only cotton fabric, let alone caters exclusively to quilters.

Now, let me say this up front: I don't sew. I can

barely even thread a needle. But if I'm anywhere near West Twenty-fifth, I always find an excuse to walk past this shop. I just love looking through the window at all that gorgeous fabric—florals, checks, plaids, polka dots, abstracts, geometrics, and pastoral prints with landscapes, animals, and birds, as well as edgy urban designs of cityscapes, taxicabs, even maps of the subway. It always makes me wish that I'd spent a little more of my youth bolstering my creative side. Assuming I have one, which seems doubtful.

I've never ventured through the door of The City Quilter. What would be the point? But that day I spotted this fabulous red paisley in the back left corner of the display. It was the exact color of the sweater Brian bought in Italy right after we were married. He wore it until it was threadbare. I was thinking about going inside to get a closer look when my phone rang.

Lanie was calling. She didn't wait for me to say hello or offer a greeting herself, just started talking, assuming I'd be interested in whatever she had to say, which is usually true.

"You will not *believe* this, Gayla. I'm at the consignment shop, and I've found the most *stunning* vintage mink coat. Stunning! Princess cut, *enormous* collar, perfect condition, with stripes of—wait for it—lunaraine and platinum—"

"Lunaraine and platinum?"

"Lunaraine and platinum," she said again, as if

11

repeating the words were the same as defining them. "Brown and white. The coat has a vertical pattern of brown and white mink pelts. Exquisite! And they're *only* asking seventeen hundred—a bargain. It's too small for me, but you must have it! You *must!*"

Lanie has adopted a pattern of speech, not entirely uncommon among New Yorkers, that places emphasis on certain words, transforming them into selling points. It's the vocabulary and cadence of a woman who knows how to close the deal, which is exactly what Lanie is and why she's made such a success in real estate. But today, I wasn't buying.

"Lanie, where would I ever wear a mink coat?"

"To the opera, the ballet. The A&P. Anywhere you want. It's New York!"

"I don't think so. I couldn't stand the idea of animals dying just so I can go to the A&P looking stunning."

"They died back in the seventies, so what do you care? It's *vintage!* Oh, never mind," she said after a moment, realizing she was getting nowhere.

That's another reason Lanie is so successful: When her arguments fail to convince, she lets go and moves on. Sometimes.

"Where are you?"

"Standing outside a fabric store. What if I made Brian a quilt for his birthday?"

"Oh, please," she groaned. I could almost hear her eyes rolling.

"What? Brian's birthday is just a couple of months off. Don't you think he might like something I made myself?"

Lanie groaned again.

"No. I do not think your husband would like a quilt for his birthday. No man wants a *quilt* for his birthday."

"How do you know?"

"Because I've been married three times. I am an expert on men. And I'm telling you, no middle-aged man wants a *quilt* for his birthday. What a man in his late forties wants is a sports car, or tickets to a playoff game, or lingerie—basically the same things he wanted in his late twenties or his late teens—the three 'Ss': speed, sports, and sex. Emphasis on the third 'S.' Men aren't complicated, Gayla. They don't change that much."

"No?" I said with a smile, still holding the phone to my ear as I gazed at a blue, white, and gray quilt that hung on a wall near the checkout counter, wondering how long it took to make something like that. "Then why have you been married three times?"

"Because women *do* change. At least I did. And because of that third 'S.' And because men are all the same."

"Not all men," I said.

"Not all," she conceded. "You got the last good

one. Brian is too sweet to cheat. Or maybe he's just too British. Adultery is so impolite, don't you think?"

"Uh-huh," I agreed absently. "Utterly déclassé."

"And beneath the dignity of a viscount."

"Except Brian's not a viscount," I corrected. "Second sons don't count, remember? Especially second sons who run off and marry Americans."

"He's still an aristocrat," Lanie replied. "I think my fourth husband should be an earl."

I frowned. "Fourth husband? Is there trouble in paradise?"

Lanie has always had a thick skin, and as the years have passed it's only gotten thicker. Sometimes I can't tell if she's teasing or if she's serious. Sometimes I'm not sure she can either.

"No, Roger's a doll. But it pays to be prepared. And anyway, I think I'd make a terrific Countess of Something or Other. Or even better, *Dowager* Countess—like Maggie Smith in *Downton Abbey*. So old and opinionated and rich that nobody can dare tell me off."

"But aren't you all that now?"

"You are hilarious," Lanie replied flatly. "Anyway, tell Brian to keep an eye out for an old earl with a bad cough. After all, he owes me. If I hadn't convinced you to take that semester abroad, the two of you might never have met."

"And we'd probably still be living in a teeny-weeny one-bedroom walk-up. And Maggie would have had to elope. Who besides you could have gotten us into the Central Park Boathouse for the reception? And with only three months' notice?"

"What can I say?" Lanie said with a sigh, as if honesty would not allow her to deny it. "When you're in the fairy godmother business . . . So how is our little princess? Still in love with her prince?"

"Madly."

"Well, she'd have to be to follow him to North Carolina. I still can't understand why they didn't move to New York."

"Because Jason's dad offered him a good job and because Manhattan is too expensive for a young couple starting out."

"Expensive," Lanie countered, "but not *too* expensive. You and Brian managed. Nate managed when he lived here."

"Yes, but my darling son doesn't care where he lives, as long as it has Wi-Fi. He's too busy studying to care. You should see the picture he sent of his apartment in Edinburgh; it's one step up from a garret. Reminds me of our first apartment. Brian and I were even younger and more starry-eyed than Maggie and Jason when we got married. We thought we could live on love and ramen noodles."

"I remember," Lanie said. "You were nauseatingly precious as newlyweds. Thank heaven you got over *that*."

15

I glanced at my watch. "Listen, my lovely, aside from trying to get me to buy dead animal skins—"

"*Vintage* dead animal skins."

"Vintage dead animal skins . . . was there any reason you called?"

"Just to tell you about the coat and to make sure we're still on for tonight."

"Of course we are. Have I ever missed our Friday night drink?"

"Just checking. I'll see you later, then. Kiss-kiss. And Gayla? *Promise* me you will *not* make Brian a quilt for his birthday."

I sighed. Lanie could be such a nag sometimes. "It was just a whim. I wasn't serious."

"Good."

She rang off as abruptly as she'd rung up, but that was just Lanie's way; I was used to it.

I stuffed the phone into my bag and started walking east, but after about ten steps, I turned around, pressed the buzzer on the door to The City Quilter, waited for the answering buzz that signaled the release of the lock, and went inside. The girl at the counter was a lot younger and hipper than I figured somebody working in a quilt shop would be.

"This is a beautiful red," she said as she plunked the bolt onto the counter. "Just came in. How many yards do you want?"

"Umm . . . two?"

She unrolled the fabric from the bolt and sliced through it with something that looked like a huge pizza cutter. "What are you planning to make with it?"

"No idea," I admitted as I handed over my credit card. "I just . . . I just wanted it."

She nodded as she folded the fabric and slipped it into a white plastic bag. "We get a lot of that," she said.

Feeling inexplicably pleased after purchasing two yards of red fabric I had no use for, I continued on my way, jogging the last five blocks and getting home just in time for my phone appointment with Sandy Tolland. Things were looking up.

Sandy hadn't set an agenda when she texted that morning, asking if we could talk, but she didn't have to. I already knew what we'd be discussing.

I am an educational consultant, a kind of college admissions counselor for hire. I went into private practice almost six years ago, after years working as a guidance counselor in public schools.

Every kid I work with is an individual, but the parents are pretty similar. Maybe one in twenty approaches the process with an open mind, but most arrive with a very set agenda. Some have their hearts set on the Ivy League. Others have decided up front that their child should pursue one particular program of study in one particular field and that one particular college is the only place to do it. Still others are focused on the school that they and the members of their clan have attended since the founding of the republic.

Families come to me because they want their child to get into the "best" school. My job is to help them find and gain entrance to the *right* school, the one that lines up with the student's interests, personality, learning style, abilities, and goals. Kids latch on to the idea pretty quickly, but some of the parents, like Sandy, can take longer. You have to let them talk it out. But that's all right; I'm a good listener. I'm also good at stealth typing, another useful skill to have in my line of work.

In case you're not aware, stealth typing is the ability to hold a telephone conversation while simultaneously shopping online, answering e-mail, or editing a personal essay so quietly that the speaker on the other end of the line has no idea what the listener is doing or that they don't have her complete attention.

I am a virtuoso stealth typist. And I should be; I get a lot of practice.

I shifted the phone to a more comfortable spot on my shoulder and opened the browser on my computer.

"Sandy, I told you from day one that Yale

wasn't a realistic option for Emily, not with her SAT scores and a B-plus average. St. Michael's is a good match for her. She'll do well there, and she'll be happy."

"Karen Wittenauer's daughter got accepted to Smith." She sniffed. "Why couldn't Emily do well and be happy *there?*"

Keeping my fingers flat to prevent my nails from clicking against the keys, I typed the name of my favorite travel site into the address bar of my laptop and hit enter.

"No gymnastics," I said. "And no boys."

Sandy didn't argue. She knew that a school with no boys was a no-go for Emily.

"What about Brown? I heard it's an easier admission than some of the Ivies. Ray and Camilla Rossman's son, Chas, got in, and he's not nearly as . . ."

While Sandy listed all the august institutions of higher learning that the children of her friends had been accepted to, I closed a pop-up ad for time-shares in Florida and fought back the urge to sigh. Oh, the weight of parental expectations. Sandy would have gotten on great with my mother.

While Sandy talked through a list of second-tier but decidedly name-brand colleges on the Eastern Seaboard, I delivered short, to-the-point responses as to why each of these places was wrong for Emily, pinned new pictures to my

Pinterest boards, and tidied my workspace. I'm a big believer in the value of multitasking.

I reached up to the wall over my desk and straightened a photo of Brian and me on our honeymoon in Italy, standing in the bow of the barge with his arm over my shoulders and my head resting against his chest. We're holding glasses of Barolo and peering at the camera with satisfied, slightly sleepy smiles. We'd just come up from below, where, about an hour before, assuming I'm doing the math right, we had conceived Maggie and Nate.

We were so young. And good-looking. Brian especially. I still miss his long hair. And Italy. We should go back there someday.

Scanning through a couple of my favorite blogs, I found a photo of an old-world-looking kitchen with stone walls occupied by a woman in a chef's apron and two handsome, fortyish-looking couples who were eating bruschetta and toasting each other with big glasses of white wine and pinned it to my "Traveling Light" Pinterest board, still semi-listening as Sandy Tolland wondered what she was supposed to tell her friends whose children *did* get into the Ivies when they said they'd never heard of St. Michael's.

"Tell them it's a little gem of a school in the Midwest with a gorgeous campus modeled on Magdalen College in Oxford, small classes, a first-rate undergraduate psychology department, and a fabulous study-abroad program, and that the gymnastics coach is very excited about Emily. Tell them that you and Mark considered a number of colleges, including many in the East, but came to the conclusion that St. Michael's was the best fit for Emily. Tell them that you decided that your daughter's happiness was more important than being able to brag about getting her into the Ivy League."

"Yeah," Sandy replied in a scoffing tone. "Because they're really going to believe *that*."

Sandy laughed, and I did, too, but I knew that at least part of her was dead serious.

I liked Sandy. I liked most of the parents I work with, but sometimes . . . well, you just have to wonder. Considering all the problems that teenagers can have and all the trouble they can get into, why isn't it enough for Sandy to have a bright, pleasant, athletic, above-average daughter? Why are so few of my clients content with that? And when did getting a child into the "best" college get to be a competition among the parents?

When? At about the time people like me figured out people like Sandy would pay good money to anyone who could help their children receive fat envelopes from the small list of prestigious schools that will impress their friends and validate them as parents. I went into this line of

21

work because I wanted to help kids and their families keep their priorities straight, to avoid making the same kinds of mistakes I made, but it's gotten all turned around. Somehow I've become part of the problem.

"What about Skidmore?" Sandy asked. "Do you think she'll clear the wait list?"

"Why would you want her to? We always meant Skidmore as a backup option, remember? It's a perfectly good school, but not as good a match for Emily's personality or interests. And they don't have a gymnastics team."

"I know, but at least people have *heard* of it."

I closed my eyes and quietly pounded my head on the padded headrest of my desk chair. The only thing you can do with clients like Sandy is let them talk it out. She'd come around. But I hoped she wouldn't take too long. I had to meet Lanie at the Monkey Bar at four forty-five and pick Brian up from JFK at seven-thirty. Wait. Was I supposed to pick him up at seven-thirty? Or was it seven? I pulled a Post-it out of the dispenser and scribbled myself a reminder to call Emily at the corporate travel agency and confirm Brian's arrival time. Then I closed Pinterest and opened the word-processing program, thinking I might as well edit a couple of essays while Sandy talked.

But somehow instead of opening my files, I ended up opening Brian's, and when I tried to get out of that folder, the screen froze. I tried hitting escape, but it didn't help. I just got that spinning color wheel, the one that appears when the computer is loading, thinking, or simply mocking you. After a minute, I started hitting random keys quickly and repeatedly, growing more frustrated by the second, not caring where my commands took me as long as it was far from the rainbow rotations of that stupid wheel.

If I'd realized what was going to happen next, I might have thought twice before I started smacking those keys.

The wheel stopped spinning as suddenly as it started, and a series of documents, written by Brian, popped up on the screen in quick succession. The fourth one, the final one, a memo, dated July 2012, was written to me.

Subject: Facing Facts

Gayla, I'm sure it will come as no surprise when I tell you I am unhappy in our marriage. It's obvious that you are as well and have been for some time.

We were so young and married so quickly, without a true appreciation of how much our personalities and expectations of life differed, that perhaps our growing apart was inevitable. In any case, I don't think there is any point in casting aspersions or placing blame, but I think it is time we faced the facts about our marriage and moved on with our lives.

Before you ask: There is no one else. I did have a very brief affair with someone from work—we met only three times over a two-week period—but I was not and am not in love with her and have ended the relationship. I am ashamed to have treated you and the woman in question so badly. Though I make no excuse for my conduct, I am very sorry for and deeply regret my actions.

However, that episode forced me to take a good long look at my life and myself. I didn't like what I saw. I realized that, as Nate would say, "I don't want to be that guy."

I don't want to be a man who cheats, lies, or feigns affection for you or anyone else. Though I do think that, in the beginning, we were very much in love—at least I was; I won't presume to speak for you—those feelings have obviously faded. This being the case, if our marriage continues on its current course, I don't see how I can keep from becoming "that guy."

The long and short of it is: I am lonely. I want to love someone and be loved in return. For a short time, when we first bought the cottage, I felt there was a chance of us reviving what we used to feel for each other, but it soon became clear that this was wishful thinking on my part. And so, to avoid any further indiscretions, lies, or betrayal, as well as to give ourselves the possibility of finding real love (I'm sure you long for this as much as I do), I think we should admit defeat and consider divorce.

I anticipate that we shall end this amicably; after all, we're both grown-ups and since we're finally out of debt and your business is doing well, this shouldn't cause any serious financial hardship for either of us.

Now that the children are grown and gone—you did a marvelous job raising them, Gayla—it probably makes no sense to delay further. Still, I don't want to cast a pall on the wedding, so I'll wait a few weeks before sending this to you.

Once Maggie and Jason return from their honeymoon and have made the move to Charlotte, you and I can sit down together and figure out what we're going to say to the children and how to proceed from here. We can retain attorneys, if you'd like, but I think going to arbitration would be a less expensive and more direct route.

As I said, we can discuss. Perhaps early September would be a good time?

Divorce? He wanted a divorce?
And he'd written me a *memo* about it?
I scrolled down to the end of the file, thinking

that there had to be more to this, that it must be a joke, some kind of macabre man-humor that one of his coworkers had copied off the Internet, or that he was taking up creative writing or was working on a screenplay, or that it was . . . anything but what it appeared to be.

I read the whole thing again.

"Oh my God . . ."

It was real. It *was* exactly what it appeared to be. Brian wanted to divorce me.

Sandy, whose voice had become a white whir in my ears, finally stopped talking. "Gayla, are you all right?"

"No. I mean . . . yes." I closed my eyes, trying to steady myself. "I'm just not feeling very well. Could I call you back later?"

"There's no rush," she said in an uncharacteristically patient voice. "Tomorrow is fine. Are you sure you're all right? You don't sound like yourself. Something you ate?"

"Probably. I've got to go. Tell Emily I said hello."

"I will. And listen, Gayla, about Skidmore—"

I didn't wait for her to finish. I couldn't. I hung up the phone, ran down the hall to the bathroom, and threw up.

2

Ivy Peterman

Turning on your computer in the morning and finding the "black screen of death" instead of the essay that you stayed up to the wee hours writing is usually a pretty good indication of how the rest of your day is going to go.

"No," I declared in my most authoritative tone, the one I use to let the kids know that I have had about all I can take and that if they try to push me further, they do so at their peril. "You are not doing this to me. Not today. Boot up," I demanded, stabbing various combinations of buttons on the keyboard. "Do it now."

Nothing. Damn.

"Bethany!" I shouted. "Can you help me? I can't get the computer to turn on!"

It's kind of humiliating that I have to call on my eleven-year-old for tech support. I'm only thirty; I grew up in the digital age. I should understand these things. But I also grew up in a poor school district with no computers, ran away from home when I was sixteen, got pregnant at eighteen, married the same year, had another baby at twenty-two, ran away again at twenty-four, taking the kids but leaving my abusive husband, and spent months on the run before landing in New Bern and finally freeing myself of the abusive husband.

In the midst of all that, I missed a few things, skipped a few steps. But I'm doing my best to make up for lost time.

Bethany, who was in the bathroom, shouted back, but I couldn't make out what she was saying. I hissed at the black-screened computer, gave it an evil glare, and went in search of my daughter, only to be met by Bobby, my seven-year-old, who almost ran me down in the hall-way.

"Mommy? I need twenty-two empty toilet-paper rolls."

"Today?"

He bobbed his head. I closed my eyes and pinched the bridge of my nose, that spot where my headaches always start. This was not going to be a good day. Definitely not. I did an about-face and headed for the garage with Bobby trailing behind.

"Why didn't you tell me before?" I asked as I pried the top off the plastic bin where I keep empty toilet and paper towel rolls, egg cartons, and oatmeal boxes—the stuff of which elementary school art projects are made.

"I forgot."

Of course he did.

Bobby is my baby, so sweet you could spread

him on toast. He's also the most forgetful child on the face of the earth. Seriously. He forgets to take his lunch and bring home his spelling words. He forgets to brush his teeth, wear underwear, and turn off the faucet. Also to take the plug out of the drain, which can be a problem.

Bethany wasn't like this when she was seven. Of course, Bethany grew up fast. She had to. I still feel bad about that, but I'm doing the best I can, trying to make up for lost time.

I dug through the bin, counting cardboard toilet-paper tubes. "We've only got twelve."

Bobby's eyes went wide. "But I need twenty-two! I was supposed to bring them on Wednesday but I forgot! Mrs. Oneglia said if I didn't bring them today I'd have to stay in at recess. What am I going to do?"

"I guess you're going to stay in at recess," I said, snapping the lid back onto the bin.

"Couldn't you go to the store and—"

"Bobby. I am not buying ten rolls of bathroom tissue and pulling the paper off them just so you can have the empty tubes. I'm sorry, Bear, but you're just going to have to man up and face the music this time."

Bobby's eyes filled. I felt terrible, but I have to start being a little tougher on Bobby. It's not easy. Every time I look at his face, I remember that happy, chubby-cheeked toddler wearing that knitted brown hat with the teddy bear ears on the top, the hat that spawned his nickname, Bobby Bear—Bear for short—and I just want to squeeze him.

I've babied him too much, I know. I guess I just wanted him to have an easier time of it than Bethany. She doesn't like to talk about it, but she remembers how it was living with her dad. She saw him hit me, felt my fear, remembers the day he hit her too. She remembers running, living in shelters and the car, afraid that he'd find us one day, afraid of what would happen when he did.

Bobby doesn't. He was only eighteen months old when we ran. Bobby is carefree, happy-go-lucky, and I've wanted to keep him that way. Maybe a little too much.

"Honey, you've got to start planning ahead. Maybe staying in at recess will help you remember to do that next time."

Bobby sniffled and swiped at his nose with the back of his hand. Little boys can be so icky.

"Okay," he mumbled and trudged off, shoulders drooping. Poor baby.

"Wash your hands!" I called to him before resuming the search for my daughter.

"Bethany," I said when I found her, standing in the kitchen, staring at the toaster. "The computer won't boot up. I've got to print out my paper before class tonight. Can you fix it?"

The toaster dinged, and a pastry popped out of

the slot. Bethany grabbed it. "Can't. There's an early rehearsal for the spelling bee."

"For a spelling bee? What's to rehearse?"

Bethany pulled a paper towel off the roll and wrapped the breakfast pastry in it. "I don't know. Mr. Zwicker said that all the finalists have to be there, or we don't get to spell. You're coming, aren't you? It's at two-thirty."

"Of course," I said. Truthfully, I'd forgotten about it, but I knew that Evelyn, my boss, would be fine with me taking off an hour. That's one of the nice things about working in a quilt shop. The money isn't great, but Evelyn understands how hard it is to combine work and mother-hood.

"That's not all you're eating for breakfast, is it?"

"No time," she said, and slipped her backpack onto her shoulders. "And there's nothing in the fridge anyway."

I tore a banana from the bunch sitting on the counter. "Here. Take this with you. What am I going to do about the computer? My paper is due tonight. I was up until two finishing it. When I turned on the computer, it flashed for a second and then—"

"Mommy," she said in her best teen-in-training, "adults are idiots" tone. "Did you save the document?"

"Yes, right before I shut down."

"Then you're fine. Just get into the Cloud when you get to work."

"The Cloud?"

"It's this big, shared memory that lets you access your documents from any computer and backs everything up automatically. Drew installed it a couple of weeks ago, remember? Never mind," she sighed, realizing I had no clue what she meant. She grabbed a scrap of paper and a pen from the junk drawer and scribbled out a chain of letters. "Just go to this address, log in with this user name and this password, look in the file, find your paper, and print it out."

"Thanks, Bethy."

Bringing the banana that she'd left on the table, probably intentionally, I walked her to the door and kissed her good-bye. When I went into the living room, Bobby was sitting cross-legged on the floor, watching television.

"I washed my hands!" he announced.

"Thank you. That's very—"

I stopped and tipped my head to the side, hearing the sound of rushing water. By the time I ran into the hallway, water had breached the bathroom door and was beginning to pool on the wooden floor.

"Bobby!"

Not a good day. Not at all.

～ 3 ～

Gayla

After rinsing out my mouth and spending half an hour pacing around the apartment like a caged animal in a zoo, circling walls that pressed too close, I grabbed my keys and purse and left, unable to endure one more minute trapped in those rooms. Too impatient to wait for the elevator, I ran down six flights of stairs, flew through the lobby without returning the doorman's greeting, and fled into the street.

The temperature was hovering just above the freezing mark during this, the most miserable May on record, and I was wearing only slacks and a blouse. A few people stared at me, possibly wondering what the lady with the tears streaming down her face was doing pounding down the sidewalk without a coat. I ducked into the minimart on the corner and bought three packs of cigarettes.

I'd smoked my last cigarette shortly after I learned of my pregnancy, giving my final pack of Benson & Hedges a burial at sea, tossing them overboard and watching as they swirled and disappeared into the white wake of the barge engines. When they were gone, I turned from the railing and walked away, and that was that. I never experienced withdrawal, never even thought about cigarettes after that day.

Now I was desperate for a smoke. My hands shook as I tore at the cellophane and paper packaging, pulled out a slender tube of tobacco, lit the end, and inhaled as quickly and deeply as I could, ravenous for nicotine and answers.

What had happened between this cigarette and my last? What had made my husband turn away from me and the promises we'd made to each other? What was I supposed to do with those promises now? And with my life?

It was cold and getting colder, but I didn't want to go back to the apartment. I couldn't. But I couldn't keep walking around Manhattan with no coat and no plan either. I jogged two blocks to the parking garage and asked the attendant to bring up our car. Five minutes later, I was behind the wheel and driving north.

I turned the heat on full blast while simultaneously cracking open the window, hoping to keep the smoke from smelling up the car. I opened the ashtray, a thing I'd never had occasion to do before, squashed my cigarette butt into the pristine little receptacle, and immediately lit up another. The nicotine, or perhaps the simple act of breathing deeply, calmed me.

But I still didn't know what I was supposed to do next. I couldn't just pick up my husband

34

curbside at the United terminal, kiss him hello, and pretend everything was all right. One look at Brian's face and I knew I'd fall apart, sob and wail and end up looking pathetic and foolish— because I was. Because I'd never seen it coming.

I couldn't face Brian, but I couldn't just leave him waiting at the airport either. He'd be worried that something had happened to me. Or, it occurred to me, he wouldn't be worried. And that would be worse.

I rested my cigarette on the edge of the ashtray and started digging through my purse for my cell phone, keeping one eye on the road as I did so, knowing I was breaking a lot of very good laws. Brian was in the air at that moment. I could leave him a voice mail. But what would I say?

I needed a story . . . a burst pipe at the cottage? Having to run up to Connecticut to deal with the situation? He'd believe that; we'd had plumbing problems since day one. Once I was out of town, I could shut off my phone and ignore his calls for at least a day or two without arousing suspicion. Three years after we'd purchased the cottage, cell reception in New Bern was still spotty. I needed time by myself to figure out what I was supposed to do next—contact a lawyer, or do whatever it was people did when they got divorced.

Divorced.

Even after reading that letter—no, memo—

even then, it was hard to believe this was happening to me, to us.

Glancing in my rearview mirror to make sure the coast was clear of police cruisers, I hit Brian's number on my speed dial, the first in the list, and waited for his voice mail to pick up. Except it didn't. Brian did. He started talking even before I could get in a word.

"My connection is delayed—again." He groaned. "I honestly don't know why I go through Chicago. Anyway, I'm at the gate, and they say we'll be boarding in about a half hour, so, assuming they're telling the truth, I should be home in time for dinner. Did you cook anything?"

"No, I—"

"Then let's go out. Italian?"

"I can't, sweet—" I started to call him "sweetheart." The endearment is nearly automatic by now, but I stopped myself. "I . . . I can't pick you up either. You'll have to get a cab. Drew texted me. . . . I'm driving up to Connecticut."

"Don't tell me," he said in a resigned tone. "That bloody furnace. I was hoping it'd last till spring. But why do you have to go up? Can't you just call a repairman?"

The sound of his voice pulled me up short. He sounded so normal, as if nothing had changed between us.

Obviously we'd moved past the "tell me what

you're wearing" stage many years ago. This is what our conversations are like now. We talk about the kids, our schedules, our jobs, and . . . things like bills and broken furnaces. I never thought that meant we were unhappy. The conversation wasn't exciting, but discussing domestic details was just part of married life, wasn't it? And, in a way, it made me feel secure. Obviously, I was wrong. Maybe I'd been hearing what I wanted to hear all along.

"Not the furnace. It's . . . a burst pipe. And there's water in the . . ." I paused for a moment, took another run at it, trying to launch into the story I'd rehearsed, but I couldn't do it. I'm a terrible liar.

"Brian, I accidentally opened some of your documents on my computer. I saw the letter you wrote—the memo."

"The memo," he repeated. I could almost hear the shrug in his voice. He had no idea what I was talking about. "What memo?"

"*The* memo," I snapped. "The memo you wrote to *me*. Saying you're unhappy in our marriage, that you had an affair and that you want a divorce."

"You got into my computer? You read my documents?"

"Excuse me!" I shot back. "You're angry with *me?* You wrote me a memo to tell me you're divorcing me. A memo, Brian! Who does that?"

"I'm *not* divorcing you! I never sent it!"

"But you wrote it."

"But I never *sent* it. After the wedding, I changed my mind. I realized what a mistake it was, all that I'd be giving up, and so I deleted it. You must have opened up the trash folder somehow. I don't know how you could have—"

He stopped, took in a big breath, and let it out in a long, deflated whoosh.

"Oh God, Gayla. I'm sorry. You have to believe me. I didn't mean it."

The lining of my throat felt thick. "You had an affair."

He was quiet for a moment. "It wasn't an affair so much as it was . . . a mistake. I thought about telling you, but then, once I'd made up my mind to see things through, I realized that if I told you about it I'd only be doing it to salve my guilt. I never thought you'd have to know about it."

"And that makes it okay?"

"Listen to me, Gayla. It's over. I haven't seen her since August. Or called her. That doesn't make it all right, but it truly is over. I kept it from you because I hoped you'd never have to know. What would be the point in hurting you if it was over? But I have. And I'm sorry."

"Who is she?" I spat, ignoring his apology.

"Just someone I met at the office. Gayla! It was three times. It didn't—"

"Brian, if you tell me it didn't mean anything, I swear I'm going to hang up! Because it did. It means you aren't happy and you don't love me anymore."

"That's not true."

"You said you're not happy. You even said *we* aren't happy. You don't get to decide that for me, Brian. Only I get to say if I'm happy or not, all right?" I swallowed hard, trying to keep my anger from dissolving into tears.

"Where are you now?" he asked. "Turn around and come home. I'll get a cab from the airport and meet you at home. We need to talk about this. Please."

"I can't. Not today."

He was quiet again, perhaps hoping I would say something. I didn't.

"Tomorrow I'll rent a car and drive to Connecticut—"

"Don't," I said quickly. "I don't want to see you right now. Maybe in a few days, but not now. Brian, I have to go. I forgot my Bluetooth, and there are cops everywhere. I'm going to get a ticket. I'll call you in a couple of days."

My thumb hovered over the end button on my cell but was stayed by the frantic sound of his voice.

"Gayla! Don't hang up!"

I waited, saying nothing.

"I am so sorry."

He waited for my response, hoping, I guess, perhaps even expecting, that I would say what I always said: that I forgave him, that it didn't matter, that everything was going to be all right. It was something I'd said often and easily in the last twenty-six years because it *had* been easy, because it had always been true. Until now.

For the first time in my life, I didn't know what to say to my husband.

The rain was coming down in sheets and the visibility was so poor that I pulled off at a rest stop to wait for things to clear up.

I lit another cigarette, this time without bothering to crack open a window, no longer caring if the car smelled like smoke. My phone chirruped cheerily to announce an incoming call. I looked at the screen.

Oh, no . . . Lanie. It was twelve minutes after five, which meant she'd been sitting at the Monkey Bar, waiting for me to show up for exactly twenty-seven minutes. Lanie is always on time.

"Where *are* you?" she asked, raising her voice to be heard over a background buzz of voices and clinking glassware.

"I should have called. I'm sorry. Something came up—very last-minute. I'm driving up to Connecticut."

"Connecticut? Now? Why are you . . . Hold on a minute."

She put the phone down. I heard a scratchy static sound and a mumbled exchange with the bartender, something about extra olives. Lanie likes her martinis dirty.

When she returned she said, "Less than four hours ago you said you were going to meet me here, remember?"

"I know. I'm sorry. It was very last-minute, but I have to go to the cottage for the weekend—"

"The weekend? But you're coming for brunch on Sunday. You are *not* canceling," she said. It was a statement, not a question. "Not again. I already put in my catering order at Balthazar—goat cheese tart with caramelized onions, pastry basket, fruit platter, the works. You have to come."

I screwed my eyes shut. Brunch with Lanie and Roger. I'd forgotten.

Brian hadn't wanted to go, but I talked him into it. He doesn't like Roger. I don't like Roger either, but what can you do when your friends marry the wrong people? We'd begged off Lanie's last three invitations. I couldn't say no.

"Lanie. I'm so sorry. I know I promised, but I . . . I just can't."

There was a brief pause, just long enough for her to swallow a mouthful of olive-infused gin. I braced myself, expecting an explosion, but she surprised me.

"Gayla," she said, "something is wrong. Tell me."

She was direct as always, but uncharacteristically gentle. It cut me to the quick. Between sobs, I told her everything, pouring out the whole story minute by minute, from the conversation with Sandy Tolland to pulling off the freeway to wait out the rain. A part of me thought it was a mistake, but I couldn't stop myself.

"You're kidding. Brian?" she asked, sounding genuinely disappointed. "I thought he was the last monogamous man on the planet. Damn. They really *are* all the same. Oh, my darling. I know it feels like your heart is breaking—believe me, I do—but you've *got* to pull yourself together. Time is of the essence. Gayla? Are you listening?"

Too choked up to speak, I sniffled. Lanie took that as a yes.

"Get out a pen and write this down," she instructed me and began reciting a series of numbers. "Libby Burrell is the best divorce lawyer in town, a barracuda. Call her right this second. She'll still be at the office; she always is. Has no life at all."

"Not now, Lanie. Not yet. I need time to think things through."

"Gayla," she said impatiently, "don't be an idiot. If you want to avoid financial destruction, you have to act now. The best defense is a good offense, so beat him to the punch. Call Libby and get the ball rolling tonight. Forget that crap about arbitration; there's no such thing as an amicable divorce. After you talk to Libby, freeze all your credit cards. Remember how Bill ran up all our cards to the limit, buying jewelry for that slut?"

I did remember. Bill was Lanie's first husband and a serial adulterer. It had taken years for her to clean up her credit scores.

"Then," she continued, "you've got to get to the checking account before Brian does and transfer all the money into your personal account. Don't wait until Monday; you can do it online."

"I don't have a personal account. Everything is held jointly."

She sighed heavily, as if such stupidity was not to be believed.

"Okay. So on Monday, you go to the bank, open an account in your name, and transfer everything. You've got to do it first thing, Gayla, before Brian does. If he hasn't already. Have you checked your balance today?"

I rubbed my eyes, trying to push away the pain that was forming behind the sockets.

"I think you're jumping the gun. I haven't made any decisions yet."

"Haven't made any decisions? Sweetie, you don't *get* to decide. It's a done thing. For crap's sake, Gayla; he wrote you a *memo*."

"But he didn't send it. He says he changed his mind."

"Gayla," she said in a wearily patient tone. "Don't be so naïve. He only said that because now he knows that you *know*. He knows that's what you want to believe, so he's using that to buy himself some time, so he can outflank you. It's the same line that Simon fed me. . . ."

Simon was Lanie's second husband, the personal trainer she met at her gym, the one she was married to for less than two years. The one she still paid alimony to.

"Brian's not like that."

There was a pause, a tinkle of ice, and a sigh.

"Gayla. Darling. I don't mean to sound cruel, but given the situation, I think it's safe to say that you don't know *what* Brian is like."

I winced, cut by the accuracy of her statement. If I knew my husband as well as I thought I did, or even a little bit, shouldn't I have seen this coming? But I still didn't believe that Brian was trying to trick me. No matter what Lanie said, he wouldn't do some-thing so underhanded, and I told her so.

"Okay, fine. For the moment, let's assume you're right. Let's assume he wanted a divorce but then he changed his mind. Gayla," she said as quietly as she could while still making herself heard over the tinkle and hum of happy hour, "what's to say that tomorrow he won't change it again? Do you want to spend the rest of your life waiting for the other shoe to drop?"

My stomach lurched, responding to Lanie's gift for summing up my most secret fears and saying them aloud. Fortunately, I'd already lost my lunch back at the apartment, so instead of throwing up again, I swallowed back the taste of bile and repeated my position. "I need time to think."

"Fine," she said, obviously irritated. "Take all you want. But don't blame me if you wind up bankrupt and living in a fifth-floor walk-up."

"I won't," I said, knowing that in spite of her heavy-handed approach, she really was concerned about me. "Thanks, Lanie."

"Thanks yourself, Stubborn," she said, her irritation abating slightly. "You're just saying that because you know I'd never let that happen to you. No friend of mine is going to have to climb more than one flight of stairs to her front door. Worst case, you can always move into our guest room."

I smiled. "You think Roger would be all right with that?"

"Who cares what Roger thinks? It's my name on the mortgage. Learn from my example, lovey. Prenups. The avenue to lasting marital harmony. Speaking of Roger, I'm supposed to meet him for dinner. Are you going to be all right? I'll call first thing tomorrow to see how you're doing."

"Oh," I said doubtfully, "you don't have to do that. I'm fine. And the reception is so bad at the cottage."

"Stop trying to be so brave. You need a friend right now, Gayla. You really do."

True enough. But was Lanie the friend I needed?

For years that had stretched into decades, the answer to that question had always been yes. Now I wasn't so sure.

⁓❦ 4 ❦⁓

Ivy

Nothing went right that day.

Cleaning up the flood in the bathroom made me late for work. Normally that wouldn't be a big deal, but Evelyn and Margot are off at a trade show, so it was my job to open the shop. Though I was only ten minutes late, three scowling women were already pacing in front of the door when I arrived.

I apologized, but it didn't seem to make any difference. They were really snippy about it, especially after I told them that we were out of the interfacing they wanted. When I informed them that the 25 percent off coupon they wanted to use had expired two months before, the scales tipped from snippy to snotty.

All three had gray hair and pinched lips and looked so much alike that I thought they must be sisters. The tallest one did the talking.

"What? We drove all the way from Hartford because we'd heard that this shop had such good customer service! I can't *believe* you're not going to honor your coupon. I want to speak to the owner. We drove two *hours* to get here!"

Unless they were driving golf carts, no way did it take them that long to get to New Bern from Hartford. Maybe they came by broomstick? I was tempted to ask but instead I just said, "I'm sorry, but Evelyn's not here right now."

"Well, this is ridiculous!" Tall Sister snapped, flinging the expired coupon down on the counter. "We are *never* coming to this shop again. Never! We're going to tell everyone in our guild about how you've treated us. And it's a big guild. Very big! I don't know why Carol raved about this place. Terrible shop. Tired fabrics, tiny selection, and *rude* clerks," she said, pinching her lips together even more tightly and glaring at me before turning to her companions.

"Come on, girls. Let's get out of here."

And that was that. They stormed off—and without paying for the fabric that they'd asked me to cut for them. Can you believe it? I put the yardage under the counter on the off chance that somebody else would come in wanting those particular fabrics in those particular lengths. More than likely, I'll end up having to put them on the remnant table, marked with a 25 percent discount. Maybe it would have been smarter to just honor the coupon, but I wasn't going to give them the satisfaction, not after they'd been so nasty.

When Virginia, Evelyn's mother, who is well into her eighties but still as sharp as a tack and continues to teach quilting and work in the shop several afternoons a week, arrived to take over for me at around eleven, I told her what had happened. By then I was starting to worry about whether or not I'd done the right thing.

"Tosh!" she said, dismissing my concerns as she picked up Petunia, the enormous tomcat who goes everywhere with her, and deposited him in his accustomed spot in the front window. "I bet they don't even belong to a guild. And if they do, I bet everyone in the guild has their number. Most quilters are kind as can be, but every barrel is bound to have a few crab apples."

I went to the workroom to cut and package Internet orders, happy to leave Virginia downstairs to deal with the crab apples. We were way behind on fulfillment. Judith, our intern, was supposed to come in at noon and help me, but she didn't show. When I called the Stanton Center, they told me she'd gone back to her boyfriend, the man responsible for her broken nose and dislocated shoulder.

I called the elementary school and asked them to let Bethany know that I wouldn't be able to make it to the spelling bee. I was disappointed, but not one-tenth as disappointed as I was about Judith. I really thought she was going to make it.

Being financially independent and having job skills makes it a lot easier for victims of domestic violence to escape that cycle. That's why we started the community internship program, a program I coordinate. Our interns are much less likely to return to their abusers than those who don't get job training, but still, it happens.

People who've never been in that situation find this hard to fathom, but I get it. Time after time, Hodge would beat me and then beg my forgiveness, promise me it would never happen again. Time after time, I believed him. Until the next time.

The day he hit Bethany was the day I knew I had to get out. If not for my kids, I'd probably never have found the courage to run or to keep from going back. It just breaks my heart that Judith is gone. I feel like I've failed her.

Working at Cobbled Court Quilts is fun. I love the people I work with. Margot is the kindest person I've ever met. Virginia is like the grandma I never had. And Evelyn . . . well, Evelyn is just amazing. How many small business owners would let me spend 25 percent of my time coordinating the internship program, a program that involves eight different businesses in New Bern, not just her quilt shop, and still pay my full salary? Nobody I can think of. But what I really love about working here is working with the interns. I can never repay those who helped me escape the cycle, but I can help others who are still trapped, cheer them on, let them stand on my shoulders, give them a boost over the wall to freedom and safety.

That's why I decided to get my GED and start taking classes at the community college, because someday I want to help run a women's shelter, maybe even be the director. Not for the money, though more money would be nice, but because that's where my heart is—with the women.

Even though I skipped lunch, I spent the rest of the day playing catch-up—and losing. I was late leaving work and late picking up the kids from after-school care. Bethany never got my message about why I couldn't make it to the spelling bee. I felt terrible. Even after I explained what happened, said we were going out for pizza to celebrate her victory (also because I hadn't had time to get to the market), and solemnly promised I'd be there for the regional competition, she was still sulky and refused to talk to me. Bobby filled the silence, jabbering about school and some group called Boys' Brigade that his friends had joined, and begging me to let him join too. Though I was only half listening, I said he could as long as it didn't cost anything. It sounded like it'd be good for him, a way to spend more time with other boys. When it comes to raising Bobby, I sometimes feel like I'm flying blind. Bethany is easier; I know what to do with a girl. Well, some of the time. As she sat there, barely eating, refusing to look at me or speak to me while Bobby babbled happily about camping trips and bowling tournaments, I couldn't help but wonder how I was ever going to survive the teen years.

After feeding the kids and picking up the sitter, I drove to the community college as fast as I could. I took a seat in the back of the room, hoping my tardiness would go unnoticed. No such luck. Dr. Verstandig stopped the lecture to tell me that Dr. Streeter wanted me to drop by his office after class.

He did? Why would the head of the humanities department want to see me?

As soon as class was over, I went to Dr. Streeter's office and knocked on the door, clutching my textbook to my chest as if that might stop my heart from pounding.

When I'm in the presence of a male authority figure—a policeman, a judge, or even Reverend Tucker, who has to be the nicest man on the face of the earth—I feel anxious, like I've been caught doing something wrong and am about to be punished for it.

The psychology class that I took last term helped me understand why. It's all mixed up with how I was raised, the guilt I still feel over my father's death when I was little, and, of course, the years of abuse I endured from my husband, who used to fly into a rage over even the tiniest infraction of rules that I sometimes wasn't even aware of. I could write a ten-page, footnoted, A-plus paper on the causes and effects of my particular brand of anxiety. But being able to explain it isn't the same as being able to control it.

I knocked again, a little louder. Dr. Streeter's deep voice came from the other side of the door. "It's unlocked!"

Dr. Streeter, dressed in the shapeless brown sweater-vest he wears no matter the season, sat bent over his desk with the end of a pencil wedged between his teeth, chewing on the eraser and reading an essay. He held his hand up when I entered, so I stood still and silent, waiting for him to finish. He shook his white head and scribbled a note in the margin of the paper before looking up, first with a frown and then with a delighted smile, which made me feel much better.

"Ivy!" he boomed, throwing out his arms as if he expected me to run into them.

Dr. Streeter acts in plays at the local theater. He talks as if he's trying to make sure they hear him in the cheap seats and uses a lot of sweeping hand gestures.

"Sit! Sit! Sit! Just clear those papers off the

chair—move them anywhere. That's right. What can I do for you?"

"Dr. Verstandig said you wanted to see me?"

"I did? Oh, yes!" he exclaimed, his face brightening. "I did! I wanted to talk to you about something."

Dr. Streeter is probably pushing seventy-five, but I don't think his forgetfulness has anything to do with age. I'm sure he was as much the absentminded academic at thirty as he is now, his office littered with papers, probably wearing that same ugly sweater-vest, and perfectly content with his life.

He turned to face me, and his ancient leather and wood swivel chair squeaked in protest. "How are your classes going?"

"Class," I corrected. "I can only take one per semester, remember? So far, I've got a ninety-two average in Dr. Verstandig's class."

"Good. Very good. Not that I'm surprised," he said, snatching a piece of paper from under a glass paperweight and holding it at arm's length so he could read it without his glasses. "I was looking over your transcript. Algebra was a bit of a bumpy road, but you've earned high marks in every other course. Well done, Ivy. Very well done."

He was such a nice man. Why had I been so worried about meeting with him? One of these days I simply had to grow up and get over it.

"Thanks. As of next semester, I'll be a sophomore. Only took three years. I'll probably be a grandmother before I'm a graduate, but I'll get there eventually."

He made his hands into a chapel and rested his chin on the steeple of his fingers. "What if you were able to graduate in two years? Or even a little sooner?"

"How could I do that?"

He began patting his pockets, then burrowing through the papers on his desk until he located a bright blue brochure with a picture on the front of a man and a woman dressed in business suits and carrying textbooks under their arms.

"This appeared in my in-box last week. Carrillon College is starting a new accelerated degree program in nonprofit management and leadership. It's designed for people like you, adults who have spent some time in the workforce but have not yet finished their undergraduate work. The head of the program happens to be an old friend; she assured me that all your credits would transfer. They would also award you credit for your work experience, an entire semester's worth."

A whole semester of college credit for work I'd already done? No books, no tests, no tuition? And best of all, no time? At my current rate, it would take me a year and a half to complete one semester's worth of classes. There had to be a catch.

I took the brochure from the professor's outstretched hand. "How does that work? Do they award more credits per class than other colleges? Is it an online program?"

Dr. Streeter shook his head. "No, no. They will give credit for work experience, but you'll have to take the rest of the classes on campus, three credits a class, and accumulate one hundred and twenty credits to graduate.

"Look," he said, grabbing an old envelope and scribbling his calculations on the back. "You've already got thirty credits from us. Carrillon will grant you fifteen more for work experience, which means you only need seventy-five more. If you take six classes for three semesters and seven classes for one, you graduate in two years— sooner if you do the summer term. Carrillon assumes that adult students will be utterly focused on work and capable of taking more than five classes a term. Which is true. Unlike my younger students, you're not spending your time watching videos of cats running into screen doors on YouTube or posting pictures of food to your Facebook page."

"No. I'm too busy working full-time and taking care of my two small children for that. Or anything else! Do you know how long it's been since I was on a date, Professor? Neither do I."

This unexpected mention of my personal life made the old man blush, and my snappish tone brought a wounded expression to his face, making me regret my outburst. Why had I jumped on him like that? He meant no harm.

And why embarrass both of us by bringing up the vast wasteland that was my dating life? Or lack thereof? Actually, I've never been on a date, not once. After I ran away from home, I ended up living on the street, then working in a strip club—sort of. I thought I was being hired as a coat-check girl in a restaurant, only later finding out what kind of place it was and that they expected me to do a lot more than hang up coats. Sounds crazy, I know, but I fell for it. Stupid of me. Anyway, Hodge scooped me up from the gutter and took me home with him. I was as grateful as a rescued puppy and just as willing to please. Before long I was pregnant, married, and trapped, entirely dependent upon him for everything. And he never even had to buy me dinner. How stupid can you get?

So, no. I've never been on a date. But it isn't like I spend my Saturday nights downing quarts of ice cream, sighing over movies on Lifetime, and moaning for a man. I'm too busy for that. Too busy for everything aside from working, studying, and caring for my kids. The only thing I do for me is go to the weekly meeting of my quilt circle. Some weeks I'm too swamped even for that, let alone a boyfriend.

Okay, I do have occasional fantasies about

Ryan Reynolds showing up on my doorstep with roses and a swooningly sultry expression on his gorgeous face. I'm human, after all. But it's never going to happen. And that's probably a good thing, because even though Ryan Reynolds *seems* like the most perfectly perfect man possible, if I actually were able to have a relationship with him, I'm sure he'd turn out to be a jerk or worse. I have some sort of invisible magnetic pull that draws jerks to me. So sure, yes. It *might* be nice to have a man in my life, but I don't see it happening.

Dr. Streeter was a lifelong bachelor with no obligations to anything but his work and studies. He had no clue how hard it was for me to find the time, money, and child care to take even one night class per week. But he meant well; I could see that.

"I'm sorry, Professor. I appreciate your confidence in me, but I'm a single mother. I just can't put my life on hold for the next two years. Even if I could, where would I find the tuition money? How much does this cost anyway?"

His face lit up again. "That's what is so wonderful. A donor is underwriting a portion of the costs, so Carrillon is able to charge a reduced, flat-rate tuition—eight thousand dollars a semester no matter how many courses you take. So if you were to—"

"Eight thousand dollars a semester!" I gasped,

and then laughed, wondering what kind of heiress he thought he was talking to. Seriously, Dr. Streeter needed to climb down from the ivory tower and spend some time in *my* world, where a blown-out tire or trip to the dentist meant the difference between being able to scrape together money for tuition or having to sit out the semester.

"Thirty-two thousand total? That's more than I make in a year! Even if I had that kind of money, what do you expect my family to live on while I'm going to school?"

Dr. Streeter, who had been nodding the whole time I talked, said, "It would be a difficult undertaking, Ivy. I realize that. But you're going to end up spending that much on your education anyway—probably more. You're just going to do it slower. Tuition costs rise every year. What will a class cost you nine years from now when you finally graduate? How much earning power will you give up in those extra seven years when you won't have a degree? Time is an irreplaceable commodity, Ivy. You've got to look at this long term."

"I understand what you're saying, Dr. Streeter, but . . ." I sighed, suddenly very tired. I looked at my watch. "I've got to go. My babysitter has to be home by nine."

I walked toward the door. "Thank you, Professor. I really appreciate your encouragement, but there's just no way I can make this work. Not now."

Dr. Streeter's swivel chair squeaked as he got to his feet. "Here," he said, taking the blue brochure I'd left on his desk and placing it on top of my book. "Hold on to this for a while. Maybe something will happen to make you change your mind—a miracle or something. Who knows? Maybe you'll win the lottery."

"Professor," I said wearily, "I've never even bought a ticket."

"Then maybe it's time you did. Act of faith, eh?"

He smiled and rested a big hand on my shoulder. "At least think about it. Promise me you will."

I *did* think about it. For about as long as it took to walk from Dr. Streeter's office to my car. Then I slid off the rainbow and back into reality, driving home with the windshield wipers going full blast, thinking about the stuff that mattered.

What was I going to do about my broken computer? The tech guys at the office-supply store would charge me seventy-five bucks just to run a diagnostic and who knew how much more for repairs? It might be cheaper just to buy a new one, but I didn't have that kind of money right now. Speaking of money, the bill for the car taxes was still sitting on my desk. How was I going to scrape up $168.52 to pay it? Had I remembered to send in an order for more interfacing before I'd left work? Or to call the pediatrician and schedule the kids' school physicals, so I wouldn't be scrambling to get them an appointment in August? Would that spot of drywall near the bathroom floor, the part that got soaked in this morning's Bobby-induced flood, dry out or would I have to patch it? Could I squeeze in a trip to the market during my lunch break tomorrow?

Fifty balls to keep in the air and only two hands to juggle with. I opened my mouth wide, unclenching and stretching my jaw, trying to relieve the building tension.

What was Dr. Streeter thinking? No way could I go to college full-time, especially a college in Delaware. Delaware! He neglected to mention Carrillon's location, but it was listed right there on the brochure. I'm sure Delaware is lovely, but no way was I moving.

New Bern is my home now and, more important, my kids' home. Bobby doesn't remember living anywhere else. He loves New Bern—we all do. Our friends, Evelyn and Charlie, Abigail and Franklin, Margot, Virginia, Tessa, Madelyn, and Philippa are all here. They're my support system; I depend on them. Not the way I did at first, of course. After all, they've got their own lives to live. Evelyn and Charlie are busy running their two businesses, the quilt shop and the Grill on the Green restaurant. Abigail and Franklin spend half their time traveling. Margot is married now and busy with her family. Philippa is occupied by her duties at the church and taking care of her baby, Tim. Madelyn has her hands full running the inn, and Tessa is busy filling the deluge of orders for her herbal soaps and lotions. Even Garrett, who for years was my regular babysitter on quilt circle nights, isn't available now. He'd been working and living above the quilt shop, waiting to see if Liza, his former girlfriend, was ever going to move back from Chicago. I guess he must have gotten tired of waiting, because about two months ago, he moved to the city. Who can blame him? New Bern isn't exactly a haven for the young and single.

But I love it here. In New Bern I feel happy, accepted, and most important, safe. I can't imagine living anywhere else, not for all the diplomas in Delaware.

The house was quiet. Drew was sitting at the kitchen table studying but started to pack up his books as soon as he saw me.

"Everybody asleep?"

He nodded. "Bethany gave me a little grief about bedtime but not much, and Bobby was in there singing to himself for a while."

I smiled. "Yeah, he does that."

I drove Drew back home. I hated to leave the kids alone, even for ten minutes, but what else could I do?

"Can you just drop me off?" Drew asked, pointing to a narrow opening in a hedge that marks the entrance to the Olivers' driveway, just a couple of hundred feet from his own. "I have to go check on the house in case they decide to come up for the weekend."

"Drew, are you sure? It's pouring. Why don't you wait until tomorrow? Nobody will know the difference. It's supposed to rain all weekend, and if they haven't been up since Christmas, it's not very likely they're going to show up now."

I've never met Gayla and Brian Oliver, the people from New York who bought the cottage next door to Drew about three years ago, but I almost felt sorry for these strangers who either didn't appreciate what they had or couldn't carve out time to enjoy it. And maybe it sounds strange, but in a way, I felt sorry for the house too. It looked lonely. And neglected. The grass was overgrown, the driveway was cratered with potholes, and the hedges needed trimming. So sad.

"The Olivers pay me to check on the house on Tuesday and Friday, so that's what I have to do. I'll be fine walking home." He pulled his black hoodie up. "Oh, I almost forgot. I fixed your computer."

"You did! Thanks! What was wrong with it?"

"Dead battery. Power cord came loose from the socket."

I smacked my hand against my forehead. "I'm an idiot."

Drew grinned, then hopped out of the car and ran to the cottage, leaping over puddles, dashing between raindrops.

What a sweet kid.

I poured ginger ale into a glass filled with ice, watching it fizz and bubble, took a piece of cold pizza from the box in the refrigerator, carried everything into my room, sat down in my favorite chair, a wingback upholstered with blue corduroy that I bought at a tag sale for twelve dollars, and opened my laptop. The computer gave a series of encouraging blips when I pressed the power button, booting up without a problem. I still felt like an idiot, but not as idiotic as I would have felt if I'd spent seventy-five dollars to have the guy at Staples "fix" it by plugging in the power cord. Things were looking up.

I love this last hour of the day, when the kids are asleep and the house is quiet, when the lights are low and the air is still and no one is asking me for anything. On an ideal day, I'd use this time for quilting. I leave my sewing machine set up in a corner of the dining room, so I can take advantage of every spare moment. But even when

I have to do homework or catch up on e-mail instead of sew, being able to do so in peace and quiet is so, so nice.

I bit the point off the pizza slice and logged in to my e-mail, sipping ginger ale while I waited for the program to open. By the time I finished deleting the spam, links to blogs I don't have time to read, and ads for things I can't afford to buy, there wasn't too much left to deal with. Donna Walsh wanted to discuss bringing in another intern to take Judith's place; I told her I'd call her in the morning. Philippa was looking for volunteers to help out with Vacation Bible School in July; I said I would bake cookies and help decorate. Margot's e-mail, with the subject line "National Girlfriend Appreciation Day," contained a poem celebrating the importance of girlfriends and instructed me to forward the message to the special women in my life, including the one who sent it to me. I did return it to Margot, with "Xs" and "Os" for kisses and hugs, but didn't forward it to anyone else. Not so much because I don't do forwards (though I don't) but because I knew that Margot would already have sent it to Evelyn, Abigail, Tessa, Madelyn, Virginia, and Philippa. We are one another's special women. I don't need a poem to remind me of that, but sometimes it's nice to get one just the same.

I didn't recognize the address on the last e-mail,

so I deleted it without opening it, thinking it was just more spam. I hovered the cursor above the red button in the upper left corner, ready to click it and shut down the program, but something stopped me.

Sheila Fenton . . . Whom did I know named Sheila Fenton? A customer from the shop? Somebody I'd met at church? Or at the Stanton Center? Nothing concrete came to mind, but the name sounded familiar.

I took another drink of ginger ale, clicked on the trash folder, opened the message, and started to read.

Dear Ms. Peterman,

As the Family Reunification Caseworker assigned to your case, number 780-533, I am writing to inform you that your former husband, Hodge Edelman, has nearly completed his prison sentence, reduced for good behavior, and will be released in sixty days.

In an interview I conducted with him earlier this week, Mr. Edelman expressed a desire to see his minor children, Bethany and Robert, upon his release and to seek . . .

My fingers went slack, and the glass I was holding slipped and fell onto the wooden floor in a collage of ice, broken glass, and ginger-colored fizz. But I didn't notice any of that, not until I got out of the chair and stepped on a shard of glass, drawing blood, turning the bubbles pink.

Until that moment, none of it seemed quite real; I was hoping that I'd fallen asleep in my chair, was having a bad dream, and would wake up soon. But I hadn't, and I didn't. The stabbing pain in my foot, the pounding of my heart, the pink bubbles, testified to the truth.

Hodge was getting out of prison and coming to New Bern. He wanted to see Bethany and Bobby, to be reunited with them. And, according to Sheila Fenton and the state of Connecticut, he could. And there was nothing I could do to prevent it.

❦ 5 ❧

Gayla

Pouring rain and an overturned tractor-trailer on I-95 added hours to my trip. When I finally did arrive at the cottage, I almost ran over Drew Kelleher.

He was walking down the dark driveway wearing jeans and a black sweatshirt. I didn't see him until the last second. Thank heaven my brakes are good.

When the car lurched to a stop, Drew, who didn't seem to realize how close I'd come to hitting him, just waved and walked up to the car.

"Hey, Mrs. Oliver," he said when I rolled down the window.

"Drew?" Truthfully, I wasn't 100 percent sure.

If anything is wrong at the house, Drew sends me a text, but I'd seen him in person only once, on that weekend he helped stack the wood and Brian offered him sixty dollars a month to keep an eye on the house. He'd been a skinny kid of fourteen then. Now he was seventeen, a foot taller, and twenty pounds heavier, with muscled shoulders and the beginnings of a beard.

"What are you doing out here?"

"Checking on the house."

"In this weather? You could have waited until tomorrow. Hop in. I'll give you a ride home. You're going to catch pneumonia out here."

I shook my head as he loped around the car to the passenger door, wondering why he hadn't worn something warmer and more waterproof than a black hoodie.

"I was just about to text you," he said, pushing the sodden fleece hood from his head. "The furnace is out."

"Seriously?" Apparently, Brian's prophecy had proven correct. "Great timing. Oh, well. I can start a fire. It's not that cold." I pulled onto the grass and made a U-turn.

"I carried some extra wood from the pile to the porch, just in case you showed up. Do you want me to ask my dad to come take a look at the furnace?"

He'd brought in extra wood? Even though we hadn't been here since Christmas? What a nice kid.

"Don't worry. I'll call a repairman tomorrow. Drew, I almost didn't recognize you. I bet you've grown a foot since I last saw you. What are you, six-two?"

"Six-three-and-half." He smiled, proud of his height. "Dad is always griping about how much I eat."

"I bet. You're a junior now, right? Have you decided where you want to go to college?"

He shrugged. "Maybe UConn, but I haven't really—Wait! Turn here!" he exclaimed, pointing to the right. I pulled up in front of a white cape-style house with green shutters. Drew thanked me for the ride.

"Hey, I'm going to be up here for a few days, maybe even a few weeks, so you won't need to come by for a while."

His face fell. "Oh. Okay, sure. Let me know when you need me again."

"Drew, I'm going to pay you anyway."

He shook his head. "I can't let you do that, Mrs. Oliver. Not if I'm not doing any work for you."

"Of course you can. We have a deal. Don't!" I said, holding up my hand to stave off his protest. "I'm paying you like I always do. It's called a retainer—a payment that someone makes so you'll reserve your time for them. Whether they use the time or not is their problem. That's how people pay me, and that's how I'm paying you, so no arguments, all right? By the way, 'retainer' is an SAT word. Memorize it."

He smiled, but I could tell that he still wasn't comfortable with being paid for work he hadn't performed.

"Well, if you need anything while you're here, Mrs. Oliver, just let me know. You're low on kindling. I can chop some for you if you want."

"I'll be fine."

He opened the car door. "Oh, Mrs. Oliver, one more thing. The Christmas tree is still up in the living room. I was going to take it down, but I didn't know if maybe you still wanted it?" He raised his shoulders questioningly, making it clear that, had it been him, he'd have removed the tree, but on the other hand, you never could tell what crazy stuff people from the city might do.

"Great," I sighed. "I asked Brian to throw it out before we left, but I guess he must have forgotten. That's okay. I can do it."

He pulled his wet hoodie back over his head and got out, then turned around and stooped down, peering at me through the open door with a concerned look.

"Mrs. Oliver, are you okay? You look kind of . . . Well . . . is anything wrong?"

My throat tightened. "I've had a cold. It's been going around. But I'm getting better. I'm fine."

"Okay. Well, if you need anything . . ."

"Good night, Drew."

The cottage was like an icebox. Drew was right: The iron dinosaur in the cellar must have finally given up the ghost. I searched through the closet and found my ski parka, then snapped on the lights in the kitchen.

The mice were back. They'd left little calling cards on the countertops. Disgusting. I wouldn't be able to prepare a thing in the kitchen until I bleached and scrubbed every surface. But cooking was the last thing on my mind; food would have choked me.

When I went into the living room, I found the Christmas tree, still in a stand in the corner, circled by a little moat of dropped needles, so brown and bare it was nearly skeletal, with one lonely, overlooked glass bulb clinging bravely to a naked branch. The very last thing I'd asked Brian to do when we left at the holidays was to toss the tree out. Maybe he hadn't been listening. Maybe he had other things on his mind.

When I got down on the floor and unscrewed the bolts from the stand, the tree toppled side-ways onto the floor, losing the last of its needles and smashing the glass bulb into silver-green shards. I opened the back door and tossed the tree skeleton outside, then grabbed a broom and swept up the mess.

The exercise did nothing to warm me. If anything, the house seemed colder than when I'd first arrived. I brought in a load of wood from the back porch and, tossing in a few handfuls of dried Christmas tree needles for tinder, started a fire in the fireplace.

I was exhausted, but my head was too full for sleep. I dug through a kitchen cabinet and found an unopened bottle of scotch, a Christmas gift from our insurance agent, and poured a little into a glass. The unfamiliar taste was harsh and initially unpleasant. It burned my throat but warmed and loosened my limbs, and after a minute, I found the sensation soothing.

I filled the glass to the top, carried it into the living room, settled myself into a chair in front of the fireplace, and started to cry again. I stayed there the rest of the night, draining the glass and refilling it twice more, sobbing until I was as used up as the discarded tree skeleton, now so stripped of color and dried out that it was hard to remember how splendid, fresh, and fine it had been when we found it and brought it home, the way Brian and I had been once upon a time.

I was only nineteen when we'd met, little more than a child. But from the moment I laid eyes on him, I had loved him. I couldn't help myself.

● ● ●

Three days after my eighteenth birthday, I received a letter informing me that I'd been granted admission to Princeton University. I was thrilled. So were my parents. Why wouldn't we be? I was a poor girl from a lower-middle-class background, the first of my family to be admitted to college. And not just any college, but Princeton! One of the most elite universities in the country, the college that my parents had dreamed of sending me to since forever, though I'm still not sure why. Whatever the reason, my father tacked a Princeton Tigers pennant to my bedroom wall before I was even born, and for the next eighteen years, there it stayed, reminding me of what was expected of me, goading me to work harder, do better, be worthy of the sacrifices my parents had made for me.

The arrival of that fat envelope marked the culmination of all their hopes, and mine as well. I wanted to go to Princeton—of course I did. How could I not? I'd never considered any other avenue; I never knew there *were* any. But within weeks of my arrival on campus, it was clear that I was not born to be a Tiger.

For one thing, I was quickly acquainted with the fact that I was not nearly as special or academically gifted as I had been led to believe. Sure, I'd been on the top of the ladder at my high school, but at Princeton, I was average at best, as my first-semester grade point confirmed. This isn't an uncommon experience among college freshmen; I've talked a number of my former clients through the shock of discovering just how small a fish they are when suddenly dropped into a bigger pond. My discontent ran deeper than that. I just didn't fit in at Princeton.

Many, though far from all, of my classmates were a lot wealthier than me, but the gulf that separated us was more than economic. They were miles more sophisticated than I was, better read and better traveled. I'd never been farther from home than the Jersey shore, and though I'd read Shakespeare's plays in their entirety and written that drama column for our school paper, my experience with professional theater was limited to two trips to see the Rockettes at Radio City Music Hall at Christmas.

Realizing how limited my life experience was in comparison to everyone else's, I was tongue-tied in the classroom and socially awkward. My clothes, my unfashionably frizzy hair, even my vocabulary was out of place at Princeton. The only friend I had was my roommate, Lanie Micelli, a pert, pretty, and driven girl, the daughter of a trucking magnate from Chicago. Lanie's freshman GPA was just as low as mine was, and she fell in and out of love nearly every week, but she knew how to get on in life.

Lanie took me under her wing. She lent me

clothes, made me read *Cosmopolitan* magazine, taught me to smoke, tried to chemically straighten my hair—a well-intentioned act with disastrous results—and introduced me to a string of her cast-off boyfriends, with similarly disastrous results. Finally, Lanie came to the conclusion that what I needed was broadening and a change of atmosphere.

"Do a summer semester in London," she counseled. "Smoke some pot, visit some clubs, sleep with the bass player in a punk band. If you have time, maybe tour a few museums and see a play in the East End. You know what your problem is, Gayla?"

"You mean besides having bad hair?"

"See? That's what I'm talking about. You're too damned serious. Quit thinking so hard! Go to Europe and do something your parents would disapprove of. You'll be a new woman when you come back; I promise."

I was too scared to smoke pot, but I did rip the knees out of a pair of perfectly good jeans, stick a bunch of safety pins on my jacket, and go to some clubs, only to discover that punk music was dead, or at least in remission, and much too angry for my taste. Following a tip from a girl at Marks & Spencer who sold me a tube of pink glitter lip gloss, I found a little club that hosted bands that were less screeching.

Warrior Poets played the kind of music that

wouldn't be out of place among today's current crop of singer-songwriters, with thoughtful lyrics and hummable guitar interludes, played acoustically. The band was just okay, but the bass player was divine.

Brian kept his eyes closed during almost every song, like he wasn't playing for anybody but himself. I couldn't stop myself from staring at him. His hair was long then and flopped down over his brows when he bent his head forward. His jeans were ripped at the knees, not because he'd torn them but because he'd didn't care about clothes. He didn't have to. Then, as now, everything he put on his tall, lean body looked absolutely fabulous. His fingers were long and slender, like mine. He pressed and strummed and stroked them along the strings and neck of his guitar with a delicacy and skill I found swooningly sensual.

By the third set, he must have felt me staring at him because he kept opening his eyes in the middle of songs, looking up at me, even fumbling a chord once, drawing a scathing glance from the lead singer. At the end of the night, he came to my table and offered to buy me a beer. Of course, I was already totally enamored, but the second Brian opened his mouth, it was all over for me. Few nineteen-year-old girls can resist a gorgeous musician, but a gorgeous musician with a British accent? Forget about it.

When the club closed, we found a restaurant that served bacon and eggs all night and told each other the stories of our lives. Brian's was much more interesting than mine. He was twenty-one years old, the second son of a distinguished family. I don't think he intended to tell me that part, because the minute it came out, he turned red and started fiddling with his silverware.

"It's not a big deal," he said.

"It sounds kind of glamorous to me."

Brian shook his head. "Three hundred years ago, maybe. Now 'viscount' is just a title. Comes with no lands or rights but plenty of responsibilities. Well, not responsibilities as much as pressures."

"Such as?"

"To look more important than you are and maintain a lifestyle you really can't afford, like keeping a big, drafty, impractical house that's been in the family since the reign of George the Fourth, or sending your sons to Harrow because that's where we've always gone, that kind of thing. Keeping up appearances. It's ridiculous. My brother, James, will inherit it all someday—title, house, and headaches."

"And that doesn't bother you?"

"Not a bit. I'm free to do and be whatever I want. Of course, my parents don't agree. When I told my father I was dropping out of university to compose and play music, he almost had a heart attack."

"You mean you *wrote* those songs?"

He dipped his head forward. His sleek chestnut hair flopped over his brow.

"Most of them." He smiled. "The good ones."

"Even the one about the phone booth? Wow! That was my favorite. That's so cool! I never knew anyone who made their living writing songs."

"Well," he said with a shrug, "I haven't actually sold any. Not yet. But I own all the songs. And if we ever make it big . . ."

He let the end of his sentence trail off as he cut bacon into bite-sized pieces. "I'm starting to think it might never happen, not with Warrior Poets. Will doesn't have much of a voice. Trevor's a decent enough drummer but only when he's sober, which isn't very often. I'm cashing in at the end of the run."

"What will you do then?"

"Go to Italy. I'm going to live on a barge for July and August, just float from place to place, drink wine, eat pasta, write songs, and perform for passengers in the evening. I saw an advert from a tour company, so I sent in a tape and got the job. I'll stay in the crew quarters. It'll be tight, but that doesn't matter."

"Wow. But won't your parents be mad?"

He grinned. "What can they do to stop me?"

Brian was more conventional than his rebellious words would have implied. Though he could absolutely have gotten me into bed on that first night, no question about it, we didn't sleep together for another three weeks. It was my first time, and it was . . . lovely. Beyond lovely.

In the morning, as soon as I stirred next to him, he pulled me into his arms, brushed the hair away from my face, and asked me to marry him.

The wedding took place a few days later, at the registry office. The surroundings were dingy and the ceremony was perfunctory, but I couldn't have been happier. I called my parents to tell them the news and not to bother sending the check for my fall tuition; I was dropping out of Princeton.

My mother sobbed herself hysterical, and my father unleashed more oaths than I'd ever heard strung together at one time, then slammed down the receiver without saying good-bye. It was a horrible confrontation, but at least it was short. The polite but terrifically tense tea we shared with Brian's parents and brother at a dreary seaside hotel in Bristol was interminable.

We were quiet when we went up to our room that night, a little morose, but another session of passionate lovemaking drove away all shadows and thoughts of our families. We were complete in each other. In the morning, we took a train back to London, and the day after that, we left for Italy.

Brian had called the tour owners and talked them into letting me come along as a chef's assistant. The chef, a short, grizzled, grumpy Italian man named Mario, didn't like women in his kitchen. Since I didn't know the first thing about cookery, this was lucky for everyone. My duties were limited to table setting, clearing, and washing up. There were only sixteen passengers aboard, so this wasn't too taxing and left me plenty of time to spend with Brian during the day and to sit with the other passengers night after night, listening to him play his guitar and sing.

His voice was good, very good. If Brian had been the lead singer, I was convinced that the Warrior Poets would have made it big. I shared this observation with Brian one night as we lay squeezed together in our cabin's single bed.

"You think so, do you?"

"Don't laugh! I'm serious. But I'm glad things turned out the way they did."

He rolled toward me and pushed the Princeton T-shirt that served as my nightgown off my shoulder.

"Oh, yes?" he murmured, kissing a line from my neck to the swell of my breast. "Why is that?"

"Because this way I get you all to myself."

It was a lovely honeymoon. We drifted lazily through the canals of Venice, then to the islands of Torcello and Burano, then down the Brenta River to Murano and to Padua before turning around and retracing our route to Venice. Brian didn't get nearly as much composing done as he'd planned, but he didn't seem to care. At the end of August, the captain of the *Lucia Dolce* asked us to stay on. I lost count of how many times we made the circle from Venice to Padua and back, but we never tired of it. We made new discoveries about Italy and each other on every trip.

Given the frequency and vigor of our love-making, we should have anticipated what came next, but somehow we didn't. Perhaps circling the same route for so long, never considering where things began or ended, lulled us into believing that life could always be exactly like this. But it had to come to an end, and it did, just before our six-month anniversary, when we learned I was pregnant with twins.

When a young doctor at the clinic in Padua, delighted by the opportunity to use his brand-new ultrasound machine, explained in broken English that my nausea and bloating were not the result of a bad ciopinno, Brian was stunned, then thrilled. We went back to the barge and shared the news with the crew, who threw us a party, toasting our babies with shots of limoncello. Brian joined in. I drank lemonade.

The following day, everyone except me had

thick heads. Brian and I had our first argument. But we worked through it and started talking about what to do next, ultimately deciding on going to the States.

Beyond that, we didn't have much of a plan. We knew we needed to find a place to live and a job for Brian that would support all of us, at least until the babies were old enough that I could go back to work. I suggested we go to New Jersey, maybe live with my folks for a while, but Brian was having nothing to do with that. We would go to New York. It was, he insisted, the only city for a musician. I was a little concerned about finding an affordable place to live but took comfort in the fact that we wouldn't need a big place. After all, we'd lived in a cabin the size of a closet for six months and been pretty happy, hadn't we? We'd figure it out.

When he cut his hair on the night before our flight to New York, I shed a few tears, but a part of me was relieved to be going home. Life on the barge was paradise, but it couldn't last. Eventually, you've got to go over the garden wall and into the real world. The babies forced us to make the leap. You can't stay in Eden forever. Eventually, you've got to wake up from the dream, face the facts, and deal with life as it is instead of how you imagined it to be.

I thought I already had, all those years ago. Maybe I was wrong.

6

Ivy

Remembering the advice of Arnie, my attorney, I uncrossed my arms from my chest, deliberately attempting to adopt a less hostile posture.

"Sheila Fenton is just doing her job," he'd told me. Be as cooperative as you can. She's going to be calling a lot of the shots once Hodge is released, so we want her on our side."

"Why? Why does this person who doesn't know me or my children have that kind of power over us?" I threw up my hands and resumed pacing from one end of Arnie's office to the other. "I still can't believe this. After all Hodge has done, why should he be allowed to just waltz in and turn our lives upside down again? Why?"

Arnie shifted his weight to one side of his desk chair, propped his elbow on the armrest, rested his chin on his fist, and tried to explain it to me yet again. "Because in the eyes of the law, barring extreme circumstances, a father has a right to see his children."

I stopped in my tracks and spun around to face Arnie, laying my hands flat on his desk and leaning toward him. "He subjected me to years of emotional and physical abuse, he broke my hand by slamming a car door on it, and he slapped Bethany so hard that he left a bruise on her face! How much more extreme do the circumstances have to be?"

"More. Look, if you'd been able to document Bethany's injuries when he hit her, we might have had a chance to terminate his parental rights, but as things stand, there just isn't enough evidence to do that."

"But what if the kids don't want to see him? What about *their* rights?"

"That's why Sheila is involved," Arnie said patiently. "She's supposed to be looking out for everybody's best interests. I've worked with her before, Ivy. Sheila is fair, but she's tough. She knows all the angles and tricks that parents try to pull. So whatever you do, do not try to coach the kids about what to say during the meeting. She'll see right through that. If I were you, I wouldn't say anything to the kids right now. Let Sheila explain the situation to them."

I slumped down into one of Arnie's extra chairs. "Well, Bethany's not going to want to see him; I can tell you that right now."

"I'm sure that's true, but there is no way she'll be allowed to refuse."

"Why? Just because she's eleven? She knows what her father is, Arnie. She remembers what he's capable of."

"I realize that. If it were up to me, Hodge

wouldn't be able to have any contact with any of you ever again. But it isn't. It's up to the law and Sheila Fenton. In this instance, Sheila *is* the law. So when you meet her, be cooperative and non-combative. Remember what I said, Ivy. We want this woman on our side."

In the ten days that had passed since I received that first, explosive e-mail, Sheila Fenton and I had exchanged a number of e-mails and had one face-to-face meeting with Arnie present. I still couldn't tell if she was on our side or not.

She was pleasant without being exactly warm, giving away nothing, maintaining an even temper even when Bethany shook her head violently from side to side and shouted, "No! I don't want to see him! And I'm *not* going to, ever again. I hate him! Nobody can make me see him if I don't want to!"

"Bethany," Sheila said evenly, "I can see that you're upset, but your father has said that he would very much like to see you again. A judge has said he's entitled to do that, so you *do* have to see him."

Bethany whipped her head toward me, eyes wide, looking for my support. She had it; I didn't think she should have to see Hodge if she didn't want to. But I also knew that my opinion wouldn't carry any weight in a courtroom and that trying to argue Bethany's point for her not only would be fighting a losing battle, but also might end up prejudicing Sheila Fenton's opinion of me. I had to find a way to comply with the legal realities while doing what I could to protect my kids.

"Honey, give it a chance." I reached out to take her hand, but she snatched it away.

"I don't want to see him. He hit me! And he hit you too." Eyes blazing, she turned back to Sheila. "He used to hit her all the time. He slammed her hand in the door of a car. I was little, but I remember."

Sheila nodded, her expression patient but immovable. "I know. I've seen the police report and your mother's medical files. But I've seen your father too. He's very anxious to see you. And I've talked to the people who have been working with him at the prison. They say he's been a very good, cooperative prisoner. He hasn't been involved in one fight or violent incident in the last five years. That's why he's being released early. The parole board thinks he's been rehabilitated," she said, looking at me and then at my daughter, simplifying her explanation so Bethany would be able to understand. "They think he's learned from his mistakes and has changed. Five years is a long time."

People can change. I really believe that. But just because people can change doesn't mean that Hodge has. Sheila Fenton doesn't know him like I do.

Bethany looked at me again. She didn't say

anything, but her eyes begged me to do some-thing.

"Will she have to be alone with him?" I asked.

"No. Definitely not," Mrs. Fenton said, address-ing herself to Bethany. "Especially at first, your visits with your dad will be supervised. Some-one will be with you all the time. Later, if things go well, that might change, but we would talk about it first and make sure you were feeling comfortable with the idea."

Sheila clasped her hands together and leaned closer to my daughter. "Your dad really is anxious to see you again and to be part of your life. He wrote you a letter," she said, reaching into her pocket and pulling out a white envelope.

"I don't want it."

Sheila's eyes shifted in my direction, seeking my support, I suppose, but I didn't say anything. I know that Arnie said I should be cooperative, but if Bethany didn't want to read that letter, then she didn't have to.

Bobby was sitting in the waiting room while all this was going on. Sheila had thought it best to speak to the children separately, so she could explain everything to them at an age-appropriate level.

I didn't suppose Bobby would be as distressed by the situation as Bethany was, but I really wasn't prepared for his response to the news of Hodge's imminent return. He was excited, elated.

And full of questions I didn't know how to answer.

"He's coming home! Really?"

"Yes. Well, not home exactly. Your daddy and I aren't married anymore, so he can't stay with us."

This didn't seem to faze him; lots of his friends have divorced parents too.

"I've got a big bed. He can stay in my room! I don't mind sharing."

"No, honey. He can't stay in your room either. He doesn't . . . We don't . . ."

I looked at Sheila, hoping she'd step in, grateful when she did.

"Bobby," she said calmly, "your father is coming to New Bern, and he wants to see you, but he can't stay at your house. It's more like he's coming for a visit."

"When is he coming? How long is he going to stay? Can we go down to the dock and pick him up?"

"Dock?" I asked. "What dock?"

"The dock at the ocean," he said simply. "Where they park the ships."

Sheila gave me a quick glance, as if thinking I might be able to explain what was going on in Bobby's mind, but I had no clue. She figured it out, though, and a lot quicker than I did.

"Bobby, where do you think your dad is right now? On a ship?"

"Uh-huh. On an aircraft carrier. In China. He's in the navy. That's why he's been gone so long. China is really far away, like on the whole other side of the planet."

Sheila kept her eyes on Bobby's as he spoke, nodding slowly. "I see. Did you figure this out on your own? Or did somebody explain it to you? Your mom?"

Bobby shook his head vigorously. "No. Bethany said that it makes Mommy sad to talk about him, so I shouldn't."

"Then, Bethany told you about your father? That he went to China on an aircraft carrier?"

"Uh-huh," he answered solemnly, then turned toward me and grabbed my hand. "But he's coming back, so you can stop being divorced now. Okay?"

For a minute, I just didn't know what to say. He looked so hopeful and innocent, because he was. I held out my arms, and he immediately snuggled into them, the way he always does.

I kissed the top of his head. "I love you, Bear. Do you know that?"

"I love you too, Mommy."

Sheila, sitting in the chair opposite from us, folded her hands under her chin and gave me a questioning look. I nodded. I was going to have to tell him the truth; I already knew that.

7

Gayla

For about a week, I became somebody I didn't recognize.

The first three days were taken up mostly with crying, drinking, and chain-smoking. There was also a certain amount of ignoring calls from Brian, then answering the calls and bursting into fresh waves of sobbing as soon as he started talking, after which I would hang up on him. Eventually, I just switched the phone off.

That was the really pitiful part of my pity party, those first three days. When the scotch ran out and when I had cried so many tears that you could have twisted me like a pretzel and not wrung out one more drop of liquid, I started cleaning. And cursing. And breaking things.

I had to do something.

Trash bag in hand, I banished the last traces of Christmas, throwing out the greeting cards, a bright green tin still containing a litter of cookie crumbs and sprinkles of red sugar (no wonder we had mice), a terra-cotta pot containing a dud of an amaryllis bulb, crumpled ribbons and wrapping paper, and various other bits that had been overlooked in our rush to beat the post-holiday traffic back to the city.

I scrubbed all traces of visiting rodents from the countertops and appliances, emptied the refrigerator, and wiped down the cupboards. I got down on my hands and knees and scrubbed the wood floors and baseboards with such vehemence that I broke a sweat and raised splinters. I moved furniture and rolled up rugs. I swept and mopped and wiped and scrubbed, working until my hands were raw and my eyes watered from bleach fumes. When that was done, I started cleaning closets. My life was a shambles, but my closets would be in perfect order.

The first box I opened was filled with dozens of how-to books that I'd bought and never really read or used. There were books on how to make candles, scrap quilts, jewelry, knitted scarves, woven baskets, homemade bread, pasta, and pickles. There were books on how to plant a garden—grow herbs, flowers, and vegetables—make compost, upholster furniture, design a tree house, write poetry, and draw with the right side of your brain.

That's what really put me over the edge—the books.

It suddenly occurred to me that if I had two lifetimes in front of me rather than the last half of only one, I wouldn't have time to master more than a fraction of the skills contained in those books. Even so, year after year, I kept buying those books, telling myself that someday, after the kids were out of diapers, or out of kindergarten, or out of college, that when I finished my degree, or got out of debt, or retired, I would have time and money and permission to do what *I* wanted to do, to *live* life instead of just getting through it.

I'd put myself on hold, thinking it would be worth it in the end, that one day, someday, when the time was right and I had fulfilled my responsibilities to my parents, my husband, my children, and my clients, it would be my turn, *our* turn, that Brian and I would finally get to be together and happy. I had believed that this house, which Brian had insisted we buy three years before, was a kind of down payment on that life we would live *together* and share *together* in that someday that was always just a little farther over the horizon.

How stupid was that? How stupid was I?

Very stupid. Fabulously stupid. Naïvely and foolishly and trustingly stupid. The magnitude of my gullibility was too great to put into words, or at least the sort of words I was accustomed to using.

That's when the cursing began.

Words I haven't used since I was in college and trying to convince people of my worldliness, words I've never used in my life, acidic and searingly profane, spouted from my mouth like lava from a volcano.

For the first time in my life, I understood how crimes of passion came to pass. At that moment, if she, the Other, walked through the door, there was no doubt in my mind that I could have inflicted serious bodily harm upon her. I had never been so furious, so emotionally out of control. It was frightening but at the same time strangely exhilarating. I don't think I realized—not until that moment—how hard I had worked for so many years to keep a lid on my emotions, desires, and disappointments. Initially, my rage was directed only at the Other, but it quickly expanded to encompass the unjust, uncaring universe in general and my faithless, thoughtless, heartbreaking husband in particular.

I ripped the top off another box. It was filled with paperbacks, all belonging to Brian. I kicked at the box, and then, one by one, flung the books into a garbage bag, along with one from my box, a book about rekindling marital romance. I ripped off the front cover of that one, then the back cover, and various pages, whole chapters at a time, and threw them in the bag with the rest.

The next box was filled with old clothes, boots, and gloves. Every single item that belonged to Brian ended up in the trash bag, even his ice skates. When the bag was full, I carted it to the back door, got another bag, and went on a rampage, opening closets and drawers, pulling out everything I could find that belonged to Brian and tossing it all into the trash bag, staying my hand only when it came to his guitar, the one he'd been playing when I first saw him in London.

When I was done, when I had banished every trace of Brian from the house, I ran across the yard in the rain to the old barn that served as our garage, carrying three big black trash bags and a cardboard box. My load was unwieldy and the ground was like a soggy sponge. I didn't see the stone sticking up from the ground, the one that tripped me and sent me tumbling.

I landed flat on my face in the pouring rain, surrounded by books and papers and clothing and crumpled Christmas wrapping.

After lying there a moment to make sure that nothing was broken, I groaned and got up. My jeans were muddy. So was my sweater. And I was missing a shoe.

I found it, slipped my mud-sodden sock back into it, spit out a few more profanities, and then picked up everything and threw it into the big blue trash can as quickly as I could before running back into the house, water dripping from my hair, mud squelching over the top of my left shoe. I was soaked, filthy, and so angry I was ready to explode. In a way, that's what I did.

I stood in the kitchen, dripping mud and spitting expletives, feeling powerless and furious. I pounded on the kitchen table, leaving a muddy crescent, the shape of a curled fist, then spun around to the sideboard and snatched a delicate, bone-china teacup with yellow daisies painted on the side, one from the set my mother had given me when the twins were born.

I hurled it as hard as I could against the far wall. It shattered into a million pieces, or maybe just a hundred. It didn't matter; the effect was the same: destructive and oddly satisfying. Especially when the echo of exploding crockery was coupled with the report of gunshot-loud profanity.

I grabbed another cup from the shelf, flung it, and smashed it. And another. And another. Until they were gone, smashed to smithereens. All six of them. The only thing left was the matching daisy-painted teapot.

When it was over, I walked through the kitchen over the broken teacups, the ceramic shards crackling beneath the soles of my shoes, my breathing ragged from the exertion of my labors, climbed the stairs, took a shower, and went to bed.

It was the best night's sleep I'd had in four days. I woke up feeling calmer, able to think clearly. For a while.

While I showered and dressed, I began thinking practically about my situation, considering what my life might look like if Brian wasn't in it.

In a brief moment of lucidity, I had taken Lanie's advice and placed a call to her divorce lawyer, Libby Burrell, who gave me a quick overview of the procedures, the timeframes, and the ravages that divorce would likely cause to my life, my family, and my finances. The last point was driven home with particular emphasis when she informed me that she would require a fifty-thousand-dollar retainer before taking me on as a client.

"It's obviously a lot of money," she said in response to my gasp. "But I think that figure is in line with the reputation and results you can expect from our firm, as well as the importance of the path you're about to take. For some couples, divorce is the only option. But this isn't a step you should take lightly, Gayla."

The conversation was so depressing that it brought on another crying jag as well as a trip to the liquor store for a second bottle of scotch. But she had a point. Getting a divorce would change my life completely. I needed to be prepared for that, to think carefully about what came next. There was a lot to think about.

One of my biggest, most immediate concerns was housing. Where would I live after the divorce? Without Brian's income, I obviously couldn't afford to keep our apartment. What could I afford? A prewar studio in the Village with quirky neighbors, real wood floors, and a bathroom the size of a phone booth? Something more spacious but in the outer boroughs? Or New Jersey? Lanie's spare bedroom? Would I live alone? Get a roommate? A cat?

After the divorce, which of our friends would be his and which would be mine? And where would the kids spend the holidays—at his place or mine? Or would I pass my turkey baster on to the next generation, letting Maggie take over the organization and execution of Thanksgiving, Christmas, and Easter dinners? Or would we meet on neutral territory, become one of those families who celebrate Thanksgiving in hotels and learn to live without leftovers, or spend Christmas in a condo in Hawaii, forgoing gifts because there's no room in the luggage?

Would the dissolution of our marriage be amicable and equitable, as Brian posited? Or vicious and grasping, as Lanie predicted?

And when it was final, would I date? Would I go to bed with other men? Would they expect that? After how long? Did I even *want* to sleep with other men? Would other men want to sleep with me? Maybe not. Maybe I'd never have sex again. Or maybe I *would,* but then the guy would never call me again. How humiliating would that be?

On the other hand, I thought as I went down-stairs to the kitchen, plugged in the coffeemaker, and started sweeping up the broken teacups while waiting for the coffee to brew, maybe it would be great.

Maybe some kind, handsome, fun-loving man with good hair would be interested in me. Maybe he would listen to me, *really* listen—as opposed to talking on his phone and pretending to listen—and find me interesting. No, fascinating. Fascinating was better. And maybe I'd feel the same way about him. And maybe, after some time had passed and I was ready, say, two or three months, I'd invite him to come inside after one of our dates, and he'd stay. No, he'd *ask* if he could stay. And I'd say yes. And we'd kiss passionately and go to the bedroom and get undressed. And I wouldn't be embarrassed because by then I'd be in better shape because I would have started going to the gym again. And the sex would be great—so great! Better than it had ever been with Brian—not that I was sure exactly what it would take to make it better than it had been with Brian. I had no basis for comparison. But it would be better. Much better. And I'd realize what I'd been missing all those years. What *had* I been missing all those years?

Would I marry again? How would the kids take it? What if they didn't like my new husband? What if he didn't like them? No. Not a possibility. I wasn't going to marry anyone who wasn't crazy about my kids.

Would Brian marry again? Definitely. Memo or no memo, Brian was the marrying kind. He said that woman he'd slept with meant nothing to him, but she'd probably figure out how to get her hooks into him. That kind always did.

And Brian, the stupid sap, would be too clueless to know what was going on, or how ridiculous he looked running around with some bimbo half his age. Of course, I didn't actually know how old she was, but she had to be younger than him, a *lot* younger. And after his money. That kind always was. Except she was probably so stupid that she didn't realize he didn't *have* any money, not really.

But he'd probably end up spending our kids' inheritance buying her an enormous, vulgar engagement ring anyway, and showing up at family gatherings, reunions, weddings, and the birthday parties of our yet-unborn grandchildren, dangling his trophy wife from his arm like a bauble from a bracelet, showing off her big diamond. And her big boobs. And her . . . Damn him!

The volcano erupted again. I grabbed a sugar bowl from the sideboard and lobbed it like a grenade against the wall, smashing it to smithereens.

I felt better.

But also a little foolish, especially since I had only just finished sweeping up the shards of the teacups. And because I had really liked that tea set.

Continuing to smash family heirlooms against the wall didn't seem like a good idea, so I drove to Goodwill and bought a whole crateful of mismatched china plates, cups, bowls, and saucers for six dollars.

For the next several days, night or day, whenever I felt the lava beginning to bubble, I would go outside and hurl dishes against a stone wall until the threat of eruption had passed. Better there than in the kitchen.

It wasn't dignified, but it kept me together, sort of. And it was a great sleeping pill, better than Ambien.

Three nights later, I had a dream.

I dreamed that Brian showed up at the cottage with a moving van and her, the Other. I don't remember what she looked like, or even seeing her face. In my dream she was always turned away from me or standing in a shadow, but I knew she was beautiful and younger than me. She had blond hair that reached past her shoulder blades, falling in a golden cascade down her back. I remember him standing on the porch of the cottage, with me in the doorway, as he looked over his shoulder back to her, saying, "She always wears it loose." I remember following his adoring gaze back to where she was standing, next to the moving van, watching her turn slightly to one side, seeing a bulge beneath her blouse, realizing she was pregnant, pregnant with my husband's child. I remember the look of bliss on Brian's face and him saying, "Twins. We're going to need more space. The nursery furniture is in the van, so if you'll just get out of the way . . ."

I remember slamming the door in his face and locking it, Brian shouting to let them in, that I was being ridiculous, that I'd brought it all on myself, and then pounding his fist against the door, shouting and pounding.

Gasping, I bolted upright in my bed. My heart was pounding, and my throat felt raw. My eyes were hot, filled with unshed tears.

I got up as quickly as I could, ran downstairs in my pajamas, grabbed a raincoat off the hook by the back door, stuffed my feet into a pair of green Wellington boots, snapped on the porch lights, and ran to the wall.

It was dark and raining, but it didn't matter. I was used to it by now; it had rained every day that week. I reached into the crate where I kept the dishes, grabbed a blue saucer, heaved it at the wall, and missed. No matter.

I grabbed a second saucer, a plate, two cups, a bowl, throwing them as hard and fast as I could against the wall of rounded stones, hurling curses, sobbing my frustration, howling for vindication, finding none.

I smashed every piece of crockery left in the crate, at least a dozen pieces, but it didn't help—

not like it had before. Desperate for relief, frightened of my own fury, I looked around for something else to throw or kick or do. Something *I* could control.

A rusted shovel was resting against the silver-gray boards of the barn. I grabbed it, circled to the side of the house, and started digging.

The grass was soft after so many days of rain. My boots made muddy impressions in the sod as I pushed the metal blade into the ground and scooped up green shovelfuls of sod.

It was easy going at first, too easy, but the soil was harder a few inches below the sod, partially frozen and unyielding, studded with stones. I had to pound the blade against the dirt and stomp my foot against the top of the shovel to gain even a few inches' entrance into the earth. My breath became labored as I continued to dig, adding more and more soil to the growing pile, grunting as I wedged the metal blade under the edges of flinty stones, pried them loose, and tossed them into another pile, the cold rain falling from above, dripping from the edge of my hood and onto my bare hands so they slipped against the wooden handle of the shovel, making the work even harder.

I didn't care. I wanted it to be hard, so hard that it would tax every muscle of my body and clear every thought from my mind. I dug and grunted and sweated and cursed and cried, my tears mixing with the rain, sinking into the soil. I dug until my hands were blistered, until my arms were shaking and so heavy that I couldn't lift them.

After a time—I don't know how long—the sun rose and the rain stopped. So did I.

I loosened my grasp on the shovel and watched it drop to the ground, then trudged into the house, pulled off my boots and coat, and collapsed onto the living room sofa, too exhausted to climb the stairs.

It was enough. I was done.

❧ 8 ☙

Gayla

Somebody was knocking.

I sat up, blinking as my eyes adjusted to daylight and my brain cleared enough to remember what I was doing on the sofa and why my clothes were wet.

"Be right there!"

Maybe it was Drew. Or Jehovah's Witnesses. Who else could it be? I didn't know anyone in New Bern.

The man standing on the back porch had blue eyes and brown hair that needed trimming. Not a Jehovah's Witness. Jehovah's Witnesses had short hair and wore dress shirts and ties, not flannel shirts and jeans. My inner New Yorker felt nervous about opening the door to a strange man, but I did it anyway. I couldn't very well leave him standing there.

I opened the door a couple of inches, ready to slam it closed, just in case.

"I'm Dan." When the announcement of his name elicited no spark of recognition from me, he said, "Dan Kelleher? Drew's dad?"

"Oh. Oh, right!" I grabbed his outstretched hand. "Hi!"

I knew about Drew's father, but we'd never met. If I hadn't been so groggy, I might have guessed. He had Drew's eyes and sharp-angled jaw. However, the senior Mr. Kelleher was just a little shorter than his son, probably about six-two, and more filled out. His voice was deeper, too, so deep he could have gotten a job as the midnight DJ on the cool-jazz radio station.

"Gayla Oliver," I said. "Nice to meet you."

I opened the door wider and smiled, even though the act of smiling made my head hurt. What time was it? Late, I was sure—too late to still be in my pajamas and sporting a bed head.

"Would you like to come in?" I asked, sincerely hoping the answer was no.

"Just for a minute. I don't want to keep you from anything."

He stepped through the door and scanned my

kitchen, which was spotless. Aside from the books heaped on the table. And two empty bottles of scotch sitting on the counter.

"I have a cold," I said, sniffling to back up my claim.

"Uh-huh," he said, raising his eyebrows in a way that made it clear he wasn't buying my story. "You shouldn't go out in the rain like that. You could catch pneumonia."

He'd seen me? Digging holes in the dark and rain in my pajamas? Great.

The Realtor, Wendy Whatever-Her-Name-Is, had sworn that the trees on our property were so thick the neighbors couldn't see us. I guess she was wrong.

Dan Kelleher shoved his hands in his pockets. "Listen, Mrs. Oliver . . ."

"Call me Gayla."

"Gayla." He nodded, cleared his throat, looked down at his shoes. "Right, Gayla. The thing is, I don't want to pry into your private business or anything, but with the leaves not out on the trees yet and our place so close to yours . . ." He lifted his eyes to mine. "It's just that the noise really carries, you know? And I have to get up pretty early these days."

I felt my cheeks flush. I knew where this was going.

"I'm so sorry. I didn't realize. I've been having trouble sleeping lately and . . ." I shrugged and threw my hands out. "For some reason it just helps if I throw dishes at rocks. And curse."

"Uh-huh," he said, drawing out the first syllable and clipping the second, turning the affirmation into an expression of doubt. "And dig holes in the middle of the night?"

"Yes. Well. I wanted to get a start on my gardening." I reached up to smooth down my damp hair. "Probably not a great idea in this weather."

"Probably not. That's another reason why I came by. Thought you might want to borrow my rototiller."

"Your rototiller?"

"It'll turn the soil about fifty times quicker than you can with a shovel, and it'll dig the beds deeper. You ever use one before?" I shook my head. "I'll show you how. The starter is a little temperamental, but you'll get the hang of it. How big a garden are you putting in?"

I coughed, buying time to come up with an answer that wouldn't make me sound any crazier than I already did.

"I hadn't quite decided. I'm still trying to figure out what I'm doing," I said, tilting my head toward the pile of books. "I've never gardened before."

His eyebrows moved toward each other, becoming a singular, curious line. "Are you moving up here full-time?"

"No, no," I assured him. "I'm just here for a few weeks. Or months. Not sure yet."

"Vacation?"

Boy, this guy had a lot of questions. I thought New Englanders were supposed to be stand-offish.

"More like . . . a sabbatical. I decided it was time to take a break, try a change of scenery. You know how it is."

"Uh-huh," he said again, picking up one of the books from the table. "What do you want to grow—flowers or vegetables?"

"Both?"

"Well, if you want flowers, start with day lilies. They're practically foolproof. Coneflowers are good too. Stay away from roses," he advised, tossing aside *Rose Cultivation for Beginners*. "And peonies. And begonias. Definitely not orchids," he said, discarding three more titles. "Vegetables are easy as long as you keep them weeded and watered. But steer clear of the exotic stuff—asparagus, artichokes, that kind of thing. Other than that, you should be fine."

He extracted two books from the pile.

"Read these," he commanded. "The others will just confuse you."

I was about to ask him why he knew so much but then remembered that he owned a land-scaping company. Plants were his business.

"Thanks," I said, meaning it. It was a relief to

have my horticultural catalog winnowed down to two useful books. Maybe I would read them. In fact, I knew I would. Because whether I'd planned on it or not, I was going to have to put in a garden; the man was lending me his rototiller.

"Well, I should get going," he said. "Come outside for a second, and I'll show you how to use the tiller. Or should I show your husband?"

"He's not here. Works in the city. Travels a lot. You know how it is." I shrugged.

Once again, two eyebrows became one. This time, however, I got the feeling that he did know exactly how it was.

"Uh-huh. Well, if you need anything, just yell. Would you like me to bring in some more firewood? It's kind of cold in here. You ought to turn up the heat."

"Oh," I said, dismissing his offer with a wave of my hand. "The furnace is out. I need to call a repairman."

"Really?" he asked, his expression making it clear that he found this much more interesting than anything I'd said previously.

"Let me take a look; might be something simple. Those furnace guys charge ninety bucks just to show up. Does this lead to the basement?"

He disappeared through the door before I had a chance to respond. I followed him. What choice did I have? Dan Kelleher was a take-charge kind of guy.

● ● ●

Rototilling, as it turns out, is extremely satisfying. I had no idea.

It took three tries before I got the engine to turn over, but once I did, the red monster bucked and roared, chewing up the ground and leaving a trail of espresso-colored earth in its wake. Keeping the machine on a semi-straight path required physical strength, but I was focused and determined, gratified by the sensation of actually accomplish-ing something besides smoking, drinking, cursing, and smashing dishes.

I might not have planned to take up gardening. I'd have gone through with it only to keep Dan Kelleher from thinking I was a complete nut job, which he probably did anyway. But now that I was out here, I was really getting into it.

Watching the swaths of green disappear under the powerful churning of the blades made me feel powerful too. When that dark brown earth was cleared of stones and weeds and roots, freed from inertia and the presumptuous grass that grew there just because it always had, the patch of land could become anything I chose to make it. It was a clean slate, an empty canvas.

I could enclose it in white pickets and put in pathways of gray-white gravel or stepping stones and nested masses of moss that divided the space into identical and evenly placed beds, a tidy garden where flowers grew in orderly, color-coordinated rows, a sensible garden where no weed would dare to sprout. Or I could cut green branches from the saplings in the woods, then bend them and tie them and turn them into rustic trellises and archways covered with twisting green vines and flowers shaped like bells and trumpets. Or I could create a garden with no beds at all, no paths, no structure or reason, just one blue folding chair placed in the center so a person could rest and think, or rest and not think, as the sun shone down on a sea of brilliant wildflowers in blue, purple, orange, and pink, carelessly sown as I walked barefoot over the warm, soft earth, scattering seeds across the welcoming soil with wide and generous sweeps of my arm, leaving them to grow as they willed, leaving it to nature, knowing there are no ugly flowers.

Or, if I wanted to, I could grow vegetables: green beans and zucchini and peppers, and cherry tomatoes so small they could be popped whole into the mouth and so delicious they would never make it into the house because I would eat them while I stood in the garden, picking them from the vines and crushing them against the roof of my mouth, releasing sun-warmed juice that tasted like summer on my tongue.

I could grow lilies and pansies and carnations and irises. I could grow herbs or lavender. Or sweet-scented roses. Who cared what Dan

Kelleher said about it being beyond me? He didn't know me. If I wanted to grow roses, then I would grow roses. Or peonies. Or anything else that struck my fancy. Because I could.

Because *I* could.

I stopped in my tracks. The tiller, blades still churning, bucked and urged me forward, but I stood where I was, struck by the enormity of that thought.

For the first time in my life, I was not responsible to or for anyone but myself. My parents were dead. My children were grown. My husband didn't love me anymore.

For different reasons and at different times of my life, the truth of those statements had brought me to tears and despair, made me feel empty and alone. But there was another way to look at it.

Empty. Alone. I've always associated those words with anguish, confusion, and, in some sense, failure. But if emptiness is a void, isn't it also the state that precedes fullness? Is it not a moment of supreme anticipation, the season of preparation when there are no rocks or roots or weeds or impediments before you, only bare earth and possibilities? And if being alone forces you to stand apart, doesn't it also separate you from the responsibility of bowing to the opinions and expectations of others?

For the first time in my life, I didn't have to please or answer to anyone but myself. I was empty. I was alone. I didn't belong to anyone.

What a relief.

A relief? Had I actually said that? Even in my own mind, had I actually allowed myself to think that the potential ending of my marriage was cause for relief?

But at that moment, it was true. Why try to pretend otherwise?

I pushed the tiller forward again, erasing another strip of green under the blades, trying to sort things out, to sieve out the guilt and see my feelings as they were instead of how I thought they were supposed to be.

For as long as I could remember, I'd had to worry about pleasing my parents, trying to live up to the expectations and role they had assigned me from birth. Then about being my children's mother, making sure they ate properly, brushed their teeth, learned to say "please" and "thank you," knew that I loved them, believed in them, was always ready to go to bat for them. And then being Brian's wife, loving him, supporting him, trying to read his mood, to cheer him on, to fight fair, making allowances for him, excuses for him, making myself attractive for him, making a home for all of us, making more money so the whole burden of bills wouldn't fall on his shoulders, working at home, working at work, working at everything, trying to be the woman who "has it all" and, in the end, having nothing.

For the previous seven days, that knowledge had driven me to despair. But now I realized that having nothing meant that I, too, was a blank slate. I was free to be or do anything I chose.

So what did I choose? If I had only myself to please, what would please me? How did I want to spend my time, effort, thoughts, and heart? Where should I—

A tremendous clank-bang, a sound like a hammer striking a broken brass bell, jarred me from my thoughts. The red monster bucked and jerked. I lost my grip on the handlebars and jumped back, frightened. It bucked again and tipped onto its side with the motor still running and the blades churning, throwing clods of dirt into the air.

I switched off the engine as quickly as I could and knelt down to inspect the damage. I'd hit a rock, a big one. But there were no dents that I could see. Thank heaven! I really wasn't in the mood to explain a broken rototiller to Dan Kelleher.

He already thought I was crazy. He clearly hadn't bought my story about Brian not coming with me because he was traveling or about me being on sabbatical. Well, big deal. I wasn't trying to impress Dan Kelleher. I wasn't trying to impress anybody.

Besides that, I decided, I wasn't lying. I *was* on sabbatical. From here on out, if anybody asked me what I was doing in New Bern, I would say I was taking a sabbatical until the end of the summer. My seniors had all gotten their acceptance letters, so I could afford to take some time off. I needed a break—from everything.

Come fall, I could write that fifty-thousand-dollar check to Libby Burrell and start the ball rolling on the divorce. But right now and for the rest of the summer, I would take a step back, focus on myself, on living and enjoying my life. It occurred to me that Brian might file divorce papers before the end of summer. Well, if he did, then he did. I'd cross that bridge when I came to it. In the meantime, I was on sabbatical.

Of course, most sabbaticals involve some sort of project, lists of goals and plans of action. Normally that sort of thing would be right up my alley, but not now. Now I wanted something new, and maybe the new thing I needed was *not* to have a plan.

Unless . . . Unless "new" is the plan.

That was it! I would spend my sabbatical trying new things—things I'd always wanted to try but had never had time for. Something new every day. Or maybe every couple of days? Or even once a week? After all, there were apartment buildings in Manhattan with larger populations than the village of New Bern. How many new things could there be to do in a town this size?

But I had already tried one new thing: rototilling. My edges weren't as straight as they could have been, but I hadn't cut off any toes or broken the machine. Not bad for a first try.

I flopped on my behind in the dirt to catch my breath, still feeling the vibration of the big motor running through my hands and forearms, and laughed out loud.

The patch of tilled soil that stretched out before me was about forty feet long and twenty-five feet wide, a footprint almost as big as our apartment in the city! Holy crap!

I'd been so focused on keeping the machine running in a straight line and so lost in my thoughts that I'd tilled under at least a third of the side yard. Thank heaven for that rock in my path. If it hadn't stopped me, I probably wouldn't have any yard left.

But I was going to have a garden all right. A *big* one.

❧ 9 ☙

Ivy

"But why can't he?" Bobby whined, stretching out the "why" and thumping the back of my seat with his shoe.

"I told you it's because he won't be here until the end of next month. Even when he does get here, you'll meet with him in Mrs. Fenton's office at first. It will take a while before the two of you can go off and do things on your own."

"But why not? I don't—"

"Bobby! Quit kicking the seat!" I shouted.

The kicking stopped, but when I looked at his reflection in the rearview mirror, I saw his eyes filled with tears. I shouldn't have yelled, but I'd had about all I could take.

How could I explain to my barely seven-year-old son that if I had my way, Hodge would *never* see him without supervision? Bobby didn't understand why I was so on edge. It must be so confusing for him. It was confusing for me too.

"I'm sorry, sweetie. I didn't mean to yell. Just please don't kick the back of my seat anymore, okay?"

"Okay," he said glumly. "But I wish he was coming home *now*. I want him to be my partner in the bowling tournament. The tournament is only a couple of months away. We have to start practicing now!"

"I can be your partner if you want."

"It's Boys' Brigade! Only boys are allowed!"

I turned the car into the Kellehers' driveway. "Okay, okay! I was just trying to help," I said, and then muttered under my breath, "I am *so* ready for a night without kids."

I pulled up under a tree near the front of the house and put the car in park. Normally, Drew hears my car in the driveway and comes out of the house on his own. A minute passed with no sign of him. I was just about to get out of the car and go knock on the door when Drew's father, Dan, came outside.

"Drew's running a little bit late," he said, leaning down and looking through the driver's side window. "But he should be back in a minute. Want to come inside and wait?"

"That's all right," I said. "How long do you think he'll be?"

"Not long. I loaned my rototiller to the neighbor and he drove the truck over there to pick it up. Should be back any second. You sure you don't want to come in?"

I shook my head. "That's all right. We're fine out here."

Dan seems like a nice enough guy, nice looking too. Good hair, a little long, but I like that. I say hello if I see him around town, and I give him a wave whenever I pick Drew up for babysitting, but we'd never had a real conversation. I'd feel awkward sitting in his living room, trying to think of things to say while I waited for Drew to show up. I'm lousy at small talk.

Having refused his invitation twice, I figured Dan would go back in the house. Instead, he stayed where he was, leaning down to my window but leaving one hand resting on the roof of the car, smiling at us. He had big arms. Not beefy, not like one of those guys who spent all their spare time working out, but he was muscular, wide at the shoulders, like somebody who spent his time working outside, doing physical labor, which was exactly what he did. He was one of the best landscapers in the county. Even if I hadn't known that already, I might have guessed it by looking at his yard. It was beautiful; the grass was green and lush. And even now when the leaves on the trees were slow to emerge and the flowers were only just beginning to bud, his planters looked beautiful, as if he'd worked out a plan so they would look good at any time of year, summer or winter. Maybe he had.

Anyway, it was awkward to have him standing there by my car, smiling through the open window but saying nothing. I wanted to tell him that he didn't have to entertain us and could go back inside, but I figured that might sound rude, so I just sat there trying to think of something I could say. He beat me to it.

"You must be Bobby," he said after a moment and raised his hand in greeting. "I'm Dan. Nice to meet you. I've heard a lot about you."

"Yeah," Bobby said morosely, keeping his eyes on a red Matchbox car he was playing with, moving it back and forth across the seat without looking up.

"Bobby!" I hissed, turning around to glare at him.

"Nice to meet you too," he mumbled, barely glancing at Dan.

I gave him "the look" and turned back toward the front.

"Sorry. We're having kind of a rough week. So . . . ," I said, stretching out the word, searching for something to say. "You loaned your rototiller to a neighbor?"

What a stupid thing to say. Hadn't he just said that? I suck at small talk.

"Uh-huh. To Gayla Oliver."

"Oh? The people who own the cottage? You mean they actually showed up?"

"Not them. Just the wife, Gayla." He shook his head and made a puffing sound with his lips.

"I think she might be kind of a loon. Showed up here all on her own about a week and a half ago. Don't know where the husband is. Everything was fine at first. I probably wouldn't have known she was here if Drew hadn't told me about it. But a few days ago, at about three in the morning, I woke up and heard all this noise coming from over there, cursing and the sound of breaking dishes. At first, I thought maybe the husband had shown up and they were having a fight, but I only heard a woman's voice. After about ten minutes, it stopped."

"Weird."

"Yeah, right?"

He leaned closer, and I caught a whiff of

verbena. Aftershave? Or maybe just soap. Whatever it was, it smelled good.

"It happened again the next night," he said. "Twice: once just after midnight and again around four. And the next night too. Every time it happened, it took me at least half an hour to fall back asleep."

"Did you ever find out what was going on?"

"Uh-huh. The night before last, I woke up around three-thirty. It was just like before, the sound of a woman cussing and dishes breaking, coming from that side of the property," he said, tipping his head toward a line of trees on the northern edge of the lot. "I finally decided that enough was enough, so I got dressed and went over there. It was pouring rain, but there she was, wearing a coat over her pajamas, cussing like a sailor and throwing plates at a rock wall. Crazy."

"In the rain? In her pajamas? Really?"

When Dan first called Gayla Oliver a loon, I felt a little uncomfortable. I don't like gossip to begin with, and this seemed kind of a harsh thing to say about somebody you'd barely met, but it seemed like he had a point. And really, given all that had been going on next door, how could you not want to tell somebody about it?

I propped my elbow up on the window ledge. By this time I was genuinely interested in the story—I couldn't help myself.

"I saw her through the trees. I was about to yell at her to knock it off," he said, sounding a little apologetic. "I mean, people are entitled to do what they want on their own property, but I hadn't slept in four nights. Then, all of a sudden, she stopped throwing stuff and started to just sob, really sob, like somebody had died or something. Then she grabbed a shovel and disappeared around the side of the house—"

"A shovel?"

"Uh-huh. At that point, I was starting to worry about her, so I followed her. She started digging a hole—"

"In the middle of the night? Why?"

"No idea," he said. "I stood there and watched her for a while. You know, just to make sure she was okay. I didn't know what else to do. Finally, I went home and went back to bed. The next morning I went over there to check on her—"

"And lend her your rototiller."

He took his arm off the roof of the car, straightened up a bit, and hooked his thumb into his belt loops. "Well, I was just looking for some reason to go over there and check on her. I didn't want to embarrass her or anything, but . . . yeah . . ." He moved his head slowly from side to side, and made a sucking sound with his teeth. "Weird. I don't know exactly what's going on, but I'm guessing it has something to do with the husband. They aren't up here very often, but she's never come up without him before. And the way she's acting . . .

"I kind of lost it after my wife walked out," he went on. "I mean, not completely. I couldn't; I had Drew to think about. Otherwise, who knows what would have happened? I started chopping down trees just to keep from going off the deep end, cleared this whole side by myself," he said, making a sweeping motion with his arm. "Cut and stacked five cords of wood before I got a grip. Pretty rough. But I guess it's that way for everybody, right?" He shrugged. "Divorce makes you crazy. You probably know what I'm talking about."

He gave me an expectant look, obviously expecting me to agree with him or share my life story or something. . . . The awkward feeling returned. Didn't he already know about me? New Bern being the way it is—a town where everybody knows everybody else's business and has no problem talking about it—I figured he would. On the other hand, what made me suppose I was so fascinating that other people spent their time talking about me?

"I'm not sure I'm a very good example. My husband and I . . ."

I faltered, not sure how to explain my marital history to a man I hardly knew.

"For me it was a kind of relief," I said. "It was ugly. And complicated. And he . . . he left town right after the divorce."

121

"He's in jail. That's kind of like time-out for grown-ups." Bobby's high-pitched voice took me by surprise. He'd been so quiet for so long that I'd almost forgotten he was sitting within earshot.

I blushed and shifted my eyes from Dan's. Hodge is the one convicted of fraud. He's the one doing time. The only crime I'm guilty of is being stupid enough to marry him. Even so, every time someone finds out that my ex-husband is a felon, I'm overcome with shame.

I guess that's why I never sat down and told Bobby where his dad had gone. I guess that's why Bethany invented that story about Hodge being away at sea—because she feels the same way. Both of us wanted to spare him that embarrassment, the indignity of guilt by association with a father he doesn't even remember.

"He's coming back pretty soon. But," Bobby grumbled, giving the back of my seat a kick, "*not* in time to help me practice for the bowling tournament."

"Stop it, Bobby! I told you before."

I turned back to Dan. "There's this bowling tournament near the end of August," I said, trying to explain things to him, though I wasn't sure why. It wasn't like it concerned him. I guess I just was trying to fill the silence. Or maybe I didn't want him to think I'd raised a rude child. "I offered to be his partner, but it's sponsored by Boys' Brigade and . . . Oh, look! Drew is back!"

Saved by the bell. What a relief.

Drew hopped out of the truck and came loping across the lawn. "Sorry I'm late. We were loading the tiller into the truck, and Mrs. Oliver cut her hand on the blade."

Dan frowned. "Why'd she grab it by the blade? Is she all right?"

"It wasn't that deep. I helped her bandage it up."

"Why'd you let her help you anyway?" Dan asked. "It isn't that heavy."

Maybe not for Dan, I thought, glancing at the rototiller before sneaking another glance at those muscled arms, but I wouldn't be able to lift it on my own.

"I know," Drew said, sounding just slightly annoyed. "I told her that, but she wouldn't listen."

He turned his face to me. "I'm really sorry. I hope I haven't made you late for your date. Hey, where's Bethany?"

"She's at a sleepover," I said. "Don't worry about it. I'm meeting a few of my girlfriends for dinner and some quilting. It doesn't matter what time I show up."

"Well, sorry anyway," he said as he opened the passenger door and climbed in. "Hey, Bobby. Looks like we're going to have a boys' night, right? Want to play Candy Land?"

Bobby made a face. "Candy Land is boring," he said. "Can we watch *Star Wars* instead?"

"Absolutely. That's my favorite."

"Mine too!"

It was true. Bobby has watched that movie about ten thousand times.

"Hey, Drew," Dan said, stooping down so he could see his son's face. "Bobby joined Boys' Brigade and he needs a partner for the bowling tournament. Think you might be up for the job?"

"No!" Bobby shouted before Drew could even answer. "Drew can't be my partner. It's a father-son bowling tournament. Only fathers and sons can be in it."

My cheeks had felt warm at several points in the last few minutes, but now they were flaming. I was so embarrassed. Dan must think my son was a total brat. At that moment, I was inclined to agree with him. Next time I came to pick Drew up for babysitting, I was going to wait for him out on the road.

"I'm a father," Dan said without missing a beat. "And you're a son. What if I was your partner?"

Bobby squashed his lips together and wiped his nose with the back of his hand. "Are you any good?"

Was he any good? Did he actually just ask him that? I was mortified. I wished the earth would open up and swallow me right then and there.

"He's very good," Drew assured him. "He can wipe up the floor with me."

"You don't have to do that," I said, gripping the

window ledge and looking up at Dan. "Really. I'm sure you've got better things to do with your time."

Dan shifted his shoulders and took a step back from the car. "Not really. And it'll be fun. I love to bowl, and Drew here," he said, jerking his chin in his son's direction, "he's too busy to go bowling with his old man. So whaddaya say, Bobby? Can I be your bowling partner?"

"I guess so. Okay. But maybe just for practice. When my dad comes home, I want him to be my partner."

"Fine with me. Hey! This'll be great!" Dan thumped the car door with his hand twice, as if he was truly excited about going bowling with a seven-year-old boy. "Tell you what, on Sunday afternoon, Drew and I will take you to the alley, and we'll get in a little practice."

"Dan, you don't have to—"

"It's okay," he said, waving away my concerns with a sweep of his hand. "I want to. It'll be fun. See you on Sunday, Bobby."

"See you, Dan!" Bobby waved his hand and grinned at him, displaying a gap where his front tooth used to be. Dan grinned back.

"Hey, Ivy. Do you want me to come pick up Drew for you later?"

"Oh . . . you don't have to do that. It's not that far."

"I know, but Bobby will probably be asleep by

then. You don't want to leave him alone while you're bringing Drew back."

He was right; I didn't. It took only ten minutes round trip, but ten minutes was long enough for something to go wrong. He was only seven. And if Bethany wasn't home . . .

"Well, if you're sure you don't mind, I'd really appreciate that."

"No problem," he said. "My pleasure."

When we got to the top of the driveway, I looked in the rearview mirror. Dan was going back inside. After the door closed behind him, I took a right and headed toward town.

"Your dad seems like a nice guy."

"He's okay." Drew grinned. "For a dad."

ꙮ 10 ꙮ

Ivy

Quilt circle meetings were usually held in the workroom above the shop, but we were down a few people that night. Abigail wouldn't be back from Bermuda until Monday—it seemed like she and Franklin were spending more and more of their time there—and somebody had given Virginia, who loves sports, tickets to a Connecticut Sun basketball game. Tessa was out with Lee, celebrating their anniversary, and

Madelyn was busy hosting a wedding rehearsal dinner at the inn. Philippa had planned to join us, but there had been a death in the congregation, so she'd been called upon to comfort the family. Since we were such a small group, Margot suggested we meet at her house for dinner and quilting. Paul had just remodeled the attic over the garage into a new sewing room for Margot and she wanted to show it off.

I love all my quilting friends, but Evelyn and Margot are probably my favorites. I was looking forward to our evening together.

I see Evelyn and Margot almost every day at the quilt shop, so they already knew all about the situation with Hodge and had offered their sympathy and encouragement. I appreciate their support, but it doesn't really change anything. In the last week, I'd talked to everyone I could think of who might conceivably know of some way to keep Hodge away from my kids. They all said the same thing: Once he is released, Hodge has a legal right to see his children. There's nothing I can do to prevent it.

Even so, Evelyn, Margot, and I probably will end up rehashing the whole Hodge thing yet again tonight. Not because it will change anything but just because I need to vent. It's a woman thing, I guess. Tell a man about a problem, and he automatically assumes you're asking him for advice. He'll think you're asking him to fix it, when, really, you're just looking for a listening ear. Men just don't get it.

But Evelyn does. Margot does. All my quilting friends do. And they're trustworthy, too, which is very important. On quilt circle nights, we can talk about anything and everything, knowing that what's said in the circle stays in the circle.

I've really missed that. I've been so over-whelmed—with work, school, kids, and now having to fit in extra appointments with Arnie and Sheila Fenton and the therapist who is supposed to be helping the kids deal with Hodge's reentry into society and their lives—that I had to miss our last two meetings.

I probably would have done the same tonight, but Margot said I *had* to come, that it would be such fun, that she couldn't wait to show off her new sewing room, and she was going to make a pan of her special moussaka, which she knows I love, just so I wouldn't say no. Margot can be very convincing when she wants to be.

I stood on the stoop, but the door opened before I was able to press the bell. Paul, Margot's husband, grinned when he saw me standing there.

"Hi, Ivy! Come on in. The kids and I are going out for pizza, so the three of you can have the place to yourselves.

"Honey! Ivy's here!" he shouted in the direction of the kitchen, and then turned toward the stairs and clapped his hands together three times.

"James! Olivia! If you're not in the car in ten seconds, I'm leaving without you!"

There was a sound of female laughter coming from the kitchen and a sudden thunder of tennis shoes on the stairway. James, Paul's fourteen-year-old son, and Olivia, the eight-year-old niece Margot had adopted when her sister was killed in a car accident, raced down the stairs, barely stopping to say hello to me before running out the front door to the car. Margot appeared a moment later.

"Ivy!" she squealed, hugging me as tightly as if it had been months instead of hours since we'd last seen each other. "Now we can start the party!"

Margot kissed Paul good-bye, thanking him for getting the kids out from underfoot. Paul kissed her back, saying it was no problem, that she deserved a break, headed halfway out the door, and then turned around, grabbed her around the waist, and kissed her again, as if he could hardly bear being parted from her for even a few hours.

If it hadn't been so sweet, it would have been nauseating. Paul is such a terrific guy. It took Margot more than forty years to find Mr. Right, but obviously, he'd been worth the wait. Too bad it can't work out like that for everybody.

When they finally managed to pull themselves apart, Margot collapsed with her back against the door. "Isn't he wonderful?"

She sighed and started toward the kitchen

without waiting for me to answer because, as we both knew, this was a rhetorical question. Paul *was* wonderful, and that was all there was to it.

"Evelyn's already in the kitchen, scraping the burned spots off the garlic bread. We were so busy talking that she forgot it was still in the broiler." Margot giggled as we entered the kitchen. "You'd think, what with being married to the man who owns the best restaurant in town, she'd have picked up a few things by now. Wouldn't you?"

"I heard that," Evelyn said, pointing a butter knife coated with black crumbs at Margot, who giggled in response.

Evelyn put down her knife and gave me a hug. Then, without saying another word, she handed me a glass of white wine. I must have looked like I needed it.

"If anything," Evelyn said as she placed semi-scorched pieces of garlic bread on a plate, "being married to Charlie has eroded my culinary skills. He's such a great cook that I hardly even bother to try anymore. What's the point?"

"Aw," Margot murmured as she pulled a pan of moussaka from the oven and carried it to the kitchen table. "Charlie is such a sweetheart."

"He is that."

Evelyn picked up the wine bottle, poured another half glass for herself and Margot, then looked at mine and did a double take.

"Whoa! You got to the bottom of that pretty quick. I'll pour you another if you want, but maybe you should have something to eat first?"

Evelyn stared at me with an expression of concern, her fingers wrapped around the neck of the bottle. Margot, who had just placed the moussaka on a trivet in the middle of the table, turned to look at me and frowned.

"Ivy, are you all right? You look a little—"

In answer to her question and before she even had time to complete her thought, I burst into tears. And when I say "burst," that's exactly what I mean—a breaking apart and pouring out, an explosion of tears, complete with hiccups, shoulder spasms, and a runny nose. There was nothing ladylike or delicate about this crying jag. It was ugly, and it came out of nowhere.

Margot and Evelyn rushed to my side, putting arms around my shoulders and tissues in my hand, begging me to tell them what was wrong. It was several minutes before I was able to speak. Even then, I had a hard time answering their question because I honestly wasn't sure what to say.

"It's because Hodge is coming back, isn't it?" Margot said, patting my back as I sobbed. "You poor thing. It must be so stressful."

"Yes . . . I . . ." I sniffled a huge, disgusting-sounding sniffle and grabbed another handful of tissues from the box. "I mean, yes. That's it,

I guess. But it's not *just* that . . . I don't know."

"Is it because of me and Paul? Because I was saying how wonderful he is? And that Charlie is a sweetheart? I should be more sensitive. I know how it is, being alone and single when it seems like everybody in the world is happily married. Was it that?"

"Partly, I guess," I said, giving up on the wad of soggy tissues and wiping my eyes with the back of my hand. "Every man I've known has brought me nothing but trouble, but . . . sometimes I just wish things were different. I don't want Hodge back; I wouldn't ever want that. But there were times, especially early on, when he was sweet to me, said nice things to me. It made me feel good, you know? Just to think that somebody found me attractive and wanted to take care of me a little." My eyes filled and I swiped at them again.

"It's just hard to know that I'll never have that. So, yes, that's part of it. But I don't think that's the whole reason. Not exactly."

"Well, is it school?" Margot asked, keeping her bright blue eyes fixed on mine.

"No. Yes. Not entirely . . ."

I took in several deep breaths, making a conscious effort to get a grip while Margot continued to quiz me.

"What about work? The shop? Or maybe it's the internship program. I know you're worried about Judith. Or is it the kids? Are you feeling stressed-out?"

"Uh-huh," I replied, nodding after each question.

Evelyn had gone to the sink and refilled my empty wineglass with water. She pulled up a kitchen chair, sat down across from me, watched while I drank, and then took the empty glass from me.

"You know what I think it is?" she said. "Everything."

My eyes swam with liquid. Tears ran down my cheeks. She'd hit the nail on the head. That was what was wrong with my life—everything.

Absolutely everything.

We talked all through dinner. Or rather, I talked. Margot and Evelyn listened, nodding in sympathy, laughing in solidarity with me, tearing up for the same reason, filling my plate, and filling my glass, letting me let it out. Being my friends.

I don't know how long they sat there listening to me, only that it was a long time. Evelyn never moved. Neither did Margot, not even when Paul poked his head in the door to let her know they were home. She just smiled at him and made a kiss noise with her lips. He said he'd make sure the kids got to bed and that Margot should take her time, not to worry. I think he must have gotten a glimpse of my red eyes and runny mascara and figured out what was going on. Paul is a nice guy. Margot deserves a nice guy like Paul.

In a way, I think that's what I was really crying about.

If nice people like Margot and Evelyn deserve to have nice things happen to them, and those things *do* happen, then what does that say about people like me? People who can't seem to catch a break? Do I deserve the misery that has come my way? Have I brought it on myself? Am I being punished for something?

I didn't say that to Evelyn and Margot—not in so many words—because I already knew how they would respond. They would tell me that I'm wrong and that lots of good things have happened to me.

Look at your kids, they would say. *They are happy and healthy and they love you! And look what a wonderful home you have. The cutest little carriage house imaginable, the one you used to walk past when you first came to New Bern but never dreamed you'd be lucky enough to live in. And now you do! Look at your job. You'd never worked a day in your life until you came to Cobbled Court. Now you're head of a whole department! Not to mention your work with New Beginnings. Dozens of women have found meaningful work and the confidence to leave their abusers and never go back because of the internship program you coordinate! And look at your friends. Seriously, could anyone have more loving and loyal friends? Definitely not! All kinds of good things have happened to you! Millions of people would love to be in your shoes!*

It was all true. I knew that without even having to bring up the subject, which is why I didn't. But even so . . .

After a while, I looked around and realized that the wine bottle and the moussaka pan were both empty.

"What time is it?"

Margot craned her neck, trying to see the clock on the microwave oven.

"Ten forty-three."

"Is it? Oh, my gosh! I've got to go. I told Drew I'd be home by eleven. I'm sorry. I talked away all our quilting time. And I still haven't seen your new sewing room!"

"Don't worry about it," Margot said dismissively. "You'll see it another time. It's not going anywhere. Tonight you needed to talk more than you needed to stitch. We'll make up for it next week."

She got to her feet, picked up the moussaka pan, and carried it to the sink. Evelyn gathered up the empty glasses. I jumped up, too, and quickly started clearing away the plates. I was in a hurry to get home, but I couldn't very well leave without helping clean up.

"I'm not sure if I'll be able to come next week or not. Things are so crazy right now, and I've still got one more paper to write for my poetry class. I haven't even had a chance to turn on my sewing machine in weeks!"

Evelyn took a stack of plates from my hands and smiled.

"Here, let me do it. You need to get home to Bobby. I'll stay and help Margot clean up."

"Are you sure?" I asked uncertainly. I hated to eat and run, but I really did need to get going.

"It's no problem. Charlie won't be home from the restaurant for another half hour at least. I'm in no rush. But listen, Ivy," she said, putting her hand on my shoulder after she set the plates down on the counter. "I'm worried about you. I know you've got real, legitimate reasons for feeling the way you do. But I think your biggest problem is that you're exhausted, overworked, and over-whelmed. You're the mom. You're trying to do everything for everybody else.

"Every single thing you're dealing with right now is important. You're not wasting time or mis-reading your priorities. Believe me, I get it. I remember what it was like when Garrett was little. Every night, I went to bed feeling like I was failing, that I hadn't been able to give anyone or anything the kind of attention it deserved. There were never enough hours in the day. And I only had one child and a husband to help carry the load. It's ten times harder for you!

"But I will tell you something that I learned

along the way, something that every young mom needs to know: If you're not good to yourself, you can't be any good to anybody else either."

Evelyn Dixon is my boss, but she's also my friend. She doesn't offer advice lightly or often. But when she does, it's good. It's the very best.

"So," she said, keeping my gaze, "will we see you at quilt circle next week?"

I smiled. "Definitely." I gave her a hug and then rushed out the door, hurrying home to my son.

❦ 11 ❦

Gayla

The fitness instructor was named Tiffany. What a surprise.

She was five foot six and blond and had a waist measurement that matched her age, both of which I judged to be about twenty-three. Except for the ample amount concentrated in her chest, she had not an ounce of fat on her body. She wore a headset with a black microphone that extended from a wire and hovered in front of her mouth like a fat, lazy housefly.

"Woo-hoo! Yeah!" she whooped, bouncing to the beat of the bongos. "Let's pick up the pace, ladies! Bikini season is almost here! C'mon,

Gayla! Right knee, left knee, double jump! That's it! You can do it!"

I raised my right knee and then my left but skipped the double jump, taking a moment to catch my breath and loathe Tiffany.

How did she presume to know what I could and couldn't do? At her age, how did she presume to know *anything?* But I hoped she knew a few things, like CPR. Or how to dial 911. Another two minutes of this and I was going to have a heart attack. Dear God! Who had decided to put this skinny little girl with the big mouth and the big boobs in charge? She was a chit. An embryo. I had sweaters older than her!

I wished she would swallow her microphone. I wished she would fall and break her leg. Not really. But I wished I could find the idiot who invented Zumba and sue him for my pain and suffering. Or at least for my public humiliation, which was even greater.

The first thing I decided to do with my summer sabbatical was join the gym. Strictly speaking, this didn't qualify as a new experience for me. I had joined gyms before—often—but joining was usually about as far as I got. Especially in the years since I'd put out my shingle, my commitment to personal fitness has wavered somewhere between shallow and nonexistent. I know it's important, but so are a lot of things, and since my weight has remained pretty consistent over the years, I hadn't thought too much about working out. Not until yesterday, when I caught a glimpse of myself in the mirror while I was changing my sweater. Somehow, while I was busy being so busy, my muffin top had spilled over the waistband of my jeans and become a cake. It wasn't pretty.

So back to the gym I went, as I had so often before. But this time would be different. This time I'd actually work out, not just fill in the paperwork and write the check. And this time, in keeping with the theme of my sabbatical, instead of listlessly walking on the treadmill, I would take classes, try something new and different. There were plenty to choose from: yoga, Pilates, and group cycling, as well as classes with more intriguing names like Tabata, Muscle Max (which sounded both intriguing and painful), and, of course, Zumba!

The brochure said that it utilized "hypnotic" Latin rhythms and dance movements that would zap the calories and further promised that Zumba would make me think I was "at a party . . . not at the gym!"

The idea of going to a party instead of the gym sounded good to me, and since I had once bought a Jane Fonda video back in the day, I decided that Zumba was the way to go. And it might have been, if not for the trampolines.

Yes, you heard me right—trampolines.

Every person in Tiffany's class had his or her own individual trampoline, about eighteen inches in diameter, upon which we were expected to dance and bounce to these "hypnotic Latin rhythms" and, somehow, not fall off. I'm sure that's somebody's idea of a party, but not mine. My ancestors came from Scotland, Belgium, and Norway. I'm certainly proud of my heritage, but traditionally, we are not people known for busting a move. In fact, I'm pretty sure that the phrase "frog in a blender" was invented as a specific reference to my people.

While I jerked, stumbled, bumbled, and gasped for breath, Tiffany and the others bounced, whooped, and swiveled their hips in a way that, when I was in school, would have gotten you expelled from the junior high dance.

It was awful and made more so by the fact that, since it was my first time, Tiffany had insisted on moving me to the front of the class where she could "keep an eye on me." Right. She and everyone else. There were mirrors everywhere, and when I looked into them—it was impossible not to—not only did I see myself sweating, red faced, and flailing two and a half beats behind the music; I saw the faces of the other students, trying to pretend they weren't looking at me and weren't about to burst out laughing. On top of everything else, my heart was having its own little dance party, a rumba.

I was gasping. I was sweating.

When the music transitioned to a song that was even louder and faster and Tiffany shouted, "Good job! Great warm-up, gang! Now let's pick up the pace and really go for it!" I thought I would die, or maybe I just wished I would.

While Tiffany scolded me for having "gringa hips," I tried to give myself a pep talk.

I could do this. All I had to do was get through the rest of the class; that was all. After that, I'd never have to take Zumba or touch another trampoline for as long as I lived, but right now, I just had to keep up and keep going. This had been a mistake, but I couldn't quit, not now. I'd never quit anything in my life. Never. No matter how much I despised it. Not once in my entire life.

Which meant that quitting would be a new experience. . . .

My face split into a grin as the implications of this realization became apparent to me, that just because I hadn't quit before didn't mean I couldn't now and that, contrary to the mantras I had memorized in childhood, quitting doesn't necessarily make you a "quitter"—especially if the thing you are quitting is something you absolutely do not and never will enjoy and that just might end up putting you in the hospital. In that instance, quitting wasn't a character flaw. If anything, it was a sign of intelligence and maturity.

Yes! That was it! I wasn't a quitter; I was a grown-up.

Tiffany let out a "woo-hoo!" so everybody would know how much fun they were having. Everyone waggled their Latin hips and "woo-hooed" back—the suck-ups. Everyone except me.

I dropped my arms to my sides and stopped what I was doing, right between "cha" and "cha." I stepped off the trampoline, grabbed my towel, and limped to the door. When I glanced in the mirror, I saw a look of confusion cross Tiffany's face.

"Gayla? Are you all right?"

"Yes."

"Getting a drink of water?"

"Yes."

"Then coming right back?"

I threw the towel over my shoulder.

"No."

My elation over quitting was short-lived, lasting just as long as it took me to down two of those little paper cones of water and collapse onto the bench in the ladies' locker room.

"Ohhhhh," I moaned, bending down and letting my arms dangle to the floor, too exhausted to move. "Kill me now."

The metallic clang of a locker door and the sound of laughter startled me into a sitting position. A woman with wet hair and a smile on her face poked her head around a bank of lockers.

"Sorry," I said. "I didn't realize anyone else was in here."

"You all right?"

I nodded and mopped the sweat off my forehead and neck with a towel. "I'm fine. It's just that I haven't darkened the door of a gym since the Reagan administration, and for reasons beyond comprehension, I decided to give Zumba a try."

"How was it?" she asked, doing up the buttons on her blouse.

"The longest eight minutes of my life."

She laughed again and sat down on the bench next to me. "I'm Tessa Woodruff."

"Gayla Oliver," I responded. "Nice to meet you."

She retrieved a pair of tennis shoes from under the bench and started putting them on. "So what possessed you to try Zumba your first time out?"

"I think it was a mixture of audacity and stupidity," I said, bending down to untie my own shoes. "Also, it was just something new. I'm trying a little experiment."

"What kind of experiment?"

She looked genuinely interested, and so—leaving out the parts about Brian's memo, his affair, and my emotional meltdown—I told her about the weekend cottage I so rarely found the time to enjoy, my plans for the summer, the sabbatical, my quest for new experiences, and how it was coming so far. She listened intently, chuckling when I told her about getting carried away with the rototiller.

"That's a terrific idea," she said, giving every appearance of sincerity. "Seriously, I think more people ought to take a sabbatical. We all get so wrapped up in our routines and activities that sometimes I think we mistake activity for accomplishment. We forget that life is meant to be *lived,* not just endured."

She told me about how she and her husband, a former accountant, spent years living in Boston and doing work they hated, not realizing until after their son went to college that what they both wanted was a simpler existence, to live in a small town where he could farm and she could open a little shop to sell soaps and lotions made from herbs she grew herself. Their idea was good, but their timing couldn't have been worse. Like me, they had gone into business just before the economic tsunami. Her shop hadn't made it, and they'd nearly lost the farm, too, but things were better now. She was still growing herbs and producing soaps, lotions, and shampoos, but now in miniature sizes, selling them to boutique hotel chains that wanted unique bath amenities for their guests.

"Let me tell you," she said as she put her arms

through the sleeves of her blue cardigan, "it was scary for a while there, but it all worked out in the end. You know, even if it hadn't, I think I still would have been glad that we tried. Anyway, I think your sabbatical idea is brilliant. I really do." She stood up and started stuffing her workout gear into a bag.

"We'll see. I've only been at it for a day and a half. I'm kind of wondering how many new experiences there are to be had around here."

She lifted her head and stared at me. "In New Bern? Are you kidding?"

I blushed, concerned that I'd offended her.

"I didn't mean it that way. It's just that, there's so much to do in New York . . . the theater, the museums. And then there are all the restaurants, the shopping."

Tessa settled the straps of her workout bag onto her shoulder and then paused, giving me an appraising look.

"Do you want to go to the Blue Bean and grab a cup of coffee?"

Coffee? After talking to me for five minutes she was inviting me to go for coffee? I hardly knew her.

But she did seem nice, really genuine, and after so many days on my own, it might be nice to talk to somebody. And the Blue Bean served great lattes. If I ordered something other than my usual medium, skim-milk, double-shot, extra-foam latte, it would count as a new experience, right? On the other hand, just showing up would count as a new experience, too—I'd never had coffee with a stranger. It might be fun. And if it turned out that Tessa Woodruff wasn't as nice as she appeared to be, then no big deal. It was only coffee. So why not take the chance?

"It'll take me about ten minutes to shower and change."

"Perfect! That's exactly how much time I'll need to dry my hair."

12

Gayla

For the first time since my hasty flight to New Bern, the sun was out. So were the people.

The benches near the courthouse were occupied by men and women in suits with jackets removed, attorneys or clerks or perhaps jurors, taking advantage of the lunch hour to get some fresh air. The doors to several of the retail establishments were ajar, and shopkeepers stood on the thresholds, their faces turned toward the sun, soaking in the rays like flowers long deprived of light.

As we walked up Commerce Street toward the Blue Bean, Tessa informed me that the fine weather was supposed to be with us at least through the weekend. "At least that's what the weather report said. You picked the right week to put in a garden."

The Blue Bean Coffee Shop and Bakery stands on the corner of Commerce and Maple. As we got closer, I caught an irresistible whiff of cinnamon and baking butter and realized that my appetite had returned with a vengeance. If I ever hoped to banish the bulge from my waistline, giving in to the siren song of a freshly baked cinnamon roll was the last thing I should be doing, but the smell was too tempting to resist. One wouldn't kill me, would it? I could start dieting tomorrow. And I *had* gone to the gym that morning. After eight minutes of Zumba agony, surely I deserved a treat.

I had nearly justified my fall from nutritional grace in my mind when, only yards from the door of the Blue Bean, Tessa took a right turn into a cobblestone-paved alley.

"Where are you going?"

"I just want to pop into the quilt shop for a minute. I'm out of gray thread."

"New Bern has a quilt shop?"

Tessa turned to me with a bemused expression. "Cobbled Court Quilts. You've never heard of it? How long did you say you've lived here?"

"Three years. But we've never really lived here. We just come up on weekends, and not all that often," I said, trying to explain my ignorance to Tessa, who continued to look at me as if she was wondering if I walked through life with my eyes closed. "I've walked by this alley, of course, but never walked down it. I figured it was all just offices. I mean, who'd be crazy enough to open a retail business down here?"

"Evelyn Dixon would," Tessa said with a laugh. "Everybody thought she was crazy when she started out. The alley is too narrow for cars, so there's no place to park, and there's almost zero walk-by traffic. A lot of people never realize there is anything interesting down here, just like you did. But once people find Cobbled Court Quilts, they become customers for life. Evelyn has a lot to do with that. She probably is a little crazy, but in all the right ways. People love her.

"Also, there's just something about this place. It's so quiet and quaint. From a purely practical standpoint, it *is* a terrible location," Tessa admitted, "but for some reason, this turns out to be the perfect spot for a quilt shop. Whenever I come down this alley and walk into the courtyard, I feel like I've entered a simpler and less cynical age."

She was right about that. As we got to the end of the alley and entered a wide cobblestone courtyard, tucked away from the noise and bustle of Commerce Street, I, too, had a sense of going back in time. With its red-painted door, bowfront window where a fat tabby cat snoozed among a display of blue and yellow floral fabrics, and flower boxes newly planted with cheerful-faced pansies to match the window display, Cobbled Court Quilts was the definition of quaint. Quaint but impractical.

Probably the rent was cheaper here than in the Commerce Street storefronts, but even so, I couldn't imagine how they stayed in business. Maybe Tessa was right—maybe finding this quaint little quilt shop was worth the effort, but how many people would be willing to undergo that effort? And seriously, how many quilters could there be in a town the size of New Bern?

When Tessa opened the red door, we were greeted by the sound of raucous laughter. Actually, it was more like cackling than laughing, coming from a knot of five women who were clustered around another woman, who seemed to be showing the others something that they all found utterly hilarious. But when the bunch of little bells that were tied to the door jingled to announce our arrival, their laughter subsided. Six beaming faces turned in our direction and cried out, "Tessa!"

Tessa introduced me to Evelyn Dixon, the owner; Margot Matthews, who worked in the shop; and Virginia, Evelyn's mother, who taught quilting and was the owner of the cat I'd seen curled in the window. She also introduced me to Ivy Peterman, another shop employee, whose eyes darted immediately in my direction when Tessa said my name but who wouldn't make eye contact when she shook my hand. Strange girl.

Next I met Abigail Spaulding, who I soon came to realize owned a lot of the rest of New Bern, and Madelyn Beecher, who had grown up in New Bern with Tessa, moved to New York, and returned a few years before to . . .

"Open the Beecher Cottage Inn," I said, finishing Tessa's sentence for her. I turned to Madelyn. "You probably don't remember, but my husband and I stayed with you on our very first trip to New Bern."

"I remember you. Your husband is British, has a very posh accent. You came in the fall. Two years ago? No," she corrected herself. "It was three. You bought the cottage next to Dan Kelleher."

"You've got an amazing memory."

"It's a small town," she said, dismissing the compliment. "There aren't many people who come for a weekend and end up buying a house the same day. I wondered what happened to you. Once you bought the cottage I supposed I might run into you again but never did."

"Well," I said apologetically, "we had good intentions of coming up every weekend, but it didn't work out that way. Never enough time; you know how it is."

Tessa placed her hand on my shoulder. "Gayla

is spending the summer in New Bern, undertaking a very interesting project. Go ahead," she prompted. "Tell them about it."

"Oh . . . ," I said, feeling awkward and put on the spot. "I'm taking a sabbatical."

"So you're a professor? How fortunate for you," Abigail said without giving me time to correct her. "How I wish *I* could take a sabbatical. It must be such a pleasure to just take some time for yourself now and then."

Ivy, the youngest of the group, who looked to be in her late twenties or early thirties, rolled her eyes. "Abigail, you just got back from two months in Bermuda. What exactly do you need a sabbatical *from?*"

"From all this travel," she replied without a trace of irony, as though the answer should be obvious to anyone. "The packing, the unpacking, the itineraries, the lines at airport security, those horrible X-ray machines. I don't care what the government says; I'm sure they're just exuding radiation. Travel used to be such an elegant adventure. Now . . ." She lifted her hands in a hopeless gesture. "Simply exhausting."

Evelyn and her mother, Virginia, smiled and exchanged knowing glances. They clearly had Abigail's number. So did I—sort of.

Manhattan is crawling with Abigails: eccentric, grande dame types, opinionated, very used to getting their way, and very rich. Old money. I could tell by the diamonds in her ears—modestly sized, but perfectly matched and flawless. New money likes bigger stones, more bling. But there was something about her that didn't quite fit the stereotype. For one thing, what was she doing in a quilt shop? Society matron types don't usually go in for that kind of thing. She was definitely a character, an intriguing one.

"And of course," Abigail continued, "there are all the things I have to crowd into my schedule when Franklin and I *are* in New Bern. Do you know that we have a dinner scheduled every night this week? And trying to coordinate our calendars has become a Herculean task. Everyone is so overscheduled these days. It used to be that when you asked how someone was, they said, 'Fine.' Now the answer is 'Busy.' Everyone I know lives in a state of incessant busyness." She sighed dramatically. "How I long for a simple evening at home in front of the fire and a home-cooked meal. . . ."

Evelyn shot another glance at her mother. "But, Abbie," she said, "you don't cook."

"No, but Hilda does. After a fashion." Abigail turned to fill me in. "Hilda is my housekeeper. She's really not much at cooking, or ironing either, come to think of it. But her tuna noodle casserole is divine."

Ivy's eyes went wide. "*You* like tuna noodle casserole?"

Abigail drew her shoulders back and raised her chin to an offended angle. "Is that so surprising? Now and again, we all crave the comforts of childhood and a simpler existence, don't we? A break from our harried existence? You know," she said, giving them a look that was simultaneously haughty and hurt, "I may not work for a salary the way all of you do, but that doesn't mean I don't *work*. I have responsibilities, you know. . . ."

The tall blonde with the pretty blue eyes, Margot, tsked her tongue and put an arm over the older woman's shoulders.

"Of course you do. All the boards you sit on, the charities you support. New Bern wouldn't be the same without you, Abigail. Everyone in town knows that."

Abigail smiled benevolently. "I do what I can."

"Yes, we know. You're very generous," Tessa said quickly, bringing the conversational tangent to an abrupt end.

Abigail set her lips into a disapproving line and lifted one perfectly tweezed eyebrow, annoyed that Tessa had interrupted her interruption.

"Gayla didn't get a chance to tell you what she's going to *do* with her sabbatical," Tessa said. "She's going to spend it trying new experiences. Isn't that great?"

Though the others looked vaguely interested in the idea, they didn't seem to find it quite as intriguing as Tessa did. But they laughed when she told them about my disastrous attempt at Zumba. Virginia, who looked to be in her mid-eighties, told me that she went to the gym three times a week and said I'd be most welcome to join the "Ageless Wonders" class.

"It's not as tame as it sounds. Look at this!" she exclaimed, then rolled up her sleeve and flexed her arm, summoning a distinct knot of muscle from beneath the freckled flesh of her biceps.

"Pretty impressive," I said.

Virginia rolled down her sleeve. "You are looking at the Cobbled Court Arm Wrestling Champion."

"Don't challenge her to a match," Margot said soberly. "Or if you do, don't play for money."

Tessa told them more about my exploits, making them sound far nobler than they were. She didn't know that the idea of a sabbatical was born, not from nobility but from a desperate attempt to salvage my sanity. But she didn't need to know that, did she?

"Anyway," Tessa said after she finished telling them about my other adventures, "I was thinking that maybe this is something *we* could try, all of us together. Kind of a summer project."

Evelyn, who had moved behind the counter during the discussion and was folding a pile of fabric into tidy little squares, gave her a doubtful glance.

"It's a nice idea, Tessa, but I don't see how I'd

154

find the time. I'm teaching three classes this summer and so is Mom. Margot just told me she wants to offer a quilting camp for children. . . ."

"I don't know how popular it will be," Margot said. "But it will be fun, even if we only have a couple of students. Olivia wants to come, so that's one at least."

Tessa leaned over and whispered in my ear, "Olivia is her niece. Margot's sister was killed in a car accident, so Margot adopted her."

"You can count Bethany in too," Ivy said. "That'll solve at least part of my summer child care problem."

"Ivy, you know the children arc always welcome at our house," Abigail said. "Franklin is already planning to take Bobby on some fishing trips this summer, and I promised to teach Bethany to play tennis."

"Really?" Ivy smiled with relief. "That'd be such a help, Abigail! Drew is a great sitter; the kids love him. But his dad needs him to help with the landscaping business in the summer, so he's not always available. I've enrolled them in some day camps, too, but I've still got gaps to cover."

"Drew Kelleher?" I asked. "I know him; he keeps an eye on our place for us. Really a nice kid."

Ivy gave me the strangest look—guilty, like I'd just caught her in a lie.

"Oh, yes . . . uh . . ."

Ivy cleared her throat and, once again, refused to maintain eye contact with me. She seemed terribly shy around strangers. Maybe that's why they had her working upstairs, cutting fabric on her own. She wouldn't have been very good around customers.

"Drew babysits for me all the time. So I heard all about . . . I mean, I heard that the neighbor from New York was around for the summer. I guess that's you, huh?" Her eyes darted to my face and then away just as quickly. "I heard you're putting in a garden?"

"Yes. Something else that's new to me. I have no clue what I'm doing, but Drew's father, Dan, gave me some advice and lent me a rototiller. He seems like a nice guy."

Ivy chewed on her lower lip and dropped her gaze to the floor. "He is. I mean, I guess he is. I don't really know him. I just, you know . . . I just see him now and then when I pick Drew up for babysitting."

"Summer is a crazy time around here," Evelyn said, returning to the previous subject. "We bring in sixty percent of our annual income during those four months. A sabbatical sounds like a nice idea, but I just don't see how we can manage it."

"I know," Tessa said. "I've got to grow and harvest my herbs for the year, and Lee needs help with the farm too. I wasn't thinking of us taking an *actual* sabbatical, not the kind where you go off someplace. But what if we all did at least one new thing this summer? Wouldn't that be fun?" she asked, looking at the assembled faces. "Abigail, weren't you just saying that we're all overscheduled? Too busy to enjoy life?"

"Yes, but it seems to me that what you're proposing would simply add one more item to our already overcrowded to-do lists."

"It wouldn't be like that," Tessa insisted, shaking her head. "This wouldn't be something we *have* to do but something we *want* to do. We'd be carving out time for ourselves. Isn't there something you've always wanted to try but haven't had time for?"

Abigail considered this momentarily. "No," she said. "Everything I've ever wanted to do, I have."

Evelyn laughed as she placed the last of the folded fabric squares in a basket. "Oh, come on, Abbie! I know you've lived life a little larger than the rest of us, but nobody gets to live out all their fantasies. Not even you. I can think of a dozen new things I'd like to try. Surely you can come up with *one*."

"Perhaps one." Abigail gave a grudging shrug. "But I'm already certain I have no talent for it, and when I'm proven right and fail miserably, I'm not anxious to be the butt of everyone's jokes."

Evelyn came out from behind the counter and

leaned against it, crossing one arm over her waist, propping her elbow on that arm, and resting her chin in her hand.

"You know," she said philosophically, "just the other day I was talking to a very busy woman and giving her a big speech about how she had to make time for herself. But it suddenly occurs to me that I'm guilty of the same thing. Maybe I need to take some of my own advice. Lack of time isn't the only reason we don't follow through with some of the things we dream of doing. Sometimes fear gets in the way too."

"Well, I can understand how Abigail feels," Madelyn said. "There's something I've been thinking about doing for the longest time, but it is a little daunting. But on the other hand, if I don't do it now, when will I? I'm not getting any younger."

"You can say that again," Virginia puffed. "I've had all kinds of things on my bucket list, things I always told myself I'd find time for one of these days. But time is running out, and before I kick it, I'd like to check a couple of things off my list. And you know something?" she said with finality. "I'm going to!"

"So am I!" Margot exclaimed. "I've got two things on my list. Well . . . maybe three," she stammered and blushed a deep crimson and turned to Tessa. "Do we have to tell everybody what we want to do?"

"Not if you don't want to," Tessa said. "But I do think we should all make a commitment to try at least one new thing this summer. We don't have to go into specifics, but we should all commit that no matter how it turns out, we'll tell the others about our experiences. We can share our experiences at quilt circle."

Tessa obviously had a gift for organization and implementation—also for cheerleading. I could almost hear the shaking of pom-poms as she grinned at her friends and said, "What do you think, ladies? Should we do it? Who's with me?"

Virginia put her hand up first, quickly followed by Margot, Evelyn, Madelyn, and, of course, Tessa. Hands still in the air, the five of them stared at Abigail, who lifted hers as well but without enthusiasm.

"Ivy?" Evelyn said, turning to the younger woman, who was standing a little way from the others, with one arm wrapped protectively across her torso and her hand held near her mouth, chewing on the nail of her little finger.

"I'm thinking," Ivy said. "Give me a minute."

They did. When it had passed, Ivy raised her hand. Slowly.

"Great!" Tessa enthused, then turned toward me. "Gayla, the circle meets on Fridays. Is that good for you?"

"Yes. I mean . . . I'm sorry, but . . . what?"

Surely she didn't intend for me to be part of all this. We'd only just met.

"You're already doing the sabbatical anyway, so why not join in the fun?"

"Oh, you're nice to invite me, but," I said, making my face an apology, "I'm not really a joiner."

It was true. The only thing I'd ever joined willingly—more or less willingly—was the PTA. Over the years, I had reluctantly been a part of a couple of women's networking groups, and for a couple of years when I was working in the school, I had a weekly lunch with two of the other guidance counselors, but I didn't enjoy it. Women, I have found, can often be their own worst enemies—gossiping and snarking behind one another's backs. Who needs it? Lanie was my only real friend. Of course, she could be snarky, too, but never toward me. But I had to admit these women seemed different.

"Come on," Margot urged. "It'll be fun!"

"Maybe she doesn't want to," Abigail said. "She said she's not a joiner. Neither am I. Or at least I wasn't until I met you and Evelyn. But you shouldn't press her, Margot. She's only just met us. She may not even like us."

"Oh, it's not that," I rushed to assure them. "It's just . . . I don't want to horn in on your club."

"It's not a club," Evelyn said. "It's a circle; it can expand or contract as the occasion calls for it. It started with me, Margot, Abigail, and Liza, Abigail's niece. She lives in Chicago now. Then we added Ivy to the circle, then Tessa and Madelyn, and then Philippa—she's one of the pastors at the community church. It's not open to the whole world, but it's not a membership thing either. When we find somebody interesting, we make room for them in the circle. Simple as that."

"But I don't know how to quilt," I protested. "I never even learned to sew."

"Not at all?"

"Not even a button. I wanted to take home ec in high school, but my mother made me take calculus instead. But it's a funny thing," I said slowly, realizing what a strange coincidence it was. "A couple of weeks ago, I was walking along Twenty-fifth and passed this quilt shop . . ."

"The City Quilter?" Evelyn asked. "I love that shop."

"Me too. I saw this gorgeous red fabric through the window and ended up going in and buying two yards. I don't know what possessed me," I said with an incredulous laugh. "I saw that fabric and just had to have it."

Evelyn's smile widened as I spoke. She looked to Virginia, who gave her a wink and then looked at the others, who all started to laugh.

"What?" I asked. "What's so funny?"

"Nothing," Evelyn replied with a knowing

shake of her head. "But whether you know it or not, deep down inside, you're a quilter. It's only a matter of time."

"Just because I bought a couple of yards of fabric?"

"I've seen it before," she said sagely.

"But I told you, I don't know how to quilt. I don't even own a sewing machine."

"Then it'll qualify as a new experience, won't it? And your timing is perfect: We're going to start a group project next week."

Madelyn, who had been standing to one side, fingering a bolt of orange fabric with blue and white stars, looked up. "We are?"

"We are," Evelyn confirmed. "All of us."

❧ 13 ❧

Ivy

Bethany reached into the box and pulled out a purple terry-cloth baby bib with a little yellow duck appliquéd on the front.

"How about this?"

I smiled. I hadn't seen that bib in ages. It was one of the first things I'd bought after finding out I was pregnant. Both of the kids had used it; the pale orange stains testified to their love of strained sweet potatoes.

"Definitely," I said. "Put it with the rest of it."

Bethany tossed it to Bobby, who peered into the shopping bag we had filled with an assortment of old clothing, ribbons, buttons, and photographs. Bobby's old bear hat was inside too, the one that had earned him his nickname.

"What are you going to do with all this stuff?" he asked.

"I'm honestly not sure," I said. "We're starting a new project at quilt circle and Evelyn said we should bring things that evoke strong memories for us."

"Like when you made the log cabin quilt?" Bethany asked.

She was talking about my first quilt, the one I'd made when we were still living in the women's shelter.

Evelyn had been teaching a beginner's class to the residents and asked us to incorporate a piece of fabric that was important to us into our project. All the red center patches of my quilt were cut from pieces of the kids' outgrown clothes.

It's hard to explain, but somehow, making that quilt made me feel capable. It helped me realize that I wasn't the worthless, helpless, useless creature that Hodge had made me believe I was. That quilt changed me, changed everything. Without it, I might have taken Judith's path, returning to a man who had abused me so badly for so many years. I don't think it's too much of a stretch to say that quilting may have saved my life.

"I think it's similar," I said, answering Bethany's question, "but she told us to bring a lot of different pieces and not just fabrics but anything that could conceivably be sewn onto a quilt."

"What's this for?" Bobby asked, reaching into the bag and pulling out a photograph that had been taken a couple of summers previously during a picnic at Lake Waramaug.

Margot had come along. She took the kids down to splash in the water while I read a book for one of my classes. When they returned, I was asleep on the picnic quilt. The kids snuck up quietly, then jumped on me and tickled me while Margot snapped the picture. It shows the kids dripping water and squealing with laughter, their mouths ringed with a stain of purple Popsicle. I'm laughing, too, and my sunglasses are tilted sideways as I squeeze and tickle them back. It's my favorite family portrait.

"You can't sew a picture into a quilt," Bobby said.

"No, but I can copy the picture onto a special kind of fabric. Then I'll be able to stitch it just like any other piece of fabric."

"Really? Wow, that is so cool! Hold on a second!"

Bobby jumped to his feet and ran to his bedroom. I heard him opening drawers and digging around, the sound of objects being dumped onto the floor.

"Bear? Don't go leave stuff on the floor!" I shouted. "I've got to vacuum in there later!"

"Do you think he heard me?" I asked Bethany, who was still sorting through the box of old keepsakes.

"Oh, he heard you. But that doesn't mean he's going to listen to you," she said matter-of-factly, like the miniature adult she was.

How can two children from the same genetic pool, raised by the same mother, be so different?

Bethany spied something at the bottom of the box. Her mouth opened into an "O" of delight, and her eyes lit up like blue beacons. Suddenly she was a child again, just eleven, and I was her mom.

"Look! Mom, look! My old hair ribbons!"

She held them up so I could see. They were frayed at the ends, skinnier in the middle, and creased from the hundreds of times they'd been tied into bows at the base of her pigtails.

"Do you remember?" she asked excitedly. "Do you remember how I wouldn't leave the house without them?"

I nodded. "One blue and one green."

"Because I couldn't decide on just one favorite color." She giggled at the foolishness of her younger self. "Can these go in the quilt?"

"Oh, I think they have to."

I dropped the ribbons into the bag, one blue and one green, as Bobby came thundering down the hallway.

"I found it! It was mixed up with my baseball cards!" he exclaimed, waving the picture over his head before handing it to me, facedown. I turned it over.

It was a photo of Hodge and me, taken before we were married, soon after I found out I was pregnant with Bethany. Hodge had his arm around my shoulders. I looked up at him with adoring eyes. We smiled at each other.

"Where did you get this?"

"In a box next to the trash can. I found it a long time ago and put it away and lost it.

"Now you can copy the picture onto some fabric and sew it into your quilt. Then we can all be in it," he said excitedly. "The whole family!"

The picture ended up in the bag with the ribbons, the bib, the buttons, and other memorabilia.

Bobby was so excited and so insistent. I didn't know how to say no to him or how to explain why I'd rather not include that picture in my quilt, that I didn't want to think about the foolish girl I had been back then or be reminded of the terrible things that came after. I wanted to forget all that. Up until recently, I'd done a pretty good job of it. And then Hodge got time off for good behavior—

one of the more ironic ironies in the history of the world—and ruined everything. Yet again.

I couldn't explain that to my son, a seven-year-old child who didn't know about any of that and shouldn't have to. Instead, I told him that since I really didn't know what Evelyn had in mind and how the project was supposed to come together, the items in the bag were just things I *might* end up using.

"It's good to have a lot of options," I said casually as I stowed the box of keepsakes on the closet shelf and put the shopping bag on the counter, "but I'll just have to wait and see what turns out to be useful and what doesn't. I probably have way more stuff in here than I need."

I could feel Bethany's eyes on me as I talked. I knew that she knew I had no intention of including Hodge's picture in my project, but she didn't say anything.

We've gotten pretty good at keeping secrets.

14

Gayla

Sabbatical or no sabbatical, I still had to work. Thankfully, telecommunications made telecommuting easy, even in a location as centrally isolated as New Bern. So in the morning I booted up my laptop, answered my e-mail, and made a few calls.

Tyler Mattox, a rising senior with procrastination issues, promised to get in contact with William and Mary, Washington and Lee, and the University of Virginia and make appointments for campus visits during his family's summer vacation to Williamsburg. Jen Wells, Blake Neidermeyer, and Zachary Allen all confirmed that they had, as promised, enrolled in summer SAT-preparation courses. And Sandy Tolland, as I'd predicted, was now singing the praises of St. Michael's College. Her attitude had undergone a rapid adjustment after she received a call from the gymnastics coach, who offered Emily a significant athletic scholarship. St. Michael's might not be the Ivy League, but the promise of a scholarship would supply Sandy with the bragging rights she craved. More important, Emily would fit in beautifully there. Problem solved. I was happy for them both.

With my most pressing work wrapped up by eleven, I decided to reward myself with a visit to the demonstration gardens of the famous White Flower Farms in Litchfield, something I'd been meaning to do for years. I could tick another item off my sabbatical wish list and garner some inspiration for my own garden.

As it happened, my visit coincided with the opening day of TomatoMania. I'd never heard of it before, but apparently it was an annual and highly anticipated event. The parking lot was absolutely packed. Three men wearing neon-orange vests directed traffic and tried to keep the chaos to a minimum. After finally finding a place to park, I followed the line of people, chose a little red wagon from one of the many parked near the end of the lot—apparently these were to take the place of shopping carts—and trudged up a little hill to a grassy field, where literally thousands upon thousands of tomato plants in scores of different varieties were offered for sale.

People were loading up their carts as quickly as they could, choosing plants by the dozen and lining up to purchase them at a white tent that housed outdoor checkout counters. It was all a little crazy, but after a long cold winter and a long cold spring, I guess people were just anxious for the start of summer.

I moved on to the flower gardens and green-houses, which were even more incredible than I could have imagined. There were acres and acres of flower beds, some planted with late-blooming tulips in big blocks of color so beautiful they took your breath away, others that included a greater variety of plants—for example, clumps of lavender next to white roses just coming into bloom with green clusters of lamb's ear to provide texture and balance—but were laid out in a way that made you appreciate and notice each individual plant.

The greenhouses were lovely too. My favorite was devoted entirely to begonias, hundreds of them, with succulent, waxy green leaves and brilliant blooms of scarlet, purple, flaming orange, and canary yellow. They were stunning.

One thing I learned from my visit to White Flower Farms is that using a smaller variety of plants but placing them in groups would provide a greater visual impact than mixing them up, and I knew that was something I wanted to do in my garden. But other than that, I was a bit overwhelmed. In the end, I just ended up buying six tomato plants and going home. I just had no idea where to begin.

Fortunately for me, that question sort of answered itself.

When I returned to the cottage, there was a blue Prius parked in the driveway. It belonged to Tessa Woodruff.

"Hope you don't mind me dropping by unannounced," she said, opening her trunk to reveal three big plastic gardening flats filled with potted plants. "But I thought I'd bring over a few herbs to help you get started on your gardening.

"That's Lavender Goodwin Creek," she said, pointing to one of the pots. "It withstands heat better than some of the other varieties and makes a wonderful sachet, has a kind of rosemary scent to it. This variety is called Lavender Silver Mist. You can recognize it by the silvery shimmer of the leaves. It blooms a little later in the summer and is very pretty in fresh arrangements. And over here, you've got Lavender Grosso, so named because it gets to be very, very big. It doesn't look like much now, but you'll want to put that near the back of the bed; otherwise, it'll end up blocking the view of the other plants."

She leaned closer to the plants and breathed in. "Don't they smell wonderful?"

"They do," I agreed. "It's awfully nice of you to bring these, but you shouldn't have gone to all this trouble."

She waved off my comments. "I had to do a little thinning in my own garden. Where should I put these?" She grabbed one of the flats, lifting it out of the trunk.

I took the box that held my tomato plants out of my own car and led the way. When we rounded the corner of the house and Tessa caught site of my still plantless garden, her eyes went wide.

"Wow! Are you putting in a garden or planting crops?"

Seeing it the way she did, an absolutely enormous patch of dirt with undulating edges that testified to my inexperience in the use and control of rototillers, I felt a bit embarrassed.

"I told you, I got a little carried away."

She nodded. "I get it. How do you think I ended up with a quarter acre planted in lavender? I had to go into the soap business simply to justify it. I brought you some other herbs too," she said, nodding to plastic pots filled with small but vigorous-looking plants.

"There's rosemary, sage, bergamot, verbena, basil, and mint. Keep an eye on that and cut it back frequently; mint can take over your whole garden if you're not careful. It's so hardy it's practically a weed. The rest of these are pretty sturdy too, and I think we're finally past the threat of frost, so you can plant them today if you want.

"This one is English thyme. Gives a wonderful flavor to chicken and vegetables, or in soup. I cook with it so often that I keep some in the kitchen window, but this one needs a bigger pot. See?" She set the flat on the ground, picked up one of the plastic pots, and yanked out the plant so I could see a tangle of straw-colored roots, wrapped around the soil like a tight-woven bird's nest.

"It's root-bound. When you replant it, just pull those apart. Don't worry—you won't hurt it," she assured me when she saw the look of horror on my face as she tore into the straw-colored knot, pulling so hard and in opposite directions that they actually made a ripping sound. "It looks

172

savage, I know, but tearing at the roots helps break up that old growth and forces the plant to send out more roots. It's the same thing with the lavender. Once it's mature and established, you've got to prune it way back, cut out the dead wood so it'll have room to spread, and you'll get new, hardier flowers the next season. Now, with the rosemary, you'll want to—"

She stopped in midsentence and laughed at herself.

"Sorry. I'm talking too much. Here," she said, and placed the thyme plant, wounded roots and all, in my open hand. "Take it. You'll figure it out."

"Tessa, this is so generous of you."

"Well, the plants would have gotten thrown away otherwise, and you've got plenty of space. These should fill up"—her eyes twinkled as she looked over my shoulder, assessing the ginormous swath of turned soil—"a tenth of your garden."

I turned around to face my would-be garden and shook my head. She was right. I could plant ten times the amount of herbs Tessa brought, and I still wouldn't have enough to fill up even a corner of the ground I'd torn up.

"What am I going to do with all this? I mean, how many tomatoes can one person eat?"

"Gayla, I hate to be the one to break it to you, but this area is too shady to grow tomatoes. If you want to do that, you're going to have to till up another bed, over on the south side of the house."

"Another? You've got to be kidding."

Tessa shook her head and laughed. So did I.

"Am I a mess or what? Seriously," I said, spreading my arms to encompass the enormous patch of naked ground, "what am I going to do with all this?"

"Anything you want," she said, walking into the middle of the patch. "You've got all the room in the world to work with. The fact that you're starting from scratch is a plus. You won't have to tear anything out, just plant it, water it, weed it, and watch it bloom."

"Still seems like a lot of work."

"It won't be so bad once everything is established, but the planting is going to be a big job. Plus," she mused, "you'll need to install some hardscape—stone footpaths, edging for the beds. And maybe an arbor, right over there. As kind of an entrance. And you'll really need to put in some larger plantings—maybe boxwood hedges?—something to define the space that stays green year-round. The best-designed gardens are pretty in winter and summer. But that will involve some heavy work. You'll need some extra pairs of hands. I'd help you myself, but this time of year, I'm so busy with my own garden, and Lee needs my help with the farm."

"I've got help," I said. "I'm hiring the neighbor

boy, Drew Kelleher, to help take care of my lawn this summer."

Tessa's face brightened. "That's right! I forgot you live next door to the Kellehers. Well, there's your answer right there. Dan Kelleher is one of the best landscape designers in town, and he grows his own nursery stock. You are going to need a *lot* of plants, and Dan's prices are very reasonable."

"Oh . . . I really don't think I'll need to bring in Dan," I said, recalling my embarrassing encounter with my neighbor. "Drew and I can handle it."

"Drew is a hard worker, but he's just a kid. You need somebody who really knows what will and won't grow in this soil. Nobody is better than Dan. Lee consults him all the time. The fact that he lives next door to you is just icing on the cake, makes everything easier."

"Oh, I don't think so," I said hesitantly. "I don't think Dan likes me."

"Doesn't like you?" Tessa's eyes widened in disbelief. "You must be kidding. Dan likes everybody. Wasn't he the one who lent you his rototiller?"

"Yes, but—"

"See what I mean? That's Dan all over. He's the first person to help out a neighbor or donate his time for a good cause. Did you know that he installed all the landscaping around the library for free? And he gave them the plants at cost.

"Dan is kind of quiet around me," she went on, "but he talks to Lee with no problem. Maybe he's shy around women. I don't know the details—it happened a long time before Lee and I moved here—but his wife walked out when Drew was just a baby. He never remarried, not even after all these years."

Dan Kelleher was divorced? I had no idea. Of course, I'd never bothered to ask. Drew had worked for us for three years, but I knew almost nothing about him or his dad. Some neighbor I was.

"Maybe you're right," I said. "Maybe I should give him a call."

"I would," Tessa replied, casting her eyes from one end of the enormous brown expanse to the other.

"It's either that or buy a bag of grass seed. A really big one."

❧ 15 ❧

Ivy

The semester was over! I had turned in the last paper for my English class and taken my final exam! After three years of work, I was officially a sophomore. If that wasn't a reason to blow my diet, I didn't know what was.

I fixed myself a celebratory bowl of maple walnut ice cream and garnished it with three Oreo cookies, then carried it into the living room and settled down on the sofa. The kids were asleep, and my classes were done! I booted up my computer and did something I hadn't done in months—wasted time.

After watching an old episode of *The Office* on Hulu, I popped over to OneKingsLane.com and drooled over a pair of vintage botanical prints mounted in ornate gold-leaf frames that would have looked fabulous hanging over my bed, as well as a gold, cream, and taupe rug, hand-woven in Turkey, that would have gone perfectly with my tag-sale-find sofa, and a gorgeous cream-colored sofa with button-back upholstery and curved arms (totally impractical for a woman with two kids) that made me want to haul my current couch to the dump.

The prices were excellent, 40 to 50 percent off retail. Even so, they were way out of my budget, so I logged in to my long-neglected Pinterest account and pinned them to my "My Style" board. The chances of my ever owning furniture that fancy fell somewhere between slim and none, but at least in digital terms, the prints, the rug, and the sofa now belonged to me.

Next, I did a little sleuthing around the boards of other users and found several pairs of boots that I repinned to my "Releasing My Inner

Cowgirl" board—one blood-red, one bright red, and one turquoise with silver stitching. Gorgeous. I've never owned a pair of cowboy boots, ridden a horse, or visited a ranch, but for some reason, the whole cowgirl thing is hugely appealing to me.

Maybe I should give horseback riding a try, I thought. *Would that qualify as my sabbatical activity?*

On the other hand, no. I liked the *idea* of being a cowgirl, but if I ever tried to actually ride an actual horse, I was pretty sure I'd have a panic attack or break my leg, probably both. Horses are beautiful, but they're also big and unpredictable.

Besides, what had popped into my mind when Evelyn brought up the question of things we'd been longing to do but had lacked the time or courage to try had nothing to do with horseflesh. But what I had in mind was just as unpredictable and, as far as I was concerned, even scarier.

How had I let them talk me into this whole sabbatical thing anyway? Peer pressure—that was how.

Everybody was already in, even Abigail, who is normally the first in the group to throw cold water on just about any idea that would force her out of her comfort zone. Then they just stood there, staring at me. So I raised my hand. What else could I do?

I could have told them that Gayla Oliver was crazy; that's what.

I could have told them she goes outside in her pajamas in the rain and breaks dishes and digs holes in the dirt and cusses so loud it turns the air blue and wakes the neighbors and that the whole sabbatical idea was just as crazy as she was—maybe more.

But that would have been mean.

And when she was standing there in the quilt shop, she didn't *seem* crazy. A little bit sad maybe, but otherwise perfectly normal and nice.

I didn't doubt that she'd done all the things Dan had said she'd done; I'm sure he wouldn't make something like that up. He was nice, too—very nice. He'd come to pick Drew up after baby-sitting so I wouldn't have to leave Bobby alone, *and* he'd volunteered to take Bobby bowling. A guy like that wouldn't make up stories about his next-door neighbor.

And just because Gayla Oliver was acting crazy didn't mean she was crazy, only that something, or someone, was making her crazy. Probably the latter. Probably her husband.

Well, we'd all been there at one time or another, hadn't we? Some of us had made multiple trips round the bend, driven to distraction by some man.

Which made the fact that I was even *thinking* of doing what I was thinking of doing completely crazy! Just as crazy as throwing dishes at rocks in the middle of the night. Crazier.

And yet . . . I was thinking about it. Or at least nibbling around the edges of it. I had been for days, even before Tessa brought up the sabbatical idea, ever since that e-mail had shown up in my inbox a few days ago, the one from "It's Only Coffee."

I'd deleted it just as soon as I figured out what it was about, before I even finished reading it. Then ten minutes later, I got into the trash folder, opened the e-mail, read it again—all the way through this time—and moved it to my miscellaneous folder, where I wouldn't have to see it.

But I knew it was there. And I thought about it. A lot. More than I cared to admit.

And then Tessa dragged Gayla into the shop with her sad eyes and her crazy idea about taking a sabbatical, and next thing you know, they were all staring at me and I raised my hand and now I was in too!

What had I been thinking?

Well, at least if it turned out to be a disaster, as it absolutely and definitely would, I didn't have to tell them about it—not in detail. All I'd have to do is say that I had done it—given the thing I'd been too scared to try a shot—that it had been just as awful as I'd predicted, a complete train wreck, and that would be that. I would have fulfilled my promise to the group and could move on and deal with the many other train wrecks in my life.

End of story.

I put my hand against my forehead, rubbed my face, and pinched the bridge of my nose. I didn't want to do this. I really, really didn't. But I knew I was going to, so I might as well get it over with. No time like the present, right? I logged in to my e-mail account and then clicked on my miscellaneous folder.

There it was. Right where I left it.

"It's Only Coffee!"
A Discreet Dating Service
for Discerning Singles

Are you tired of the bar scene? Of trying to find the love of your life over dried-out Buffalo wings and 2-for-1 well drinks during happy hour? Of being set up on blind dates by well-meaning but completely clueless friends, relatives, or coworkers? Of gritting your teeth and counting the uncomfortable minutes until the waiter brings the check at the end of a dinner date with a stranger you have abso-lutely nothing in common with?

Then "It's Only Coffee!" is just right for you!

After you fill out a personal, 120-question profile, the experienced professionals at "It's Only Coffee!" will look over your answers, carefully match you with other singles whose profiles and personalities mesh with yours, and send you a list of potential partners, complete with recent photos and a brief biography.

You choose the profiles that interest you, and your "It's Only Coffee!" personal dating coach will make arrangements for you and your potential partner to meet for a 20-minute coffee date.

Why 20 minutes? Because studies have shown that most people can make an accurate assessment of their compatibility with a potential life partner within the first 20 minutes of meeting them.

When your date is finished, you check in with your personal dating coach. If the partner you thought had potential turns out not to be your cup of tea, no problem! You'll move on to the next person. If the date went well, your coach will arrange for another, longer date and you might just be on the road to finding the loving life partner you've been dreaming of!

Don't think that a 20-minute coffee date can set you on the road to romance? Just click on this link to watch short videos from just 10 of the more than **10,000 couples** who have found love with the discreet professional guidance and support of the dating experts at "It's Only Coffee!"

Still not convinced? Then take advantage
of this **FREE** offer!
**Join us for an "It's Only Coffee!"
speed-dating event on June 15th!**

During this 30-minute speed-dating party,
you will enjoy free beverages at a local
coffeehouse and the chance to go on five
6-minute "mini-dates" with attractive and
eligible singles in your area.

Five mini-dates means five chances to find
the love you deserve! Click on the link below
to register for this FREE onetime offer!

**Why wait? Take a chance on love! Take a
chance on yourself! After all . . .
"It's Only Coffee!"**

I took in a deep breath and blew it out slowly to
a count of five, employing the same breathing
technique that had helped me endure the births of
two children without anesthesia. Then I moved
my cursor over the registration link and let it
hover there. I took in and blew out another
breath, closed my eyes, and clicked.
I was in.

❦ 16 ❧

Ivy

Someday, somebody is going to invent a tape dispenser that cuts the tape cleanly without twisting it into a sticky knotted mess, and when they do, I will buy them a medal and make them a quilt to go with it.

Cursing under my breath, I grabbed a pair of cheap scissors, cut the twisted tape, tore it off the box, and tried again, with better results. I was just putting the last label on the last box when Vesta Richardson, the new intern, cried out, "Oh, no!" I spun around and saw her standing at the table with a rotary cutter in her hand and tears in her eyes.

"What's the matter? Did you cut yourself?"

Rotary cutter blades are as sharp as any knife and potentially just as dangerous. We put fresh blades in all the cutters every morning. It makes slicing through stacks of fabric quicker and cleaner, but it can do the same thing to human flesh. If you don't handle them properly, a rotary cutter can do damage serious enough to require stitches. The first thing I'd done that morning was give Vesta a lesson on how to use the cutters safely, then stood and watched her work for half an hour until I was convinced she had it under control. Even so, accidents happen, especially with new employees.

I grabbed the first aid kit from a drawer and rushed to Vesta's side. "Which hand? Let me see."

She shook her head quickly from side to side and took in a big shuddering breath. "Not my hand," she said in a choked voice. "It's the fabric. I cut the strip two inches instead of two and a half."

"Is that what you're crying about?" She nodded, and I put an arm around her shoulder. "Don't worry about it. I do it all the time. Everybody does."

"I'm so sorry. I'll pay for the wasted fabric."

"Don't be silly. If we made every employee pay for miscut fabric, nobody would ever bring home a paycheck. Seriously, don't worry about it. Just toss it into the scrap basket. We'll find a way to use it later."

"Are you sure?" she asked, blinking her eyes and sniffling.

"I'm sure. It's just about time to close up. Can you do me a favor and take these last boxes down to the post office? Then you can go home."

"I can stay and help you clean up first," Vesta said earnestly. "I don't mind."

"That's all right. I don't want to miss the last postal pickup."

Vesta gathered up her things and loaded the boxes and padded envelopes containing the afternoon's orders into the plastic mailing bin, while I started stacking up bolts of fabric and putting away the rulers.

"See you next week, Ivy."

"Thanks for your help," I said, looking up with a smile. "You had a great first day, Vesta. Really great. You learn fast."

Her tears of a moment before were replaced by a smile. "Thanks!"

She descended the stairs from the workroom. I could hear the murmur of voices as Virginia and Margot wished her good night and the jingle of bells as Vesta opened the front door of the shop. I walked over to the tall window and watched as she crossed the courtyard to the alley, saying a little prayer that God would give her protection and the courage to stick with the program.

I had a good feeling about Vesta. She was bright but still so fragile. Her reaction to cutting that strip the wrong size was a perfect example. She was terrified of making even a tiny mistake, probably because her abuser had punished her severely for the tiniest of infractions or errors. That was something we'd have to work on. I'd have to help her understand that making mistakes is just part of being human. I needed to teach that girl how to quilt. Nothing on earth will help you bring that lesson home more quickly.

It was nearly four-thirty, time to clean up for quilt circle. Evelyn, Virginia, and Margot would come up right after they closed the shop at five, which, in theory, was when our meetings began, but our true starting times were more fluid than that. People would wander in anytime between five and five-thirty. Abigail was nearly always late. And Gayla? I wasn't sure she'd show up at all. She'd looked a little bit like a deer in the headlights when Evelyn invited her to join in.

I was glad to have a little time alone before the others came trooping up the stairs. The workroom belongs to Evelyn, of course, just like the rest of the shop, but sometimes it feels like my own private sanctuary. I couldn't ask for a prettier space to spend my days: a big open space with beautiful old wooden floors, exposed brick walls, and a set of tall windows that flood the room with light even in winter. And much of the time, I have it all to myself, which suits me fine. It's not that I'm antisocial or anything; I'm just not quite as outgoing as some of my friends. I'm not sure I'm as welcoming as they are either.

If the truth were known, I admitted to myself as I grabbed a broom and started sweeping up stray threads from the floor, I'd just as soon Gayla Oliver didn't join the circle. It wasn't that I had anything against her; I hardly knew her. That was the point. I felt comfortable with our group the way it was. I could talk to them about anything without worrying that they'd judge or misunderstand me. It wouldn't be the same if we brought in a new person. I wouldn't feel like I could talk as freely. And, at that moment, I really did have a lot on my mind.

As the day of Hodge's release drew closer, the kids were acting up more and more. They were bickering with each other and talking back to me. Bethany looked daggers through me, furious that I wasn't doing something to stop it. If I could have, I would have, believe me! But as Arnie and everyone else kept reiterating, my best hope was to cooperate with the process and with Sheila Fenton, hoping she'd take a liking to me and lean a little in my direction. That's what I was trying to do.

It didn't seem to be working. When I saw her a couple of days ago, she suggested, without coming right out and saying so, that my attitude toward Hodge might be influencing Bethany, that I was undermining her willingness to reunite with her father.

So there you have it: Bethany was mad at me for being too cooperative and Sheila Fenton was accusing me of not being cooperative enough.

On top of that, the day before, Donna Walsh had called to inform me of some new directions at New Beginnings. She said it was going to become a stand-alone charity, continuing to partner with the Stanton Center but with separate funding and a separate board. That would allow Donna and her staff to focus strictly on providing emergency counseling and shelter for families in a domestic violence crisis and permit New Beginnings to concentrate on helping the female heads of those families to move forward once they were out of immediate danger.

"It's been in the works for some time," Donna told me. "I didn't want to say anything until it was signed and sealed because I didn't want to get your hopes up."

"My hopes?"

"New Beginnings needs an executive director. I think you should apply for the position."

I didn't laugh at Donna's suggestion, but it was hard not to. Why would she think they'd hire someone with only four years' work experience and no degree for a job like that?

"Because you've been part of the program from day one," she said. "You know the clients and understand their needs. I'm not saying you're a shoo-in for the job, Ivy, but I'm sure they'd at least give you an interview. They'll have to after they read the wonderful letter of recommendation I'm going to write for you."

"You'd do that for me?"

"Of course. I talked to Abigail, and she's willing to write you a recommendation too. So what do you say? Are you going to apply?"

Was I? Honestly, I wasn't sure. If the timing

had been different, if I wasn't so distracted and busy, if I'd already finished my degree or had a little more experience under my belt, then I'd have done so in a heartbeat. A directorship at New Beginnings was my dream job. Who knew when an opportunity like that might come along again? Maybe years. Maybe never.

But what was the point of putting myself through the work of writing a résumé, the agony of enduring an interview—or several interviews—and the humiliation and rejection that would follow when I learned I hadn't gotten the job, as I surely wouldn't, because the people who did the hiring felt I was inexperienced, under-educated, and completely unsuited for the job, as they certainly would? Donna meant well, but thinking that someone like me could get a job like that wasn't just a long shot; it was a no shot.

As I reached this conclusion, it occurred to me that I'd be better off *not* discussing any of this with the quilt circle. They were the best friends anyone could hope to have, but they were also natural-born cheerleaders, optimistic no matter the odds. If I told them about the job, they'd start shaking their pom-poms and doing what they do. Virginia would say something about missing 100 percent of the shots you don't take, Tessa would say that I was letting my fear get the best of me, Abigail would start making calls and pulling strings, Margot would offer to help write my résumé, Tessa would give me an encouraging wink and a brownie, Evelyn would put her arm around me and tell me she believed in me and always had, and next thing you knew, they'd suck me into the fantasy, getting my hopes up only to have them smashed on the rocks of reality.

Right. Better *not* to discuss this with the circle, I concluded as the sound of footsteps on the stairs signaled the arrival of the others. After all, I was already registered to go on five speed dates. Surely that was enough embarrassment and humiliation for one summer.

"Well, we don't really have any," Evelyn explained when Gayla, who had shown up in spite of my predictions to the contrary, asked about our rules and procedures.

"The only real agenda is making a little space in the week to spend time with people we enjoy, doing something we like. We decided from the very first—no rules, no leader, no officers, no agendas, and *no* obligations."

"Except for me," Madelyn said as she opened a plastic storage container and started arranging brownies on a plate. "I am obligated to bake and bring the brownies every week. You should hear the whining if I forget."

"The others take turns bringing wine and other snacks," Virginia said, "but I always bring sparkling cider." Virginia pried the cap off a green glass bottle and filled her glass before putting one of Madelyn's brownies onto a paper plate.

"I don't touch alcohol. Except for that little slug of bourbon Madelyn adds to the brownies. The alcohol evaporates while they're baking. Everybody knows that."

"Okay," Gayla said after taking a sip of the wine that Tessa had just poured into her glass. "So the only real rule is that there aren't any rules. But don't you make quilts together? As a group?"

Evelyn bent over to plug her sewing machine into an extension cord that snaked beneath the tables grouped together in the middle of the room.

"Now and then," she said, her voice coming from under the table. "When there's a special occasion, like when we made the quilt for Margot's wedding. And sometimes we'll make charity quilts."

She popped up from under the table, sat down, and picked up a spool of blue thread. "I came to New Bern from Texas after my divorce. I put every dime I had into the business and came this close to going bankrupt," she said, licking her fingertips and using them to wet the end of the thread.

"Then things got really interesting. I found out I had breast cancer and ended up having a mastectomy. It was kind of ironic because I got my diagnosis just a couple of days before we were hosting a Quilt Pink event for breast cancer research. They don't have nationally organized Quilt Pink fund-raisers anymore," Evelyn said, threading the blue cotton through the eye of her needle, "but I still organize a local event every year. We make some quilts, auction them off, and send in the proceeds.

"Last year, we raised over six thousand dollars. Of course, part of that is because Abigail always runs up the bids. She refuses to let any of the quilts we make go for less than eight hundred dollars. Sometimes the people who are bidding against her find that irritating, but, oh, well," Evelyn said with a wink. "It's all for a good cause."

"We've also made quilts to raise money for the Stanton Center," I said as I unpacked my sewing notions and the collection of memorabilia Evelyn had asked us to bring. "But aside from that, it's unusual for us to be working on a group project.

"Speaking of which," I said, holding up one of Bethany's old hair ribbons, "what am I supposed to do with this?"

"Glad you asked," Evelyn said, and swiveled her sewing chair so she could see everyone. "When we were talking about our sabbatical project and how we're so busy living life that we don't actually get a chance to enjoy it, I started thinking that the same thing is true even when it comes to quilting. Right now, the biggest buzzwords in quilting are 'quick' and 'easy.' It seems like everybody who comes into the shop is looking for a pattern that fits that description; they're so focused on getting something stitched up and out the door in record time that they're not really enjoying the process."

"I don't know if that's quite true," Abigail said. "There's a certain satisfaction in seeing something finished. I like checking things off my to-do list."

"So do I," Evelyn conceded, "and there are definitely times when a quick and easy quilt is exactly what is called for. But as long as we're spending the summer trying new things, why don't we change our pace? And our tactics? This summer, instead of quilting something that's quick and easy, let's try something slow and special."

Madelyn, who was circling the tables, offering brownies to anyone who hadn't had one yet and seconds to those who had, asked, "Such as? Not that it makes much difference to me. I never seem to finish any of my quilts," she said with a sigh, "even the supposedly quick and easy ones. But I'm just curious as to what you had in mind."

"Crazy quilting," Evelyn replied, pulling a few books out of the project bag that sat at her feet and passing them around. "It's one of the earliest, most time-honored techniques in quilting, but I don't think any of us have ever tried it."

"Oh, I have," Virginia said. "Not since I was a girl, though. My grandmother made crazy quilts and taught me some of her techniques. Hers were really scrappy, made entirely out of old clothes. Grandma used denim, corduroy, wool, even velvet, if she had some on hand, backed them with flannel, and hand-embroidered the seams with all kinds of fancy stitching. She made them as wedding quilts for all her grandchildren, including me."

"I remember that quilt," Evelyn said. "The one you and Dad had on your bed when I was little. That was a beautiful quilt."

"It was very warm—great for Wisconsin winters. But it was also so heavy you could barely move under it." Virginia smiled, her eyes crinkling up at the corners. "Your dad called it the birth-control quilt. He said Grandma made them heavy just to save herself the work of having to make quilts for scores of great-grands."

Evelyn laughed. "Sounds like something Dad would say."

"Oh, your father was a great joker. I could never stay mad at him for long, not even when I wanted to. About the time I was ready to blow my top, he'd say something to make me laugh, and then I'd forget what I was mad about. Such an irritating man," she said, with a smile that belied her words.

"Anyway," she said, waving off the memories. "I think it'd be fun to do some crazy quilting. But let's just keep them small, so we can take our time and enjoy the process."

Evelyn nodded. "Exactly what I was thinking. If we make wall hangings instead of quilts, we'll be able to slow down, take our time choosing our materials, using fabrics and trims that are really meaningful to us, finish them with beautiful hand-embroidery, and create something really special, a quilt we can truly feel proud of."

Gayla, who had been silent during this whole exchange, frowning in concentration as she studied the pictures in one of the books Evelyn had passed out, looked up.

"Hand-embroidery? I don't know how to thread a needle, let alone embroider something." She closed the book and held it out to Evelyn.

"Thanks, but I don't think I'm ready for this. Besides, I don't really have anything to work with here, not anymore." She looked away quickly, casting her eyes to the floor as if she'd just realized she'd said more than she intended.

"I . . . I just finished clearing out my closets. Spring cleaning—you know how it is," she said, her eyes darting quickly to Evelyn's face and then back down to the floor. "So I don't really have anything left that has any meaning or memories attached to it. Not here in Connecticut.

Maybe I should just wait until later, when you're back to doing quick and easy projects," she said, giving an awkward little laugh.

A murmur of protest broke out as everyone assured Gayla that she was up to the task—she really was—that it wouldn't be as difficult as it looked, and that they wanted her to join in. Everyone, including me, was very insistent. Perhaps they were just being kind, as they always are. But perhaps there was more to it. Perhaps they sensed that Gayla was dealing with more than she was willing to admit to.

I didn't just sense it—I knew it. Sane people don't just go outside in the middle of the night and throw dishes at rocks. I didn't know Gayla well, but I knew her well enough to know that she wasn't crazy, not permanently. But something— or someone—was making her crazy. And sad. She didn't say so, but you could see it in her eyes, especially when she thought no one was looking at her.

I hadn't wanted Gayla to join our group, but seeing that look on her face and knowing what I knew about her changed my mind. She needed us. She might not realize it, but she did, just like I had when I came to New Bern, nearly five years ago.

"I don't know how to embroider either. Maybe we can learn together. And we don't *have* to use fabric from old clothes, do we?" I asked, turning to Evelyn. "Just something that is special to us, right? What about that red fabric you found at City Quilter? It's special because it is the very first fabric you ever bought."

"Oh, I don't know," Gayla began to protest, "I'm not sure that counts."

"Of course it counts," Evelyn said. "There are no real rules to this. You can make it up as you go along. And your project doesn't have to be about your memories of the past, Gayla. It could be about memories you're making right now."

"Like your garden!" I interrupted. "What better way to preserve the memory of making a garden than by creating a quilt?"

Gayla's eyes went a little wide. "How did you know I'm putting in a garden?"

"Oh," I said, feeling a little flush of heat in my cheeks, "because Drew babysits for me, remember? Dan has been nice enough to come pick him up once I'm home, so I don't have to leave the kids alone. He's been taking Bobby bowling too. They're going to enter a tournament."

Abigail arched an inquisitive eyebrow. "He is? They are? How very kind. And interesting."

"Dan told me all about you," I said, ignoring Abigail. "I mean . . . about your garden. He told me all about it."

"Dan Kelleher is putting in your garden?" Virginia asked.

Gayla nodded. "Tessa convinced me that I

needed some help. It's a big space, and Dan lives right next door."

"He is a good man," Abigail said, standing up and walking across the room to pour herself another half glass of wine. "Not as creative as my landscape designer but capable enough. And much better looking," she said, giving me a sideways glance before turning back to Gayla. "So what is Dan planning for your garden?"

"We're still working on that," Gayla said. "We haven't decided on what to plant in the beds, but we're going to have four square beds in the center and then two long rectangular beds on either end. We'll have boxwood hedge borders and paths between the beds—"

"Sounds a lot like a quilt," Evelyn said, gesturing to a quilt on the wall, pointing to the different components to explain her terminology. "See? The flower beds are the blocks, the hedges are the borders, and the pathways running between are the sashing."

"You're right; there actually is a certain similarity," Gayla said. "How funny. The paths will either have plain white pea gravel or bluestones set in beds of moss. I can't quite decide. The north-south pathway will have white entrance arches, and the east-west pathway will have a garden bench on each end, also painted white."

"That sounds beautiful!" Margot exclaimed. "I'd love to see it!"

"There's nothing to see at the moment, but maybe you can all come over when it's finished."

"A garden party," Abigail murmured, taking her seat again. "What a lovely idea. However, I won't be available for the next few weeks. In fact, this is the last time I'll be able to come to quilt circle until late July."

"Don't tell me you're going on another trip," Virginia said. "I thought you and Franklin were staying in New Bern for the rest of the summer."

"We are," Abigail said, breaking a tiny corner off her half brownie. "It's just that I'm going to be occupied on Friday night, and every night, for the next six weeks."

I rolled my eyes. "I'll bite. What is it that's going to keep you so busy, Abigail? You obviously want to tell us."

Abigail took a sip from her wineglass. "Can't tell you. It's a surprise. But I *will* tell you that it has something to do with my summer sabbatical. Following Gayla's example, I am taking a sabbatical from quilting, from board meetings, as well as all my other charitable and community obligations, so I can try something I've always wanted to do but never thought I'd have the time for. I wasn't too keen on this project to begin with, but now that I've started, I'm quite enthusiastic about the idea. How is everyone else coming with their sabbaticals?"

There was another round of murmuring in

answer to Abigail's question, explaining how busy the week had been and how they had meant to get started but just hadn't found the time.

"For what it's worth," I said, "I made a plan to try something new, but haven't actually done it yet. And before you ask, Abigail, no, I am *not* going to tell you what I'm planning to do. Maybe I will when it's over, but I'm not making any promises."

Abigail gave a snort of disgust. "Oh, come now! Surely someone, besides myself, has made some real progress on this project. Margot? What about you?"

All eyes turned to Margot, who instantly blushed.

"Aha!" Abigail exclaimed. "You did try something new! And from the look on your face, I'd say it was either a grand success or an unqualified disaster. Tell us everything."

"I did try some new things this week," Margot admitted, briefly shifting her eyes to her lap before raising them again. "But nothing all that earth-shattering. My parents came over to watch the kids so Paul and I could go into the city. We got a hotel, went out to dinner, and then to the ballet. I've always wanted to go, so I did. We did."

"Did you enjoy it?" Madelyn asked. "What did you see?"

"*Swan Lake*. And I loved it!" Margot exclaimed, as if her reaction had surprised even herself. "The music! The costumes! Oh, and the dancers. So graceful. It was so beautiful that I actually cried. I couldn't help myself.

"We're already making plans to go again next year. In fact, Paul thinks we should try another overnight in the city later this summer. We've never been to the opera either. So I'd say it was a success." A playful little smile tugged at her lips. "Definitely a success."

Abigail tapped her finger against her lips. "I sense we aren't getting the whole story. You said you tried *some* new things, which would indicate that there is more to this than you've told us so far. Something a bit more adventurous? Something new that you tried *after* the ballet? Back at the hotel room?"

Once again, everyone looked at Margot, who blushed even pinker than she had the first time.

"Margot!" Abigail exclaimed with a triumphant grin. "Who knew you had it in you? No wonder Paul wants to go back to the city before summer's end."

"Abigail! Stop that!" Margot laughed, grabbed an empty pincushion from the table, and tossed it toward Abigail, who caught it with one hand.

"Oh, don't be such a prude," Abigail said. "Every marriage needs a little spicing up now and then, so good for you. Well done. Of course, you've only been married for a few months, so you don't need quite as much spice as the rest of us. What do you say, Margot? Any tips you'd like to share with the group?"

"Sorry," Margot said with a prim little smile, "you'll just have to figure it out for yourself."

"Well," Abigail sighed. "I suppose every woman is entitled to keep a few secrets from her friends. But just a few," she cautioned, giving me another quick glance before drinking the last of her wine.

❧ 17 ☙

Gayla

I sat at the kitchen table, shoulders tense, the tip of my tongue sticking out the side of my mouth, the way it does when I'm trying to concentrate, practicing my lazy daisy stitch. It's not very hard, in theory. All I had to do was sew tiny white loops on a piece of pale blue cotton I was using for practice, catch one end of the loop with a teeny anchoring stitch to make a petal, and then repeat the process five times to make a flower. Simple, right?

Except it wasn't. Not for me.

My thread kept getting twisted, and not one of my petals was the same size as the others, which meant that my flowers ended up looking bedraggled, like they'd been through a hard rain.

I hadn't even started working on my actual quilt, and already it was a disaster.

Ivy had come over earlier in the day. We practiced our embroidery together while her kids played hide-and-seek outside, briefly. After about thirty minutes, the kids had come inside arguing, insisting Ivy referee some alleged rule infraction. But she'd been here long enough to show me some of the base blocks of her quilt, with its gorgeous, colorful patches, and for me to watch her master the lazy daisy *and* the French knot. I'd been practicing for two solid hours, and the only thing I could really sew well so far was the stem stitch.

This was hopeless. Everybody else would end up making beautiful heirloom quilts, and I'd just have a rag with some knotty embroidery. If I wasn't so competitive, I'd call up Evelyn and bow out, quit while I was ahead. Then again, if I wasn't so competitive, I wouldn't care how my quilt turned out; I'd just "enjoy the process," as Evelyn advised. Living in the moment sounds good in theory, but like sewing daisies, it's harder than it looks.

Disgusted and hungry, I finally put my sewing aside and started working on dinner, nibbling on cheese and crackers while I fried garlic and onions in olive oil and opened a can of crushed tomatoes with basil to make pasta sauce.

How long would it be until I could use actual

tomatoes, ones I'd grown in my garden, to make sauce? So far, my six tomato plants, which I'd planted in pots rather than risk another go-round with Dan's rototiller, hadn't produced anything besides little yellow flowers. How long did it take to go from tomato blossom to a fully ripe tomato? Weeks? Months?

I dipped a piece of cracker in the pot, tasted the sauce, and reached for the oregano but paused when I heard the crack and pop of rubber on gravel. Someone was coming up the driveway. Looking out the kitchen window, I saw a silver sedan with New York plates emerge from the wall of the privet hedge.

Brian was at the wheel.

"I wish you would have called before you came up here," I said coldly, handing Brian the glass of water he had requested upon entering the kitchen.

He glanced longingly at the plate of crackers and cheese I'd left on the counter, but I pretended not to notice. Nobody had invited him up here. If he wanted a snack, then he could go back to the city. Manhattan had delis on every street corner.

"I did call," he said in a voice that was carefully nonconfrontational, as if he'd made up his mind not to get into an argument with me and spent the northward drive coaching himself on how to avoid doing so. "I left several messages, but you never called back. I was starting to get worried, so I decided to rent a car and drive up here, just to make sure you're all right."

"Well," I said, holding my arms out from my sides, "sorry to have put you to all that trouble, but as you can see, I'm fine. I haven't slit my wrists or put my head in an oven or anything. You can go home now."

"Any chance I can talk you into coming with me?" he asked, and smiled *that* smile, the impish, boyish smile he always uses when he's trying to get around me, to win me over, the one that almost always works.

"No."

His smile vanished, replaced by an expression of disappointment. Too bad. Honestly, what did he expect?

We weren't talking about him forgetting to pick up the dry cleaning like he'd promised or not calling to say his meeting was running late and he wouldn't be home for dinner. We weren't even talking about him neglecting to tell me that he was taking a job that would double his travel schedule or making up his mind to buy a cottage in the country without even consulting me first. This time we were talking about betrayal, about breaking his vows and my heart, making me doubt myself and everything I'd done with my life. That's not something you get past with a smile and an apology.

"Brian, why are you here?"

"I canceled my trip to Houston."

Was he scheduled to be in Houston that day? Probably. He was always going somewhere. I'd stopped trying to keep track years before.

"And this matters to me, how?"

I turned my back on him and covered the cheese and crackers with plastic wrap.

"Gayla, hang on a minute. Just hear me out? Please?"

I turned around to face him, crossing my arms over my chest.

"I'm sorry."

"You're sorry?" I repeated, shaking my head at the inadequacy of his remark. "Am I supposed to forget everything you wrote and the fact that you slept with another woman because you've said you're sorry? You can't seriously think it's that easy. What do you want from me?"

"Nothing!" He spread his hands as if trying to prove that he wasn't hiding anything. "Except . . . a chance to try to do what I should have done in the first place: tell you the truth, face-to-face."

I stared at him, saying nothing. The ball was in his court. He wanted to talk? Fine. He could talk. But if he thought I was going to make it easy for him, he was wrong.

He shoved the fingers of his left hand into his hair, making a mess of it, the way he always did when he couldn't figure out how to say something.

"Writing that memo was a terrifically stupid thing to do," he began, speaking quickly, as if he was afraid I might cut him off. "And cowardly. I should have talked to you before things got so out of hand. . . ."

Out of hand? How polite. Was that British for "before I bedded some tart at the office"? I was about to ask him that, but he beat me to the punch.

"I mean, before I cheated." He sighed heavily, started again. "Look. I don't care for her, Gayla. I never did, which makes it even worse. We'd been flirting for weeks—months, really. I knew she was interested, and it made me feel . . . attractive, I suppose. It was exciting to have some-body hanging on every word. It stoked my ego.

"About a year ago, we were at a conference, about the same time that the Dyson-Marks deal fell apart. It's not an excuse, but Mike Barrows had just chewed me out for letting the deal go south. I was sitting at the bar, feeling sorry for myself. Deanna walked by and slipped her room key in my pocket."

I closed my eyes, overcome by the mental images of what came next—Brian's hand sliding into the pocket of his jacket, her over-the-shoulder glance as she walked toward the door, the locking of their eyes, the silent agreement, the decent interval before his exit so no one would guess where he was going, the way he tossed back the last of his whiskey, left a tip for the bartender, the ride in the elevator, the chance to change his mind, letting it pass, looking left and right to make sure no one from the company was in the hallway, the hesitation, the knock, her opening the door, and him locking it.

"It was a mistake; even at the time, I knew it."

"Then why did you see her again?"

"Some misplaced sense of loyalty, I think." He pulled a chair out from the table and sank wearily into it. "Having a one-off seemed so sordid, like I was using her. But of course, that's exactly what I was doing. I saw her again the next week, twice, when we were back at headquarters. I took her out to dinner and wrote e-mails back and forth, trying to convince myself that we had a relationship. I couldn't pull it off, not for long, so I ended it. God . . ."

He covered his face with his hands, pressing his fingers hard against his creased forehead, rubbing at his skin as if he was trying to scrub away the memory of what he'd done.

"Gayla, I am so sorry. I'm sorry for the affair, but I'm also sorry that I didn't come to you and talk honestly about our problems. But I didn't think there was any point. I thought you were staying in the marriage out of some sense of duty." He cast his eyes toward the ceiling. "I realize it sounds stupid, but I honestly thought that divorce would come as a relief to you."

I shifted my eyes away from his and took a step

back, wanting to put some distance between myself and the realization that, at some level, he'd read me right.

"I convinced myself that ending the marriage would be the kindest thing to do," he said, "practically an act of nobility, because I knew you were as unhappy as I was."

"I never said I was unhappy," I muttered.

"Oh, come on," he said, all but rolling his eyes. "Just because you didn't say it doesn't mean it wasn't true. We both know our marriage isn't what it was."

"What it was *when?*" I snapped. "When we were newlyweds and so hot for each other that we were jumping into bed three times a day? When we didn't have kids? Being in a marriage isn't like being on your honeymoon, Brian. Or having an affair. Marriage is what happens in the real world. Marriage is for grown-ups, and it's *hard.* You have to work at it."

"That's what I'm trying to do!"

He shouted in frustration and jumped to his feet, startling us both. Brian isn't given to emotional outbursts. It's just not his way. His flash of temper was just that, a flash, extinguished as quickly as it had ignited, but not without some effort on his part. He stuffed his hands in his pockets and stared at the floor.

"I can't unwrite what I wrote or undo what I've done. But," he said, looking up, "I am serious about wanting to salvage our marriage. That's why I canceled the Houston trip; I've canceled all my travel for the next month. And that's why I drove out here: to ask you to give me and our marriage another chance."

"You canceled your business trips for a whole month?" I asked, a bit incredulous and also a bit concerned. "What did Mike Barrows say about that?"

"Don't worry about it. I took care of it."

"But what did you tell—"

"It's not important," he said, shoving away my question. "I want to talk about us. I know it won't be easy, but if you're willing to try, I think we can get through this. I do."

One of the things I've most admired about Brian was his optimism, his unwavering confidence that everything would turn out okay in the end. I'm not like that. Brian has sometimes accused me of being cynical, but I prefer to think of myself as a realist. I know that wishing isn't enough. If you want something to happen, you have to work to make it so.

Brian was obviously trying to do that. Canceling his travel for an entire month was huge for him. It made a statement about the depth of his resolve that he knew would not be lost on me. I appreciated that, but the realist in me thought it was just too late.

"Brian," I said, dropping my arms to my sides,

"the things you wrote were so hurtful—in some ways even more hurtful than the affair. We've grown so far apart. Sometimes I don't think I even know you anymore.

"What you wrote was true. You don't love me anymore. . . . No, let me finish," I insisted, holding up my hand. "You *don't* love me anymore, not like you did. And, if I'm honest with myself, the same is true for me. I still like you, I still care, and I think you feel the same way toward me. But if I tell you that it's all right, that I forgive you, and if I just go home and we try to go back to pretending that everything is fine, don't you think that, before long, it'll get even worse? That in time, we might not even *like* each other?"

A solitary tear slipped down my cheek. I wiped it away and swallowed hard, determined to say what had to be said.

"You said that you never intended for me to see the memo. I have a hard time believing that."

He dipped his head low, an acknowledgment. "Perhaps you're right. I hated knowing that there was this enormous lie standing between us. Perhaps a part of me wanted you to find out about the affair."

"Well," I said, unable to keep the bitter edge from my voice, "now I know."

He moved toward me, as if he intended to take me into his arms, but I backed away, keeping my distance.

"Subconsciously, maybe I did want you to know about the affair," he admitted. "But when I said I didn't mean what I wrote, that I'd changed my mind about wanting a divorce, it was true. I know you don't believe me, but it is. Do you want to know why? And when?"

I did, but couldn't bring myself to answer, mostly because I was sure that whatever he was going to say next was a lie. How was it possible that, having finally come to that conclusion, he could simply change his mind?

He couldn't. I was sure of that. And yet . . .

"It was at Maggie's wedding. When we danced together at the reception. When I held you in my arms, you looked as beautiful as you did on our wedding day. And then I began to remember how I had felt about you when we got married and how you felt about me. We were the whole world to each other then. It all came flooding back to me that day. It was a wonderful wedding—do you remember?"

I did remember. And I remembered our mother-and-father-of-the-bride dance, how handsome he looked in his tuxedo, the surprise and tenderness I felt when I saw the tears in his eyes, the spark of hope, quickly dismissed, that something important had passed between us.

"I looked around the room and saw Nate, getting ready to go to Scotland for grad school, so grown-up and capable, and Maggie and Jason just starting out and so happy together. . . . I thought about what we've built together and how lucky we are to have such a beautiful family. And suddenly I realized I'd been a fool.

"Because it was you, Gayla. It's always been you. Let's not throw away everything we've done and been to each other because I'm a fool. Let's give each other another chance."

I pressed my hand to my head, shielding my eyes from his gaze and the memories that crowded too close.

"I just don't . . ." I sighed and looked at him. "I don't know how we get past this. Honestly, what is it you expect us to do? If you think I'm just going to come home and pretend everything is fine, think again."

He pressed his lips together for a moment and then launched into it. Clearly, he'd given this some thought.

"I think you should stay here awhile, maybe until the end of summer."

That was his big plan for saving our marriage? That we should live in different cities?

"It's just that I know you're not ready to come home," he said, reading the skepticism on my face. "I don't want to push you. You need some space. Maybe I do too. I think we need to hit the reset button on our relationship. You said yourself that you feel like you barely know me anymore. Maybe we need to spend some time getting reacquainted, just listening to each other like we were meeting for the first time. Not that I'm suggesting we forget what has passed," he said, holding up his hands in anticipation of my next objection. "Obviously, we're going to have to deal with all that, but first I think you should have a chance to decide if you even like me now or find me the least bit interesting."

"Or you me?"

"Oh, there's no question of that," he said with a smile. "I've always found you interesting. Fascinating, really."

Was he flirting with me? He was. And he was pretty good at it. Where had he picked that up? And then I remembered what he'd said about her, Deanna, the woman he'd slept with—*we'd been flirting for weeks—months, really. . . .*

"Let's cut to the chase," I said irritably. "What exactly is it that you're proposing?"

He cleared his throat and adopted a more businesslike tone. "Three things. First, that we take a break and live apart until the end of summer. I think we both need some time to clear our heads. Second, that we promise not to make any moves toward divorce during that time. Third, that we do see each other at regular intervals, spend time getting to know each other again. In short," he said, "for the next three months, I think we should date."

"I'm sorry?" I said, giving my head a little

shake, certain I hadn't heard him correctly. "Did you just say you want to date me?"

"Yes."

I blew out a long breath. This was crazy. "Brian, you can't seriously—"

"I am completely serious. You don't have to answer right now. All I'm asking you to do is think about it. Wait," he said, once again interrupting my objections before I could voice them. "I brought you something."

He turned toward the back door and picked up a bag he'd left on the floor when he first came inside. I hadn't even noticed it until now. He pulled out a notebook with brass-colored rings on the binding, covered with wheat-colored linen, and brought it to me.

"What is it?"

"A photo album. You bought it in that little shop in Soho about ten years ago—don't you remember? I've been going a little crazy since you left, haven't known what to do with myself, so I started cleaning out closets," he said, looking a little sheepish about his admission.

If only he knew.

I opened the album to the first page, saw a picture of Brian and me eating gelato in Turano; another of us sitting on the stoop of our first apartment in New York, a studio with a toilet that ran constantly and so small there wasn't room to change your mind; another picture taken in the hospital when the twins were born, Brian holding a flannel-wrapped bundle in each arm and beaming.

I remembered now. I'd spotted this album on the sale table in a cute little boutique in Soho years ago, probably more than ten. I'd started going through our family pictures and pasting the best of them in the album—started but never finished. We'd had company coming for dinner, so I had to clean everything off the dining room table. The album and photos ended up in a box under the bed. Every now and then, I'd drag out the box and toss in a few more pictures, telling myself that I was going to sit down and organize them as soon as I had a little spare time, but I never did.

"I found this in a box under the bed along with a ton of loose photographs and decided to go through them, put them in the album. Why don't you hold on to it for a while," he said. "And then let's talk in a few days, after you've had some time to think."

I closed the album and laid it on the table.

"Okay."

There was a moment, a silence, an awkward pause.

"I should get going," he said.

I didn't disagree with him, just walked him to the door.

"By the way," he said, "what's going on in the yard? Are we putting on an addition?"

I shook my head. "A garden. Dan Kelleher is helping me with the design and putting in a hardscape. That's why all those boards and rocks are out there."

"Dan Kelleher?"

"Our neighbor," I reminded him. "Drew's dad. He owns a landscaping business. Very nice guy. He fixed the furnace and didn't charge me for anything but parts."

Brian's eyebrows shot up. "The furnace broke down? Why didn't you call me?"

I put one hand on my hip and shot him a look, making it clear that we both knew the reason for that.

"I'm not saying I could have fixed it," he muttered. "But I'd have called the repairman for you, somebody legitimate, somebody who's been trained. How do you know he's done it properly?"

"Because I didn't have heat and now I do." I opened the door. "Anything else?"

"You might want to ring Maggie up. She's called twice. I told her that you'd decided to take some time off, come up here for a few weeks."

"Did she believe you?"

He shrugged. "Call her when you have a chance, will you?"

He leaned forward as if to kiss me good-bye, but I turned my head, dodging his lips. When he went out the door, I locked it behind him. It was stupid, a petty gesture, but I did it just the same.

218

I stood at the living room window, half-hidden behind the curtains, watched his rental car disappear behind the hedge, and wondered if there was any chance of this turning out well or if I'd ever be able to see him drive away without having to fight back the urge to run after him.

After I finished putting away the groceries, I made myself a cup of tea and sat down at the kitchen table to drink it—slowly. I knew that Maggie had been trying to get hold of me before Brian said anything about it; she'd left two messages on my cell phone in the previous week. I'd listened to them but put off calling her back. I couldn't do so any longer.

She wasn't fooled by my casual tone of voice or by my repetition of Brian's explanation for my sudden departure from the city— that the spring admissions season had worn me out and I was spending a few weeks at the cottage to rest and relax—but I didn't really expect her to be. Maggie is the more sensitive of the twins, also the more forthright. And she can read me like a book.

"Are you and Dad separated?" she asked.

"We're taking a break."

"Before getting a divorce?"

I took in a breath and held it for a moment, then told her the truth.

"I'm not sure. Probably."

She didn't say anything for a few seconds, but her breathing was ragged and when she spoke I could hear the tears in her voice.

We didn't talk for long. There really wasn't much to say. But I did assure her that I truly hadn't made any final decisions yet, promised I would think it through carefully before doing so, and asked her not to call Nate in Edinburgh and tell him about this, not until there was really something to tell. After I hung up, I just sat there staring at the wall. After a few minutes, I grabbed the photo album and my cigarettes off the counter where I'd left them and carried them to the back porch.

I lit up and flipped through pages filled with pictures of birthdays, trips to the beach and the zoo, photographic recordings of special days and ordinary ones, each summoning up a memory, almost all of them good.

You might suppose that seeing this evidence of all that we had and all we stood to lose if we divorced would have softened my heart toward my husband. Clearly, that's what Brian had intended when he brought it to me.

But it didn't.

As I looked through those photos, I was angry all over again. We had a beautiful family, a beautiful life—the pictures proved it. And he had tossed it all aside, carelessly and thoughtlessly ripping out my heart, tearing our family apart at the seams. And why? Because he'd had a bad week; because he'd lost the Dyson-Marks deal. That bastard! He destroyed all we'd spent our lives building on a whim and without so much as a warning.

My nose was running and my eyes were blurry with tears. I got up to get a tissue, but stumbled on an uneven floorboard and dropped the album, which landed faceup on the porch. Wiping tears away with the back of my hand, I bent down to pick up the album and saw a picture of Brian and me sitting on this very porch.

I knew exactly when that photo had been taken: nearly three years before, in early October of 2010, the same day we put in our offer on the cottage.

Sniffling, I picked up the album, returned to the chair, and looked at the photo more closely, examining our expressions. We were both smiling, but mine was a smile of surprise with a bit of confusion, perhaps even shock, mixed in. Brian's smile was one of relief, as if he'd just found the solution to a problem that had been weighing him down for some time.

And I'd never even noticed.

I hadn't noticed a lot of things. I said I'd never seen this coming, but as I studied that picture, I realized that maybe I should have. The signs were there all along.

18

Gayla

The thing you need to understand is that we are not impulsive people. Never have been. Not for a long time anyway. That's why I should have suspected something was amiss when Brian called from Indianapolis on a Wednesday in the fall of 2010 and informed me that he was whisking me off for a weekend getaway.

"This Friday? I have a mountain of work. What about next weekend?" I tucked the telephone tight between my ear and shoulder and started flipping through my day planner. "Wait. That's no good either. Maybe next month?"

"Next *month?* Gayla, I am trying to be spontaneous. Isn't that what women are always saying they want?"

"We do. I do. But maybe you could be spontaneous when I'm not quite so swamped? And Nate said he might drop by on Saturday if he has time."

Brian let out one of those half-sigh, half-growl noises he makes when he's impatient with me.

"Surely our son can keep us waiting around on the off chance that he might drop in and empty our refrigerator on another weekend, can't he?"

"But where are we going? What am I supposed to pack?"

Another sighing growl came from the westward end of the connection.

"Fine. I wanted to surprise you, but if you must know, we're going to Connecticut. You can pack a dress for dinner, but otherwise, I'm sure it will be very casual. Jeans and sweaters should do it."

I looked at my in-box and the stack of personal essays that I'd promised myself I would read through before Monday, then ran my finger down a pad of paper with a scribbled to-do list that now numbered twenty-eight. It was sweet of Brian to try to be spontaneous, but I *was* swamped. If we pushed it off for a month . . .

"Your schedule won't be any less crowded next month than it is right now," Brian said, as if reading my thoughts. "If anything it will be worse."

"I know, but if I—"

"Gayla, just spend the weekend in Connecticut with me, will you? We haven't spent three consecutive days together in the last thirty."

"Well, that's not my fault," I snapped. "I'm not the one who travels all the time."

"I'm not pointing fingers. I'm simply saying I'd like to spend a weekend in the country with my wife. Is that so unreasonable?"

"I'm sorry," I said, regretting my waspish response to what really was a very sweet invitation.

"You're right. A weekend in Connecticut sounds like fun."

"Right! Excellent!" he enthused. "Pick me up at JFK, the United terminal, at three fifteen on Friday. We'll leave from there, get out of town before the traffic."

If you want to beat the traffic out of New York on a picture-perfect Friday in fall, you have to leave the city earlier than three fifteen.

Brian got miffed when I refused to get off I-95 and try to find another route. He kept pushing his phone to his chest so whoever he was talking to wouldn't be able to hear as he pointed frantically at various exit signs and hissed, "Here! Take this one!"

I paid no attention. If you want to drive, then drive. If you want to backseat drive, then ride with somebody else.

When my cell rang for the first time, Brian glared at it as if he'd rather I *didn't* have a business to run. But since his own phone started ringing about a minute into my call and didn't stop for the rest of the trip, he didn't dare comment. And not all my calls were business related. Well, one wasn't. After we left the snarl of I-95 behind and headed west on Route 8, Maggie called me.

Maggie had graduated from Smith in the spring but stayed on to take a job in the admissions department. She called a couple of times a week, that day to tell me that, for the first time since she'd broken up with her boyfriend in May, she was going on a date.

"A date! That's great, bunny!"

I glanced toward Brian, hoping to get his attention, but he had his eyes closed in concentration, deeply embroiled in a conversation about payables with somebody named Mike. I turned my attention back to my daughter and driving.

"What's his name? How did you meet him?"

"He works in the finance department. Or maybe it was accounting? I can't remember. Something about helping manage the college's investment portfolio."

Investment portfolio? That sounded promising.

"Is he nice?"

"I guess. We were standing in line at the cafeteria and started talking about how epically vile the vegan lasagna is, and then, just like that, he asked me to the movies!"

I heard a little clicking sound, like plastic tapping against ceramic, and knew she was chewing her nails. She does that when she's nervous.

"This is probably a bad idea. He seems kind of geeky."

"Is he cute?"

"Meh. Nice eyes. But he wears hipster glasses. His hair is good, though. Brown and sort of curly, kind of flops over his forehead, just a little bit."

"Never underestimate the power of good hair," I said, glancing at Brian. "It can lead to all kinds of things."

Maggie made a gagging sound.

She knew all about the bohemian existence that followed our whirlwind marriage, our adventures in Italy that came to an end after my pregnancy precipitated our return to New York, and how we became grown-ups almost overnight, as dull and predictable as any of her friends' parents, so predictable that she sometimes accused us of making up the whole thing, inventing a backstory so we would seem more interesting than we really are.

I knew she was teasing us when she said things like that, but it bothered me a little. Sure, it was a long time ago, but it really did happen—all of it. We used to be interesting.

"So how is the aging rock star? Can I talk to him?"

I glanced at Brian. He had his eyes closed, his cell phone pressed to his ear, and was using his free hand to rub his forehead.

"Not a good time. He's on the phone and seems to be having a serious discussion about due diligence that wasn't conducted quite as diligently as it might have been."

"Well, tell him I said hello. I'll call you tomorrow and let you know how the date with

Jason the hipster geek went. Seriously, did every second woman who gave birth to a boy in 1987 just wake up from the anesthesia and decide to name her baby Jason?"

I laughed. "Give the man a chance. Jason is a nice name."

"Do you think I should wear a dress? Or does that look like I'm trying too hard?"

"Do you want to? Personally, I always feel prettier in a dress."

"So do I," she confessed. "And I found a cute one at the consignment shop. It's got these little orangey flowers on the skirt and there's a sweater that goes with it. Twelve bucks! Okay," she said, finally sounding like she was beginning to look forward to the evening. "I'll wear that! Thanks, Mom. Gotta run. Call you tomorrow!"

She rang off without giving me a chance to say good-bye. I smiled. Even though she was grown up and on her own, I loved it that she still called to ask my advice.

Brian finished his call. "Was that Maggie? How is she?"

"She's got a big date; somebody who works at the college. Jason. He helps manage the college's investment portfolio." I gave him a meaningful glance.

Brian laughed. "Do you realize how like your mother you look right now? The idea of a financier son-in-law has you all aflutter."

"It does not!" I protested. "It's not like Maggie's going to marry this boy. I'm just happy she's going out. It's been too long."

"Right that. Well, good for her. I'm going to call her back and tell her so."

He pressed Maggie's number into his cell and waited for her to pick up. After a moment he frowned and took the phone from his ear.

"Maybe she's in the shower," I offered, slowing slightly and hugging the curves as hills on each side of the road grew taller and closer, becoming a canyon as the road serpentined its way between the rocky cliffs and alongside a small but fast-moving river, mirroring the twists and turns of the rushing water.

"No," he said, still frowning, now staring intently at the screen. "It's not that. There must be some kind of . . . Wait . . . there's no coverage. No bars."

"No bars? Are you serious?"

"Not a one." A slow smile spread across his face. "Isn't that fantastic?"

Just as I was about to remind him that he had absolutely promised I would be able to keep in contact with my clients this weekend, the road took a final twisting S and the rock-faced cliffs gave way to a wider and lusher valley, with rolling, painted hills, and trees ablaze with yellow, orange, umber, sienna, cinnamon, and crimson.

"No," I said, "but this is."

●●●

I've been to plenty of little villages in New England but none as charming as New Bern. Perhaps because New Bern wasn't *trying* to be charming; it simply was. That's how it seemed to me—unpretentious and natural, self-satisfied without being smug.

The Green was a little overgrown, the streetscape signage on the smallish side. The doorways of the shops stood open to let in fresh air and customers, but there was no urgency about the latter. No one stood on the corner passing out flyers to passersby, and there were no placards advertising year-end clearance sales sitting on the sidewalks.

A child in a green sweater spun around a lamppost, hanging on with one arm. Two women with spiked hair and tattoos on their arms stepped off the curb and into the street without looking. A silver sedan stopped to let them cross. An elderly couple wearing hiking boots and olive-green fishing hats leaned on the windowsill of a shop that sold sweaters and wide-wale corduroys, licking ice cream from cones. A black lab, leashed but untethered, lay near a bench in need of paint, waiting for its owner to return. It thumped its tail in greeting when I stooped down to say hello but didn't bother to rise.

It seemed to me the whole town had an attitude a little bit like that dog. *I'm glad to see you, of course, but I hope you'll forgive me if I don't get up. I'm good where I am.* Welcoming but not fawning, comfortable in its skin, feeling no urge to impress anybody.

That was New Bern, and I liked it. I liked it from the first.

The innkeeper, an attractive woman in her mid-fifties whose face looked strangely familiar, escorted us to our room.

"Is she who I think she is?" I whispered after she left, just in case the innkeeper had supersonic hearing. "Come on," I said, snapping my fingers a couple of times as I tried to summon up a name. "You know who I'm talking about . . . that singer . . . the famous one . . ."

Brian gave me his best "are you daft?" look and loosened the knot on his tie. "Gayla, what would a famous singer be doing running a bed-and-breakfast?"

"Okay," I said, conceding his point. "Maybe not a famous singer, but I know I've seen her face before. She's definitely somebody."

Brian tossed his necktie onto the bed. "Isn't everybody?"

"You know what I mean!" I said, exasperated because I could tell by the teasing look on his face that he *did* know. We've played this game before.

Manhattan is one of the best places in the

world for celebrity sightings. I'm always on the lookout and spot them pretty often, but amid the adrenaline rush of discovery, I can never remember their names. But Brian always can, even though he is completely unimpressed by the goings-on of the rich and famous. Once, he and Nate shared a cab with Robert De Niro, but I didn't even hear about it until Nate came over for dinner a week after it happened. Brian hadn't thought it was important enough to mention.

"Who is she?" I demanded. "Somebody famous, right?"

Brian slipped his loafers from his feet and settled into a chintz-covered easy chair. "She's Madelyn Baron, Sterling Baron's widow, the man who ran the big Ponzi scheme and then killed himself in prison, remember?"

"Oh, that's right. Gosh, I guess the papers weren't lying about the feds taking all their assets. She used to live in a penthouse; now she's running a hotel."

Brian shrugged. "She looks happy enough. Maybe she prefers New Bern to New York. Seems like a nice place."

I took off my jacket and undid my hairclip, shaking my head so my hair fell loose around my shoulders. "It does. Want to take a walk into town and look around?"

He got up from the chair, crossed the room, and put his arms around me. "I kept thinking about you all during the flight out here." He kissed me on the lips, then the neck—he knows I can't resist that—and twined his fingers in my hair. "You should wear your hair down all the time."

I laughed. "It's too much work."

"I love it this way," he murmured, brushing his lips against my neck again.

I sighed and let my head fall back, arching my body against his ever so slightly, thoughts of walks and dinner driven from my mind.

"You've been traveling all week; are you sure you're not too tired?"

"Not too. Not for you," he said, raising his head and kissing me on the lips.

I pulled away, heading toward the bathroom. "I'll be right back."

He stretched out on the bed with a pillow propped behind his head and his arms crossed over his chest. "I'll be waiting."

When I emerged from the bathroom five minutes later, he was still there on the bed, snoring lightly, fast asleep.

In spite of a somewhat rocky start, we had a lovely weekend.

Brian stirred in the bed next to me the next morning, pulled me close, and picked up where he'd left off the night before. It was a nice way to start the day. With him traveling so much, it had been weeks—actually more like months—since we'd made love.

After breakfast, we drove to Washington Depot, bought some books at the Hickory Stick, a wonderful little bookstore housed in a squat and unusually curved brick building, then went on a hike in Steep Rock Preserve and had a picnic on the riverbank, serenaded by chirping birds and rushing water.

Our dinner at the Grill on the Green was delicious. Brian ordered the short ribs with root vegetables, and I had the roast chicken with mashed potatoes. Not very adventurous, I know, but cool autumn weather calls for comfort food, and I relished every bite. We spent three hours at dinner, talking about everything under the sun. I couldn't remember the last time we'd talked like that, really had a *conversation*. It was wonderful. After the server cleared our dishes, Brian reached across the table and took my hand, pressing his lips against the inside of my wrist, on that sensitive spot where the veins blush blue under the skin.

"You look lovely tonight."

"Are you flirting with me? Don't tell me you're trying to lure me into bed again," I teased, though my heart was beating a little faster. My free hand, hidden beneath the cloth, found his knee and snaked slowly up his thigh.

Brian laughed awkwardly and shifted backward

in his seat. "I didn't suppose you'd be interested in another go so soon. Perhaps I should have skipped the wine."

"Oh, this morning was wonderful," I assured him, quickly removing my hand from his leg and placing it in my lap. "It's been a perfect weekend. Maybe we should quit our jobs, move to Connecticut, and spend our days making mad, passionate love."

He laughed again. "Now, there's an idea."

On Sunday, after only forty-five minutes spent poking through antique stores, art galleries, and clothing boutiques in downtown New Bern, Brian insisted we get going.

"Let's go for a drive. There's something I want to show you."

"What?"

He smiled enigmatically. "You'll see."

Next thing I knew, we were driving down a country road to the north, in the opposite direction to New York. Brian took a sharp left into a narrow driveway lined with privet hedges on both sides and pulled up in front of a white clapboard cottage with peeling paint and a sloping porch.

He shifted the car into park and opened the door. "Well? How do you like it?"

"How do I like what?"

Still confused I got out of the car and followed

Brian to the house. The front door opened, and a short, chubby woman with gray hair and rhinestone wingtip eyeglasses stepped onto the porch.

"Brian Oliver," he said, striding forward to shake the woman's hand. "You must be Wendy. Sorry we're late."

Late? How could we be late for an appointment I didn't even know we had?

"That's all right. It's not like I had anything better to do besides sit in the office and wait for people to not buy houses. The market's been flat as a pancake for more than a year." She laughed —actually, it was more of a snort—making her rhinestone glasses bounce on the bridge of her nose.

"But if you've got the money to do it, Mr. and Mrs. Oliver, you couldn't pick a better time to buy a second home."

I looked at my husband, wide-eyed, finally realizing what he was up to.

"A second home? Brian, we can't—"

He grabbed my hand and pulled me through the door. "I can't wait for you to see it. If it looks half as good as it did online, it'll be perfect for us."

Perfect for us?

The porch was rotted as well as sloped, but not as sloped as the wooden floors, and the roof was covered with moss. The kitchen was bigger than the little galley affair in our apartment but still very small, with ugly green linoleum and untrimmed cabinets, painted beige. The only bathroom had rust stains in the tub and a flow of water that was more a drip than a stream. An impossibly steep, narrow staircase led to two tiny bedrooms tucked under ceilings so low and sharply angled that Brian could straighten his back only when standing in the center of the room.

In spite of all that, it *was* charming. And cozy. I wondered what it would be like to lie in bed on a morning in early spring and listen to raindrops patter against the moss-covered roof. Or to pull up a chair next to one of the many-paned windows and stare out onto a wide, grassy meadow dotted with huge maple trees ablaze with bright red leaves.

"It's only two acres," Wendy said apologetically. "But the trees are planted so thick along the border of the meadow that you can't see your neighbors, even in winter."

Two acres? That was more land than I'd ever dreamed of owning.

"There's an oil furnace, of course," Wendy said as she escorted us into the living room. "But this fireplace can practically heat the whole house. Well . . . the main floor."

I could believe that. The huge fireplace seemed a little out of scale in comparison to the rest of the room, but I could imagine how warm and safe the room would feel with the fireplace blazing on a cold day, how peaceful it would be to sit by that fire on a snowy night with a book and a glass of wine at hand and no phones or computers to jar your sensibilities or inhibit your focus—a simple and peaceful existence, like something from another time, which it was. No one lived like that anymore, us least of all.

Brian squatted down next to the fireplace. "What's this?" he asked, reaching out to take hold of an iron bar and swing it out into the center of the firebox.

Wendy squinted through her rhinestone rims. "That's for cooking. See that groove on the end of the bar? That's where you'd hang your soup pot. When this house was built, they were still cooking over the fire." She bent down for a closer look. "And see there? That's a beehive oven. Two hundred years ago, people baked their bread in that."

Brian sat back on his haunches and looked up at me, an enormous smile on his face. "Well? What do you think? Let's make an offer!"

"An offer? What . . . now?" I sputtered. "Today? On *this* house? Why? Brian . . . we've never even *discussed* getting a second home. And now, after forty-eight hours in Connecticut, you just want to . . ."

Brian was looking at me blankly, as if he couldn't quite grasp what was distressing me, as if *I* was the one who was behaving irrationally.

"Honey, you don't just decide to buy a house five minutes after you walk through the door!"

"We decided to buy our apartment five minutes after we walked through the door."

"That was different. If we hadn't snapped it up right away, somebody else would have, and we actually *needed* a place to live. And it was in New York. In an established building with management, and a concierge, and a super . . ." I threw up my hands.

"Brian, you don't know anything about this place! It could have rats, or termites, or God knows what. It could have a leaky basement or broken windows or . . ."

He must be joking. He had to be! Sure, we'd had the occasional romantic, wine-induced conversation about living in a farmhouse off in the country and raising chickens or peaches or something. Or buying a run-down Victorian in a little college town somewhere and restoring it to its former glory. But that wasn't for *now*. That was for . . . someday. When we had time and money and fewer responsibilities. And anyway, the reason those romantic conversations were so romantic was because, in our hearts, we both knew it was never going to happen!

"What if there's a fire? Or a blizzard? What if the roof blows off or the pipes burst? Who's going to deal with that if we're in the city? How would we even know it happened?"

Brian gave me his exasperated look, the one that says he thinks I'm being overly dramatic. "We'll get an alarm system or . . . a caretaker or something."

"People in New Bern generally just find somebody to look in on their places," Wendy said helpfully, shoving her glasses up the bridge of her nose. "There's a teenage boy, Drew Kelleher, who lives nearby. He could keep an eye on things for you."

"Sounds perfect," Brian said. And then, as if everything were settled, he reached into his pocket and pulled out a check. A single, folded check.

"Hold on! What are you doing? We can't just buy this house! We don't even know how much it costs!"

"One ninety-five," Wendy replied quickly. "The land alone is worth the price. You can't buy two flat, cleared acres this close to town for less than one seventy-five."

"Or even a studio in Manhattan," Brian added, unfolding the check. "It's a steal."

"A steal? It's one hundred and ninety-five thousand dollars!" I shouted.

Brian's grin disappeared. Wendy stared at the ceiling, trying to look invisible.

"I'll just step outside and let you two talk," she said, and made a hasty exit.

"You're mad," Brian said as soon as she was gone.

"Let's call it surprised," I said flatly.

"I thought you'd be excited. I was trying to be spontaneous."

I shook my head. I wasn't buying it. "Making an appointment with a Realtor without telling me isn't being spontaneous. Neither is taking a check out of the book and slipping it in your pocket so you can make an offer on the spot. Brian, we've never even *talked* about buying a second home. And all of a sudden . . . What is going on?"

He shoved his hands deep into his pockets.

"I was going to wait to tell you later. Don't look so worried," he said, giving me a smile that didn't quite reach his eyes. "It's good news. I'm being promoted. As of Monday, I'll be vice president of strategic acquisitions. Comes with a big increase in salary." His pseudo smile faded. "And in travel."

"*More* travel? But you already spend fifty percent of your time on the road."

"Well, now it's going to be eighty percent," he said. "The chairman thinks it's a good time to pick up some companies cheaply. They want me to acquire a company every two months. You know what that means."

I did. Trips to investigate companies, most of which would turn out to be dead ends, weeding out the weak from the strong; on-site meetings with the management teams to figure out who they'd keep and who they would let go; return trips with teams of accountants to go over books, inventories, and payables; and endless meetings with attorneys. Brian had been involved in two acquisitions in the previous year. The thought of him doing it full-time, being on the road week after week, made my heart sink.

"We'll still have weekends," he assured me. "And if we have a place out in the country, at least we could make the most of what we *will* have together. I'll be able to take some three-day weekends. And once I get settled in the job, maybe I can work out of the house, or up here, a couple of days a month."

He moved closer and wrapped his arms around my waist. "I'm sorry, Gayla. I'd have told you about the promotion and my idea about the house and all, but I didn't want to say anything until we'd seen the town. If we hated it, I figured I'd just call the Realtor and cancel the appointment, but . . . I like it here. Don't you?"

I sighed. "Do you realize how much work this place needs?"

"You're always saying I need a hobby." He spread out his hands. "This could be it. We could work on it together. It'd give us something to talk about besides the kids and work. And it would be a kind of refuge. I haven't started the job yet, but already, I can't go to the loo without that wanker Mike Barrows calling. But since we've been in New Bern?" Brian pulled his cell phone from his pocket and held it up so I could see. "No calls from the boss. Not a one. That alone is worth the price," he said with a teasing smile.

"Baby, are you sure you want this promotion?"

He shrugged. "We're buried in debt. Now we can pay it all off. Even the college loans—yours and the twins. Think how good it would feel to get out from under that. Anyway, it's not like I can turn it down. When Mike offered me the job, he said, 'You're either moving up the ladder or out the door. There's no treading water at this company, Oliver.' "

He made a puffing sound with his lips. "Barrows is a git, a total tosser. But he's right. I can't turn this down and expect to stay at Ellison-Farley. And so, to answer your question, am I sure I want this promotion? Absolutely. Who wouldn't?"

"Oh, honey." I reached up and brushed his hair off his forehead, wishing there was something more I could say, but he'd already said it all.

Brian had spent his whole career with this company, but if he turned down this opportunity, they'd probably turn him out the door. Nobody was hiring, and even if they had been, Ellison-Farley had already bought most of its competitors. Now it looked like it was going to buy up the rest. Five years ago, Brian would have had no trouble finding another job, but not now. And I couldn't support us on my income alone. Not yet.

There was no choice. Brian had to take the job.

But we'd get through it. We always had. And if I looked on the bright side, I could already see how there might be some good for us in this—not just financially, but good for *us,* as a couple.

I turned in a slow circle, taking in the sloping wooden floor, the dusty beams, the low ceilings, until I faced the fireplace, stained black from the soot of two hundred years.

Brian came up behind me and rested his chin on my shoulder. "What are you thinking?"

I reached behind and pulled his arm around my waist. "About having my way with you in front of this fireplace."

I never did have my way with him in front of the fireplace, or he with me.

Our intentions were good. For a few months, a few weeks, we spent every weekend in New Bern. But then he ended up having to stay in the Midwest for some weekend meetings, and I had to do some traveling of my own, attending conferences and visiting campuses, and we fell out of the habit of coming here and making time for each other. Somehow, I never noticed it was happening, never perceived the problem, because I truly didn't think there was one.

But Brian did.

He knew the marriage was in trouble as early as three years ago, maybe even before. He'd sensed we were drifting apart and that the distance between us would only widen if we didn't do something about it. And what he'd done was bought the cottage, thinking it would tether us one to the other, keep us connected even as time, circumstances, and simple indifference pulled us apart.

Three years ago, as we sat on the porch and I was smiling with surprise and confusion, he was smiling with relief and satisfaction because he thought he'd fixed a problem I didn't even know we had. Or maybe I just didn't want to know. It's hard to say.

I laid the photo album on the table and walked down the steps and across the grass to my would-be garden. The planters were finished, defined by borders of gray-white Belgian block, and the boxwood hedges, stubby but promising, had been planted along the outer borders. But the archway entrances had yet to be installed, the pathways were still devoid of gravel, and the soil was scraped brown and bare; no flowers had been planted so far. But as I walked between the expectant flower beds, I spied a small patch of green, the leaves of a weed with especially deep roots that had managed to survive the ravages of the rototiller.

I bent down to pull it out, but as I got closer, I could see that there wasn't just one green sprout pushing up through the earth, but dozens. I plucked out a few but realized that I needed to spend some serious time out here before we planted the new flowers, digging down deep and getting rid of the roots. Otherwise, weeds would spring up everywhere and take over my garden.

I stood up, brushed my dirty hands on the legs of my jeans, then pulled my cigarettes from my jacket pocket and lit one up, strolling through the garden and around the yard, smoking and thinking.

❦ 19 ❧

Ivy

Drip, a coffeehouse just outside of New Haven, was the location of the "It's Only Coffee!" speed-dating event. It's also where I spent the longest eighteen minutes of my life.

After checking in at the registration desk, getting my packet and a sticker with my number, twenty-three, then picking up a decaf vanilla latte from the counter, I sat down at a two-seater café table. The crowd was bigger than I'd imagined it would be. There were probably thirty tables, maybe more. A lone woman sat at each one.

Mandy, the cheery organizer of the evening's festivities, who looked to be fresh out of college and seemed unable to speak a sentence that didn't include the word "okay," wasn't exactly the kind of person I'd had in mind when I'd read about the "dating experts" in the ad copy. She clapped her hands to get the crowd's attention.

"Okay. Everyone should have gotten a piece of yellow paper in their packet with a list of five numbers on it, okay? Wave your hand if you don't have a list."

She waited while people opened their packets and pulled out the list, scanning the room for waving hands. When none appeared, her face lit up.

"Okay! Good! That's your date list, okay? The women are going to stay seated at the tables. Ladies, be sure to put the stickers with your numbers where they can be seen, okay? Okay. Guys, when I blow the whistle, you're going to look for the table that matches the first number on your list and sit down. You've got six minutes to talk to each other, and believe me, they're going to fly by, so don't be shy. Just jump right in and start talking, okay?

"When I blow the whistle again, move on to your next date, which will be the second number on the list, and so on. Remember," she cautioned, "even if you're enjoying talking to your date, when I blow the whistle you *have* to move on to your next date, okay? There are a lot of interesting people here tonight, and we want you to meet as many of them as possible.

"So. Okay. Does everybody understand the

rules? Okay? No questions? Okay!" she exclaimed and clapped her hands again. "Ready? Set? Let's date!"

At the blast of the whistle, there was a sudden murmuring and milling about as men searched for the correct women. I felt conspicuous sitting there, feeling all those sets of eyes checking me out, and so, even though I don't like sugar in my coffee, I reached for a packet and added it to my latte, just so I wouldn't have to look up.

Just about the time I was thinking, with a certain amount of relief, that no one had gotten my number this go-round, a skinny, washed-out looking man wearing skinny, washed-out jeans and a red and white plaid shirt plopped down across from me and introduced himself.

Kieran Fleischman took Mandy's advice about jumping right in to heart. Within two minutes of his sitting down, I learned that he liked watching reruns of *Father Knows Best* on the nostalgia channel, owned a metal detector and, using it, had once collected fourteen dollars and twelve cents in dropped change from under the bleachers at the Yale soccer field, and spent his weekends geocaching, which basically sounded like using electronic compasses to go on scavenger hunts. He lived with his parents but was going to be getting a place of his own as soon as he could save up the money for a deposit. Last summer, he'd been a camp counselor someplace in New

Hampshire, but the camp had been closed down because of some alleged infraction of the health code—"totally bogus," he assured me—and so he was "between opportunities."

"You haven't worked since last summer?"

"Well . . . I mow my dad's lawn every Friday, but the job market is really slow now. I've been applying for some jobs in finance, but they won't even talk to you if you don't have experience." He spread out his hands in a sort of "go figure" gesture. "I don't think I'd really like finance anyway. I've been thinking about auditioning for *American Idol* instead."

"Kieran, how old are you?"

He reached for his coffee and tossed back a big swig. "Twenty-six."

I arched my eyebrows. "Try again."

"Okay, fine. Twenty-one. Almost. I will be. In January. But hey," he said eagerly, "I've got no problem dating a cougar. I mean, look at Madonna. She's still totally hot! You're, like, thirty, right? You look really, really good for your age."

"Gee. Thanks."

"So?" he said, leaning forward. "What do you say? Can I have your number?"

"Maybe you should try Mandy instead."

At that moment, Mandy stepped up onto a chair and blew her whistle. Kieran turned around to check out our mistress of ceremonies.

"Good idea!" he exclaimed and jumped up, disappearing into the scrum of moving men.

"Good luck," I muttered and ripped open another packet of sugar just as a tall man with white hair and incredibly white teeth—as in too white to be real—who was wearing—I kid you not—an ascot and a sailing cap, the kind sea captains wear, sat down and thrust out his hand.

"Byron Smythe-Jones," he said, flashing his dentures. "Yachtsman."

"Ivy Peterman," I replied. "Human."

He threw back his head so far that I could see the hair in his nostrils—there was a lot of it—and laughed so loudly that couples at the other tables turned to look at us.

"Ha-ha-ha-ha! A woman with a sense of humor! I like that! Makes life so much more interesting, doesn't it? Helps you keep your head during emergencies too. For instance, when I was sailing in the America's Cup last year, I faced a rather sticky situation that—"

"Byron," I said, cutting to the chase, "how old are you?"

"Forty-five," he said stoutly.

I arched my brows.

"Well," he said, chuckling, "does it really matter? Age is just a state of mind, isn't it? Especially these days with all the . . . um . . . pharmaceutical enhancements that are out there. My last girlfriend was twenty-two, and she had no complaints about my performance, I promise you.

"And," he continued in a husky voice, leaning toward me, "there's something to be said for experience and maturity, don't you think? I'm sure I could . . . um . . . show you a few things, eh? You look like a girl who'd be eager to learn."

He winked slyly, and I felt my stomach lurch.

"How old are you anyway?" he asked. "About thirty? That's all right. I don't mind a woman who's a little past her prime. You look quite good for your age."

After I'd endured a detailed explanation of the differences between the various "pharmaceutical enhancements," information I could have happily lived without for the rest of my life, Mandy blew the whistle.

I could have kissed her on the lips.

As I poured a third packet of sugar into my latte, I gave myself a little pep talk, told myself to calm down and stay put, that I had just been having a run of bad luck and that my other dates couldn't possibly be as bad as the first two. But I didn't really believe me.

And in all fairness, Trace, a man about my age who worked as an assistant manager of a movie theater but was studying for his certification as a personal trainer, seemed nice enough and not nearly as hopeless as the other two. It was just that I wasn't at all interested in the difference between whey and hemp protein powders or why body mass index was a more reliable indicator of overall fitness than a number on a scale. However, he did give me some tips about isometric exercises that would help banish my "flabby abs."

"What are you—about thirty?" he asked, and then shook his head sorrowfully. "You're really too young to let yourself go like this, Ivy."

When the whistle blew for the third time, I grabbed my purse from the back of my chair and started for the door. I'd had all I could take for one night. But Mandy, who was circulating through the room, saw me, grabbed my arm, and propelled me back toward the table.

"Hey! Twenty-three," she chirped, glancing at the numbered sticker on my blouse, "we've just got two more rounds to go, twelve minutes. Why don't you wait until we're through before you head to the ladies' room, okay?"

"I'm not going to the ladies' room," I said. "I'm going home. This just isn't working out for me."

Mandy puckered her lips and made a "poor baby" face. "Oh, come on, now. Don't run off so soon, okay? It'll throw off the whole system if you go. I'll have two guys wandering around and nobody to match them with.

"Okay," she said, shrugging her shoulders, "maybe you haven't run into the man of your dreams yet; I get it. But it's early, okay? What if the very next date turned out to be your soul mate? But you missed meeting him because you gave up too soon and left early? Talk about tragic! So you just sit back down and hang in there for the next twelve minutes, okay? Remember, a girl has to kiss a lot of frogs before she meets her Prince Charming."

"Mandy. This room has nothing *but* frogs. There's not a prince in the bunch, not my prince or anyone else's. It's completely hopeless, so I'm going home now. Okay?"

I pulled my arm from her grasp. She opened her mouth to argue with me but was interrupted.

"Excuse me. I got here a little late, missed the first three rounds, but the guy at the desk said I could still get in on the final two. Is one of you number twenty-three?"

I turned around and looked up at the handsome face of a tall, tanned man with brown eyes and black hair.

"Ivy?"

"Dan?"

"I can't believe it's you," I said for the third time, shaking my head. "Seriously. You're the absolute last person I would have expected to see here. Why would you need to come to something like this?"

"I could ask you the same thing," he said.

"Well, New Bern is such a small town, and

almost everybody who lives there is married. It's hard to meet people. And to tell you the truth, I really wasn't sure if I was ready to date yet. My ex-husband was . . ."

I paused, realizing I didn't have to explain my situation to Dan. The story of how Hodge, as owner of a nursing home, had cheated the government out of close to three million dollars in fraudulent Medicare claims had been front-page news in New Bern. Everybody in town knew about that, as well as his "alleged" history of domestic abuse, hinted at rather than declared because I hadn't pressed charges, figuring that the fraud conviction would be enough to keep him in prison for many years to come. Dan knew all that and more about me because, once he'd offered to take Bobby bowling, I'd had to tell him about Hodge's upcoming release. Not all the gory details, just the basics, so he'd understand what Bobby was dealing with and why he'd made up that story about Hodge being stationed on an aircraft carrier.

"I haven't had very good luck with relationships," I said. "And honestly, I never thought I'd want to try again. But after a while . . ."

"A person gets lonely," Dan said, finishing the thought for me. "I know what you mean. I met Lila, Drew's mom, in high school. She grew up on Cape Cod, but her family moved to New Bern in the middle of her junior year. It was love at first sight, at least for me. I skipped going to college just so I wouldn't have to leave her behind in New Bern.

"Not that I was all that set on going to school. Lucky for me, it turns out I like landscaping, but the only reason I got into it was because it paid enough so Lila and I could afford to get married right away. We did, four weeks after graduation. Drew was born a week before our first anniversary."

"That was quick. You sound like me. I was only eighteen when I had Bethany."

Dan nodded. "Some would say too quick, but I'm not sorry we had him. Drew's the best thing that ever happened to me. Lila was a different matter. When Drew was six, I found out she was having an affair with my best friend. You know, even after that, I actually wanted to try to work things out, but she left anyway. Just as well. Turned out she'd been sleeping with a string of guys. I had no idea," he said, lifting the paper cup of coffee to his lips. "Maybe I just didn't want to know. I was crazy about her, but she was just too young, I guess.

"Anyway," he said, "a thing like that will make you a little gun-shy . . ."

"Makes you doubt your ability to judge people," I said.

"Exactly. Having fallen so hard the first time, being so certain you've met *the one,* how can you

254

be sure you won't make the same mistake again?"

"You can't," I said. "That's why I decided to stay away from men. But lately I've felt so alone. All my friends are married, and they seem so happy. They don't have as much time to spend with me now, not the way they used to. So I just thought that I might give this a try, you know? Test the waters a little bit and see what was out there. And since it was in New Haven and I wouldn't be meeting anyone I already knew, I figured—what the heck? If I ended up making a fool of myself, nobody would have to know about it."

Dan chuckled and nodded as he ripped the top off a packet of sugar and poured it into his coffee. "That's what I was thinking too.

"Want some?" he asked, holding out the sugar caddy.

I shook my head and held my hand over the top of my cup. "I'm good."

"Actually," he said, looking at me over the rim of his cup, "when I decided it might be time to try dating again, my first thought was to ask you out. That's why I came out to the driveway and started flirting with you that day when you came to pick up Drew—because I was hoping you might be interested."

"Wait. You were flirting with me?" I laughed. "I guess I must be out of practice on picking up the signals."

"Either that, or I'm out of practice sending them. I was trying as hard as I could to get your attention, but"—he spread out his hands—"no dice. I went back inside, licked my wounds for a week or so, and then decided to give this a shot."

I looked down into the beige pond of my latte, the foam down to just a few bubbles around the edges of the cup. He'd been flirting with me that day? Trying his hardest to get my attention? So hard that he would be willing to use my kids as a means of getting close to me?

It had been one thing to be gullible and a terrible judge of character when I was the only one who could get hurt, but now I had kids. I didn't want to be suspicious of everyone I met, and Dan seemed like a good-hearted guy, but still, I had to be careful.

"Even though you weren't interested in me, I'm glad I went outside to talk with you," he continued. "Bobby's a great kid."

"You know, you don't have to take him bowling again . . ." I stopped myself, thinking how rude that sounded. "I mean, not if you don't want to. I'm sure you've got better things to do with your time."

"Not really. Drew is so busy with school and work and girls these days that I practically have to make an appointment to see him. Seems like yesterday that he was Bobby's age. I miss having a little guy around. Seriously, I don't mind." He smiled. "I'm having as much fun as Bobby is."

I studied his expression, trying to figure out if he was sincere or just trying to win me over by complimenting my son, but there were no telltale signs, no shifting of the eyes or twitching of the lips. He looked like he always did, honest and open and really, really cute, even more than he had before.

"Can I ask you something? Does Bobby talk about his dad when he's out with you?"

Dan nodded. "Uh-huh. He's pretty excited to see him, says his dad is going to bring him a macaw from China."

"A macaw? One of those big parrots?" I closed my eyes for a moment and groaned in frustration. "Where does he get these ideas? I explained to him that Hodge has been in prison, not the navy. Why does he keep making up these stories?"

"Well," Dan said, wrapping his hands around his cup, "if I were Bobby's age and I had to choose between believing my father was a felon or believing he was a sailor, I'd pick sailor. It can't be easy for him."

"No," I murmured. "You're right. I just wish I knew how much to tell him about his dad. I don't want to sugarcoat it, but at the same time, I don't want to go into any more of the sordid details than I have to."

Dan was quiet for a moment and then took a sip of his coffee. "Are you asking my advice?"

I nodded. I guess I was.

"Keep on doing what you've been doing. Tell him the truth about his dad but not any more than he needs to know. Keep Bobby safe, but give him a chance to get to know his father again. Who knows? Maybe five years in prison really has reformed your ex. Maybe he's changed his ways and truly is ready to be a good father. If so— great. If not, he'll reveal his true nature soon enough. Bobby will pick up on it. He's a smart boy, and sooner or later, people always show you who they really are. You just have to watch and wait."

Easier said than done, especially if you're the one doing the watching, but I knew good advice when I heard it. I was about to tell Dan exactly that when Mandy appeared out of nowhere and blew her whistle.

"Okay! Last round!"

Dan smiled and shifted in his chair, but without thinking, I reached out and grabbed his hand. "Don't go," I said.

"Okay," he replied, looking pleased but surprised.

Mandy was surprised, too, but looked far from pleased as she approached our table.

"I'm sorry, sixty-two," she said, forcing a smile, "but you'll have to get up now and go to your next date, okay? There are lots of interesting people to meet tonight. I'd hate for you to miss out."

Dan glanced up at her and then at me. "Thanks, but I've already met the most interesting person in the room. Think I'll just stay where I am."

"Ha-ha," Mandy laughed nervously. "Well, I'm glad you met someone you're interested in, but really, you have to move on now. Those are the rules. I'm sure number twenty-three's next date will be here any second."

Sure enough, just at that moment, my fifth and final date of the evening did show up.

"Hello. I am Sergei," he said, grinning widely. "I date you."

I grabbed his outstretched hand and said, "Oh, Sergei. It's nice to meet you, but I was wondering if you'd mind dating someone else for this last round. You see, Dan and I would like to talk a little more . . ."

His grin faded a bit. "Hello. I am Sergei. I date you," he repeated, and then started jabbering in another language, probably Russian, but I honestly couldn't be sure.

Dan got up from the table. "Maybe we should go somewhere else to finish our conversation. Can I take you out for coffee? There's a diner a couple of blocks from here."

"Can we make it a milk shake instead? Coffee keeps me up at night."

"Okay," Dan said, and helped me to my feet.

"No!" Mandy shouted. "Not okay! I explained to everyone at the start of the evening that you had to move on to your next date when the whistle blew, that you had to go through all the numbers on your list. No lingering! Those are the rules!"

Dan held out my jacket while I slipped my arms through the sleeves. "Uh-huh. Well, I got here late, so I never heard about that part. And I've never been much of a rule follower anyway. Good night, Mandy. Thanks for a great evening.

"Sergei," he said, handing a piece of yellow paper over to the other man, who was glaring at Mandy and babbling away in Russian, "take my list. Who knows? Fourteen might turn out to be your lucky number."

❧ 20 ❧

Gayla

I still had my doubts about this whole dating thing and about putting off any decisions about divorce until the end of the summer, but that's what I'd agreed to, so I decided that if I was going to do it, I might as well do it right.

On Saturday morning I went to Kaplan's boutique in search of a dress. Almost every dress I own—all of which were still sitting in my closet in the city—is black, but when I spotted a turquoise and green checked shirt dress on the rack, I decided to try it on. Very Connecticut, I thought. If only it had come with pearls and a matching cardigan, I'd really look the part. It was definitely a departure from my usual, but it looked good on me, so I bought it.

Brian liked it. That's what he said when I opened the door that evening. Brian looked very nice, too, dressed in the Irish linen sports coat he knows I like and a blue button-down with an open collar. He smiled in response to my compliment and then, after a momentary pause, said we should probably get going.

The drive from the cottage to the restaurant was awkward. We were both on our best behavior. Brian even jumped out of the car when we parked and ran around the other side to open my door for me. It really did feel like we were on a date, a first date. Except that on our real first date, we'd had no trouble talking to each other. We'd been fascinated with each other, firing question after question, responding without the least attempt to filter our answers, eager to learn absolutely everything possible about each other, feeling no hesitancy about sharing our most carefully guarded hopes and most outlandish dreams.

Now, of course, we knew how the story turned out. We knew that desire, however deeply held, isn't always enough. That hopes are often dashed. And that life is hard. We knew about disappointment and apathy, broken promises and failures.

But we didn't talk about that because it was a date and we were being polite. So very polite. So very well behaved.

Anyway, what was the point of going over old ground? Or, as I started to think by the time the salad arrived, of talking at all. We already knew everything about each other. What more was there to say?

But Brian had an idea—actually, more of an agenda.

"Listen, Gayla. I was reading this book about . . . Well, about how to save a marriage in crisis, and I came across something I think we might want to try. It sounds a bit . . . um, touchy-feely," he said, pushing his fingers into his hair. "The sort of thing my father would utterly have disapproved of, so naturally, I thought it well worth a try."

I smiled. I wouldn't want to speak ill of the dead, and I met Brian's father only once, on the very formal and uneasy occasion of our post-nuptial tea, but I had to agree with Brian. Any communication technique that Arthur Oliver would have disapproved of was probably a good idea.

And hearing that Brian was concerned enough about saving our marriage to actually read "touchy-feely" books on the subject impressed me. Lanie, of course, would have told me that it was just another piece of maneuvering on his part, another deception, but I didn't think so. Saying he was sorry was easy enough. People say they're sorry all the time, even when what they really mean is that they're sorry they got caught, or sorry that they're being put in a situation where they've been forced to apologize. Apologies cost nothing. But taking responsibility for your actions comes at a price. It's not about what you say; it's about what you do.

Brian was here. He was trying. I had to give him points for that. I put one elbow on the table and rested my chin in my hand. It was my listening posture. I wanted him to know he had my full attention.

"Here's how it works. You'll talk, and I'll listen. Wait," he said, holding up his hand to interrupt my forthcoming interruption. "There's more to it. You talk about your life from birth through age five—anything that comes to mind at all—for twenty minutes. And I listen. I don't comment or ask questions until you're finished. And then we trade sides and repeat the process— I'll talk and you listen. What do you think?"

"You want me to talk about my life up until I was five? For twenty minutes?"

He had to be kidding. My memories of my first five years of life wouldn't take two minutes to tell. I was born, my family lived in New Jersey, my father worked at a job he hated, my mother was bitter, and they fought constantly, agreeing about only two things: that life had cheated them and that I should grow up and go to Princeton. That was it—the first five years of my life. The rest of my growing-up years were pretty similar. Brian knew all that already. What was the point in repeating it?

"I know, I know," he said. "I'm as skeptical as you are, but I was talking to Ian about it and he says that it works. When he and Pamela were having some problems, their therapist recommended they get the book and work through some of the techniques on their own. He said they were very effective."

"You talked to Ian?"

That surprised me. It really did. Ian and Brian had been rivals back in their days at Harrow. When Ian left England and moved to New York, married well, and found a high-paying job on Wall Street, the two men, bound by a common history and nationality, became friends—of a sort. Every time we went to dinner with Ian and Pamela, which, thankfully, wasn't more than twice a year, the men spent most of the evening engaged in a quiet and very British game of one-upsmanship, subtly dropping names and hinting at their accomplishments. But they never, ever discussed their failures or fears. It was hard to imagine Brian allowing Ian to see a chink in his armor. Almost as hard as it was to imagine him canceling his travel for a month.

He *was* trying. He truly was.

"You told Ian about us? That I'm living up here?"

"I didn't go into specifics," Brian assured me. "I simply told him we were having some marital issues. A few years back, when we went to that party at his house to watch the World Cup final and he'd had a few too many, I remembered him saying something about he and Pamela having gone to a marriage counselor, so I just asked him if he knew of anyone good. That's all. It's not like we're the only people on earth who have problems, you know." Brian stared at his plate, separating the croutons from the salad and shoving them to one side.

"I know," I said, taking a sip from my wineglass. "I was just surprised to hear you'd spoken to him."

"Well." Brian shrugged. "I figured it was worth asking. He said he could give me the name of the therapist if I wanted but thought that working through the book might do us just as well. And be far less expensive."

"Ah, yes." I smiled. "Trust Ian to think of that."

"Right. Have you noticed that people who bring down seven-figure annual bonuses doing nothing terribly useful are the first to whinge about the exorbitant salaries of the lesser mortals?" Brian speared a lettuce leaf. "All the same. It can't hurt to try. Shall we? Ladies first."

I took off my watch, making a joke about not wanting to go beyond my time, and laid it on the table near my empty plate. And then, after lifting my glass to my lips and taking a final swallow of wine—a swallow, not a sip—I started talking.

I began, as I always did when anyone asked about my childhood, with the Princeton Tigers pennant that my parents hung on the nursery wall even before I was born. That pennant is part of our family apocrypha, a story that my parents told regularly, a symbol of their unshakable faith in my intelligence and promise. It wasn't until my late twenties that I realized the story was less about me than them, that what it really represented was their personal determination as parents and individuals, the weight of their expectations, and their absolute need to make their lives count for something.

Why Princeton? I honestly don't know. Except that it was located in New Jersey and that the president of the company where my father worked for thirty-eight years, years that never saw him rise above the ranks of lower-middle management, had sent his son there.

"See that?" he said, pointing to the television screen when I was about four, as we watched a montage of campus buildings during a sports-cast about a recent Princeton football victory. "That's where the bigwigs go to school. That's where you're going."

I knew that, of course. I had always known that. And I was on board with it. I wanted to be a bigwig. Who wouldn't? And I wanted to make my parents proud.

I told the rest of the story, about my parents' arguments, about my mother's resentment about the size of their house and the fact that it was a "man's world," and about the time she made me solemnly promise never to learn how to type because if I did, I would spend the rest of my life doing it. I told him all of it, though he'd heard it all many years before. But my memories weren't all bad, and my parents weren't always unhappy.

I told him about summer vacations in Atlantic City, riding the roller coaster on the boardwalk with my mother five times in one day, and how she had insisted that we ride in the front car and told the operator we would stand aside and wait for the next run so we could have our preferred spot.

I told him about our Christmases—my parents loved Christmas—and how Dad would drive eighty miles to the same tree farm in Pennsylvania year after year, cutting the tree himself, the biggest he could find, so big we had to set it up in the foyer of our little Victorian house, because that was the only room tall enough. I told him how we had to stand on ladders or climb the stairs and hang over the banisters to get the decorations on the upper branches.

And I told him about the huge storm when I was five, the one that dumped close to three feet of snow in less than a day and knocked out power to the whole town. I told him about how Dad had pulled the sofas close around the fireplace and then hung quilts and blankets behind them, using pushpins to suspend them from the ceiling, making a kind of fabric den to keep the heat in, and how we had lived in that little den for most of the three days that followed, playing board games, reading aloud, cooking hot dogs and marshmallows on sticks over the fire, pretending we were camping, and how my parents had not had one fight during that entire time—not one! And how I had opened my eyes one night, stirring momentarily from sleep, and seen my father and mother lying together in front of the fireplace under a blanket, nested together like silver spoons wrapped in felt, staring into the flames, and how my father had stroked her arm with his hand, up and down, over and over again, very gently, and pressed his lips into her hair, kissing the crown of her head.

"You never told me that story before," Brian said when I was finished.

"Didn't I? Maybe not. I haven't thought about it for a long time."

We talked a little more about my childhood, about why my parents had waited so long to have me, and why there were no other children after me. I didn't know the answers. I assumed that my status as an only child had something to do with my parents' ages—Mother was thirty-three when I was born—but who knew? These things were not openly discussed in our home.

It was the same for Brian, I knew. Though when it came to taboo subjects in the Oliver household, fertility and sex were just the tip of the iceberg.

"Basically, we didn't talk about anything personal. It was acceptable to discuss what you'd done but not how you felt about it. Weather was always the first topic of discussion. I can't think why," he said in a bemused tone, "there was so little to discuss. It was always either raining or threatening rain. While you were sunbathing on the Jersey shore and riding roller coasters with your mother, my brother and I took 'bracing' walks in the rain with Father, who would share his observations about how exposure to warm climates led to indolence and widespread social decline. He had a theory that access to inexpensive transportation, the ability of ordinary people to go on holiday abroad to places like Spain and Italy, marked the beginning of the decline of the British Empire."

"Wait a minute." I laughed. "Vacations in sunny Spain brought down the empire? What about all those incursions into other continents? The whole colonization thing? India has a pretty hot climate, too, you know. So does Africa."

Brian shook his head, feigning seriousness. "Different situation entirely. The people who went to India and Africa were soldiers, disciplined, driven by duty."

"Ah. I see. But what about—"

Brian leaned across the table. "You're not following the rules," he informed me. "No questions until I'm finished."

"Sorry."

"Right. Now, where was I?" he asked, nudging his wineglass to the edge of the table, making it easier for our waitress, who had appeared from nowhere, to refill it. "Oh, yes. According to Arthur, the sight of all those happy people lolling about in cafés on a fine Mediterranean afternoon, instead of spending their days nose to the grindstone, bred dissatisfaction among the working classes and was directly related to the rise of socialism."

Brian paused, taking a test sip from his newly filled glass. I lifted my hand to a spot near my ear, as if asking for permission to speak, though I didn't wait for it to be granted. "Hold on. These were the discussions you had with your father between birth and age five? Now who's breaking the rules?"

"Point taken," he said, setting down his glass. "I don't remember when he first started discussing his theories with us, but probably not as early as that. Though he may have. The point I was trying to make is that it was permissible to talk about externals, like the weather, or sport, or world affairs—as long as it wasn't too controversial—or history. Especially the history of the Oliver family—the more ancient, the better, since we'd seen our peak well before the Protestant Reformation. But it wasn't acceptable to talk about ourselves or people we knew in anything but the most detached manner. And under no circumstances was it permissible to express or display strong emotion.

"I remember once—I must have been about five—that I wanted to go see *Mary Poppins* at the local cinema, but my parents wouldn't let me. I think Father may have objected to a classic British book being brought to the screen by an American company. In any case, I wasn't permitted to go. We were eating lunch, and I was very angry about that, so I started kicking the table leg, harder and harder. I suppose I was trying to get some sort of rise out of my parents, but it didn't work. After a few minutes, Mother simply removed me from the table and made me go sit in a chair in the hallway. I was still angry, so I started to sing as loud as I could."

He screwed his eyes shut, a smile on his lips, and said, "Can't remember all the lyrics anymore, but I remember that the chorus said something like . . .

Mary Poppins, what a lark,
Flew Jane and Michael to the park,
But all that I can do is bark,
And I shall bark until it's dark,
While I wait for Mary Poppins,
Oh when, oh when, oh when shall I see Mary
   Poppins . . .

He opened his eyes and laughed to himself. "Not much of a rhyme scheme, eh?"

"Pretty good for a five-year-old," I said. "Was that the first song you wrote?"

Brian tipped his head thoughtfully to one side and dabbed his lips with the edge of his napkin. "You know, I think it may have been. If my parents would have realized what they were unleashing, they might have just let me go see the damned film."

"Then I'm glad they didn't. Otherwise, you might never have found your musical voice."

"Perhaps not," he murmured, the bow of his lips flattening to a line. "Though it wouldn't have been any great loss to the world if I hadn't."

I was about to say that it would have been a great loss to me, but given the circumstances, it didn't seem quite an appropriate comment.

The waitress had quietly and discreetly cleared our salad plates at the end of my monologue. After that, aside from continuing to make sure our wine- and water glasses remained full, she let us alone, either out of respect for the intensity of our conversation or perhaps just because it was Saturday night, the restaurant was full, and the kitchen was running behind. Finally she brought the entrées—rack of lamb for Brian and diver scallops for me—and then disappeared.

Brian picked up his fork, looked at my plate, and frowned. "She brought you the wrong entrée."

"No, she didn't. I ordered scallops."

"You don't eat scallops."

"It's not that I don't," I said. "It's just that I haven't. Until today. As long as I'm up here, I thought I might try an experiment of my own."

I explained about the sabbatical, how the phrase I'd tossed out as a smokescreen to overly inquisitive locals had, upon further reflection, started to seem like a pretty good idea.

I told him about my ill-considered and blessedly brief attempt to master trampoline Zumba, a story he enjoyed, and my newfound quilting circle, which he approved of, saying he thought it would be good for me to make some new friends. For a moment, I thought he was about to add "some friends besides Lanie" to that remark, but if so, he restrained himself, which was probably a smart move. And I told him about the quilting itself, which he seemed to find interesting.

"What a great idea," he said. "You really need an artistic outlet."

I couldn't have agreed more, but something about the way he said it seemed a little patronizing. Of course, I reminded myself, he was just trying to be agreeable, but maybe that was the problem. Maybe he was being a little too agreeable, trying a little too hard, and I thought, maybe things were going just a little too well. Was it really supposed to be this easy? Was a nice dinner together, or even a few, and the unearthing of some nearly forgotten memories supposed to make up for the fact that he had slept with somebody else? Maybe in his mind it did.

He said that the encounter, the affair—no, let's call it what it was—the sex with that woman, that Deanna, meant nothing to him. And I could just about believe him, but it didn't mean nothing to *me,* and wasn't that what counted? I was the injured party here. I was the one called upon to make the magnanimous gesture of forgiveness, but really, was that fair? At the end of the day, what was this costing him? Not much. Not in comparison to what it had cost me—the humiliation, the heartbreak, my lost sense of self. And what it would continue to cost me if I stayed in the marriage—the fear that it could happen again, a fear that might fade in time but that I doubted could ever be erased completely.

Was that a fair trade?

My mood darkened alongside my thoughts, but Brian didn't seem to notice. He was talking, cutting his lamb into bites and dragging it through the sauce, ruining the careful design of curlicues and dots that artfully decorated his plate, a design that someone in the kitchen had spent a long time creating, and saying that he thought it was good I was getting a rest, that I had been working too hard ever since I'd opened the business, and that a sabbatical was a brilliant idea.

He was trying so hard to be nice, to be agreeable, to *appease* me.

Did he think it was that easy? From the look on his face, I could see that he did. A few more dinners like this, a call to the florist, maybe a trip to the jeweler's, and all would be forgiven.

Screw him.

That's what I wanted to say—to scream, really. Screw you! And then, quite possibly, to flip over the table, scattering the cutlery, breaking the dishes, and shattering the glasses, giving him a chance to experience chaos firsthand, to figure out how to handle the embarrassment and aftermath of an irrational act he'd never seen coming.

Crazy, right? That kind of impulse? Completely crazy. Completely unlike me. An impulse that no one who knew me, not *even* me, would ever believe I was capable of giving in to. And I didn't. But I *imagined* doing it, and that was frightening enough. What was wrong with me?

It was like I was right back at the beginning, feeling just as irrational and out of control and broken as I had on that first day. I felt like I wanted to punch someone, him, her, or even the strangers sitting around us in the restaurant innocently enjoying plates of lamb chops and rubbery, fishy scallops that tasted just as nasty as I'd always thought they would.

I hated them. I hated everything. I hated Brian most of all.

Stop! Stop right now. You're acting crazy. And unfair. He's being nice; what's wrong with that? He's apologized—more than once. What more can he do? What more do you expect him to do?

I didn't know. I really didn't. But . . . more. More than he was doing now, though I had no concept of what more looked like or when more would become enough. But after a moment and with superhuman effort, Rational Me, the Gayla I recognized, wrestled the reins from Crazy Me.

I got out of my head and came back to earth just in time to hear Brian say that, while he missed me and the apartment felt too big when I wasn't there, for the first time in a long time, he had taken his guitar out of the case and played a little music. It felt good, he said.

"Who knows?" he joked. "Maybe we should both take a sabbatical."

"Maybe," I agreed. "I have to say I'm really excited about my garden. I planted the lavender this week and a whole flat of purple salvia. I put in some hydrangea bushes too."

"Oh, yes?" Brian asked, making a miming motion with his hand, like he was signing his signature in the air, so the server would know we were ready for the check. "That's wonderful, darling. Good for you. That's something you've always talked about, isn't it?"

I nodded and touched my napkin to my lips before laying it on the tablecloth, ready to wrap up the evening and head home. "Of course, it turned into a bigger project than I would have imagined. I got a little carried away."

Brian paused in the middle of calculating the tip. "You? Carried away?" He chuckled and turned his attention back to the bill.

"I'm so grateful Dan lives right next door. It'd be too much for me to manage on my own. Don't know what I'd do without him. He comes over practically every day."

I hadn't planned on saying that. It just popped out, an unnecessary, immature, and somewhat untrue utterance by Crazy Me, a pathetic attempt to rouse my husband's jealousy. I knew I was being ridiculous, but that doesn't mean I didn't enjoy his reaction. Rational Me's grip on the reins still wasn't as tight as it should have been.

Brian looked up. "He's there every day? Why every day?"

"I told you—because it's gotten to be a big project. It's too much for me to deal with alone, especially installing the hardscape. Lifting all those huge rocks and shoveling all that dirt? I'd never be able to manage it. But Dan is incredibly strong, picks up those rocks like they're nothing. It's fascinating to watch. Dan comes highly recommended, and fortunately for us," I said with a sweet smile, "he's right next door. How lucky is that?"

Brian frowned as he slipped his credit card back into his wallet. "I don't like the idea of him coming over to the house all the time, not when I'm not there."

"Well, he's not in the house, Brian. He's in the garden. Oh, for heaven's sake. Take that look off your face. I needed help with the garden, and Dan turned out to be the perfect man for the job."

I almost said, *It just happened; it doesn't mean anything,* but managed to stop myself.

Brian slid out of the left side of the booth. I slid right.

"How much is he charging? Whatever it is, I'm not paying for it."

I picked my handbag up from the banquette and looped it over my forearm.

"Well, then. Isn't it fortunate that I am perfectly capable of paying my own way?"

The ride back to the cottage seemed even longer than the ride to town had been. Our earlier silence had been awkward, as we struggled within ourselves, trying to think of what we ought to say. This silence was more smoldering, as we struggled to keep from saying what we ought *not* to say.

Even so, when we got to the cottage, Brian once again exited the car first and jogged quickly around to the other side to open my door for me. I appreciated the gesture, his effort to move us past our moment of mutual pettiness, and so when I stood up I leaned forward and kissed him lightly on the lips and said thank you for a lovely evening.

He kissed me back, but not lightly.

He put his hand on the back of my head, running his fingers under my hair, which I'd worn loose because I knew he liked it long. He cradled my head in the bowl of his hand, making it impossible for me to pull my lips from his.

But at that moment, pulling away from him was the last thing I wanted.

My mouth fell open like a sigh, and I let go of all the tension and my right to be right because, at least for that moment, I didn't care about who was right or who had been wronged, or the balancing of scales, or the paying of debts. I just wanted him to kiss me, to feel his tongue tracing the curve of my lips, the ridge of my teeth, his body shifting mine to the right with the unyielding metal of the car at my back, so he could press his hips hard against mine while his lips moved from my mouth to the soft flesh of my neck, to that sensitive spot just at the top of my collarbone, the place that makes me melt, that made my arms lift of their own accord, fluid and thoughtless, like water birds in flight, to drape over his shoulders and around his neck, while I arched toward him so my buttons would be easier to undo, my skirt easier to raise. I opened my mouth again and closed my eyes. At any second, I was going to cry.

Because it had been so long, so long since he touched me like this, weeks upon weeks that added up to months upon months, and I didn't know, not until that moment, how much I missed this and how very much I wanted him.

He moved his lips lower, and I dropped my head back, making that small sound that I don't make at any other time, the utterance that has no exact translation, a sound that is part yielding, part possession. Brian lifted his mouth from the curve of my breast, leaned close to my ear, and whispered, "Let's go inside."

And when he said it, I knew he meant forever and for always, that if I let him come into the house, he was *in;* he would stay. Allowing him entrance would be my pact and promise to let go of all he had done, and not done, and left undone. And for a moment, I wanted him so much that I thought I could say yes. I wanted to.

But then he did something I didn't expect.

He lowered his head again, brushed his lips

across the top of my breast, his lips and then . . . his teeth. Not a bite, not precisely, but more like a bite than a kiss, something new, something he had never done before, not in the twenty-six years of our lovemaking, and I knew that this thing, this new thing that made my skin shiver and my nerves go taut, was something he had learned, and practiced, and done with her, for her, and maybe she had liked it.

I turned hard to the left, pulled my body away from his, buttoning my undone buttons and said, "I don't think so. It's not a good idea."

I ran into the house. He walked quickly after me, taking big strides, calling my name like a question, wondering what he'd done. How could he not know?

I closed the door and locked it, standing with my back pressed to the hard wood and cold glass until he gave up, walked back to the car, and drove away. As the headlights swept over the driveway, rippling across the windowpanes like water from a crystal fountain, I sank to the floor and buried my face in my hands.

❦ 21 ❦

Gayla

The next day, I brooded. And that night I had a dream. The kind of dream I haven't had in a long time, a very sensual dream.

Brian and I were walking down a street in New York—I think it was somewhere in the Village because the streets were narrow and the buildings pressed in on us closer than they do in the wide avenues of midtown. Anyway, we were walking and talking. I don't remember what about, just that it was nice and that we weren't mad at each other. I think we were window-shopping because, at one point, we stopped in front of a big display window filled with guitars, all painted red, and looked at them for a while, trying to figure out how much they cost and if we could afford one.

And then he grabbed my hand and said, "I want to show you something," and pulled me down the street and around the corner and into an alley with brick walls that had thick green grass underfoot instead of concrete. It was strange.

We walked down this alley for a little way. Brian was ahead of me; I could see only his back because he was actually pulling me and telling me to hurry. I was struggling to keep up with him because, for some reason, I was wearing these very high black stiletto heels, and they kept sinking into the grass and tripping me up. He kept pulling me, so I was sort of mad at him, but at the same time, I thought it was funny, and I started to laugh, telling him to hold on a minute for heaven's sake, hopping on one foot and then the other while I tried to take off my shoes, half bent over with my hair coming out of the clip and falling down into my face until I finally pulled out the clip and let my hair fall loose to my shoulders.

I kicked the shoes off, too, at about the same time the alley opened up into a beautiful wide meadow with a tree in the center, covered in lovely white blossoms.

Somehow I had lost Brian. He wasn't anywhere to be seen, so I started walking toward the tree, calling his name. I wasn't worried. I knew he was there somewhere. I remember how good the grass felt on my bare feet and that there was a teasing little breeze blowing, making the edge of my skirt flutter against the skin of my legs.

I got to the tree. Still no Brian, so I decided to wait for him there.

The dress I was wearing was turquoise cotton with a pattern of little green leaves. The fabric was light and thin, almost transparent, and when I leaned against the tree the rough bark felt good on my back, a gentle scratching of fingernails filed smooth. Wondering when Brian would return, I slid slowly down the length of the tree, the bark catching on the fabric of my dress as I sank toward the soft grass, my skirt inching above my knees. It was warm, and I started to feel drowsy, so I closed my eyes to doze, breathing slowly and deeply, my limbs heavy, quickly falling into the half-life that lies between slumber and consciousness.

A moment later—or it might have been an hour—someone was next to me, kissing me. I felt a hand on my shoulder, another at my waist, pressing me down, and I lay back willingly, yielding to his touch, my hand covering his as he slid the silky folds of my skirt high on my bare thighs. There was a lifting and rising and shifting sensation as he moved above me, his head so close to mine, his breath warm and sweet in my ear as I opened myself to him, and he whispered, "Let's go inside."

I stopped, confused because the voice asking for the entrance that I had been so eager to allow had an American accent. I opened my eyes, saw his face, and pulled back. The voice, the face . . . it wasn't Brian. It was Dan.

I woke in the dark and sat up in bed, confused by my surroundings, flooded by terrible sadness and a profound disappointment.

Knowing there would be no more sleep for me that night, I went downstairs and made tea. I carried my cup into the living room and sat staring out the window into the black night, feeling more alone than I'd ever felt in my life. I didn't know what to make of that dream. I didn't know what to make of a lot of things. But one thing I did know was that I couldn't deal with this by myself anymore.

22

Ivy

"I haven't gotten very far," Margot said apologetically as she turned the piece of patchwork she was stitching outward so everyone could see.

"That's all right," Virginia said. "The whole idea is to take our time and enjoy the process, right? You've got some beautiful fabrics here. Where did you find them?"

"That red silk piece is from one of my dad's old ties, and the blue paisley is from one of my mother's old blouses, but the green velvet is new. Mom made green velvet Christmas dresses for my sister and me when we were little. I don't have the dresses anymore, so I bought a scrap of velvet in the same shade as a stand-in. Does that count?" she asked, frowning a little.

"Of course it does," I said. "Your quilt, your

rules. I think it looks great so far. What else are you going to use?"

"I've got fabrics to add from Paul's, James's, and Olivia's old clothes yet. I found some extra lace from my wedding gown that I'm going to use for the trim later. Plus," she said with a nervous giggle, "I unraveled the sleeve from one of Paul's sweaters so I could use the yarn. I hope he doesn't mind. He never wears it anymore, and it was just the perfect shade of gold for the vines I want to embroider along the border."

"Bring it in to me, honey," Virginia said. "I'll rework the sleeves and turn it into a vest. Chances are he'll never know the difference. Men don't pay attention to clothes."

"Oh, would you? Thanks, Virginia!"

"Anybody else?" Evelyn asked, looking around the room. "Gayla? How is your project coming?"

"Slowly," she said. "All I've really done so far is practice my embroidery, find a few fabrics that I want to use, and . . ." She hesitated and shifted her eyes to the floor before going on. "And decided it was time to let you in on some things."

Gayla's words and the tone of her voice caught everyone's attention. One by one, we put our stitching aside and turned to look at her. The room was perfectly silent.

"I tried something new last week," she said. "I went on a date—with my husband." Her eyes scanned the circle of faces. "I'm sure you've figured it out by now, but I didn't come up to New Bern for a sabbatical. A few weeks ago, I discovered that my husband had had an affair. It was over before I found out about it, and Brian apologized and told me he wanted to salvage the marriage, but I didn't know what to do. I got in my car, started driving, and ended up here. I ran away."

So I'd guessed right. The dish throwing, the midnight ditch digging, the crazy behavior that seemed so out of character with the calm, kind, and somewhat cautious woman whose kitchen I'd sat in while practicing embroidery; it all made sense now. She'd had her life turned upside down by a cheating husband and had come here, to New Bern, to our quilt circle. Funny how that worked. But maybe it was like Tessa said: People don't choose to become part of our circle as much as the circle chooses them, expanding to make room for the people who, whether they know it or not, need it most. As I looked at the faces of my friends, I realized that at one time or another this had been true of every one of us.

Evelyn ended up in New Bern almost the same way Gayla had. After her husband divorced her for another woman, she'd gotten in her car, drove all the way from Texas to Connecticut, and never looked back. I glanced at her, wondering if she would say something, but she kept silent, listening to everything Gayla had to say.

Gayla closed her eyes for a moment and took in a deep breath, as if she had absolutely decided not to cry, then opened them and went on.

"Maybe you're wondering why I'm telling you all this now." She gave a mirthless little laugh. "I'm kind of wondering the same thing myself. I've never been one to confide in other women, but I've been watching all of you these last weeks, the way you support one another, and as I was thinking through some things, I realized that . . . well, maybe I need some help getting through this."

"Of course."

"Absolutely."

Words of encouragement came from every corner of the room, and Evelyn said, "Tell us how we can help. Have you made any decisions about your future yet?"

Gayla nodded slowly. "I have, at least in the short term. Brian had this idea that we should try dating, sort of starting over from square one. At first I thought it sounded crazy and that things had gone too far for that. But," she said, "I agreed to give it a try. I also promised I wouldn't file for divorce before the end of the summer—"

"As a kind of cooling-off period?" Tessa asked. "That seems like a smart idea."

Gayla shrugged. "Maybe. I didn't think for a minute it would work. Honestly, I think I mostly agreed to it because of the kids. I don't want

Maggie and Nate to be able to say that I hadn't even tried to save the marriage. I don't want to be the bad guy in all this. Sounds pretty selfish, I know, but that's the truth.

"Anyway, we went out on Saturday. A lot of it was awkward, but some of it was great—much better than I'd hoped. But"—she shook her head—"things didn't end well. He did something—I don't even think he realized he was doing it—but it reminded me of everything that had happened, all the lies he'd told me, and I just . . ."

Gayla took another deep breath, but this time it wasn't enough to keep her emotions in check. She moved a hand to her face, covering her eyes, and took several more big breaths, trying to collect herself.

"It was like finding out about the affair all over again. I spent the whole day crying and brooding and smoking cigarettes. I went through a whole pack. I hadn't had a cigarette for twenty-six years before this happened; now I'm smoking like a chimney." She sighed and lowered her hand from her face. "I've got to stop."

Virginia reached over and patted her hand. "You will. But maybe one problem at a time, hmm? Once your divorce is final, you can—"

Gayla shook her head. "No, you don't understand. I'm not sure I want to divorce Brian. I know it sounds crazy, but . . . I had this dream.

Dreams never make sense when you try to explain them, but when I woke up, I knew that I could never feel about anyone else the way I felt about Brian."

"So you've decided to take him back?" Madelyn queried, giving Gayla a skeptical look.

"No, I haven't decided that either. But what I *have* decided to do is to give him a chance, a real chance. Not for the kids' sake or just so I won't look bad. But because I know in my heart that if I can't resurrect my love for Brian, I'll never be able to love anyone else. At this moment, I honestly can't imagine how we can move past this, but I'm going to try. The reason I wanted you to know all this is because I think it will help if I have some . . . some friends I can talk to and who will cheer me on.

"Although," she said with a little laugh, tipping her head toward the ceiling and blinking back tears, "now that I've heard myself saying all this, I realize it sounds completely nuts. You must think I'm some kind of spineless idiot to consider taking him back."

"No, we don't," Evelyn said, handing Gayla a box of tissues. "This is one of those things that every woman has to answer for herself. My first husband cheated, too, you know. Later, after the divorce, he came to Connecticut and wanted to reconcile, but not until after his girlfriend had dumped him. He didn't want to be with me; he just didn't want to be alone. But, if he'd made that offer early on, who knows what would have happened? I might have taken him back. I certainly would have thought about it. You're not being spineless, Gayla. None of us sees you that way."

"Actually, I think you're pretty tough," Madelyn said. "Much tougher than I was in your shoes. My late husband, Sterling, was a serial adulterer. I knew about it, but I put up with it because I didn't think I could survive without him. Talk about spineless." She rolled her eyes. "I let him treat me like a doormat. But you've made a declaration about what you will and won't put up with, and you've stated, very clearly, that you're ready to walk away if he can't change his ways. That takes some guts, especially if you really love him."

"But I feel like such an idiot," Gayla said, taking a sip from her wineglass, which had been sitting untouched. "How could I not have known what was going on? How could I have ignored the signs? I keep thinking that I should have—"

"Don't!" Tessa said. "Don't beat yourself up like that. It happens. A lot more often than people think."

Tessa's sentences were clipped, her voice uncharacteristically sharp. Everyone turned to look at her. She pressed her lips together into a thin line before speaking again.

"Nobody knows about this," she said. "So I'm

going to remind everyone of our rule: What's said in the circle stays in the circle. About twenty years ago, Lee had an affair."

My eyes went wide and my hand flew to my mouth, covering my shock. Lee Woodruff had cheated? I couldn't believe it! Lee and Tessa seemed so happy together. They still held hands when they went walking. I've seen them, watched them cross Cobbled Court hand in hand when they thought no one was looking. He brings her coffee in bed every morning, and every year on her birthday, Lee buys an entire truckload of manure and spreads it over Tessa's lavender patch. Okay, maybe that doesn't sound romantic, but shoveling manure requires a lot more effort than buying a present or making dinner reservations, and Tessa, feeling the way she does about her lavender, appreciates it a lot more. I completely get that.

When I was a little girl, I used to daydream about a man who'd bring me flowers or buy me jewelry. Nothing against candy and flowers, but these days, the man who'd really make me swoon would be the man who'd mow the grass or do the dishes or fold the laundry. Funny how your ideas of romance change as you get older.

But Lee Woodruff was that man, the solid and steady kind, the kind who'd do anything for his wife, who'd never cheat. That's what I'd always believed.

"It didn't last long, but I found out about it while it was still going on," Tessa said, her eyes fixed on Gayla's. "I was completely crushed. I couldn't eat or sleep or work. I lost nine pounds in two weeks.

"Lee ended the relationship immediately," Tessa went on. "He apologized, said he'd been a fool, and promised it would never happen again, but I threw him out of the house and changed the locks on the doors anyway. A few days later, he showed up on the doorstep and begged me to give him another chance, and I did."

There was a murmuring of sympathy throughout the room. Tessa was always so cheerful. Even when she had to close her shop, For the Love of Lavender, because she and Lee were teetering on the edge of bankruptcy, she'd kept up a brave face. It was impossible to imagine her falling apart.

Madelyn frowned. "You never told me any of that. I'm your best friend, and you never told me. How could you keep that from me all this time?"

"Because it was over and done with by the time you and I renewed our friendship," Tessa said with a shrug. "So why bring it up? I wouldn't want you to think badly of Lee. He did a bad thing, but he isn't a bad man. He bent over backward to regain my trust. It wasn't easy, let me tell you. It took a long, long time before I felt able to trust him again. If I didn't know where he was every minute of every day, I'd panic."

Gayla nodded, as if she understood exactly what Tessa was talking about. So did Evelyn.

Tessa brought her empty glass to the table and refilled it before carrying the bottle around to the rest of us.

"I think this kind of thing happens a lot more than people realize. If a couple decides to stay together and work through the pain of infidelity, the affair becomes a secret. If the marriage is to survive, it almost has to."

She stopped in front of Gayla and topped off her glass. "The only reason I'm talking about this now is because I want you to know that you're not alone. If the person who did the cheating is genuinely repentant, and the couple is willing to make a serious effort to reconcile their relationship, people *can* get through this, Gayla. It's not easy, but they can. Sometimes," she said, lifting her own glass to her lips, "they even come out better on the other side. It's possible."

Gayla forced a smile. "I hope you're right."

"Can I call you tomorrow?" Tessa asked.

"That would be nice. Thanks. Anyway," Gayla said, and slapped her palms against her thighs, indicating she had said all she was willing to say for the moment. "I didn't intend to hijack the conversation. Did anybody else make progress on their sabbatical project?"

"Well," I said slowly, "I wasn't really planning on talking about this—not yet—but since Gayla opened the door . . . I went on a date this weekend too. My first ever."

"You did! Who with?"

"Really?"

"Oh, Ivy! Good for you!"

My cheeks felt hot in the face of their enthusiasm, but I couldn't keep from smiling.

"Actually, I ended up going on four dates. The first three were absolute nightmares. But the fourth . . ."

Amid much laughter, I told them all about Kieran, Captain Smythe-Jones, Trace, and even poor, frustrated Mandy. Then, amid much oohing and awing, I told them about Dan.

"Oh, Ivy! That's just wonderful!" Margot exclaimed, jumping up from her chair to give me a big hug. "I'm so happy for you!"

"Don't get carried away," I laughed. "It was a milk shake, not a proposal. Dan and I are just friends. But dating turned out to be a lot more fun than I figured it would be. I've decided to take another leap of faith too. I'm going to apply for that job at New Beginnings. I probably won't get it, but I've got nothing to lose by trying, right? Dan says you miss one hundred percent of the shots you don't take."

Evelyn frowned. "Wait a minute. I thought that's what I said. And what Donna Walsh said. And what *all* of us have said to you at one time or another." She chuckled and picked up her stitching. "I guess it just sounds more convincing from Dan Kelleher."

"I've been making a little progress on the sabbatical front too," Evelyn said as she fashioned a length of red silk ribbon into a tiny rose to embellish her crazy quilt. "Ever since I moved to New England, I've wanted to learn to sail. I kept telling myself I'd get around to it one of these days, but of course, I never did."

She paused, squinting to make sure her needle was piercing the ribbon at the perfect spot. "But this week, I thought, 'What the heck. If I don't do it now, when will I?' I found a sailing school that offers a weekend course that's just for women and signed up. Charlie is grumbling because he thinks we should do it together, but it would make me nervous if he were there. I told him he can come with me to Newport for the weekend, but he has to stay on shore until I get my certification. Then we can sail together. As long as he lets me have the tiller."

I laughed, and so did everyone else. Knowing Charlie, we could just imagine how that conversation went.

"The only problem is it's the same weekend as our Midsummer Madness sale. Can you manage without me?" Evelyn asked, looking at Margot and me.

"Absolutely. Not a problem. You and Charlie deserve some time off," I said.

Virginia, who had been quiet for several minutes, intent on embroidering a line of perfectly sized French knots on her crazy quilt, sat up a little straighter in her chair and cleared her throat.

"Evelyn's not the only one who made progress on her sabbatical project, you know." She lifted her eyes from her work and peered over the tops of her reading glasses momentarily before returning to her sewing.

"Two Sundays from now, I will turn eighty-five. I've decided to give myself a little birthday party, and I'd like all of you to come. No gifts, please. There's only going to be one present at this party, and I'm giving it to myself."

"But, Mom," Evelyn said, "Charlie and I were planning to throw you a party. He's already worked out the menu."

"Yes, I know. He accidentally left it sitting on the countertop at your house. I saw it when I came over for breakfast last week. Honey," she said, giving Evelyn a pointed look, "osso buco with porcini mushrooms and lemon zest? I don't even know what osso buco is! Baked Alaska for dessert? What's wrong with a nice piece of cake and some ice cream? I just can't stomach all that rich food anymore."

Evelyn began to protest, but Virginia shook her head.

"No," she said firmly. "I know Charlie means

well, but I've made up my mind. This birthday, I want to have things my own way. I've already made all the arrangements. I've even talked Garrett into coming in from the city to cover the shop. Wendy said she'd help, too, so you'll all be able to come. You, too, Gayla. You're part of the circle now. We'll meet at church," she informed us, "right after the first service. Plan on being gone the whole day. I've got a lot of activities planned."

"Such as?" Evelyn asked, drawing her brows together.

"Not going to tell you."

"Why not?"

"Because if I did," Virginia said, snipping off the end of her thread, "you'd try to talk me out of it."

❧ 23 ❧

Gayla

The July sun was high and hot. I could feel a trickle of sweat running down my neck. I should have remembered to bring my hat outside, but I didn't want to bother going back into the house to get it; I was nearly finished.

I grabbed the last weed by its prickly leaves, grateful for my new gardening gloves, and gave it a tug. It didn't budge. I tried again with the same results, then pulled a trowel from the pocket of my gardening apron.

By this time, I had all the equipment. Hats, hoes, rakes, trowels, watering cans, baskets, shears, nippers, and even a thick, waterproof foam kneeler to cushion my poor knees while I was weeding. Best twenty dollars I ever spent. Gardening can be an expensive hobby, I've found. I calculated the price for one of my lavender stalks at about a buck each. And that wasn't even counting the money I paid Dan for the installation.

But, I thought, as I shifted back onto my haunches and looked around at a stand of bright-faced Shasta daisies and the rose of Sharon bush I'd planted in the corner, which was just beginning to bloom, it was worth every dime I'd spent and would spend in the future.

This year, I'd planted a few flowering shrubs and other perennials, but also annuals, pansies, and geraniums and the like, so I would have color in my garden from the first. But the annuals were just placeholders for the perennials I intended to plant in the fall: lupine, daffodils, tulips, and coreopsis, which wouldn't come up until the following spring. I'd spent many afternoons at White Flower Farms since that first field trip, picking the brains of the staff and adding new flowers to my wish list, and had become a regular customer. The peace and quietness of mind I discovered while digging in the dirt, the pleasure I derived from the daily discovery of each new bud and bloom, the lessons I had learned about the value of slowing down, paying attention, and taking time to enjoy the small things, were worth the price of admission twice over.

I shifted my weight forward, thrust my trowel into the dirt four times, rocking the blade back and forth to loosen the soil around the weed, and then grasped it again and gave a good, hard tug.

"Aha!" I cried, holding the culprit in the air. "Trying to choke out my echinacea, were you? That'll teach you!"

"Gayla? Do you always talk to the weeds?"

"Ack!" I gasped and jumped, then turned around, squinting up into the sun. "Dan. I didn't hear you come up. You scared me!"

"Sorry. But really. Do you always talk to the weeds?"

"Not usually. Mostly I just talk to the plants. I heard that it helps them grow faster. But you should know that, being a landscaper."

"Uh-huh. Think I've heard that somewhere once or twice too. But since I've never met a plant that had ears . . ."

He smirked and rubbed his nose. I got to my feet.

"I was just finishing up," I said, wiping the

sweat from my brow. "Care to come inside for a glass of iced tea?"

"No, thanks. I wanted to come over and see how things are going. See if those tomato cages I brought you were working out all right."

"Yes," I said slowly, giving him a bemused look. "I told you that yesterday, when I saw you and Ivy at the Fourth of July parade, remember?"

"Oh. Right," he said, shuffling his feet. "I forgot. Good. That's good."

"Say, how is Ivy anyway? We didn't have quilt circle this week because of the holiday, so I haven't talked to her. How did her interview go? I forgot to ask."

"It's not till tomorrow. She's nervous, but I'm sure she'll do fine. She keeps telling me that her chances of getting the job are infinitesimal, but I keep telling her that a tiny chance is better than none at all. Can't hurt to try, can it?"

"No, it can't," I said with a smile, thinking what a good man he was. Just the sort that Ivy needed. It didn't hurt that he was good-looking either.

"You and Ivy have been seeing a lot of each other, haven't you?"

"Uh-huh. But we're taking it slow. With her husband coming back to New Bern soon and the kids and all . . ." He shrugged. "She's got a lot on her plate. I don't want to push her too fast."

Dan sniffed and scratched the side of his face. "Well. I guess I should let you get going. You're probably ready to get in out of the heat," he said, looking down at his feet and bobbing his head without moving one inch from where he stood.

"Dan," I said, laughing, "is there something I can do for you?"

He lifted his eyes from his shoes to my face and nodded quickly.

"There is. I hate to ask. I know you're up here on vacation, but . . . Drew just got the results of his SAT test. They were pretty bad," he said.

"How bad?"

He told me the number.

I winced. "Well, that's not the worst score I've ever heard, but it's not very good," I admitted. "But, listen, it'll be all right. A lot of kids choke on their first go-round. Tell him not to worry. I'm sure he'll do better next time."

"That's the problem," Dan said. "He says there won't be a next time.

"He's been saving up since he was fourteen to go to college. Every dime that you paid him for watching your place, the money from every babysitting job he's ever had, every lawn he's ever mowed—it's all gone into the bank. He's got close to six thousand dollars saved. Now he says he's going to take the money and buy a truck."

Dan shook his head and kicked at the ground with the toe of his work boot. "Stupid, stubborn kid. I've tried talking to him, but he says there's no point in doing it again, that he's just no good at tests."

"That's not true," I said. "He's just not used to this kind of test—that's all. Did he take any preparation classes beforehand?"

"No. I got him a book, and he read it, but that was about it."

"Right," I said. "Listen, that's not an uncommon experience. I've spent enough time around Drew to know that he's smart and can do much better on these tests. He just needs a little coaching. You tell him that I'm going to be his coach, that I've helped plenty of kids bring up their scores. He'll do much better next time—I promise. In fact, if he's willing to work with me, tell him I'll bet him twenty bucks against a set of mud flaps for this truck he says he's going to buy that he'll add at least two hundred points to his score."

"Yeah?" he asked, relief written clearly on his face. "But are you sure you don't mind? You're supposed to be on sabbatical."

"Dan, over the last five weeks I've taken up Zumba, guitar, quilting, gardening, pottery, Chinese cookery, kayaking, and watercolor painting. I even tried juggling. Some of my experiments have been successful. Others, not so much. I've enjoyed it all—well, almost all of it. But sometimes, it's nice to do something you already *know* you're good at.

"I know I can help Drew," I said. "And I'm

happy to do it. Tell him I'd like to see him for two hours, twice a week, until the next test. What days do you think would be good for him?"

"Between helping me with my landscaping clients and babysitting for Ivy, he's pretty booked," Dan said, pulling on his nose again, thinking. "Would Tuesday nights be okay? And maybe Saturday afternoons?"

"That'll be fine." I bent down to pick up my discarded trowel and placed it back in the pocket of my apron. "As long as we're finished before four on Saturday. I like to have a little extra time to get ready before Brian arrives."

"That's right," he said. "I almost forgot. You two go out every Saturday, don't you?"

"Uh-huh," I said with a smile. "Saturday night is date night."

❧ 24 ☙

Ivy

I should have worn a longer skirt.

When I sat down, my skirt hiked halfway up my thighs. I had to keep squeezing my knees together to avoid giving the panel more insight into my personal life than they'd bargained for. But from the way that Brad Boyle kept staring at my knees, I'd have sworn he was hoping I'd do exactly that.

Whoever decided that a guy like that should serve on the board of an organization that serves women—many of them survivors of domestic violence? If, by some miracle, I did manage to get the job, my first act as director of New Beginnings would be to boot Boyle from the board. The second would be to abolish the practice of conducting panel interviews. Or making the job applicant answer questions while sitting on a metal folding chair in the middle of a room with six sets of eyes staring at her. Talk about feeling exposed.

When I left for the interview, dressed in a gray jacket and black pencil skirt I'd borrowed from Margot, the last piece of advice she gave me was to just relax and be myself. If you're trying to make a list of the top ten most useless job interview tips, "relax and be yourself" would definitely make the top five. Nobody in that room was the least bit interested in discovering who I truly was or what I was capable of doing—me least of all. I was focused on keeping my knees together and telling them what they wanted to hear.

For a few minutes, it seemed like it was going pretty well.

I breezed through their questions about my personal background, speaking of how I became involved with New Beginnings without revealing too many gory details about the years of beatings, the mental and emotional abuse, the common history I share with so many of the women who come through the doors of New Beginnings and how that has ignited a desire to help repay the debt I owe to providence and the people who rescued me and helped me turn my life around by doing the same for other women.

Instead I said, "I believe my personal experiences give me a unique ability to appreciate the stresses and challenges that many of our clients are facing and will also allow me to gain their trust."

And when they asked about where I saw New Beginnings heading in the future, I emphasized the need to expand the internship program, which, as we all knew, I was already in charge of.

I said, "This program has been an enormous success for the clients of New Beginnings as well as the businesses that have taken part in it. With the right kind of leadership"—by which I meant mine, but I didn't spell that out to the panel because I didn't have to; we all understood the rules of the game we were playing—"I'm convinced we could double our current rates of participation and job placement."

Every member of the panel smiled as I said it; they loved the idea of New Beginnings helping women find full-time, good-paying jobs. So did I. Finding a job isn't the answer to every problem facing victims of domestic violence, but it sure helps.

I smiled to myself, thinking that it really was going well, much better than I'd hoped.

But that was before Brad Boyle started asking his questions.

"I'd like a little clarification on the educational portion of your résumé," he said, frowning as he scanned one of the ivory-colored sheets of paper I had distributed to the panel when I entered the room. "It says here that you graduated from high school but doesn't mention where you went to school or when you got your diploma."

Squeezing my knees together so tightly that it would have taken a crowbar and an act of Congress to pry them apart, I cleared my throat. "I got my high school equivalency diploma three years ago."

He lifted his eyes from the paper and stared at me with raised brows. "You got your GED? So you didn't graduate from a real high school?"

"I didn't graduate from a brick-and-mortar high school," I said, forcing myself to maintain eye contact, not wanting him to know how the question rattled me, "but I studied for and passed a series of tests that demonstrated I had mastered the equivalent educational standards required by the state. And I've been taking classes at the community college since then. I have a three-point-six grade average."

Boyle shifted his eyes to the left and right,

making sure his fellow interviewers heard my response.

"I see. And you're a sophomore now? After three years." He coughed. "You know, Miss Peterman, I appreciate your special circumstances. I'm sure we all do. But you're the only candidate we've interviewed who doesn't have *at least* a bachelor's degree."

My cheeks went red.

"I was encouraged to apply by Donna Walsh, the executive director at the Stanton Center—"

"Yes, we all know who Donna Walsh is." Boyle smiled patronizingly, and I took a moment to silently loathe him, even more than I had before. "She's written you a very impressive letter of recommendation, but she isn't a member of this committee. The letter that Abigail Spaulding wrote on your behalf praised you just as highly. How long have you lived in New Bern—just five years? The fact that you've gained the support of both the executive director and one of the more prominent board members of the Stanton Center in such a short period of time certainly says something about you. But I feel I should remind you that, while New Beginnings is associated with the Stanton Center, we are now a separate entity with a separate and *independent* board. I think what I'm trying to say here is that—"

Susan Cavanaugh, who I knew from my work at New Beginnings and from the quilt shop, where she was a regular customer, cut him off.

"What Brad is trying to say, Ivy, is that we're very impressed with all you've been able to accomplish personally and professionally, especially in such difficult circumstances."

She rose from her chair and extended her hand, letting me know that the interview was over.

"Thanks, Ivy," she said, clasping my hand in both of hers. "We'll be in touch just as soon as we've made our decision."

I went into the bathroom to splash cold water on my face, not because I'd been crying but because I was angry and needed to cool off before I met Dan and the kids at the bowling alley. If Brad Boyle had walked into the ladies' room at that moment, I'd have spit in his face. Or at least on his shoes.

Brad Boyle didn't walk into the bathroom, but Susan Cavanaugh did.

"You okay?" she asked.

"Did you come in here to tell me I'm hired?" I asked sarcastically. I yanked a paper towel from the dispenser. "I know I wasn't a shoo-in for this job, but what was the point of embarrassing me like that? Why did Brad have to make me feel like I was three inches tall? What a jerk!" I threw the balled-up paper towel in the trash.

"You won't get any arguments from me there,"

Susan muttered. "But Brad is looking to launch a political career. He wants to establish a reputation as a maverick, someone who can't be influenced or prodded by the old guard. And the others really are anxious to make sure that our board is operating independently of the Stanton Center. Those letters of recommendation from Donna and Abigail definitely helped you get the interview—the committee couldn't ignore them—but they also made it tougher for you to get the job.

"Don't take it so hard," she said, standing behind me and addressing my reflection as I reapplied my lipstick. "You just got caught up in the politics of it—that's all. And let's be honest, you've been doing good work at New Beginnings, but your résumé is still a little thin. If you had a college degree, I don't think the rest of the board would have gone along with Boyle. You really need to go back to school, Ivy."

"I already did."

"You know what I mean," she said. "Ivy, you are smart, hardworking, and passionate. I'd love to see you run New Beginnings. But no one is going to hire you for a position with that much responsibility without a college diploma. You need to go back to school full-time and finish your degree now. Not ten years from now."

I put the cap back on my lipstick tube and turned to face her.

"Thanks for the advice, Susan. And the minute somebody steps up to pay my tuition and bills so I *can,* I'll be happy to take it."

When I arrived at the bowling alley, Drew and Bethany were sitting on blue plastic benches, drinking soda and eating pizza while awaiting their turn to bowl. Dan was standing a few feet behind Bobby with his arms crossed over his chest, watching as my little guy crouched forward, swung his arm, and sent the ball spinning down the lane.

"Yes!" Dan cried, pumping his fist as Bobby's ball struck the pins. "Sparc! Way to go, Bob-O!"

Bobby did a little dance of celebration, wiggling his hips and waving his arms.

Dan gave Bobby a high five. "You are a champion, buddy!"

"Ha! Beat that!" Bobby said as he took his sister's place on the bench.

Bethany got to her feet slowly and picked up her ball. "Shut up, Bobby."

Dan spotted me standing in the back, grinned, and lifted his hand to greet me. I waved back and tried to smile, but I must not have been very convincing. Dan frowned and started walking toward me.

"Hey, Bobby," he called over his shoulder. "Let's be good sports, okay? Bethany hasn't had as much practice as you have."

Drew put down his drink and jumped up from his seat. "Hang on, Bethany. Let me show you how to aim the ball."

Dan kissed me on the cheek, then placed both hands on my shoulders and looked into my eyes. "I'm sorry," he said, knowing how things had gone without having to ask.

"Thanks," I sighed. "It's just that I really, really *wanted* this job, you know?"

He nodded. "I know."

"Until now, I think I was afraid to admit how much." I shrugged. "Well, I'll get over it. I always do. This is just one more item on the long list of things I've failed at. Honestly, I don't know why I even bothered to fill out the application. The whole thing was a big waste of time."

"Hey. Stop that." Dan squeezed my shoulders. "Maybe you didn't get the job this time, but another time, you will. There will be other jobs. And you're not a failure," he insisted.

I pulled away from his grasp.

"Next time? Jobs like this don't come along very often, especially in New Bern. Whoever does get the job will stay there until they drop. Of course," I said with a derisive little laugh, "maybe by then I'll actually have finished my stupid degree. Maybe *then,* when I'm about ninety, I'll finally be qualified for the job."

There was a crash of bowling pins. I looked up to see Bethany standing at the top of the lane, grinning, and Drew clapping for her. Bobby was clapping too.

He turned toward me and yelled, "Mommy! Did you see that? Bethy got a strike!"

I forced a smile, waved, and called out, "Good job, sweetie!"

As soon as she saw me, Bethany's grin was replaced by a glare. "Your turn," she said to Drew and sat down.

I made a sputtering sound with my lips and turned back to Dan. "Wonderful. And on top of everything else, my daughter hates me. Oh, and I was also treated to a snippy phone call from Sheila Fenton, reminding me that the kids' first meeting with Hodge is just weeks away and that she certainly hopes Bethany will have improved her attitude before then. As if I had any control over that! And I'm sorry, but Bethany gets to feel however she feels about Hodge. She may be a child, but she's still a person. She's got a mind of her own. And a memory."

I sank down into a chair, propped my elbows on one of the café tables, and put my head in my hands. Dan sat down next to me and rested his hand between my shoulder blades.

"Can I buy you a beer?"

I shook my head but didn't look up. "Beer makes you fat."

"How about a glass of wine, then? And a cheese-burger. I'm taking everybody out to dinner."

"You don't have to do that," I said. "I'll be okay."

"I already told the kids we were going out. I figured if you got the job, we should celebrate. And if you didn't? Well, I figured you'd need a cheeseburger. And maybe a chocolate milk shake."

"Wine is better," I mumbled into the tent of my arms. "Thanks. Sorry I'm such a grump."

"It's all right. You're entitled. Hey, I was thinking that on Sunday we could take a picnic to Tanglewood and go to the James Taylor concert, just you and me. I'll bring a whole bottle of wine and ask Drew to babysit."

"Can't," I said. "Virginia's birthday party is on Sunday."

"That's right. I forgot. Well, maybe next week. I don't know who's playing, but it doesn't matter. It'd just be nice to get away by ourselves for a few hours."

"Uh-huh," I said distractedly, then picked up my head.

"You know what makes me crazy? Susan Cavanaugh said that if I just had my diploma, they probably would have given me the job. It's so unfair! It's a piece of paper! Why should it matter? And that snotty Brad Boyle . . . he made me feel about this big," I said, pinching a couple inches of air between my thumb and fore-finger. "Susan says he wants to go into politics.

Ha! I wouldn't vote for him for dog catcher!"

"Me neither," Dan said soberly. "Can't stand that guy. Hate his guts."

His deadpan tone made me smile in spite of myself. "Do you even know Brad Boyle?"

"Nope. But that's not the point. I'm being supportive. Hate his guts. Hope he gets hit by a trash truck."

"Very funny. I should call Susan later," I said, my smile fading. "I was kind of nasty to her today."

"Why?" Dan asked. "I thought you liked her."

"I do. She tracked me down in the bathroom after the interview, trying to cheer me up, and said I should go back to school full-time. I was pretty snippy to her, but . . . she's right. Nobody is going to hire me for the job I really want until I finish my degree. Which, at this pace, will take until I'm forty! By then, they'll probably say I'm too old to do that work."

I sighed and leaned sideways, resting my head on Dan's shoulder.

"Maybe I should enroll at Carrillon."

"The college your professor told you about? The one in Delaware?"

I nodded. "That would be the fastest way to finish my degree. Probably the cheapest, too. But where would I get the money?"

Dan twisted to the side, and I had to lift my head from his shoulder.

"Wait a minute," he said. "You'd leave New Bern and move to Delaware? I thought we . . . I mean . . . I thought you liked it here. All your friends are here."

"They are. But Susan's right. If I'm ever going to make something of myself, be able to do what I really want to do, and have control over my own life, I need to get my diploma. If I went to Carrillon, I'd be finished in two years, maybe less. Then I could move back to New Bern."

I paused, taking a moment to think.

"Well, maybe I could. If there were any openings in my field. I guess I'd have to go where the work is," I mused, and then laughed, realizing how crazy I was. "What am I talking about? I'll never be able to find that kind of money, not in a million years."

Suddenly, I realized that Dan was being very quiet. I looked at him. "Hey, are you okay?"

"Sure. I'm fine."

"Yeah? Because you had kind of a funny look on your face just now."

"No. I'm fine. It's just that I thought that you . . . that we . . ." He waved his hand dismissively.

"Never mind. Doesn't matter. I'd better get back over there," he said, tipping his head toward the bowling lane, where Drew, who had just thrown a seven-ten split, was groaning and smacking himself on the head. "I'm up next."

"Hang on a second," I said slowly, giving my attention to a new idea that was forming in my mind. "Maybe I could—"

Dan was already on his feet, but I grabbed his sleeve to keep him from leaving. "Gayla has been tutoring Drew for his SAT test, right? How's that going?"

"Good. He picked up ninety-five points on his last practice test." Dan frowned. "Why do you ask?"

"I was just thinking . . . Gayla knows everything about getting kids into college. Maybe she knows about scholarships too. Not for teenagers but for people like me—adults, women who're trying to go back to school. Do you think I should ask her to help me?"

Dan was quiet. His face was serious and the look in his eyes was . . . I don't know how to describe it exactly. Only that I've never had a man look at me that way before, like he understood every part of me. It pulled me up short to see him look at me like that. For a second, it was like he'd crawled inside me.

"If that's what makes you happy, Ivy, then I think you should. I think you should have everything you want from life."

My breath caught in my throat. I started to say something but couldn't. The sound of Bobby's voice, calling for Dan to hurry up, intersected my half-formed thoughts before I could find words to explain them, either to Dan or to myself.

He smiled, bent down, and planted a kiss on the top of my head.

"Gotta go," he said. "It's my turn."

❦ 25 ❦

Gayla

I've never been much of a churchgoer.

Oh, sure, when I was growing up my parents had made me go to church on Christmas and Easter, just for form's sake. Also, I think, to hedge their bets, in case there turned out to be something to the whole God thing after all.

Personally, and especially as I reached my teen years, I thought that was pretty ridiculous. I mean, if God is really *God* with a capital "G," would he be fooled by such transparent motivations? I didn't think so. That, coupled with the fact that my parents almost never failed to have an argument in the car during these biannual pilgrimages to the local house of worship, put me off religion entirely.

But I've been waking up early recently. The summer sun starts shining in my window by five o'clock, and Sunday was no exception. So after making coffee and going out to water the garden, I decided to treat myself to breakfast at the Blue Bean.

As I was sitting at my table, finishing up a plate of blueberry waffles and a side of bacon, I looked out the window, saw people starting to arrive for the early service at the church, and thought, *What the heck?* I had to meet the others there soon anyway; why not join them for church instead of driving home only to turn around and drive back? I wanted to see the inside of the building anyway. People say it's beautiful.

And while I was there, maybe I'd say a quick prayer, a sort of thank-you note to God. Even though I'm not a big fan of organized religion, I do believe in God, at least in the broadest sense. And lately, it feels like he's been watching out for me.

A month ago, my life was a complete train wreck, and while there's still a long, long road ahead, I feel like things are back on track for Brian and me.

We've seen each other five times in the last two weeks, and each time is better than the last. Yesterday, we spent nearly the whole day together. We started off with a late-morning hike at Steep Rock Preserve—it was even more beautiful than I'd remembered—followed by iced chai lattes at Marty's Café and a trip to the Hickory Stick Bookshop in Washington Depot, where I picked up a new cookbook. On the drive back to New Bern, just as I was telling Brian about my stop-and-start efforts to teach myself guitar, we spotted a music store. Brian pulled in, saying that regular lessons might help. He was probably right, but after meeting the manager of the store, who was also the guitar teacher, a man with hooded eyes who wore a Grateful Dead T-shirt and talked more slowly than anyone I've ever met in my life, Brian decided he should probably teach me himself. I bought some new guitar strings, and we went on our way.

Later, we took in the early show at the Red Rooster Cinema, a charming sixties-throwback movie house that holds only about eighty people and has seats that date back to the Nixon administration, then went out for Chinese food.

The movie was great; so was the organic popcorn with actual butter, sold to me by a skinny girl with braids who also recommended the fair-trade green tea, but the Chinese food was *terrible*. They just don't seem to have decent Chinese in Connecticut.

I didn't let Brian stay the night—I'm just not ready for that—but I invited him inside for coffee after our dinner. He taught me two new chords on the guitar, and then he played by himself for a while. I haven't heard him play in so long. I'd almost forgotten how good he was.

Anyway, things have been going well. So well, in fact, that I decided to pull out my red fabric and make a birthday quilt for Brian. I don't care what Lanie says; I think he'll really like it. Evelyn fixed me up with a used sewing machine that she said was a good buy and would last for years, as well as a pattern, additional fabric, and a couple of private lessons. The base block for the quilt is a pinwheel surrounded by four half-square triangles, as Evelyn called them. Once you sew those, either you add four borders of fabric along the edges, with cornerstones—really just squares of fabric—in the corners or you make four flying-geese blocks and add those to the base block.

When I first saw the pattern, I thought it would be too hard, but Evelyn assured me I was up to it. The thing to do, she said, was take it step-by-step, deal with one block at a time and not try to look too far down the road. That seems like pretty good advice on a lot of levels. And it turns out to be true, certainly as far as quilt making is concerned. When I broke it down into steps, the block wasn't nearly as difficult as I'd thought at first. Well, except for the flying geese. Those took a little practice to master.

So I'm having fun quilting, meeting new people, and trying new things. The summer that started out as one of the worst in my life is showing potential to become one of the best. I'm really starting to believe that Brian and I are going to be okay. Considering where we began, that's a medium-sized miracle, so a word of appreciation to the Almighty seems warrantcd.

I paid for my breakfast, gathered my things, and walked down the Green to the New Bern Community Church.

It's a pretty building—one of the most photographed in New England, so they say. The exterior is white clapboard, with a high steeple, a bell tower, and a row of big white columns lining the front.

The organ was already playing to signal the start of the service when I arrived. I stood in the vestibule, looking for one of my friends so I could sit with them, but didn't see anyone. I accepted a photocopied weekly bulletin from a white-haired man wearing a tweed suit that seemed a little heavy for summer and went inside. I saw Evelyn, her husband, Charlie, and Virginia up toward the front. Margot and her family were there, too, but there was no room near them, so I took a seat closer to the back.

The interior is simple, the walls painted pale yellow, the window casings all in white, the wooden pews stained a warm cherry color, worn shiny and smooth from hundreds of years of contact with the hands, arms, knees, and bottoms of praying parishioners and the regular application of lemon oil, the scent of which hung faintly in the air, mixing with the aroma of melting wax from the altar candles. It was a pleasant smell, a peaceful surrounding, an atmosphere that spoke of constancy and the passage of time and made you think that, somehow, things would be all right in the end. Maybe that's why people go to church—because they want to believe that, somehow, it all turns out.

My mind wandered during the sermon. I was too busy taking in my surroundings and the faces of the people near me to give the minister my complete attention, but I enjoyed the music. The choir, dressed in their red robes, numbered only about twenty, but they had a bigger sound than I'd expected. The acoustics were very good. I also liked the congregational reading, from Psalm 121, I think it was.

> I will lift up my eyes to the mountains;
> From where shall my help come?
> My help comes from the Lord,
> Who made heaven and earth.

Speaking those words out loud and in unison with other people was kind of encouraging. My concept of God is a little blurry, but maybe standing in the presence of those who have such firm hope and are willing to declare so aloud brings a hope of its own. I guess that's another reason people go to church.

When the last hymn was finished and the congregation was dismissed to go in peace, the organist played the postlude, and I filed out with the rest, murmuring "good morning" to the people who greeted me first. I stopped to shake the hand of the minister, Reverend Tucker, who said it was nice to meet me and seemed sincere. I echoed his words, relieved that he hadn't asked how I liked the sermon, because I hadn't heard that much of it.

The summer sunshine was blinding after I left the cool confines of the church. I was standing outside the door, blinking, when I heard someone calling my name and turned to see Philippa, Tessa, Evelyn, and Virginia standing in a cluster on the far side of the steps.

"Gayla!" Philippa exclaimed, and gave me a big hug. It was funny to see her dressed in her black clerical robes and collar. I've only ever seen her at quilt circle, and she always wears her street clothes to our meetings.

"So glad you came to the services," she said.

"Well, I'm glad I was able to come," I replied, meaning it. "Where is everybody?"

"Abigail is getting a cup of coffee for the road," Tessa said. "Margot and Ivy are picking up their broods from Sunday school class. Madelyn doesn't go to church, but she should be here any minute."

I turned to Virginia. "Happy birthday! How does it feel to be eighty-five?"

"About the same as it did to be eighty-four. You

know something? Aside from the pain in my knees and fuzzy eyesight, I really don't feel a lot different than I did when I was forty. My thoughts are just as disorganized as they were when I was twenty. Where is this wisdom that's supposed to come with age? That's what I'd like to know."

"Oh, don't give us that, old woman. Nobody's buying it." Charlie, Evelyn's husband, approached carrying three cardboard cups of coffee in his big hands.

"You're just as wise as an owl and everybody knows it," Charlie said in his burred Irish brogue as he gave one of the cups to his mother-in-law. "Cream and two sugars for you, Virginia. Black with one sugar for my bride," he said, giving Evelyn a peck as he handed over her cup. "And black with no sugar for me. Though I don't know how I'll manage to choke it down. Philippa, the coffee in this church is as tasteless as day-old dishwater. How many scoops are they putting into the pot when they brew it?"

"Charlie, I don't know," she said wearily. "But if you'd like to join the hospitality committee, I'm sure they'd welcome your input on the proper preparation."

"You know," he said, "I might just do that."

"Yes?" Philippa said, looking surprised. "Well, we'd be glad for the help. Call me on Monday, and I'll give you the particulars. And you," she said, embracing Virginia, who was so tiny she nearly disappeared in the folds of Philippa's black robe, "have a very happy birthday. I'm so sorry I won't be able to join the festivities."

"You're not coming?" I asked.

Philippa shook her head. "Sunday is a workday for me. I'm leading children's church at the second service, and after that, I've got a counseling session. But I want to hear all the details," she said. "Take a lot of pictures."

"I'll be in charge of that." Madelyn, who had just mounted the steps and joined us, took a shiny black camera bag from her shoulder and held it up. "Look! A Nikon D80! They cost over eight hundred new, but I found it at a tag sale for about a quarter of that. Never been used. It's my sabbatical project. I've always wanted to take up photography."

Our group expanded as the others arrived. Abigail approached, coffee cup in hand, with her husband, Franklin, trailing behind. Since she'd been absent from the quilt circle for so many weeks, her arrival was marked by many exclamations, hugs, and questions about when she would tell everyone what she'd been doing with her Friday nights. "Soon enough," she said, giving an enigmatic smile, but that was all she was willing to say.

Margot and her husband, Paul, were next, but he didn't stay for long. She kissed him good-bye and reminded him that she'd left a casserole in the refrigerator. Ivy was last to arrive. She handed her children off to Franklin, who had volunteered to watch them for the afternoon, telling her kids to be good.

"So are we all here?" Virginia asked, looking around expectantly. "Let's get this show on the road! We've got to be in Ellington by ten-thirty."

"So we're going to Ellington?" Evelyn asked. "What's in Ellington?"

"You'll see soon enough," Virginia said, lifting her chin.

She marched down the steps toward the parking lot with Evelyn and all the rest of us following in her wake, wondering what she was up to.

"Who's driving?" Virginia asked.

"No one," Abigail replied. "I've arranged for transportation, so we can all ride together."

"Oh, my goodness! Will you look at that," Virginia exclaimed as we rounded the corner of the building.

A sleek, black, stretch limousine was waiting for us. The driver, a burly man who introduced himself as Daryl, was polishing the hood with a chamois cloth.

"I have *always* wanted to ride in one of these things," Virginia said excitedly, her eyes wide as she walked around the shining vehicle. "Cross another item off my bucket list! Thank you, Abigail."

"It's my birthday present to you. Personally, I

think the stretch versions are a little vulgar, but it'll be roomy enough to hold all of us comfortably. And you'll find a supply of chilled sparkling cider inside."

Madelyn raised her eyebrows. "Nothing stronger?"

"It's not even lunchtime yet," Abigail reminded her. "Shall we be on our way?"

"Hang on a minute," Madelyn said, and opened her camera bag. "Let's get a picture first."

Everyone lined up in front of the black behemoth while Madelyn fiddled with her camera, muttering to herself. She took six shots, rearranging us into different groupings for each one before asking Daryl to stand in for her so she could be in the last picture.

When we were finished, Daryl gave the camera back to Madelyn. "By the way, where am I driving?" he asked.

Virginia pushed up on her tiptoes and whispered something in his ear. Daryl laughed.

"Seriously?"

Virginia bobbed her head, and Daryl laughed again.

"All right. It's your day. I guess you can do whatever you want." Giving a little bow, he opened the door. "Ladies, your chariot awaits."

The trip took a bit over an hour.

After oohing and aahing over the car's fancy

interior, teasing Abigail about being a cheapskate for not ordering a limo with a hot tub inside, and toasting Virginia's happiness and continued good health with flutes of sparkling cider, we did what we always did when we got together: We started stitching.

"See?" Evelyn said when she saw me pull a plastic zipper bag containing my crazy quilt from my purse. "You were born to quilt. I knew it from the moment I saw you."

"I don't know about that. You'd think a person born to quilt would be able to master a French knot in less than a week. But I finally got it down; the lazy daisy stitch too! Aside from gardening, quilting is the thing I enjoy most. I work on it whenever I've got a spare moment. Now that I have some of the stitches mastered, handwork is relaxing for me; it helps clear my head."

"That's great to hear," Evelyn said, opening up her own purse and pulling out her project. "How is your other quilt coming, the one you're making for your husband?"

"Good! I finished all the blocks, even the ones with the flying geese units. But I'm a little worried about putting them together. Wouldn't it be easier to just sew them into strips instead of using all those zigzag seams?"

Evelyn shook her head as she threaded a needle. "Setting the blocks on point isn't nearly as hard as it looks. There aren't any zigzags involved, even though it looks like there are. You'll need to add some setting triangles to the ends, but after that, you will be sewing them into strips."

"Really?" I asked doubtfully.

"Really. Bring your blocks into the shop next week, and I'll show you what I mean."

"Okay, thanks." I unfolded my crazy quilt, which measured about thirty inches square, and smoothed it out on my lap. "Small as it is, you'd think I'd be further along by now."

Evelyn put aside the little fabric hexagon she was stitching, using a technique I had recently learned was known as English paper piecing, and leaned over to examine my work.

"It's coming along great," she said. "Your herringbone stitches are perfect. And those green featherstitches along the yellow floral make a nice transition to the deeper gold patch next to it. Incorporating these touches of black was a good idea—makes the brighter patches pop. But," she said, brushing her fingers across the black patch, "it's an awfully thick piece of cotton. We don't have anything like that in the shop. Where did you get it?"

I bit my lower lip. "Yes . . . I've been meaning to talk to you about that. How much do you think the napkins cost at your husband's restaurant?"

Evelyn tilted her head to one side, as if she thought she'd misheard me. "I'm sorry?"

"Grill on the Green was the first restaurant

Brian took me to in New Bern. It was also the location of our first date since . . . well, since I came up for the summer. It has a lot of memories for me, so last time I was there I . . . I took one of the black napkins."

I looked down at my lap, blushing with embarrassment. "I'm sorry. I can pay for it. I always intended to, but your husband wasn't in the restaurant at the time, and I didn't quite know how to explain it to the waitress. How much do I owe him? Would twenty be enough?" I asked, reaching for my wallet.

"Twenty dollars?" Evelyn laughed. "For one napkin? Don't be silly. Charlie won't care. He's spent enough time with me and this crew to know that even the most law-abiding quilter can go a little crazy in hot pursuit of a fabric. And I think he'd be honored to have a little piece of his restaurant in your quilt. Don't give it another thought."

"But I've got to pay him back somehow. How about if I bring him some flowers from my garden instead? So he can put them on the tables."

"If that would make you feel better, sure. He'd like that."

"I've got a bumper crop of daisies," I said. "I'll bring him some of those. Hey, how did your sailing lessons go? You haven't said a thing about it."

Evelyn's eyes were fixed on her hexagon patch, but her face lit up at the mention of sailing. "I was planning to wait until next Friday to give the full report; today is Mom's day. But since you ask, it was fantastic! At first, I was all thumbs, and during my first attempt at tacking, I forgot to duck and got whacked in the head by the boom, but by the end of the second day, I was feeling pretty comfortable. By day three, I completely fell in love with sailing. In fact, I loved it so much that I've decided to buy myself a sailboat."

"Wow," I said as I wrapped my thread three times around the needle, poked the tip through the fabric, and pulled, creating a perfectly formed French knot. "So should we start calling you Captain?"

"Well, maybe just Skipper. I'm now licensed to captain a boat up to twenty-eight feet in length, but the boat I'm buying is only half that size. Just a little day sailer, but it'll be perfect to take out on the lake. I found it used online for a very good price. It even comes with a tow trailer."

"That's so great, Evelyn. You must feel really proud of yourself."

"You know," she said in a slightly philosophical tone, "I really do. You get to a certain age and I think you quit looking for new adventures." She tied off her thread and clipped it with a pair of embroidery scissors that hung from a ribbon around her neck.

"Of course, every day is an adventure when you own your own business, but this was different, maybe because it was physically and mentally challenging. Like a lot of quilters, I tend to be pretty good at sitting still for long periods of time," she said with a self-deprecating smile. "Anyway, it reminded me that you're never too old to try something new, and I have you to thank for it. If not for you and the sabbatical project, it might never have happened."

I looked over at Virginia, who was sitting on the far side of the car, squinting at the screen of her new smartphone, making occasional grumbling noises as she tried to get to the next level of Angry Birds.

"Hmm . . . I'm willing to take credit for the sailing, Evelyn. But the part about realizing that you're never too old to try new things? I don't think you'd have to look very far to be reminded of that."

Evelyn followed my gaze to the far end of the car and laughed. "You've got a point."

The limousine made a wide turn to the right, and Daryl shifted his eyes upward, looking at all of us in the rearview mirror. "Ladies, we have arrived at Ellington Airport."

"Ellington Airport?" Evelyn frowned and twisted in her seat so she could see out the window. Her eyes went wide.

"No! Absolutely not!" She gasped and spun around to face Virginia. "Mom! Have you lost your mind?"

26

Ivy

Standing a few feet away from the limousine, I craned my neck and put my hand above my brow, squinting beneath its shade, searching for a speck of bright red in the cloudless blue sky.

"There it is!" I called out, turning to the others and pointing to the northwest.

Everyone crowded around me, trying to catch sight of the red speck.

"You're right!" Margot exclaimed, hinging her neck backward. "Isn't this exciting?"

Evelyn covered her face with her hands. "Oh, dear Lord . . ."

Abigail patted her on the back. "Everything will be fine."

"Abbie's right," I said. "It's not like she's up there alone. She'll be tethered to the instructor. You heard what he said: He's done this hundreds of times."

"And Tessa's up there too," Madelyn said, twisting the lens on her camera. "I don't know what possessed her to join the party at the last minute. She wasn't like this when we were kids— I can tell you that. Back then, *I* was the brave one."

She lifted the camera to her eyes, pointed it at Evelyn, who still had her face buried in her hands, and snapped a picture.

"Could you not do that right now?" Evelyn said, giving Madelyn an uncharacteristically smoldering glare.

"Sorry. I was practicing. I don't want to miss the shot."

Gayla, who was standing right next to Margot, pointed skyward.

"Look! I think the doors are opening."

"Yes! Here they come!"

"I can't look," Evelyn said, then looked anyway, tilting her face sunward just like the rest of us, watching the plane that buzzed like a fat bee overhead.

I held my breath. I think we all did. My heart was pounding, too, but I have to say, I felt so happy. I don't know why exactly. It's just so cool that I know these women, these amazing, fabulous, incredibly brave women. It gives me hope that, someday, I'll be amazing too. When I'm eighty-five, I want to be just as stubborn and adventurous as Virginia.

After a few seconds that felt much longer, two blue-black shapes appeared in the sky and started plummeting toward the earth like stones, and we let out a collective gasp.

After a few more incredibly long seconds, Evelyn cried out, "Oh, Lord! Oh, no! What happened? Their parachutes aren't opening!"

"They will in a moment," Abigail assured her, sounding none too sure herself. "They're still in free fall. Remember? The instructor said they'd be in free fall for about a minute before they opened the parachutes. Everything is fine."

"That's right," I said, putting my arm around Evelyn. "See how high up they still are? Oh, wait! There it is! The chutes are opening. See?"

Margot clutched her hands to her breast, standing there with tears in her eyes. "Oh! How beautiful! They look like red and yellow blossoms falling from the sky."

Suddenly, my eyes were tearing too, partly from relief that Tessa and Virginia, the grandma I never had, were safe, but also from sheer wonder. What must they be feeling right then? What does the world look like when you're floating with angels?

Beautiful. Limitless. Full of possibilities.

As the shapes drifted closer to the earth, we could see them more clearly, recognized that each shape was actually two people, saw their faces, realized that the red parachute belonged to Virginia and her instructor, who was strapped to her like a shell on a turtle, and the yellow one was for Tessa and her instructor.

When the parachutes were about two hundred feet from the ground, I could hear the sound of laughter and whooping coming from above, which grew louder the closer they sank to earth. We all began running into the grassy field, heading toward the spot where it looked like they were going to land, laughing and clapping and crying.

Virginia was grinning from ear to ear when she landed. So was Tessa. Madelyn snapped pictures as fast as she could, trying to capture the moment.

"That was fantastic! Let's go again!" Virginia exclaimed as her instructor, Gary, unclipped her from her harness.

"Not in my lifetime!" Evelyn said, hugging her mother tight to her. "I wouldn't survive another morning like this one."

"Well, maybe on my ninetieth," she said to Gary. "She'll have calmed down by then."

"It's a date, Virginia. I'll jump with you any-time."

We buzzed around the two jumpers like bees around a hive.

"Did you have fun?"

"What was it like?"

"Were you scared?"

Tessa, who was beaming, said, "Absolutely! I almost changed my mind, but then Virginia jumped out, and I figured if she could do it, then so could I."

"Well, I was pretty nervous myself for a second," Virginia admitted. "When Gary here asked if I was ready to bail out, I suddenly thought, 'Good Lord, Virginia. Have you lost your senses? You're about to jump out of a perfectly good airplane.' " She laughed.

"And then I thought, 'What the heck. I've got to get down from here somehow. Might as well take the most direct route.' "

After we took more pictures and Tessa and Virginia changed out of their jumpsuits, we got back into the limousine. Virginia whispered another address into Daryl's ear.

"Excellent choice," he said, and made a left turn out of the driveway of the airfield, heading south.

"Another surprise?" Evelyn asked. "I'm not sure I can take much more."

"Don't be such a party pooper. You'll like this one," Virginia said. "I promise."

She was right.

Rein's, in Vernon, is as close to a real New York delicatessen as you're going to find in Connecticut. Some people ordered Reuben sandwiches, others ordered pastrami, Abigail had smoked whitefish salad, and Virginia ordered a hot dog and French fries.

"Mom, it's your birthday. Don't you want to get something a little more adventurous?" Evelyn asked.

"The last thing anyone can accuse me of being today is unadventurous. I *like* hot dogs."

"Okay, have it your way."

"I will," said Virginia. "After eighty-five years, I've earned it."

It wasn't fancy, but no one could fault Virginia on her choice of restaurant. The food at Rein's, including the chocolate cake with birthday candles that the waitress brought out as Virginia was opening the gifts she'd told us not to bring, was delicious, and the portions were huge. Everyone went home with a doggie bag.

Another advantage of Rein's was the location, a strip mall that included, among other things, a terrific shop called Quilting by the Yard.

The instant we got through the door, everybody scattered, scampering off in different directions in search of textile treasures. Gayla, who was sticking close to me, looked confused.

"I don't get it," she said as we walked between rows of shelving loaded with floral prints. "They're like kids in a candy store, even Evelyn. She owns her own shop—doesn't she already have enough fabric?"

"There's no such thing as enough fabric," I said, looking left and right, searching for something I couldn't live without. "Only more. Cobbled Court is a pretty big shop, but there's no way Evelyn can carry all the fabric lines she might want to. Quilters are always looking for something new and inspiring."

We took a loop to the left and found a whole wall of batiks, more than I'd ever seen in one shop at one time.

"Like this!" I exclaimed, reaching out for a gorgeous bolt of bottle-green batik printed with a design of purple and blue dragonflies. I bought a yard of that and two more of a modern, peachy-pink print with blue squiggles that I thought would make a cute skirt for Bethany. If money were no object, I could have bought a lot more, but it is, and I don't have a discount at Quilting by the Yard.

Gayla did pretty well, but didn't go overboard, buying a pack of ten fat quarter "blenders" that I told her would blend well in just about any of her future projects and help build her fabric stash, as well as some skeins of gorgeous, hand-dyed perle cotton threads that would look beautiful stitched into her crazy quilt project. I wouldn't have minded buying some myself, but they were a little beyond my budget. But, without my asking or even hinting about it, Gayla said she was going to pull a few yards off each skein to share them with me.

When I told her she didn't have to do that, she laughed and said, "But I'll never be able to use all this. Not at the rate I'm going."

I really like Gayla, and not just because she offered to share her thread with me. Not even because, when I somewhat awkwardly brought up the subject of Carrillon College and how expensive it would be for ordinary people to afford a program like that, she jumped in before I was even finished and said, "You know, I don't usually deal with adult students, but I'm sure there are scholarships available for people in your situation. Why don't you let me check it out?"

That's what I mean. Given all that she's dealing with right now, you'd think that helping me or anyone would be the last thing on Gayla's mind. But she's very considerate. And funny. Not backslapping funny—she's too quiet for that— but now and then she gets in these little one-liners that crack me up. She's brave, too—really brave.

If my husband cheated on me, I don't know if I'd be able to forgive him and keep the marriage together, but I admire her for trying. And for telling us about it and asking for our support. That took guts. And I think it helped too. I hope so. I know that Tessa has been calling her regularly, checking in on her. It must help her to be able to talk to somebody who's been there.

I think people need that, just the way that I try to mentor women who've been abused, and Evelyn sometimes coaches women who've been diagnosed with breast cancer. Being able to talk to someone who's already gone through it gives the other person hope, helps them feel less alone. Maybe that's some of the reason we have to go through trials like this, so we'll be ready to help the next person who's walking that road.

Well, whatever the reason, I like Gayla. I can't believe there was ever a time when I didn't want to include her in the circle. She's one of us now. She fits right in.

While the others lingered in the quilt shop, Gayla and I went to check out some of the other stores in the strip mall. Neither of us saw anything we wanted—not until Gayla found a used book and record store.

Other than a couple of romances, I've been taking a break from reading this summer. I have enough reading to do during the semester. And I don't own a record player, so looking through dusty bins of old vinyl records wasn't too appealing either. I was just following Gayla, keeping her company, figuring we'd be out of there in a minute.

In fact, we were heading out the door when Gayla spotted something in the glass display counter, gasped, and said, "Holy—It can't be!" She bent over the case, her face practically touching the glass. "Oh, my gosh. It is! I can't believe it."

I walked up next to her and peered through the glass at an album with a picture of a dark-haired man wearing earphones, a plaid shirt, and a rumpled gray jacket and holding a guitar on his lap.

"What is it?"

Gayla closed her eyes, took in a deep breath, and opened them again, as if she thought she might be seeing a mirage. "It's an album, an incredibly rare one," she said quietly. "There's a track on here of Noel Gallagher singing 'Wonderwall' as a solo, accompanying himself on acoustic guitar. It was recorded live in Japan in 2002. It's a very rare recording, almost impossible to find."

"Do you collect old records?"

She shook her head. "No, but I know someone who does. How much do you want for this?" she asked the clerk.

The figure he quoted her was a car payment for me—a couple of them. Gayla's not cheap, but she doesn't spend money she doesn't need to spend either; I've watched her. But she wrote out that check without a second thought.

"It's for Brian," she explained. "Our anniversary is next weekend. Twenty-seven years. He'll be over the moon when he sees this."

After what her husband did, she was excited about buying him an expensive anniversary present. She must really love him. I wonder if I'll ever be able to love someone that much. Someone like Dan?

He's good to me and good to my kids; that counts for a lot in my book. And of course, he's completely gorgeous. Those eyes. And that body. I went over to his house to pick Drew up one day and saw him working in the yard without his shirt on. I've never seen a man with shoulder muscles like that, not in real life—magazine models don't count.

Dan and I have kissed a few times, once or twice pretty passionately, but that's as far as it's gone. But I've been thinking about doing more than kissing him, and I have to say, that surprised me. When I was married to Hodge, I never really cared about sex. Of course, we *had* sex; I've got two kids. But it was hardly ever my idea.

All that's changed since I've started going out with Dan. Now I have all kinds of ideas. Sometimes I have to stop, take a breath, and force myself to think about something else. It's very distracting. I made five fabric miscuts last week; I usually make only one or two. But all these ideas I've been having . . . are they good ideas?

For a second, on that day in the bowling alley when he looked at me in a way that stopped my breath, I thought that maybe I could love Dan. That maybe I did. But then I started thinking about my quilt circle friends and all the marriages, divorces, and betrayals they have known.

On the day Gayla told us about her husband's affair, there were eight women in the room. Eight smart, attractive, caring women. Six of them, including me, had been deceived by men who professed love for them. Only Virginia and Margot have gone unscathed. Those aren't good odds.

Okay, Abigail didn't love her first husband, Woolley Wynne, and she even told him so before they got married, so maybe she doesn't count. And looking back, I realize that I didn't love Hodge. I needed him, or thought I did, but that's not the same thing; I know that now. So maybe I don't count either.

And yes, Tessa and Lee were able to work through their differences, get past the betrayal, and rekindle their love. It looks like Gayla and Brian might be doing that, too, which is great. And sure, Abigail and Evelyn would both say that on the second trip to the altar they found real and lasting love, but how do they know for sure? They've been married only a few years. And Margot is practically a newlywed. How do they know? How does anyone know? Who's to say that in a year, or five, or twenty, they won't get their hearts broken?

Dan cares about me. But who's to say that won't change? Or that I'm not wrong about him? After all, I was wrong about Hodge.

Could I love Dan? Really love him? I'm not sure. Maybe.

But I'm not sure I want to love him. Not unless I could be 100 percent certain that it would last, that things would never change, and that he would never hurt me or my children.

I want a guarantee against heartbreak, a life-time guarantee. And the thing is, there aren't any. So where does that leave me?

ᵕ°ᵍ᷍᷍ 27 ᷍᷍ᵍ°ᵕ

Ivy

Personal angst aside, I had a really good time at Virginia's birthday party. We've never taken a field trip—not all of us together—but as we drove back to New Bern we decided we should do it more often. It was fun.

By the time Daryl parked in the church lot and then jumped out to open the door for us, it was a little after five. After saying our good-byes and wishing Virginia happy birthday one more time, everybody except Margot and Abigail, who had to stay for a meeting at the church, got in their cars and drove off.

I stopped to put some gas in my car and pick up a gallon of milk and a carton of eggs at the minimart, thinking we'd have breakfast for dinner, then drove to Abigail and Franklin's house to pick up the kids.

Franklin answered the door. "Did you have a good time?"

"The best. Virginia went skydiving! Can you

believe it? Tessa too. We went to this fabulous deli for lunch and then shopping at a wonderful quilt shop in Vernon. And we got to ride in a limo! My first time! Of course, I'm sure Abbie already told you about that, but it was great. Really great. Thanks so much for keeping an eye on the kids so I could go, Franklin. Were they good?"

"Of course," he said. "They always are. We went to play mini-golf and then came back and spent the afternoon in the pool."

I smiled. Franklin and Abigail are sort of surrogate grandparents for Bethany and Bobby. They love coming here. Of course, sometimes Abigail spoils them, but I guess that's all right. That's what grandparents are supposed to do, right?

"Well, I really appreciate you taking them for me." I leaned over and kissed him on the cheek. "But we'd better get out of your hair. I bet you're tired after such a long day. Bobby! Bethany!"

Franklin put his hand on my arm. "Hang on a minute, Ivy. We need to talk before you go. About Bethany."

My good mood instantly dissipated.

"What did she do? Whatever it is, I'm sorry." I blew out an exasperated breath. "She's been such a pain lately."

"Nothing," he rushed to assure me, lifting his hands. "Nothing bad. She's a good girl, Ivy. And far more intelligent than any eleven-year-old I've ever met. But she's very upset about this reunification process she's being forced into by her father." Franklin cleared his throat. "And she's hired me to be her lawyer."

Bobby stayed in the living room watching television while Franklin, Bethany, and I talked in his study.

"What do you mean, you hired Franklin as your lawyer? Where did you ever get such an idea? And how do you think you're going to pay him?"

Bethany, who was sitting opposite me in one of the leather chairs that flanked Franklin's unlit fireplace, glared at me.

"I read about it on the Internet. There's a girl a little bit older than me whose parents are getting divorced. Her parents were so busy fighting with each other that nobody was thinking about what *she* wanted, so she decided she needed personal representation and hired her own attorney."

She crossed her arms over her chest. Personal representation. Attorney. Where did she pick up words like that? Franklin was right; Bethany was smart. Too smart for her own good sometimes. Definitely too smart for mine.

"I've paid Uncle Franklin a retainer of forty-six dollars, everything I had in my savings account. And I told him I can either pay him the rest out of my allowance when it comes in every week or I'll come and clean his office for him every Saturday morning."

Franklin lifted a hand. "We're still negotiating that part," he said. "I've accepted Bethany's retainer, but none of it has been applied to her account. Like most attorneys, I offer my initial consultation gratis."

"That means free of charge," Bethany informed me. "It's Latin."

My mouth dropped open, literally. Was he serious? Was she?

"Don't look at me like that," Bethany said. "I had to do something. I don't want to see him, not even if somebody else is there. We did that before he was sent to jail, remember? It was awful. I don't want to see him at all. I told you that, but you won't listen to me. No one is listening to me!"

I covered my face with my hands and rubbed my forehead. "Bethany," I said, after lowering them, "it's not that I'm not listening to you. It's that there's nothing I can do about this! Believe me, I've tried. I've asked Arnie about this a hundred times, but he says there's no way around it. Your dad wants to meet with you and your brother. He insists on it. And according to the law, he has a right to do that."

"But what about my rights?" Bethany said, clutching the arms of the chair. "You don't have to see him! Arnie got a restraining order for you! Why didn't he get one for me?"

"Because . . . because it's different for me, baby. I don't feel safe around your dad. He used to hit me, and—"

"He hit me too," she said, her voice low and accusatory and much too hard for a little girl who had skinned knees and a crush on the lead singer for One Direction. "Remember?"

"I know," I said softly. "That's why I finally ran away from him, remember? Because it was the only thing I could do to protect you. Because you're the most important thing in the world to me. And I'm still trying to protect you. I'm doing everything I can, but my hands are tied.

"The law is the law," I continued. "You can't change it. The best I can do is cooperate with the legal process and do everything I can to make sure that your visits with your father are supervised and stay that way."

I turned my head and wiped the tears from my eyes. I felt so powerless. She and Bobby mean the world to me. Doesn't she know that? If there was anything I could do that would keep Hodge from them, I would.

"Tell her, Franklin. Arnie knows what he's talking about. He's a good lawyer, isn't he?"

"Yes, he is. One of the best in the county. And I'd know," Franklin said, swiveling his head toward Bethany and then back to me, "since he works at my firm. But, Ivy, you've made one assertion that isn't entirely correct."

Franklin rose from his chair and stood next to the fireplace, resting one arm across the mantel, turning toward us and raising his voice just slightly, as if he were addressing a jury.

"The law is not *the* law, as you claim. Not always. Very often the law is what the court *interprets* it to be, and that can differ, depending on the circumstances of the case, the individuals involved in the suit, and the viewpoint of the judge.

"And Bethany," he said, smiling down at my daughter, "has brought something to my attention that Arnie may have overlooked, something I think we should take under consideration."

He raised his brows and looked at Bethany, who picked up on his cue.

"Well," she said, "after I found out about the girl on the Internet who got her own lawyer, I wondered if there might be some other things that had happened in courts that might help change the mind of the judge. Some . . ."

She looked questioningly at Franklin.

"Precedents," he said. "Legal precedents."

"Right. Legal precedents. So I started going to the library to see what I could find. Mrs. Baxter, the research librarian, helped me. First of all, I found out that, according to the state of Connecti-cut, if I was twelve instead of eleven, the court

351

would have to at least listen to what I want. Even then, the judge might still say I had to meet with my dad, but the court would have to hear me out. Well, I'm going to be twelve in six more months, and that just didn't seem fair to me. Why should it make such a big difference?

"So Mrs. Baxter and I did some more research, and we found some cases where the court decided that some people who were a few months younger than the age of preference—that's the age you have to be for the court to take what you want into consideration," she explained, "were able to get the judge to say that they were old enough to make their own decisions and deny visitation to a parent they didn't want to have contact with."

"Is that true?" I asked Franklin, who nodded. "Why didn't Arnie tell me that?"

"Probably because he didn't think of it. Unless Bethany had brought it to my attention, I doubt I'd have thought of it either. It just doesn't happen very often," Franklin said. "And when it does, there's usually been a record of documented abuse of the child. Hodge did strike Bethany. We know that, but there was no legal complaint filed at the time—"

"I didn't think to do that," I said, my eyes filling again. "I just wanted to get away. If I'd stuck around and called the police, who knows what Hodge would have done? He'd have gotten out of it somehow, told the police that it was all a big mistake. He can be so convincing. And then, once they were gone . . .”

Franklin, looking uncomfortable at the sight of my tears, took his handkerchief from his pocket and handed it to me. “It’s all right, Ivy. You were right to do what you did. At that moment, the most important thing was to get the children away from him.”

Bethany got up from her chair, walked to mine, and perched on the armrest. “Don’t cry, Mommy,” she said.

She hadn’t called me that for years. Hearing her say it now just made me want to cry more, but I swallowed hard and pulled myself together.

“Franklin,” I said, “do you really think there’s a chance you can get the judge to listen to Bethany?”

“Maybe. It depends on the judge. If it was Judge Treadlaw, the man who was presiding over the case when Margot was trying to get custody of Olivia, I don’t think we’d stand a chance. Treadlaw is a lazy judge. He’ll go exactly by the book because it’s easier. But Judge Dranginis has been overseeing this case so far, so I believe it’s worth a try. She’s a *thinking* judge, someone who will look at the big picture.

“But we’ve got to be able to convince the judge that all this is Bethany’s idea and that you’re not influencing her or trying to prejudice her against her father in any way.”

"Sheila Fenton already thinks that's exactly what is going on," I grumbled. "She thinks Bethany refuses to see Hodge because of me, and it's just not true! I've bent over backward and bit holes in my tongue to keep from saying anything bad about Hodge to the kids. Sometimes I think I've gone too far," I said, thinking of Bobby and how little he understood about how and why we'd come to New Bern. "But I wanted them to make up their own minds."

"And they will," Franklin assured me. "Who-ever is supervising the visits will make sure Bobby is safe, and time will take care of the rest. If Hodge has really changed his ways, good. And if he hasn't, Bobby will see through it. Bethany's not the only intelligent child you've raised," he said, giving her a wink. "And I think the fact that Bethany took the initiative to hire me as her lawyer will work in our favor," he continued. "It will help underscore the fact that her desire to prohibit contact with her father truly was her idea."

"Okay, but I can't let you take the case for a forty-six-dollar retainer. I've got a little money put by," I said, wondering if the tires on my car would hold out a few more months. "I can write you a check tomorrow."

"No!" Bethany exclaimed, removing her arm from my shoulder. "I want to do it myself! Uncle Franklin and I worked out a deal. He needs my

354

help. I'm not just going to clean his office; I'm going to help organize his files too. I've got a whole system worked out with color-coded tabs and everything."

"Bethany and I have discussed this," Franklin said. "We're going to work out a contract for exchange of services. If I can show that to the judge, it will help underscore the fact that Bethany is doing this on her own.

"And she's right, Ivy. I could use the help; you've seen my office. Ever since Mrs. Simpson retired, I can't find anything. I'll be Bethany's lawyer, and she'll be my junior clerk. It'd be excellent training for a future attorney," he said, ruffling Bethany's hair with his hand. "This young lady has a gift for argument."

"She certainly does," I mumbled.

"So can I do it, Mom? Can I?" she begged, her eyes wide and innocent.

"If you want to. I'm still not sure this will work, but I guess you can't lose anything by trying, can you?"

28

Gayla

Brian moaned and clapped his hand to his chest. "Oh! This is amazing."

"Yeah?"

"Fantastic! Absolutely the best *aloo gobi* I've ever had in my life. Better than that curry place we used to go to in London, in the East End. Remember?"

"The one on Brick Lane. What was the name of that place?" It came to me, and I snapped my fingers. "Sheba! Really? Better than Sheba?"

"Better than Sheba."

He picked up his fork. "Darling," he mumbled, his mouth full of *aloo gobi*, "where did you learn to make Indian food like this?"

I poured a little more wine into my glass and rested my chin on my hand, smiling at him through the flickering light of the candle.

"Well, you know how I like to buy cookbooks?"

He nodded. I took a bite of tandoori chicken and washed it down with a sip of sauvignon blanc.

"Funny thing, but since I've come to New Bern, I've actually found time to start reading them."

I laughed and Brian laughed, too, and he was so

beautiful, and the night was so beautiful, and everything was so perfect that I could have cried from sheer happiness.

Brian touched the rim of his glass to mine. "Happy anniversary, darling."

"Happy anniversary."

I swallowed my wine and rested my cheek on my hand, giving him a coy look. "Do you want to open your present?"

"You don't want to wait until after dinner?"

"No," I said, and jumped up from my chair and grabbed his gift from the sideboard, where I'd left it. "I can't wait for you to open it."

Brian swiped a starched white napkin across his mouth—I'd set the table with my best dishes and linens for the occasion—and tossed it on the table.

"Good, because I can't wait for you to open yours either." He reached into the inside pocket of his jacket and pulled out a blue envelope.

"You first," I insisted, coming back to my seat and thrusting the package into his hands.

"Let's see," he said, teasing me. "A big, flat, skinny square. Hmm . . . too small for a Ferrari. I'm guessing it's an album. Something for my collection? Brilliant!"

"Open it!"

He did, and the look on his face was all I'd hoped it would be. He was absolutely floored.

"You are kidding," he said, his eyes widening

as he tore the paper away. "Is this what I think . . . It is! I can't believe it!" He looked up at me with a stunned expression. "Darling, it's fantastic! Where in the world did you find it?"

"A used book and record shop in Vernon." I laughed. "Can you stand it? I've searched every used record store in Manhattan for this, spent hours online, hoping I'd find one for you, and it turns up in some little hole-in-the-wall shop in the middle of Connecticut. Do you like it?"

"Like it?" He gave me an incredulous look. "Of course I like it. I love it. It's probably the best present I've ever received. Thank you, darling."

He pushed himself halfway up in his chair, leaned across the table to give me a kiss, and then sat down again and turned the album around, examining the back.

"This is just amazing. I can't wait to listen to it. Noel Gallagher singing 'Wonderwall,' live and unplugged, just his voice and a guitar, at some little club in Japan. Can you imagine what it would have been like to actually be in the audience?"

"Do you remember what year 'Wonderwall' was released?"

"Nineteen ninety-five," he said without hesitation.

"That's right," I said. "The same year we got the apartment, remember? The twins were in second grade. After so many years of scrimping and saving, renting that tiny one-bedroom, we finally moved into a bigger place. I'd just finished my undergraduate work and we were so happy, remember? I thought that finally everything was going to be easier, better. We both thought so.

"You used to sit on the chair in the kitchen while I was making dinner and the kids were running in and out, and you'd sing 'Wonderwall.' When you got to that one line, about maybe being the one that saves me, you'd sing it right to me, like it was true. Like you thought I was the one person in the world who could save you. And, the thing is," I said, swallowing back tears, "I thought the same thing about you."

He got up from his chair, came around to my side of the table, and took me in his arms. "I love you; do you know that? I really do. And I'm sorry. I was such an idiot."

"Don't," I whispered. "You don't need to apologize again. I forgive you."

"Do you really?"

I nodded, and we stood there for a moment, holding each other tight. I didn't want to let go, but after a minute, Brian loosened his grip a little.

"Now it's your turn," he said, and picked the blue envelope up from the table.

It looked like a card. Last year the only thing he'd given me on our anniversary was a card. I wasn't disappointed—not really. After all, I'd only given him socks. I hadn't been expecting anything extravagant. The longer we'd been married, the more practical we'd become in our gift giving. And that, I now saw, was part of the problem. We'd gotten practical about our relationship, too, complacent, supposing it would just go on like it always had. We'd forgotten to take delight in each other. Now we were learning to do that again. And to remember all we'd done and been for each other over the years and take delight in that too.

"What is it?" I asked, knowing from the self-satisfied smile on his lips that it wasn't just a card.

"Just open it."

I slipped my finger under the edge of the envelope and pulled up the flap. "Oh, Brian," I breathed, my hand lifting to my mouth to cover my surprise. "Oh, sweetheart. I can't believe it! Italy? We're really going back to Italy?"

"And Scotland," he said. "As long as we're going to Europe, I thought we'd spend a few days with Nate."

"Oh, sweetheart! What a wonderful idea!"

Brian's little smile expanded into a grin. "I cashed in my airline miles since the beginning of time. All these years I've spent on the road finally paid off. After Scotland, we'll spend a few days in Tuscany, touring the vineyards and taking that couples cooking class you told me about. I booked us into a beautiful boutique hotel, used to be an old monastery.

"And here's the *big* surprise," he said, though I couldn't imagine anything bigger than what he'd already told me. "We'll be spending the second week floating down the Brenta on the *Lucia Dolce*. No crew cabin this time. I've booked the best suite on the barge."

I gasped. "The *Lucia Dolce*? You're kidding. You mean it's still operating after all these years?" I laughed with surprise as Brian nodded his head.

"She had a complete overhaul about four years ago and looks better than ever. Vincent retired, and his son, Alex, took over as captain. But Mario is still in the galley and grumpy as ever, they tell me. He's seventy-one now and refuses to retire."

"Seventy-one! Was he only forty-six when we were on the barge? That's the same age we are now. At the time, I thought he was ancient."

"Back then, anybody over thirty seemed ancient to us."

Brian wrapped his arms around my waist. "There's just one problem. I had to use airline miles for our tickets—even coach class to Europe costs the earth these days, and if I had to pay for tickets, we wouldn't be able to afford the rest of the trip. I wasn't able to get us seats until mid-September, after the school year starts." He drew his brows into a questioning line. "Do you still want to go?"

"Of course I want to go! What a question!" I laughed.

"You sure? Last time I tried to surprise you with a trip, you were convinced your clients would die if you were out of touch with them for a weekend, let alone two weeks."

I reached up and pushed his hair from his forehead, then slid my fingers down his temple, cheek, and neck, to the skin just above his collar opening, sliding my hand underneath his shirt as I kissed him.

"That was before. Things are different now. It'll take a little juggling, and I might have to put in some longer hours before and after the trip, but I'll figure out a way. I can't think of anyplace I'd rather be than Italy in September. Or anyone I'd rather be there with than you."

I kissed him again, and he kissed me back, so sweetly, taking his time. He moved closer, stroking my hair, sliding his hand down my back and letting it linger there a moment before reaching the front, undoing the top button of my dress, tracing a trail of slow kisses along the curve of my neck to my collarbone, his lips brushing over that soft spot of flesh that makes me melt. I kissed the top of his head, bent low and still lower as his lips moved from my neck to the swell of my breasts.

He reached for the second button, but I pushed his hand away and undid it myself and the next, and the next, and the next, stepping back so he could watch as I opened the dress, slipped the fabric slowly back over the curve of my shoulders, and let it slide off my arms and fall to the floor in a silken heap.

I lifted my eyes to his. "I think we can finish dinner later, don't you?"

"Brilliant idea," he said with a soft little laugh. "Indian food is delicious reheated."

I smiled and moved backward, taking hold of his hand as I stepped over the folds of my discarded dress and urged him toward the staircase.

"It's even better for breakfast."

🐾 29 🐾

Gayla

On Monday morning, my cell phone rang. It was Lanie, and for the first time in a long time, I didn't let the call go to voice mail.

"Good morning, my darling!"

"Good morning yourself," she said suspiciously. "What are you up to? You sound nauseatingly cheerful."

"Nothing," I said. "Just washing the breakfast dishes before I go outside to water the garden."

"Oh. How are you? How are things?"

"Great! Couldn't be better. Brian left at about

five-thirty. He had to get back to the city for a breakfast meeting."

"Wait a minute. You mean he spent the *night* there?"

I turned on the faucet and rinsed toast crumbs from a plate.

"I mean he spent two nights here—Saturday and Sunday. And I'm pretty sure that he'll be spending weekends in New Bern from now on— at least through Labor Day. Then I'll have to shut up the house and go back to New York."

"Oh, my God," she moaned. "You slept with him. You lost your mind, and you slept with him. Gayla, that was the stupidest . . ."

Lanie sputtered on, but I wasn't listening. Nothing could put me in a bad mood that day, not even Lanie's prognostications of misery.

She'd been wrong about Brian and me, wrong in her predictions about the impossibility of us repairing our broken marriage, and I wanted her to know it.

"But I won't be in Manhattan for long," I said, talking right over her. "Just long enough to get my clients on track for the school year, answer the backlog of mail, and pack my bags. Brian and I are going to Italy for two weeks! He arranged the whole thing himself and surprised me on Saturday night. We'll spend the first week visiting Nate in Scotland and then touring the vineyards in Tuscany and the second barging on the *Lucia Dolce*. Isn't that romantic? It'll be like a second honeymoon!"

Lanie, who had finally stopped sputtering and started listening, let out a deep sigh.

"Gayla," she said, her voice deliberately patient, "I understand you haven't had sex in a very long time and that the postcoital high is making you a little giddy, but you've *got* to listen to me. I'm saying this as a friend. Letting Brian sleep over on weekends, agreeing to go to Italy with him—it's a mistake. I know that right this second, everything seems hunky-dory, and you're certain your problems are over, but you're *wrong*. A man who strays once is going to stray again; he can't help himself."

I groaned and shut off the faucet. "Lanie, don't be such a—"

"No!" she barked. "You've *got* to hear me out. I know what I'm talking about."

I was quiet. Even though I'd spent the last several weeks avoiding her calls or returning them only when I was pretty sure she wouldn't pick up, Lanie was my friend. I'd sit still and listen to what she had to say.

But she didn't say anything, not for a few moments. When she finally spoke, her voice was strange, uncharacteristically flat, as if she were trying to recount the story without reliving any of the emotions that had accompanied it.

"A few weeks after I threw Simon out of the

apartment, he called up and begged to see me. Stupidly, I said yes. He took me out to dinner at the Plaza, made an abject apology, told me he'd broken it off, and promised never, ever to see her again, then pulled a Tiffany's box with a diamond tennis bracelet out of his pocket.

"I was all over him after that. I couldn't even wait to get back to the apartment to get my hands on him, so we went to the front desk and got a room. The only thing they had was a junior suite, eight hundred dollars for the night. But we got our money's worth. We did it in the bathtub, on the sofa . . . even on top of the minibar. It was amazing. Makeup sex always is. But it also clouds your judgment.

"Two weeks after our orgy at the Plaza, I found out he was seeing another woman—not the yoga instructor, so technically he hadn't broken his promise—that's what he kept screaming at me while I smashed the hood of his car with a baseball bat. He was seeing a different woman—actually, two different women. And when the bills came in a week later, I found out he'd charged the Tiffany's bracelet to my credit card."

I put my hand over my eyes, wishing I could block out the sound of her voice. "Lanie, why are you doing this? I know all about what happened between you and Simon, and I'm sorry for it, but that has nothing to do with Brian and me. We've worked through the worst of our problems. I know we've got more work to do, but everything is going to be fine. And we're more in love than ever. Why can't you just accept that and be happy for me?"

"Because I know how this turns out!" she barked. "And I care too much to just sit idly by and watch you careen over the cliff. Do you know what I did the day *after* I smashed Simon's car with a baseball bat?"

I nodded and moved the phone to my other ear. "You went to Rio for Mardi Gras. I remember because your mother called to say you'd flown off spur of the moment and could I go to your apartment and feed your cat while you were gone."

"Wrong. That's just what my mother said. I was actually in the hospital. After the baseball bat incident," she went on, her voice a little less flat, a little more bitter, "I went home and swallowed a whole bottle of sleeping pills and washed them down with vodka. The only reason I survived is because Mom came over to borrow some earrings and found me. After they pumped my stomach, I spent a week in the psychiatric ward."

My mouth dropped open. I'd had no idea. She'd kept it a secret all these years, even from me.

"Lanie, I . . . I'm so sorry. Why didn't you tell me?"

"Because I was embarrassed!" she snapped. "I felt stupid enough the first time, but to let him make a fool of me a *second* time? And then to try and kill myself over him? No, worse than that—to *fail* to kill myself over him. How pathetic is that?"

She choked out a single, mirthless laugh. "Let me tell you, Gayla, when they break your heart a second time, there's not enough glue on the planet to put Humpty-Dumpty together again. After I got out of the hospital, I adopted a strict one-strike-and-you're-out policy. No man gets a second chance to make a fool of me. Because no man *deserves* a second chance."

"Brian does," I said quietly. "I know you don't think so, but you're wrong. He's genuinely sorry for what he's done. He keeps apologizing, but it's over now. I've forgiven him."

"I don't believe you," she said. "Forgetting to put the milk back in the refrigerator, or even drinking it all and putting the carton back in empty; that you can forgive. Even forgetting your birthday is a forgivable offense. But when they forget they're married? No. That's a bridge too far, my friend. Even for you."

"But I have. I've forgiven him completely."

"If you've been able to forgive him, then why does he feel like he needs to keep apologizing?"

I took in a breath and held it for a moment, not knowing how to answer.

"Be careful, Gayla. I don't want to open the door to your apartment one day to find *you* lying on the floor, unconscious and covered in vomit."

~⊱ 30 ⊰~

Ivy

It was quilt circle night, and once again, we were going on a field trip.

Other than her appearance at Virginia's party, Abigail had been missing in action all summer, busy working on her sabbatical project. We still didn't know what she was up to, only that we would find out tonight.

Abigail had given us instructions to meet at her house promptly at five-thirty, to dress for an evening out and not worry about having dinner beforehand because refreshments would be provided, and to feel free to bring our family members and that she hoped we would. However, she needed to know in advance exactly how many people would be attending. Other than that, we had no inkling of what would be going on that evening.

I'd picked the kids up early from day camp at three and brought them to the shop for the rest of the afternoon. For a while, Bobby drew pictures, mostly of him bowling. Then he played with Virginia's cat, Petunia, before going outside and racing circles around the cobblestone courtyard, pretending he was a NASCAR driver. Bethany, inspired by my most recent project, sat down at one of the workroom sewing machines and started making a crazy patchwork pillow for her bedroom while I cut baby quilt kits.

"I told her she could use scraps and trims from the box of miscuts," I told Evelyn when she came upstairs. "I hope that was all right."

"Of course it is." Evelyn smiled and looked across the room at Bethany, who had her earbuds in and was completely absorbed in her music and sewing. "I can't believe how she's grown. When I first met her she barely came up to my waist, and she was so shy. Hardly had a word to say for herself."

"Oh, that's not a problem anymore," I said. "You should have heard her at the hearing with Judge Dranginis; she had plenty to say. And she wasn't emotional or the least bit nervous. She laid out her facts just like Franklin told her to. She explained to the judge how Hodge had hit her when she was younger, that she had no desire to have further contact with him, that this was her idea, not mine, and that, the way she saw it, it didn't seem right or fair to force her to have contact with her dad just because she was eleven instead of twelve."

Evelyn laughed and pulled up a chair and started assembling kits, taking the patches I'd cut, organizing them into groups, and slipping them into clear plastic bags with a pattern.

"And what did the judge say to that?"

"She asked her a few questions, especially about what had given Bethany the idea to hire Franklin as her lawyer and how she'd gone about doing her legal research—I think she just wanted to make sure Bethany wasn't simply reciting something we'd taught her to say. Then she looked at her, said she'd rarely had the pleasure of hearing an argument stated so clearly and concisely and that if some of the lawyers in town would do the same, justice would be a lot swifter, and then granted her request. Just like that. And just in time."

"You were lucky to get a hearing so quickly," she said, putting aside a finished kit and starting on another.

"That was all Franklin's doing. He was able to convince the court that it was an emergency since Hodge arrives in New Bern next week. I'm *not* looking forward to it," I said. "But it is what it is."

I stepped away from the cutting table and peered through the window down into the court-yard. Bobby was standing on top of one of the brick planters, bowing and waving. Apparently, he'd won the race.

"Bobby's excited, though." I sighed and went back to the table. "He wants a father so much. If Hodge really can be that to him, nobody will be happier than me, but . . . I just don't know."

"Maybe things will be different now," Evelyn

said, trying to stay positive even though her tone was laced with doubt.

"Maybe," I said, my tone matching hers. "He's not a nice man, Evelyn. He never was, but I was too young and stupid to know that when I met him." I shook my head, remembering how gullible I'd been. "I just don't want Bobby to get hurt—emotionally, I mean. The father he's created in his mind is a hero. When he finds out that Hodge isn't, he'll be crushed."

"No," Evelyn said, counting out a stack of five-inch squares. "He'll be disappointed. Nobody gets through life without disappointment. But he won't be crushed. He's tougher than he looks, just like his big sister. They must get it from you."

"I don't know about that," I said, smiling as I bent over the table, lined the ruler up, and sliced through the layers of fabric. "But I do my best."

"Is this the last one?" Evelyn asked.

I shook my head. I needed to finish one more set.

"Charlie and Paul will be here in a few minutes," she said. "I thought we'd all walk over to Abigail's together. The others will meet us there. Gayla said Brian is driving in from the city, so we'll finally get to meet him. Is Dan coming?"

I looked up from my work, surprised by the question. "Abigail said family."

"I know, but you've been seeing him for a while now."

"A month. That doesn't exactly make him family."

Evelyn shrugged. "I'm sure Abbie would have been fine with you bringing him. Madelyn is bringing Jake, and they're not married."

I smiled absently and started layering another stack of fabric. "What do you think this is all about anyway?" I asked, changing the subject.

"I've been trying to figure that out. What could Abigail want to do that she's never done before? She's been just about everywhere and done just about everything."

"She doesn't know how to cook," I offered. "Or she didn't. Maybe she's learned. Maybe she's invited us all over for dinner to show off her skills."

Evelyn lifted her brows. "She took eight weeks to cook us dinner?"

"To *learn* to cook us dinner. It could take a while; she doesn't even know how to scramble an egg. And you know Abbie; she doesn't do anything halfway. She probably enrolled in a course at Le Cordon Bleu or something. We'll be having beef bourguignon and Grand Marnier soufflé for dessert."

"Sounds good to me." She glanced at the clock on the wall and got up from her chair. "You coming downstairs?"

I nodded. "Ten minutes. I just want to finish this kit so Vesta can get it ready to ship tonight. I sent her to the post office to pick up some more boxes."

"How's she working out?"

"Great," I said. "She's reliable, she learns fast, and she's getting more confident every day. I think she's going to make it."

"I'm not surprised," Evelyn said, pausing at the doorway. "She's had a good teacher."

Once again, Abigail had arranged for transportation.

When we arrived at Franklin and Abigail's house, two full-sized Ford vans were sitting in the driveway. Franklin was there to greet us, handing out boxes of cold roast chicken with sides of dill potato salad and fruit, and walnut brownies for dessert. Abigail still didn't know how to cook.

"If she was going to use a caterer," Charlie groused, "why didn't she call the Grill? I've always catered Abigail's parties."

"Because she wanted everything to be a surprise," Franklin said, climbing behind the wheel of one of the vans. "Hop in, everybody. We can eat on the way. There are coolers with drinks in each van. Paul, you want to drive the other vehicle? Margot can sit up front with you."

"Sure," Paul replied and caught the set of keys Franklin tossed to him. "Where are we going?"

"To Sherman," he said, firing up the engine.

"Just follow me. I know the way. I must have driven Abigail there fifty times by now."

Sherman, Connecticut, as it turned out, was the home of the Sherman Players, a community theater founded in 1923 that staged its shows in an old church turned playhouse.

It was opening night for their current production, Oscar Wilde's *The Importance of Being Earnest*, with our own Abigail taking the part of the formidable and haughty dowager, Lady Bracknell. To my surprise, Dr. Streeter was in it, too, playing the part of the Reverend Chasuble.

The play was very entertaining. I was worried about Bobby being able to sit still through an entire play, but he was very well behaved. All the actors were good, but Abigail was excellent and so funny. When she came out for her bow at the end of the show, everyone jumped to their feet and applauded like crazy.

"Wasn't she terrific?" I said to Madelyn, raising my voice so she could hear me over the applause.

"How could she not be?" Madelyn replied. "It was Abigail playing Abigail."

I had to smile at that. She definitely had a point.

After the curtain came down, we all hurried to congratulate Abigail and the rest of the cast at a backstage reception. When she came out of her dressing room, still in her stage makeup but wearing a robe, Franklin gave her a bouquet of roses and a kiss.

"You were wonderful, Abbie! The consummate Lady Bracknell! Better than the woman I saw play the part in London."

"Thank you, darling," she said, returning his kiss. "But I think you might be just a wee bit prejudiced."

"Were you nervous at all?" I asked. "You didn't look it."

"Nervous? I was petrified. At the last minute, the prop master gave me the fan to hold so the audience wouldn't notice how badly my hands were shaking. But once I started in on my lines, I was able to calm down. After a bit, I almost forgot the audience was there. By the second act, I was actually having fun."

"I thought you were just great!" Margot exclaimed. "So did Paul. Do you think you'll do more plays in the future?"

"Oh, *heavens* no!" Abigail exclaimed, pulling her stage fan from the pocket of her robe and waving it in front of her face. "It had been in the back of my mind for years, so I'm glad I finally tried it. But acting takes a lot more work than I realized, and a lot more time. At my age, memorizing lines is a nightmare. I've missed my evenings with all of you, and with Franklin," she said, glancing at her husband, who was standing with the men a few feet away. "It was a lovely sabbatical, but I think I'm ready to get back to real life now."

I moved off so Abigail could greet her other admirers and searched for Dr. Streeter, who was standing at the opposite end of the stage, talking to some other people. When he saw me, he threw his arms wide.

"Ivy! What a pleasure! I had no idea you were coming this evening. You should have told me."

"To tell you the truth, Professor, I didn't know myself."

I explained that I'd come with a group of Abigail's friends and that the whole thing had been a surprise.

"We had no idea that Abigail had been rehearsing a play all these weeks. In fact, I didn't even know there was a play."

"I'm not surprised. Sherman is a bit of a hike from New Bern," he said. "I'm sure I put a thousand miles on the odometer coming back and forth to rehearsals, but I do like to get back on the boards during the summer break, and I knew this would be a fun production. You can't go wrong with Wilde," he intoned. "The script is so comical that it does most of the work for you."

"Well, I thought you were wonderful."

"Thank you. I see you brought your children along," he said, his face brightening as he noticed Bobby and Bethany walking around the stage, investigating the false walls of the set. "Good for you. Children should be exposed to theater at an early age. So what have you been up to this summer?" he asked. "Have you registered for a fall class yet?"

We chatted for a bit. I told him about what was going on in the shop, my failed application for the directorship of New Beginnings, and Virginia's skydiving adventure. That tickled him. The sound of his laughter boomed across the stage.

"Eighty-five, you say!" He craned his neck to catch a glimpse of Virginia on the opposite side of the stage, sitting in a chair someone had brought to her, swinging her legs a bit because they were too short to touch the floor. "That's marvelous! Just marvelous!"

Gayla, whom I hadn't had a chance to talk to yet—she and Brian had ridden in the other van and had been so engrossed in conversation with each other during the intermission that I hadn't wanted to butt in—spotted me across the room, waved, and walked over.

"Congratulations," she said, greeting Dr. Streeter first. "It was a wonderful show. I'm Gayla Oliver, one of Ivy and Abigail's friends."

"Ah," he said, shaking her hand. "One of the quilters. A pleasure to meet you. I'm Dr. Streeter, one of Ivy's professors from the community college."

Gayla's brows lifted as she heard this. "Is that

so? Then I think both you and Ivy will be very interested in my news."

She turned to me. "Ivy, I've found several scholarship possibilities for you, including a brand-new program targeted at single mothers and offered through the Floche-Meyerson Foundation that will not only help pay for your tuition but give you a stipend for living expenses. As it turns out, the director is an old friend of mine from Hunter College. I gave her a call this morning and told her about you. She was very impressed. There are no guarantees, so you still have to fill out the application, but I'd say the chance of you getting the scholarship from them is better than half. There's not enough time to process the application before the fall term, but"—she smiled—"if things work out like I hope they will, you could be enrolled as a full-time student at Carrillon College by January."

"Ivy! That's wonderful news! Congratulations!" Dr. Streeter exclaimed.

But Margot, who had wandered over to join our group in the middle of Gayla's announcement, wasn't quite as enthusiastic.

"Carrillon College. But isn't that in Delaware? You mean you're going to leave New Bern?"

The ride home was segregated by sex. The men, aside from Bobby, who fell asleep on the last row of seats almost as soon as we were out of the parking lot, rode together in one of the vans so they could talk about whatever it is men talk about. The women gathered in the other so they could talk about me. Madelyn was at the wheel and Margot rode shotgun.

"I just don't understand why you didn't tell us about any of this before," Margot said, twisting around in her seat so she could see me better.

"Because when Dr. Streeter brought up the idea at the end of the term, I blew him off. I knew I'd never be able to come up with that kind of money"—I shrugged—"so why talk to anybody about it? I'd probably never have thought about it again if Brad Boyle hadn't been so snotty to me during my interview. After that, I saw that nobody is ever going to hire me to do what I truly want to do until I finish my degree. That's when I decided to talk to Gayla and ask if she could help me find a scholarship."

"What do you truly want to do? You mean you don't like working at the quilt shop?" Margot asked.

The confusion in her wide eyes made me feel instantly guilty, and I rushed to explain. "Of course I do. I love working with all of you, and meeting the customers, and working with the interns. It's a terrific job, but—"

"But you could do so much more," Evelyn said. "Seriously, I mean that. You've done an amazing job in the shop, Ivy. Especially considering where you started. But you could do more good working full-time with abused women. That's why I made you the liaison for the internship program with New Beginnings, because I saw that you had something special to offer."

"So you're saying you want her to go?" Margot asked.

"No. I'd miss her if she left; we all would. I can find someone else to cut quilt kits and fill orders, but I'll never find another friend like Ivy. Still, if we truly care about Ivy, then we should care enough to let her fulfill her potential and do what makes her happy."

Abigail, who was sitting in the next-to-last seat with her arm around Bethany, said, "Evelyn is right. I'll miss Ivy. And, of course," she said softly, looking down at my daughter's head, which was resting in the crook of her arm, "I'd miss the children terribly. But Ivy should have an opportunity to make something of herself and use her talents to benefit others. It'd be awfully selfish of us to wish for her to do anything else, even if it means her leaving."

"I suppose that's true," Margot said, sniffling. "But I'm still going to miss her."

"Stop that," I said. "Come on, Margot. Don't cry. I don't even know if I'm going. I haven't applied to the college *or* for the scholarship. There are no guarantees here. Gayla said that the odds of me getting the money are only about half."

"Better than half is what I said. A little better. But you're right. It's not a guarantee."

Bethany, who had been listening this whole time, twisting a piece of hair around her finger, the way she does when she's nervous, looked up at me. "How long would we be in Delaware?" she asked.

"A year and a half," I said, leaning over the seat so I could see her face. "Two at the most. But you don't have to worry about this right now, Bethy. Like I said, I'm not even sure I'll get the scholarship."

"But if you did," she said, her eyes solemn, "would you go? Would we have to leave New Bern?"

"I don't know," I answered truthfully. "Maybe."

31

Ivy

Bobby and I sat on a pair of molded plastic chairs in the hallway of Sheila Fenton's office, waiting for her to come get Bobby for his first visit with Hodge. Bobby swung his legs back and forth and kept leaning forward and looking down the hall to see if anyone was coming.

I smiled, trying to mask my nervousness. "Excited to see your dad?" I asked.

"Uh-huh. Do you think he's a good bowler?"

"I'm really not sure. You'll have to ask him."

"I bet he is," Bobby said confidently.

Bobby leaned forward yet again, looking toward the far end of the hall. This time the door opened. Sheila Fenton came out, and the sound of her heels clacking against the tile echoed through the tall ceilings of the corridor.

"Ready?" I asked, giving Bobby another smile. He bobbed his head and bit his lower lip. He was nervous too.

"Hello, Bobby," Sheila said, squatting down so she was at his level. Sheila was not happy that the judge had permitted Bethany to forbid contact with Hodge, but she's never let our differences spill over into her relationship with the kids. She's been good with them through this whole process.

"It's nice to see you today. What have you got there?" she asked, pointing to a manila envelope that Bobby was holding.

Bobby looked up at me, his eyes asking me to answer for him. Poor thing. He really was nervous.

"Bobby brought along one of the stories he wrote in school this year and some pictures he drew," I said brightly, looking down at my son, being his voice. "And some pictures of our trip to Cape Cod last year."

"I thought it might help break the ice a little," I said quietly, addressing my words to Sheila.

"Make things a little less awkward starting off."

Sheila smiled as if she meant it. "That was a good idea. Thanks."

"Sure." I gave a quick nod of acknowledgment.

I don't feel hopeful about the odds of Bobby and Hodge developing a good father-son relationship; I just don't think Hodge has it in him. But Bobby wants a dad so much, someone he can count on and look up to, someone who'll show him how to be a man. And because I love Bobby, I want that for him. Just because Hodge was cruel to me doesn't necessarily mean that he'll be that way to Bobby. Maybe, because Bobby is a boy, it will be different with him. I hope so; I really do.

"Bobby," Sheila said, looking into his big eyes, "your father is already waiting for you in the playroom. We're going to go inside in just a minute. Remember what we talked about? Because it's your first time meeting him, this will just be a short visit. I'm going to be in the room with you the whole time, so if you need to—"

There was a noise at the end of the hall, a door being shoved open and banging against the wall, a deep male voice, raised in anger, that made the hair stand up on my neck and my heart start racing, the voice that still invades my dreams sometimes, that lurches me awake, sweating and gasping—Hodge's voice, resonating from the ceilings like a clap of thunder.

"Is this your doing?" he shouted, pounding

across the tile floor with his finger pointing at me. "Are you the reason I can't see my daughter? Did you talk her into hiring that effin' lawyer? Did you?"

Sheila spun around and went into action, meeting Hodge in the middle of the hall, blocking him from getting any closer.

"Mr. Edelman!" she snapped, her voice clear and commanding, like a school principal breaking up a playground brawl. "Mr. Edelman, we talked about this! This is not the time and place to discuss this. You are here to see your son, and if you don't go back inside this *instant*," she declared, standing as straight as an arrow and pointing toward the door, "I will cancel this visit right now and then go back to my office and write a report to the court, explaining why. And if you take one more step toward Ms. Peterman, I'm going to call your probation officer and let him know that you are in violation of your restraining order, which also means that you'd be in violation of parole. Do I make myself clear? Mr. Edelman?"

Hodge was silent but restless, shifting his weight from one foot to the other, glaring at me over the top of Sheila's head, as if he was a tiger and she was the bars of a cage that separated him from his next meal. Bobby, who had been gripping my hand as tight as he could, moved behind me, peering around me at Hodge's face, his eyes wide. I reached my arm out and rested my hand protectively on his head.

After a moment, Hodge took a step back, apparently deciding to heed Sheila's warning.

"This is bullshit!" he spat, looking at Sheila and then lifting his eyes to me with a murderous glare. "Complete bullshit!" He pointed at me again, then stomped back down the hall and through the door, slamming it behind him.

When he was gone, I started to breathe again.

"It's okay," I said evenly, stroking Bobby's head with my hand. "I'm right here."

In spite of my protests, which I delivered to Sheila in a conference room while Bobby waited in the hall, the visit between Bobby and Hodge did take place that day.

"Look," Sheila said, leaning both her hands on top of the table, "I know that was upsetting for both of you, but I don't want to postpone. If we put this off another week, it's just going to mean Bobby has a week to think about what happened just now and feel more nervous about it. I want him to see his dad today, even if it's just for a few minutes, to give him a chance to see Hodge when he's not out of control. That's the best chance we'll have for getting this off on the right foot and helping him build a long-term bond with his father."

"You really think that's going to happen

now?" I said, crossing my arms over my chest.

"I don't know," she said, straightening up. "But I know we should try."

I sat in one of the plastic chairs, waiting for Bobby to come out of the playroom, fiddling with my phone, trying to balance my checkbook but giving up when I kept adding the numbers up wrong, drumming my fingers against my leg. It was a long half hour.

By prior agreement, Hodge was to stay in the building until Bobby and I were gone, so when Bobby came through the door at the end of the hallway, only Sheila was with him. When he saw me, he let go of her hand and came running down the hall toward me, wrapping his arms around my legs.

"Hi, Mommy."

I bent down and kissed the top of his head. "Hi, Bear. How did it go?"

He shifted his shoulders up and down. "Okay," he said, his face giving away nothing.

And then after a moment: "Do you think Dan would still want to be my partner for the bowling tournament?"

❧ 32 ❧

Gayla

On Thursday morning, as soon as I put the last of the breakfast dishes in the dishwasher, the phone rang. I sighed heavily, thinking it was Lanie again. I really wasn't in the mood to talk to her. But when I looked at the screen, I saw it was Brian, so, of course, I picked up right away.

"Hi, sweetheart. You're up early. I was going to call you later. A new restaurant just opened in Bantam, Al Tavolo. It's supposed to be very good. Everybody's been talking about it. Do you want me to see if I can get us a table for Saturday night?"

"It sounds great, but, darling, I'm sorry . . . I won't be able to come up after all. We've run into some problems with the Fordham acquisition. I have to fly to LA for a few days. I'm leaving this afternoon."

"What kind of problems?"

"Oh, just . . . some financial issues." He paused, coughed, and then came back on the line. "Sorry. I think I'm coming down with a cold. Anyway, it seems the CFO may have been cooking the books. I've got to get out there and deal with it as quickly as possible. I'm sorry to have to cancel our plans."

"That's all right," I said, trying hard to sound as if I meant it. "You haven't traveled for more than a month. I knew it couldn't last forever. Though I sort of hoped it might."

"I know. Me too. But listen, let's do it next weekend, all right?"

"All right," I said. "Sure."

"Brilliant. It's a date. Listen, darling, I've got to run. I haven't packed yet, and my flight leaves in three hours. I'll call you tomorrow. Love you!"

"Okay. Love you too."

I put down the phone, picked up a sponge, ran it under some water, and started wiping down the counters, trying to just go on with my morning as if nothing had happened. But something had happened. Brian was leaving town, and very suddenly.

My heart started fluttering. Little beads of sweat started popping out on my forehead, and I could feel a knot forming in the pit of my stomach. For a moment, I thought I might throw up. The anxiety I had become so familiar with during my first days in New Bern was back.

"Stop this," I said, scolding myself aloud. "He just has to go out of town. It's part of his job. It's *always* been part of his job. You knew he'd have to go back on the road eventually."

True. But, why did he have to go so suddenly? Why hadn't he said something to me before? And he'd been so vague about his reasons for leaving, chalking it up to just "financial issues." And then, when I'd asked for more specifics, he'd hesitated, even started to cough, before answering me. Was he really coming down with something, or had he just been buying himself a little time to come up with a plausible answer, something to cover a lie?

Again, I told myself to stop it, that everything was fine and that I was being silly. He wouldn't do that to me again. He'd told me he was sorry ten times, fifty times, and sworn it would never happen again. He'd *promised*.

I paced around the kitchen for a while, then went outside, got out the hoses, and started watering, but being in the garden didn't calm me, not like it usually does. I went inside and got out my crazy quilt, trying to force myself not to think or ask questions, just to focus on each individual stitch, but that was no good either. Inside of five minutes, my thread was a knotted mess, probably because my hands were shaking.

I went upstairs and opened the bottom drawer of the dresser. Since Brian was coming up regularly on weekends, he'd started leaving some things here. I tore through the pile of clothes, checking every pocket, searching for something that would either reveal his dishonesty or convince me he was telling the truth, but found nothing. I opened the closet, checked the pockets of his jacket, but didn't find anything except a receipt for gas and a ticket stub from the movie theater. I even went through his drawer in the bathroom, actually pulled out the whole thing and turned it upside down, dumping everything out on the counter. The only things I found were his toothpaste, toothbrush, several razor blades, vitamin packets, boxes of allergy medication, some bandages, and forty-three cents in change.

I went back downstairs and paced some more, then picked up the phone and dialed Tessa. She'd been through this before. She'd be able to talk me down from the ledge. After a few rings, her recorded voice came on the line, saying she wasn't home and to please leave her a message. I couldn't think of what to say, not without sounding like a complete basket case, so I pressed the end button on my cell.

I started to dial Lanie but changed my mind. Lanie would spring into action at any sign of doubt. She'd feed my anxiety and make it grow so large there'd be no way I could pull back. I couldn't talk to Lanie, not unless I had proof of Brian's deception. Where could I find that? How could I be sure? Who could I talk to?

Wait. I knew exactly who.

I hadn't called in so long. Was the number scribbled in one of my notebooks on my desk at the apartment? Or had I thought to enter it into my contact list?

I had. There it was.

"Stern and Rossman Travel. This is Emily."

"Hi, Emily. This is Gayla Oliver. I'm supposed to be picking Brian up from the airport next week but I can't find the flight information. I think I accidentally deleted it. Can you give it to me? Brian's in a meeting, and I don't want to interrupt him."

"Sure, Mrs. Oliver. I think someone else booked his ticket, but I can find the information in the computer."

I waited for a moment, barely remembering to breathe as she searched for it, the sound of fingernails clicking the keys of the keyboard coming faintly through the phone.

"Sorry for the delay. Here it is. He'll arrive at JFK on Tuesday at two forty-five. United flight number one-six-oh-four from Indianapolis."

"Indianapolis?"

My throat was tight. It felt like my heart had skipped a beat. The company headquarters was in Indianapolis. So was the other woman, Deanna.

"That's where the flight originates? It's not a connection from Los Angeles?"

"No," Emily said slowly, sounding a little confused by the question. "He's flying directly to Indianapolis today and directly back to New York on Tuesday. We don't have any other flights booked for him."

"Oh . . . I see. I must have misunderstood his plans. Thank you, Emily."

"Thank you, Mrs. Oliver. Is there anything else I can help you with today?"

"No. No, that's all. Thanks."

I pressed the end button, closed my eyes, and clutched the phone tight against my breast.

Lanie was right. It was even worse the second time.

❧ 33 ☙

Gayla

After pulling myself together, I had called Lanie. Then I called Libby Burrell. The plan was in place.

When Brian exited the airport terminal on Tuesday, a man would be waiting in baggage claim to serve him with divorce papers.

"And you're *sure* he'll be checking a bag?" Libby asked.

"Yes. Brian hates fussing with rollaboards and fighting for space in the overhead bin. And for anything longer than an overnight, he prefers a bigger suitcase."

"Well, it's lucky for us that he'll be gone a few days. We need time to fill out the paperwork and get our ducks in a row. Now, when do you think you'll be able to wire the retainer?"

"Soon," I said. "I have to move some money around and cash in a couple of investments. I'll make the deposit to the firm's account by Monday afternoon."

"Good. Just so we have it before Tuesday. Well, I think that's it for now," she said in a "let's wrap this up" tone. "I'm due in court, but before I go, how are you holding up?"

"I'm fine," I replied, lying through my teeth. "Trying to stay busy. Lanie is going to come up next Friday to help me close the house. I need to get back to the city and drum up some new clients."

Mostly so I could pay my attorney's bills, but I didn't say that to Libby.

"Good," she said. "At a time like this, working hard is the best thing. Keeps you from thinking too much. Gotta run. But if you need anything, just pick up the phone. I'm here for you, Gayla. You can count on me."

She hung up before I could say "thank you."

I didn't go to quilt circle on Friday night; I was just too depressed to see anyone. After baring my soul to my circle friends and then going on about how great everything had been going the last few weeks, even letting them meet Brian at Abigail's opening night and then listening to them tell me how handsome he was and how happy they were that things had worked out, how they admired me for sticking it out, I just couldn't face them. It would be too humiliating.

However, I did phone Tessa on Friday to explain why I wouldn't be there. She'd been my confidante and cheerleader during the last several weeks. Even though it was difficult to tell her she'd been cheering for a losing team, I felt like I owed her an explanation. Besides, if I failed to show up for quilt circle on Friday without letting them know why, I knew my phone would be ringing off the hook on Saturday morning. Some of them might even show up unannounced, bringing chicken soup, worried that I was sick. They're very good at rallying around one another in times of distress. That, too, was part of why I didn't want to see them. In the face of kindness, I knew I would fall apart, and right now, I couldn't afford to do that.

"Oh, Gayla," Tessa said, "I'm so sorry. Are you all right? Do you want me to come over?"

"No, no. I'm all right, holding it together," I said as I spotted a ceramic fragment peeking out from under the lip of the cabinet and bent down to pick it up.

Apparently, I had missed that piece when sweeping up the teapot I'd hurled against the wall earlier that day. Either I'd have to learn to restrain myself or make a trip to Goodwill and buy another box of cheap dishes, specifically for smashing. But it was too late to save my mother's teapot—or Brian's birthday quilt.

In a way, I felt even worse about that than the teapot. It wasn't a family heirloom, but it might have been. Had things worked out the way I'd hoped, that quilt might have become a symbol of all we'd endured and triumphed over, the patch-work blocks a reminder of how we'd patched our marriage back together, taking the scraps of our torn relationship and stitching them into new and beautiful patterns.

Instead, and after all that painstaking work, my quilt was a ravaged mess.

Smashing the teapot had done little to calm my ire. When I stormed out of the kitchen in search of my cigarettes—I hadn't smoked one in close to two weeks, but I knew there was half a pack hidden somewhere—my eyes fell upon the dining table and my nearly completed quilt top, lying next to my sewing machine. I snatched it up and, without thinking, tore off one of the borders, the breaking threads popping violently asunder as I pulled the seams in opposite directions. I tore off a second border as well, one of the setting triangles, and then the diagonal seam in the center of the six strips of blocks. That seam didn't separate as easily as the border had—the popping sound stopped halfway down the strip—so I tore another seam, and another after that, until my beautiful quilt was shredded into distorted ribbons clinging to the last remaining border, like the tattered battle flag of a defeated army.

Seeing it like that, realizing what I had done and what it meant, took some of the steam out of my anger. I picked up the torn remains of my quilt, folded it as best I could, and shoved it onto a shelf of the linen closet, my feelings of anger replaced by deep sadness.

I dropped the ceramic shard into the trash can and switched the phone to my other ear. "I'm going to be busy for the next few days anyway," I told Tessa. "I've got to pack up and close the house, then go back to the city and figure out what my life looks like without Brian. I've been hiding up here long enough. It's time to go home and face facts," I said, wishing I'd done that in the first place. It would have saved me a lot of additional misery. "Will you say good-bye to the others for me?"

"You mean you're not even going to see them before you go?"

"I really can't," I said, feeling guilty but standing firm. "Maybe I'll see them later in the fall, when I come back up to put the cottage on the market."

"I can't believe you're going to sell the cottage—especially after all the work you put into the garden. You love that house, Gayla."

"I do. But my business is in the city and a

second home just isn't in my budget anymore. We'll have to sell our apartment, too, and I'll have to find someplace cheaper to live. I've got a lot on my plate right now, Tessa."

"Gayla," she said gently after a moment's silence, "are you sure you want to do this? Shouldn't you at least *talk* to Brian first? Maybe there's some explanation."

"Oh, I know what the explanation is," I said bitterly. "He lied to me. He said he was going to Los Angeles on business. Instead, he's in Indianapolis with *her*. I'm done, Tessa. He lied and he broke his promise. That's all I need to know."

After she asked once again if I was sure I didn't want her to come over and I said no but thanks for offering, we said good-bye.

I didn't see her that day, but when I stepped out onto the porch on Saturday morning, I found a cardboard box sitting next to the door. Inside were two presents. One, a terrarium filled with herbs planted inside a miniature glass greenhouse with a top that lifted up so you could clip fresh herbs for cooking, was from Tessa. The handwritten card attached to it said . . .

Thought you'd like taking a little piece of New Bern back to the city. A little piece of you will always be with me.
Much love, Tessa

The second gift, which came in a Cobbled Court Quilt Shop canvas tote bag, was a collection of fabric. Each member of the circle had chosen two half yards to include in the bag: batiks from Ivy, florals from Tessa and Margot, a paisley and a stripe from Evelyn, cream-colored background fabrics from Philippa, polka dots from Madelyn, and two novelty prints with little airplanes from Virginia. There was also a packet of needles, a pincushion, a pair of embroidery scissors, a packet of lace dragonflies, and some beautiful glass buttons, also decorated with dragonflies.

The card said . . .

With much love from your Circle Sisters. Thanks for a great sabbatical, and don't forget to keep yourself in stitches!

They'd all signed their names at the bottom.

I sat down on the steps and spread that beautiful fabric out on my lap, looking at each piece, thinking about each woman who had chosen it for me. My throat felt tight, but I didn't cry. In fact, I smiled.

I was sorry that my marriage was ending this way, sorry I'd let Brian make a fool of me yet again, but I wasn't sorry I'd come to New Bern.

In a lot of ways, it had been one of the best summers I'd ever known. I had tried new things, developed new interests, made new friends, found deeper faith in myself and even in God. No, I wasn't quite ready to join a church and sign up to teach Sunday school, but I couldn't help but feel that somehow this sojourn to New Bern had been of His doing, a season of rest to strengthen me for what lay ahead, and that He had put these women in my path so I'd understand what real friendship looked like and how much it mattered.

Folding up the fabric and putting it back in the bag, I decided that I would see my friends again in the fall and ask if I could be a sort of adjunct member of the Cobbled Court Quilt Circle. I could drive up here one Friday night per month; it wasn't that far from the city.

And when I got back home, maybe I'd look for a quilt circle to join there. Since there was a really good quilt shop in New York, there were probably some really good quilt circles too. It just stood to reason. And if there weren't, I'd start my own. I could do that, even if I wasn't an expert quilter. I knew how to be a friend now. It seemed to me that was the most important part.

I got to my feet and picked up my presents, smiling as I peered through the glass walls of the terrarium and saw that Tessa had even included a tiny lavender plant among the herbs. How cute. This would be perfect sitting on the kitchen windowsill in my apartment. Or wherever I landed after the divorce.

I opened the door to go inside but stopped when I heard a car coming up the driveway.

Still smiling, I quickly put the presents down on the kitchen table and went back outside, thinking that Tessa, or maybe the whole circle, after quietly leaving their offerings on my doorstep, had decided to ignore my request for privacy and come over anyway. I was glad. I really wouldn't have felt right about leaving without saying good-bye.

But the car that emerged from behind the hedge didn't belong to Tessa or any other member of the quilt circle. It was a rental car with New York plates and Brian was driving.

What was he doing here? He wasn't supposed to be back until Tuesday. But here he was, mucking up my plans, making my life hard. As usual. What should I do? Pretend that nothing had happened and then surprise him with the divorce papers on Tuesday? Or tell him the truth, here and now?

I decided on the latter.

He jumped out of the car with a smile on his face and a bouquet of pink roses in his hand. "Surprised? I was able to wrap things up earlier than I thought. I came straight from the airport. There's something I want to talk to you about."

"That makes two of us."

I stood at the top step and crossed my arms over

my chest. Brian stopped short, trading his smile for a frown.

"What's wrong? Did something happen?"

"Yes. You lied to me. You said you were going to Los Angeles, but you really flew to Indianapolis to see Deanna. So yes. Something happened. I don't know the details, but I can make a pretty good guess."

His jaw dropped, and for a moment, he just stood there staring at me, speechless. Good. Let him stand there and experience what it felt like to be blindsided.

"I know what's going on, Brian. I know where you've been and what you've been doing, and I've had enough. I've called a lawyer. On Tuesday, I'll be serving you with divorce papers."

"What?" he shouted, throwing out his hands, one of which still held the roses. "You can't be serious!"

"I am deadly serious, Brian! I'm not putting up with this anymore. I'm not going to just sit here and do nothing while you—"

"You have no idea what you're talking about, Gayla," he barked, talking right over me. "No bloody idea!

"Yes," he said through clenched teeth, "I lied to you about going to Los Angeles. Yes, I was in Indianapolis. Do you know why? Because three weeks ago, I told Mike Barrows that I wanted a demotion—"

"A demotion? Why would you ask for a demotion?"

"So I could spend more damned time with you!"

He threw the flowers down so hard that the plastic sleeve they'd come in split, scattering roses across the grass.

"I thought that my job, that all the travel, is part of what caused us to drift apart, so I decided to ask for a demotion. I told Barrows that I'd take anything, even go back to my old sales job in Manhattan, as long as it didn't involve my being on the road more than one week a month.

"On Thursday morning, he called me back and said he had a new job for me with less travel and to come to Indianapolis right away. I wanted to tell you about it, but I thought it best to wait until everything was settled because I knew what would happen if I told you I was going to Indianapolis; I knew you'd act just like this!"

Oh, no. My cheeks went hot with shame as I realized the magnitude of my mistake and that he'd read me exactly right. He *should* have told me, but he didn't because he knew I'd go off the deep end. That was exactly what I'd done, dove headfirst into a pool of erroneous suspicions.

"Oh, Brian. I'm really—"

"When I got to Indianapolis," Brian went on, his tone clipped and angry, "Barrows informed me that he was granting my request for a demotion and putting me in charge of marketing in the New York office."

"So you've got a new job in the city?"

"No," he said sharply. "I don't. Because Deanna—yes, *that* Deanna—also happens to work in marketing, and they're transferring her to New York. I told Mike that I couldn't work in the same office with her and asked him to find me another position, any position. Even if it meant we had to move. I wasn't sure how you'd feel about moving, but I supposed you'd prefer that to my working with Deanna."

He shoved his hands in his pockets, sighed, and looked around, taking in the trees and grass and gardens. "And I thought maybe they'd send us someplace more rural, maybe even someplace like this, where you could have a garden. I thought you'd like that. I thought I might like it too."

"Well, yes," I said quickly. "I'd have to do something about my clients, but I could figure out a way to work remotely, maybe just go to New York once or twice a month for meetings. Or I could start over someplace else. It might take a while to build up my client list, but sure. If they want to move you out of state, I'm willing to do that."

"Except they're not," Brian said grimly. "Barrows told me there was no other position and that, even if there were, he wouldn't give it to me. He said that my work had slipped, that I'd missed the conference in Las Vegas and that the

Fordham deal was looking shaky because I hadn't been paying attention. I told him that if the Fordham deal was looking shaky, it was because the company was shaky, that we shouldn't be buying it and I'd told him so from the first.

"And then he reminded me of what he'd told me three years ago, that at Ellison-Farley, you're either moving up or getting out. There were no other options. And then he fired me. So I got on a plane, flew back to New York, and came out here."

"He fired you! After all these years? Oh, sweetheart."

I started to come down the steps to comfort him, but Brian lifted his hands to stop me.

"Don't! Just don't. I've had about all the drama I can take for one day, Gayla. I really have."

He gave a wry little laugh and shoved his hands back in his pockets, shaking his head. He started to pace back and forth across a little patch of grass, heedlessly stepping on the roses, crushing them beneath his shoes, looking down, but clearly not seeing anything. It was as if I wasn't even there and he was talking to himself.

"Do you know what's really funny about this? I was so mad after Barrows fired me. I was well and truly ticked. But by the time I got to the airport, I felt better. I hated working for Mike. He's a wanker, always was. And I hadn't been happy at Ellison-Farley for years, not since the merger. It wasn't the same company after that.

During the flight, I started to think that maybe things weren't so bad after all, that maybe this was a blessing in disguise. Yes, it was probably going to strain us financially, but we'd figure it out. They gave me a year's severance—they sort of had to considering how long I'd worked there. That should be enough to help us get by until I found another job. Or, I thought, maybe it'd be enough so I could start over, do something new, something I actually enjoyed."

He stopped and lifted his head to look at me.

"By the time I got to New York, I had decided that getting fired was probably the best thing that had happened to me in a long time. I thought about sending Barrows flowers, but instead, I bought some for you and drove out here as fast as I could. Because I thought that, together, we'd figure it all out."

"And we will," I said quietly. "We still can."

Brian pressed his lips into a line, standing perfectly still for a long, long moment before speaking.

"I have bent over backward trying to make up for what I did to you, Gayla. I've done absolutely everything I could think of to earn your forgiveness and regain your trust. And I thought I had. But I was wrong. This entire exercise was completely pointless."

"That's not true, Brian. I have forgiven you. If you had just—"

"No, you haven't. Because if you had," he said, his voice rising again, "then you would have talked to me, given me the benefit of the doubt. Instead, you got a lawyer!"

He shook his head again, frowning. "I shouldn't have lied to you," he said, sounding almost as angry with himself as he was with me, "but I was honestly trying to protect you. And you lied to me, too, you know. You promised me that you wouldn't make any further moves toward a divorce until the end of the summer and that if you *did* start having doubts, you'd talk to me about them first. You said you were capable of forgiving me and making a fresh start, Gayla. But it wasn't true. It was never true."

He turned away and started walking to the car.

"Where are you going?" I asked, following behind him.

"Back to New York," he said, opening the car door.

"Don't go, Brian. Please don't. I'm sorry. Come inside. Let's talk about this."

"I can't do this right now, Gayla. I've had enough."

He turned on the ignition, backed the car up, and started heading down the driveway. I ran after him; I couldn't stop myself.

But it was too late. By the time I got to the road, he was gone.

ᴇ𝑔 34 𝑔ᴇ

Ivy

Bethany plucked a grape from the fruit bowl and popped it into her mouth. "Well?" she said, propping her elbow up on the coffee table and resting her chin in her hand. "Are you making a guess or not?"

"Hang on a minute. I'm thinking. Okay," I said after a moment, "I've got it now."

"You sure?"

"Absolutely. Miss Scarlet in the drawing room with the candlestick."

Bethany opened one end of a miniature manila envelope and peeped inside. "It was the rope."

"Darn it!" I said, and smacked my knee. "I hate this game."

"Well, you're better at Clue than Candy Land. But you kind of suck at that too."

"I do not!"

I grabbed a pillow from the sofa and tossed it at Bethany's head. Giggling, she ducked, and it sailed right past her.

"Okay, maybe I do," I admitted and took a sip from a glass of iced tea. "Do you want to play again?"

I really hoped the answer was no. I've never

been very good at board games, but the kids love them. And since Bobby was out bowling with Dan, giving Bethany and me a rare "girls only" night, I'd said she could pick any game she wanted. I am better at Clue than Candy Land, but not a lot.

"I don't feel like it right now," she said. "Can we quilt instead?"

"Sure," I replied as I got up from the sofa. "That's something I never say no to."

We each went to our rooms to retrieve our project bags, then met back in the living room, putting our needles and notions on the coffee table and then settling in on the sofa.

Bethany had finished sewing her "crazy" pillow top on the machine but was adding embroidery and embellishments by hand. I was nearly finished with my crazy quilt wall hanging; at least I thought I was. I'd actually been saying that for a couple of weeks, but then I'd discover another embroidery stitch that I thought might look neat to add to one particular seam or find a scrap of ribbon that would look pretty made into a flower. That's the thing about crazy quilting; you almost can't overdo it. Almost. But I thought I might be getting close.

The last thing I'd decided to add to my quilt was a button tree. In my very first attempt at needle-turn appliqué, I appliquéd a tree trunk on the lower left quarter of the quilt. It turned out pretty well, if I do say so myself. One of the things I like about taking my time and quilting by hand is that I tend to catch my mistakes early on, so if I don't like the way something looks, I just pull out a few stitches and try again.

Once the tree trunk was appliquéd onto the quilt top, I took some of the dark-brown yarn I'd unraveled from Bobby's old bear hat and couched it along the length of the trunk, stitching it to the lighter brown fabric to give it a bark-like look. Then I got out my button box and started sewing on buttons of all different colors and sizes above the trunk where the leaves should be. Of course, those buttons look nothing like real leaves. They were more like children's drawings of leaves, cheerful and whimsical.

For a while, we just sewed without speaking, enjoying each other's company and the breeze coming from the fan that I'd placed in front of the open screen door. The temperatures had been up in the mid-nineties all day, so I'd opened the front and back doors to let the air circulate through the house.

Bethany finished stitching a pink daisy onto her pillow top and then reached for another color thread. "Mom, do you *want* to move to Delaware?"

Ah. I'd been wondering when she'd bring that up. I knew she'd been thinking about it ever since the night of Abigail's play, but she hadn't said anything and neither had I, even though I'd been thinking about it too. One thing I know about my daughter is that there's no point in trying to make her talk about something until she's good and ready.

I tied off my thread, snipped it, and laid the quilt on my lap to give her my full attention.

"It's not that I want to move to Delaware or anywhere else. But I want to make a good life for us, and it'll be easier to do that if I finish my degree."

"But we already have a good life. I like living in New Bern. We don't know anybody in Delaware."

"I know. I like living here too. We've made good friends here."

"Wouldn't you miss them? And what about Dan? Wouldn't you miss him? I think he'd miss you."

Her question, as well as her observation, took me by surprise. I reached for another button and threaded my needle again, giving myself time to figure out how to answer. "Dan and I are friends—good friends, I think—but that—"

"I really like him," she interrupted. "So does Bobby. We think he'd be a good husband."

We? Had she and Bobby talked about this?

"Dan is a nice man," I said, choosing my words carefully. "I like him a lot. And I think he likes me too. But we haven't known each other very long, Bethy. And I just think that . . ."

I hesitated, not sure how to explain to her that time wasn't the only thing that made me hesitant about developing a deeper relationship with Dan.

At that moment, the whole concept of marriage was a question mark in my mind. I had my children, friends, and a fulfilling life. What did I need to get married for? Yes, I was lonely sometimes. And yes, sometimes I felt a great void in my life, but who didn't? Who goes through life completely fulfilled? And really, considering the risks and the potential for pain, was marriage worth it?

I put a knot in the end of my thread and started sewing on another button. "Well, I just think it's better not to rush. These things take time."

"But," she said, spreading her hands, "how are you going to get the time if we go to Delaware? Don't you *want* to be in love?"

Wow. I didn't see that one coming. Kids really have a way of cutting to the chase, don't they?

Did I want to be in love?

When I was younger, I'd have said yes without a moment of hesitation. But I wasn't younger now, and love had turned out to be a lot more complicated than I'd thought it would be. And it wasn't always easy to know when you'd found it.

Look at Gayla. Even after her husband cheated on her, she'd agreed to try again, to work out their problems. When I saw the two of them together at the play, I truly believed they had.

I hadn't talked to Brian much that night, but I'd watched him. He'd seemed so devoted to Gayla. He held her hand during the play, brought her a glass of soda during the intermission, helped her get into her sweater when it was time to go. And when he looked at her, it was with such . . . I don't know how to describe it exactly, but he had the same expression in his eyes that Dan did that night at the bowling alley, the look that took my breath away and scared me so much that I'd made myself pull back from him, frightened of where a look like that might be leading. Until a few days ago, I might have described it as love, but now, I wasn't so sure. If the expression on Brian Oliver's face had been the look of true love, how could he have cheated on her again?

Did I want to be in love? Even after all I've been through, the answer is still yes. But only if I could be sure that the person I'd fallen in love with shared my feelings and could be trusted absolutely. But, honestly, I'm not sure if that's possible.

"I think everyone wants to be in love, Bethy. But it's not the only thing I want," I said truthfully. "I want to do something meaningful with my life, to make the world a little bit better."

She frowned a bit, as if she was trying to make sense of my words. "You've made the world better being our mom," she said, so simply that I had to swallow to keep my eyes from tears. "And

413

you've made the world better for a lot of people in New Bern, too—Vesta and all those people who come to work with you in the quilt shop. And your friends, too—Aunt Abigail and Evelyn and Margot and Virginia. You've helped them a lot. Why can't you just keep doing that? You don't need a college degree to know how to help people. You're already pretty smart."

"Thanks, honey. I do think I've helped people at the quilt shop, but if I had more education, I could help even more people and do it in ways that I can't right now."

She still looked unconvinced, so I tried another tack.

"Bethy, remember how Uncle Franklin was able to help you with the judge? He was able to do that because he went to school to learn how to be a good lawyer. He was always a smart man, but he had to get the right kind of training to be able to do the kind of work he really loved and to be able to help people like you. If I can get my degree, I'll be able to help women who are in trouble, some who might even be in terrible danger, the way that Donna Walsh and the people she works with helped me when I was in danger. I think that's very important, and I think I'd be good at it."

Bethany lifted her thumb to her mouth and chewed on her nail, thinking. "And that's what you want more than anything?" she asked after a moment's consideration.

"No," I said. "The thing I want more than anything is for you and Bobby to be happy, so if leaving New Bern, even for just a couple of years, would make you unhappy, then we won't go. And, hey, I might not even get the scholarship. That's all right too. I can always keep on taking one class at a time, the way I have been."

"But then it would take you a long time to graduate, right?"

"About nine or ten years. Hey! I've got an idea," I said in a teasing voice. "Maybe you and I could have our graduation parties at the same time!"

Bethany rolled her eyes and laughed. "That's a terrible idea," she said, and then, after a pause, became serious.

"Mom, if you get that scholarship, I think you ought to go for it."

"Yeah? Even if it meant leaving New Bern for a while?"

She nodded.

"But," she said, adding a caveat, "*only* if we can come back during the summers. I love summer in New Bern."

"So do I. Come here, punkin," I said, lifting up one of my arms. She smiled and scooted across the sofa for a hug. "You're an amazing kid—do you know that?"

I kissed her on top of her head. "It's so hot. You know what I think we should do? I think we should go outside and run through the sprinkler."

Bethany's head popped up, her eyes wide. "Really? Even though it's getting dark?"

"Really. Come on. Last one to get on their swimsuit is a rotten egg!"

Five minutes later, we were outside, running across the wet grass in our bare feet, having a great time. It was dusk rather than dark; the August sun was taking its time slipping over the horizon, and clouds of fireflies flickered in the sultry summer air.

At first, we simply ran through the water, hopping across the sprinkler head, enjoying the feeling of the cool spray on our hot skin. But then Bethany started to get silly, picked up the sprinkler and chased me with it. Laughing, I grabbed it away from her, unscrewed the sprinkler from the hose, and sprayed it right at her in retaliation. Her screeches of protest blended with waves of giggling; she was literally doubled over with laughter.

"Mom, stop it! I'm serious. Quit! You're making me laugh so hard I'm going to pee my pants! Mom!" she hooted as she straightened up, holding her hands up to stave off the spray of water.

But then her expression changed, her smile disintegrated, and her eyes went wide. Her voice changed, too, becoming suddenly concerned, then alarmed. "Mom? Mommy!"

I turned around to see what was scaring her and saw Hodge, standing not fifteen feet from us with that expression I remembered so well, the smoldering glare that came just before the explosion. But he didn't explode. He just stood there.

I could feel Bethany shift to her left, moving behind me. For a moment, I considered telling her to run inside and call the police, but Hodge was standing between us and the door, and though he looked furious, he still hadn't made a move toward us. I wanted to keep it that way.

I let the hose drop from my hand and felt the cold water start pooling into the indentations of the wet sod. "You can't be here. I have a restraining order," I said, trying to keep my voice strong.

His lip curled. "Yeah? Well, you know what you can do with your restraining order?" he asked, and then gave a vivid answer. "I'm here to see my daughter. I have a *right* to see my daughter. But *you've* poisoned her against me!" he shouted. "You told her a bunch of lies about me and—"

"I didn't tell her anything about you. She *knows* about you, and she's scared of you. Look at her! She's scared of you, Hodge! And it's because of crap like this!"

"I want to see my daughter," he growled. "I have a right."

"She has rights too. You need to leave, Hodge. You need to go now."

Twin beams of light swept across the lawn: the headlights from Dan's truck. I felt an enormous sense of relief, but it was fleeting.

If Dan jumped out of the truck to rescue me, pounding across the grass to save the day by beating the stuffing out of Hodge, it would be putting a lit match next to a keg of gunpowder. Hodge had always been incredibly jealous. It wasn't the natural jealousy that comes with love and affection, the desire to stand first in the heart of someone you truly care about, but the jealousy born of the need to possess and control another human being. When we were married, if any man got within fifty miles of me, no matter who he might be, or if I so much as looked sideways at another man, Hodge would fly into a murderous rage.

I closed my eyes for a moment, praying that Dan had more sense than my former husband, that he'd keep his head cool and his testosterone in check.

The truck door opened. Dan climbed out and ambled toward us. Bobby stayed where he was, staring through the window with big eyes.

"Hi. Something going on here?"

Dan was looking at me. So was Hodge. He curled his fingers into a fist, but still, he didn't move.

"Who's this? Your boyfriend? Bobby told me about him. Boy, you just couldn't wait until I was out of the way, could you? Slut."

"Don't you call her that!" Bethany shouted, shifting back to the right. "Don't call her names!"

I twisted my neck so I could see her and said softly, "It's okay, baby. Just stay behind me, all right?" When she complied, I turned around again and spoke to Hodge. "Dan is a friend of mine."

"I'll bet."

Dan had moved into a position on the opposite side of Hodge, about the same distance from him as I was. "You seem pretty upset," he said calmly, "but there's nothing to be gained in this."

He pulled his cell phone from the pocket of his jeans so Hodge could see it.

"I know Ivy has a restraining order against you. If I dial 911 right now, the police are going to show up, clap you in cuffs, and take you back to jail. I don't think you want that to happen, particularly with your son watching. I don't want that either."

Hodge snapped his head toward Dan, and when he did, in the light that came from the porch, I could see there were tears in his eyes.

"What do you know about it? What do you know about my son?"

"I know he's a really nice kid," Dan said evenly. "I know that he'd like to get to know you better, but right now, you're making that kind of hard.

You coming over here when you're not supposed to, yelling at his mother, and calling her filthy names isn't going to do anything but drive him away. Understand? I think you should leave now before things get any worse."

Hodge looked at Bobby, still sitting in the car with the window rolled up, then at Bethany, who was half-hidden behind me. The light was getting dimmer, and it was harder to see his eyes, but it seemed to me that he was actually thinking over what Dan had said.

After a moment, and to my shock, his fist unclenched, and his hand dropped to his side. "All right," he said.

And then, not to me but to Bethany, he said, "I'm sorry."

He started walking away, down the driveway and around the corner, his shoulders drooping. For a minute, I almost felt sorry for him. But I was also happy to see him go.

When he was gone, Bethany started to cry, and so did I. Relief, I suppose. Dan came toward us, crossing the now muddy grass with big, manly strides, oblivious to the fact that his shoes were being ruined, and hugged us both, wrapping one arm around my shoulders and using the other to squeeze Bethany, who was clinging to him for all she was worth.

"You okay?" he asked anxiously. "Did he hurt you?"

I shook my head and sniffled. "No. I honestly think he was trying not to."

"Do you want me to call the police? He's walking. They can pick him up on the road."

"Don't. I'm going to have to talk to Arnie and Franklin about what happened, but let's not call the police unless we have to."

"Are you sure?" Dan said, peering into my eyes.

"He wasn't always like this," I said quietly. "Nobody is born that angry; somebody made him that way. I'm not going to let him hurt me or my children, but I don't want to hurt him either. Not unless I have to."

"Well," Dan said, "if he'd taken one more step toward you and Bethany, I'd have no problem hurting him, but I guess this is your call."

He kissed me, and I kissed him back, wanting more but breaking away, feeling Bethany's eyes on us.

Dan ran his hand over my scraggly wet hair. "You're a mess," he said with a soft laugh, and then, "Let's everybody go inside and have some ice cream. We picked up a gallon of chocolate chip on our way home from the bowling alley." He looked back toward the truck. "Bob-O! Bring in that ice cream, will you, buddy?"

Dan bent down and, as big as she was and as soaked as she was, picked Bethany up. She wrapped her arms and legs around him and rested her head on his shoulder. Bobby, who had jumped out of the truck, ran up behind carrying a plastic grocery sack. "Hey! I want a ride too!"

"Not right now," I said. "You'll break poor Dan's back."

"No, he won't," Dan said, and crouched down. "Hop on, buddy!"

Bobby did, scrambling up Dan's back and clinging to him like a baby orangutan. We walked toward the house, Dan lumbering along with his heavy load, his shirt getting soaked from Bethany's sopping hair and swimsuit. I ran ahead to open the screen door for him.

As they walked across the threshold, Bobby, his face beaming, turned back to look at me. "See? He can do it, Mommy! Dan is superstrong!"

"Yes," I said. "Yes, he is."

ᵛᴇᵍ 35 ᵍᴿᵛ

Gayla

Over the following two days, I must have left a dozen messages for Brian, but he didn't return any of my calls.

Obviously, he was angry with me, and really, I couldn't blame him. I wish he had told me the truth about where he was going and why, but I also wish I'd given him the benefit of the doubt before assuming the worst about him. If I had, none of this would have happened. I'd apologized at least ten times via voice mail, once or twice even calling back a second time because I got cut off before I could finish. I think it's really over this time.

I called Libby Burrell and told her to put things on hold for now; I won't be the first one to file. Even so, every time I hear something outside, I think it's someone coming up the driveway to serve me with papers. Nothing so far, but the writing is on the wall. It's just a matter of time.

I called Brian yet again this morning, more from habit than hope. While I was in the middle of the call, I heard a beep, indicating that someone was calling in, and clicked over to answer, hoping that Brian might have seen my name on the screen, relented, and returned my call while I was still leaving a message.

But it wasn't Brian. It was Lanie. As usual, she launched right into her monologue without even saying hello or giving me a chance to get a word in.

"Congratulations," she said. "I'm glad to see you've *finally* come to grips with reality. I know this is hard for you, Gayla, but it's the smart move; it really is. And things will get better with time, you'll see. Say, after you get packed up and back to the city on Friday, why don't you stay with Roger and me for a few days? We've been invited to a party at Josie and Jerry Dane's place on Saturday. You should tag along. Josie's brother is coming. He's head of the derivatives division at Allied National. *Very* handsome and recently divorced, ripe for a rebound."

What? Was she seriously talking about setting me up? I wasn't even divorced yet. I wasn't even in the *process* of getting divorced yet. Okay, it was probably inevitable at this point—I'd said as much to her when we talked the day before—but trying to set me up with single men was jumping the gun and a little insensitive, even for Lanie.

"Lanie. I'm not ready. Really. And it's nice of you to want me to stay with you, but I really just want to get home, unpack, and lie low for a few days. Maybe reorganize my closets. Cleaning always makes me feel better."

"I'm sure it does." She chuckled. "But you can't tear your closets apart right *now*. You've got to keep your place pristine, at least for the next few days. I don't think it'll take longer than that; the market is really heating up. But until then, it'll be easier for you to stay somewhere else."

I shook my head, utterly confused. "What won't take longer than that? Why do I have to keep my place pristine? Lanie, I have no idea what you're talking about."

She sighed impatiently. "I'm *talking* about the apartment."

"The apartment? What about it?"

"Oh, come on, Gayla. You don't need to be coy with me. True, I was a little miffed when I looked through the new listings this morning and saw you'd gone with another Realtor, but I figured that Brian had insisted on using someone else. Men can be so spiteful during a divorce. But who cares? The main thing is to sell your place, find a new one, and make a fresh start."

"Wait a minute," I said, feeling dazed and a little panicky. "Brian listed the apartment for sale?"

"Yes. Didn't he tell you?" She clucked her tongue and said, "I can't believe he did that without telling you. What a louse. Maybe the Realtor was pushing him to get it on the market before the weekend and figured they would get your signature on the paperwork when you got back to town on Friday. Still, they shouldn't do it that way. It's unethical. Be sure to tell Libby about this when you talk to her next.

"I was thinking that we can start looking for new apartments for you over the weekend," she went on. "I already made a couple of appointments for showings, assuming the places I have in mind are still for sale by Saturday. The market is hot again: If you see something you like, you've got to be ready to make an offer that day. It may be a little soon for you, but I spotted this great one-bedroom on East Eighty-sixth—"

"Lanie, I don't think—"

"I know, I know," she said. "It's on the other

side of the city and Eighty-sixth is a high street. But the neighborhood is nice, and the apartment is huge! It's even got a balcony so you can grow some plants if you want."

My head was pounding. I covered my eyes with my hand to shut out the light. "Lanie, I just can't talk about this right now. I have to go. I'll call you later."

"Okay, but don't—"

I hung up the phone without saying good-bye. I couldn't bear to listen to any more.

I went out to the garden and sat down on one of the benches.

The hydrangeas were in full bloom now; the fluffy white flowers, really a congregation of hundreds of smaller blossoms, reminded me of elongated popcorn balls. The butterfly bush, now grown nearly as high as my chest, was blooming, too, the dark-purple blossoms doing their job well, attracting the attention of three beautiful monarch butterflies that flitted languidly from flower to flower, having their fill of sweet nectar.

Though it was only in its first year and the hedges were still stubby, and the roses only just beginning to climb the lattice of the arbor, it was a beautiful garden. I had put a lot of myself into its creation and care. This time next year, it would be more beautiful still, but someone else would be sitting here watching the butterflies.

I hoped they would love it as much as I did.

I heard the sound of a car coming up the driveway. I got to my feet with a certain resignation, thinking that whoever was in the car had come to serve me with divorce papers. But I was wrong.

Philippa had the top down on her red Jetta convertible. She waved to me as she came up the driveway.

She got out of the car and walked toward the garden. "I was hoping to find you at home. You're headed back to New York at the end of the week, right?" She walked beneath the arbor, her shoes making a crunching sound on the pea gravel path. "I just couldn't let you go without saying good-bye. May I?" She tilted her head toward the bench.

"Is this an official visit?" I asked, looking at her white clerical collar.

"Well, I thought I'd dress for the occasion."

I scooted over to make room for her.

"Tessa said that you weren't in the mood to see anyone, but that was a few days ago. I thought you might need someone to talk to about now."

She was right.

After my conversation with Lanie, I knew there was nothing I could do to prevent the divorce, so I wasn't looking for anyone's advice. At this point, it was what it was. But I did feel the need to process the events that had brought us here and come to grips with my role in that. I wanted, in short, to make my confession.

And when I had finished, Philippa asked, "Do you believe you truly forgave Brian?"

I took in a big breath and let it out again, considering her question. "No. I *said* I did. I think I even believed I had. But no. Everything was fine as long as Brian was nearby, taking me to dinner, coming up every weekend, picking up the phone ten times a day, so I knew exactly where he was every second, but the minute he was out of my sight, I was sure he was back to his old tricks. I was an idiot."

"No, you weren't," Philippa replied. "Brian had given you cause for suspicion before. It was perfectly reasonable and right for you to feel the need to keep tabs on him at first. Gayla, you wouldn't be human—or very smart—if his behavior hadn't raised some red flags in your mind," she said, twisting slightly on the bench so she could look me in the eye.

"Contrary to the old adage, forgiveness *doesn't* mean forgetting or turning a blind eye. In some instances, doing so can actually mean enabling someone to engage in unethical or sinful behavior, which can be a kind of sin unto itself. Jesus told us to be as wise as serpents and as innocent as doves."

I lifted my brows and gave her a skeptical look. She laughed.

"Yeah, I know. That's a tough one to get your head around. My point is, when we truly forgive another person, we don't pretend that nothing happened. We just choose to believe the best about them until we're faced with proof of the worst."

"I wish I'd done that with Brian," I said, giving a heavy sigh. "If I had brought my suspicions to him right away and asked him what was going on, we wouldn't be halfway to divorce court now. Of course, I'd still have chewed him out for not telling me the truth from the start," I said, still irritated that he hadn't done so.

"And you'd have been justified," Philippa said evenly. "You deserve complete honesty from Brian, just as he does from you. That has to be a nonnegotiable for the two of you."

"Yeah. I'll remember that next time," I said, unable to keep the bitterness from my voice. "Not that there's going to *be* a next time. It's too late for us now."

"Well," Philippa said in a regretful tone, "if what you're telling me is accurate, that's probably true. Even so, it's not too late for you to forgive Brian."

I shot her a look. Hadn't she been listening? Brian wouldn't answer my phone calls. He'd put our apartment up for sale.

"My marriage is over," I said. "What's the point?"

"Forgiveness isn't just something you do for someone else," she countered. "It's something you do for yourself as well. Forgiveness has a lot more practical value than most people realize."

Seeing my confusion, she tried to explain.

"In the book of Matthew, there is a parable about a king whose servant has incurred an enormous debt. He owed his master ten thousand talents, which basically translates into hundreds of millions in today's dollars, an astronomical amount. Even so, the king decides to forgive the debt. Why? Because the king is just incredibly noble and selfless? Because he doesn't care about money?"

She looked at me as if she actually thought I might have an answer to this. I gave it my best guess.

"None of the above?"

She smiled. "Right. The king forgives the debt because he knows that there is no way in the world that he can collect on it. Some debts are just too big to be repaid.

"You see," she continued, shifting her weight and pulling one knee up on the bench, "this king was smart enough to realize that if he insisted on repayment, not only would he never live long enough to see the debt satisfied; he would spend the rest of his life worrying and thinking about that debt. By releasing his debtor, wiping the slate clean, he was really releasing himself.

"Brian owes you an unforgivable debt. Nothing he can do or say can wind back the clock or make his offense disappear completely, not even divorce. Even though Brian has done all he can to make things right, he can't. Think about it. What could he possibly do to balance the scales?"

"Nothing," I said softly, letting my gaze drift out over the garden.

"Right. Which means that, finally, logically, the job of forgiveness lies with you. No one else has the power to release this debt."

"How am I supposed to do that?" I said, spreading my hands. "I get it in theory, but how does that really work?"

"It's a process; I can tell you that," she said, tilting her head slightly to one side and giving me a sympathetic look, as if she truly understood the challenge she was putting before me. "When those stray thoughts, doubts, and suspicions come into your head, you have to shout them down, say, 'No. That debt is paid. I'm not going there. I chose forgiveness.' If you do, those thoughts will become less frequent. In time, they'll disappear completely."

"But what if you forgive someone, and then it turns out it was a mistake?" I asked. "What if they go out and make a fool of you again?"

Philippa nodded slowly, her warm brown eyes filled with compassion. "Well, that's what it all comes down to, isn't it? When someone betrays us, we feel like fools, and so we want to hold them accountable to prevent them from doing it again. But the thing is, if someone is determined to betray you, they will, no matter how tightly you hold the reins. Think about it; you were trying your very best to keep tabs on Brian every moment of every day, but it isn't possible, is it? Not for any length of time. And so, the second he slipped from your control, you went into a tailspin, causing yourself all kinds of unnecessary anguish and anxiety. And if it turns out that your forgiveness was undeserved, it only proves that he was the foolish one, not you.

"Don't you see, Gayla?" she asked urgently, leaning toward me. "If you truly release Brian from the burden of a debt he has no possibility of repaying, you're not just freeing him but freeing yourself. There's no profit in doing anything else. Every debt we choose to hold on to actually has a hold on us."

36

Ivy

Bobby crouched over, swung back his ball, released it, and then stood at the end of the alley with his fists clenched and his face clenched, too, waiting for the rattle of pins. Three of the four remaining fell with a clatter, and the last one even swayed a bit, but in the end, it stayed upright.

"Oh, darn it," I mumbled to myself before shouting, "That's okay, sweetie! Good job, Bear!"

Everyone clapped, but Bobby stamped his foot in frustration. Dan came up to pat him on the shoulder, then bent down and said something to him. I couldn't hear him above the voices and applause of tournament spectators and the constant thunder of toppling bowling pins, but whatever it was seemed to help. Smiling, Bobby turned around and gave Dan a high five before they went back to their seats to await the next round.

"So you decided not to try and have his probation revoked?" Evelyn asked before taking a sip from the diet soda Charlie had just brought her.

Margot and Virginia were keeping an eye on the store, but Evelyn and Charlie had come to watch the tournament. Abigail and Franklin were there, too, sitting at the next table with Bethany and Charlie, devouring orders of nachos and mozzarella sticks between rounds. Evelyn, who was watching her weight, decided to sit with me, removed from temptation.

"You know, I thought about it, but in the long run, what would be the point? He'd be out again in a couple of years anyway. And knowing that I'd been responsible for sending him back would only make him angrier and more bitter and, potentially, more of a threat."

"Well, you're a better woman than I am," Evelyn said with a questioning tilt of her head. "If I'd been in your shoes, I'm not sure I could have been so forgiving."

"It's not a matter of forgiveness—not really. I'm just tired of having Hodge's shadow looming over every aspect of our lives. If I sent him back to prison, I'd just spend more years worrying about what would happen when he was released. I don't want to live my life like that anymore, Evelyn. And, honestly, I really believe the agreement we reached will be better and safer for the kids."

"So you actually agreed to meet with him?"

"It was Franklin's idea. I had doubts at first, but I was perfectly safe. Franklin was there, and so were Sheila Fenton and Hodge's probation officer. Hodge wasn't exactly cordial, but he wasn't hostile either, not like he had been. I'm not saying he's suddenly been transformed, but I think he's come to realize that a lot of the misery in his life has been of his own making. You know, he was the one who said he just didn't think it was a good idea for him to stay in New Bern and suggested they find another halfway house for him."

"Really?" Evelyn asked. "That's a surprise."

"I thought so too. The judge had to sign off on it, but they found him a placement in Pennsylvania, far enough away so I don't have to worry about running into him on the street but close enough so he can drive up one Saturday a month to see Bobby. They've also found him a job. He's going to be doing janitorial work in a lab, but if things work out, they could promote him to technician. I think it'll be good for him to work again."

"And Bobby's all right with seeing Hodge? The scene at the house didn't scare him?"

"A little," I admitted. "But he's still interested in continuing the visitations. I'm fine with that as long as they are supervised. Bobby doesn't think of Hodge as a hero figure anymore, but he still wants to know his dad. If that's what he wants, then I don't think I should try to prevent it. In a way, I almost wish Bethany would be willing to do the same thing."

Evelyn, who had been sipping soda through a straw, sputtered when she heard this.

"What?" she gasped, coughing a bit, as if she'd swallowed wrong. "You can't be serious. Why does he deserve any—"

I held up one hand to stop her protests. "Hang on! Hear me out. I'm not thinking about Hodge; I was thinking of Bethany. I honestly think it might help her. When I was sitting across the table from him, for the first time in probably ten years, I wasn't afraid. I realized that he wasn't super-human, a monster who might be lurking around any corner waiting to hurt me. He's just a sad, damaged, and broken man who has no power over me. Not unless I choose to give it to him, and I don't. I can't tell you how freeing that's been."

Finally, Evelyn smiled. "You've certainly come a long way from the timid, secretive lady who came through my door five years ago. You're a tower of strength, Ivy. You really are. I admire you so much."

I laughed and rolled my eyes. "Oh, stop it!"

"No, I mean it," she said. "I think you're amazing. You're going to do great things going forward, Ivy. I just know it. How are things going with the scholarship?"

"I sent in the application, but I won't hear anything for a few months. But," I said, "when I picked up the mail today, there was a letter saying I'd won a twenty-five-hundred-dollar scholarship from another organization. It's not a ton of money, but it'll be enough so I can afford to take two classes this semester instead of one. That is," I said slowly, making my voice a question, "if you wouldn't mind me coming into work half an hour late on Mondays, Wednesdays, and Fridays? I found an early-morning class that I'd like to register for. I can take a shorter lunch hour to make up the time."

"Of course," she said. "Not a problem."

"Thanks."

Evelyn cast a longing glance toward Charlie or, more accurately, his rapidly disappearing order of nachos, then took another sip of soda.

"So how are things going with you and Dan?"

"Fine."

"Fine? I thought you really liked him."

"I do. Probably too much," I said with a sigh. "It's starting to get complicated."

Evelyn laid her hand on my arm. "Do you want to talk about it?"

"With you?"

Evelyn nodded, and I paused for a moment, thinking about how dear she was to me and what good advice she'd given me over the years. If I told her about the depth of my feelings for him and how my desire to be with him was starting to get tangled up with my dreams for the future, she'd probably have something very wise to say about it. But this was something I had to deal with myself. And I planned to, that very day. But nobody else needed to know that. Sometimes, you've just got to go it alone.

"Not really," I said with a little laugh.

Evelyn laughed too. "Fair enough."

Bobby and Dan ended up placing third in the tournament, which was pretty impressive considering Bobby's age. He was the youngest competitor to win a trophy, and since this was his first, he was very excited, already talking about next year's tournament.

I'd made arrangements for the kids to spend the afternoon at Abigail and Franklin's after the tournament. I was going to take Dan out to lunch. There were some things I wanted to get straight with him.

After we said good-bye to the kids, I drove to the Gooseboro Drive-In and ordered deluxe cheeseburgers, fries, and strawberry shakes to go. Then we drove a few more miles up the road to Mount Tom Park and found a table under a tree, close enough to the lake so we could see the water but not so close that the happy shrieks of splashing children would make it hard to talk.

"I'd planned on making us a really fancy picnic," I said apologetically, "but the week kind of got away from me."

"This is perfect," he said, squeezing a tube of ketchup onto his fries. "I love a good burger."

"I know."

Dan took a big bite of his cheeseburger, groaning with pleasure as he chewed. I smiled, dipped a fry into some ketchup, and took a bite, but I really wasn't feeling that hungry. After swallowing and taking a drink of milk shake, Dan looked at me and frowned, a small crease of concern forming between his brows.

"Something on your mind, Ivy? Because I have

the definite feeling that I've been called to a meeting—the kind where they hand you a pink slip."

I pressed my lips together and shook my head, looking away from him to give myself a chance to figure out how to tell him what was on my mind.

"We've had a great summer together," I began. "The kids and me. But especially me. With you, I mean," I stammered, realizing it could have sounded like the kids and I had had a nice summer. "We all liked spending time with you. I think I liked it even more than the kids."

"Uh-huh," Dan said slowly, drawing out the first syllable and clipping off the last, his face somber. "I'm listening."

"What I'm trying to say is, there are things I want to do with my life, things that matter to me. At seventeen, my plans for my life were pretty murky. After I met and married Hodge, they disappeared completely. I sort of submerged my personality into his, trying to be whatever it was I thought would make him happy."

"I'm not Hodge," he said in a low voice, keeping his eyes fixed on mine.

"I know you're not. That's why this is so hard." I looked away for a moment, staring at the blue expanse and collecting my thoughts.

"I really, really want to finish my degree, and I don't want to take ten years to do it. That is

439

hugely important to me. I don't want to let anything get in the way of that. But since meeting you . . . I guess what I'm trying to say is that I'm really confused about my feelings for you."

"I'm not," Dan said, his face as serious as his tone. "I'm not the least bit confused about my feelings for you. I love you. Plain and simple."

His unexpected declaration and the look on his face, that same look that had stolen my breath and knocked the rust from my unused heart on that day in the bowling alley, did it again—took my breath away. But just for a moment.

"You . . . you love me?"

"I do. I've known it ever since our first date. It took me all of five minutes to fall in love with you."

My heart started to race. I felt a flush of heat on my neck and cheeks.

"But I . . . I love you too!"

Dan's sober mask split, revealing an expression of joy, quickly followed by one of confusion.

"You do? Then why are you trying to break up with me?"

"Break up with you?" Now it was my turn to be confused. "I'm not. I was just trying to tell you that I mailed in my application for that scholarship today, the big one, and if I get it, I've definitely decided that I'm going to move to Delaware. But after I graduate, I'm coming right back to New Bern. What I was going to ask you is, if I were to end up going away, would you be willing to sort of . . . wait for me?"

The joyous expression was back. Dan started to laugh, shaking his head back and forth as if he couldn't believe I'd asked such a silly question.

"Well, of course I'll wait for you! I'll wait till hell freezes over if I have to! I'd walk over hot coals for you, Ivy. Don't you know that by now?"

I shook my head and grinned, beaming with happiness. I hadn't known that. But I knew now, and it was the best feeling in the world. I couldn't imagine ever feeling any happier than I did right at that moment.

But before I had a chance to say so, or to kiss him, or to jump into his arms or do any of the things that I felt like doing, he said something that wiped the smile right off my face.

"But why do we need to wait?" he asked, pushing his food to one side and planting both elbows on the table, leaning toward me. "Why don't you just go to college in Connecticut?"

"Because I told you," I said, my emotions swinging from joy to disappointment in the space of a few sentences. "I want to get my degree, and I don't want to take another decade doing it. I do love you, Dan. I love you very much. But I'm not going to abandon everything *I* want out of life. I gave up on myself once; I won't do it again. Not even for you."

"I'm not asking you to," he said urgently,

reaching across the table to grab my hands. "Look, if we were all living in the same house— you, me, Drew, and the kids—our expenses would be a lot less. You wouldn't be paying any rent, and my house is already paid for. You could afford to cut back on your hours at the shop and take more classes. If the scholarship money comes through, you could even go full-time. You wouldn't have to pay for sitters. My business slacks off after Labor Day, so I could pick the kids up from school. Of course, in the summertime I work pretty long days, but you don't take classes then anyway. During the school year, I could take care of everything, even make dinner if you were in class or studying. I'm a pretty decent cook," he said, and then laughed. "Well, good enough. I've been cooking for Drew and me for years. Nobody's gotten ptomaine poisoning so far."

I laughed, too, not because his joke was so funny but because I couldn't believe how lucky I was. A kindhearted, hardworking man, a man who was strong without having to prove it, who looked better in a pair of jeans and a T-shirt than any man I'd ever met, a man who loved my kids and was willing to cook for them and for me, loved me. And I loved him back. I'd tried not to, but in the end, I couldn't help myself. It all would have been so perfect, but for one thing.

"Dan, we can't move in with you. I love you so

much, but the kids . . . they're young and impressionable. And even if they weren't, I wouldn't feel right about us living together."

Dan's brows shot up. "Living together? Ivy, I'm not asking you to move in with me. I'm asking you to marry me."

"Marry you!"

He couldn't be serious. Could he?

On Memorial Day, I hadn't known Dan Kelleher well enough to do more than wave and say hello when I picked Drew up to babysit. It wasn't even Labor Day yet, but he was asking me to marry him. Was that a good idea? Falling in love and getting married were easy enough, but as I'd been reminded only too well over the course of the summer, staying in love and staying married were a lot harder. Any way you sliced it, choosing love was a risk, a big one.

"Dan, we've only known each other for a few weeks. Don't you think this is kind of crazy?"

"Two months," he corrected. "If it'll make you feel better, we can have a long engagement. We could get married at Christmas."

"Christmas! That's only four months away!"

"Right. Which means we'll have known each other for three times as long as we do now."

He reached for my hand. "Ivy, I know you're scared. I know that you've been burned before; we both have. But that was a long time ago. We were so young that we didn't really know what we were getting ourselves into. But we do now. We're old enough to know what love looks like and acts like and that even when you are in love, marriage is hard and that you've got to work at it. We know that even when you do that, there are no guarantees. Marriage is a risk. But it's a risk I'm willing to take, Ivy. Because I'm old enough now to know what I want, and it's you."

Dan swung his legs over the picnic bench, got to his feet, and walked around to my side of the table. I twisted my body to the side, watching as he sank down on one knee and took both my hands in his.

"Ivy, I want to spend the rest of my life getting to know you, but even if I spent the next fifty years doing that, I wouldn't be any more sure than I am right this second. You are the woman for me, the only woman I do love and will love for the rest of my life. We can wait for the wedding if that's what you want. But please, say yes. Say that you'll marry me."

There it was again, the look of love that beamed straight into my heart, the look I beamed right back to him, the one that brought tears of happiness to my eyes and stole my breath. And my reason. But not for long.

Was this crazy? Maybe. But I knew what I wanted now, and the truth of it was, I *had* wanted it almost from the moment Mandy blew that stupid whistle and Dan refused to budge from my table. I hadn't been willing to admit it before, not even to myself, but that was the moment I fell in love with him. And as long as I was being honest with myself . . .

"Yes, Dan," I whispered. "Oh, yes! I've never wanted anything more in my life."

❧ 37 ☙

Gayla

After my talk with Philippa, I decided to go back to the city a day earlier than I'd planned. If Brian wouldn't take my calls, I'd just have to talk to him in person. I got up early the next morning and drove to Manhattan. When I pulled into the garage, Marcus, the parking attendant, smiled and said, "Hey! Mrs. Oliver! Good to see you. Where've you been all these weeks?"

"Good to see you too, Marcus. I spent the summer in Connecticut."

"That's nice. Pretty up there, with the trees and all. Cooler too." He shook his head and pulled at his collar. "Jeez, but it's been hot."

I had a similar conversation with Henry, the doorman.

"Well, I'm glad you're back, Mrs. Oliver."

"Thanks, Henry," I said, walking through the open door.

Henry frowned. "Um . . . Mrs. Oliver? Are you thinking about going to your apartment?"

"Yes," I answered, surprised by his question. "I'm looking for Mr. Oliver."

"He left about half an hour ago."

"Did he say where he was going?"

"No, ma'am. But I put a couple of big suit-cases in the trunk of his rental car."

My heart sank. Brian always used big suitcases if he was going to be gone longer than a few days. Two suitcases could mean he'd be gone anywhere from a couple of weeks to a couple of months. I'd missed him and there was no telling when he'd be back. Or if he'd be back.

"I see. Well, I'll just go upstairs and wait for him."

"Oh, you can't do that, Mrs. Oliver!" Henry ducked his head, embarrassed. "I mean, you can. It's still your apartment, but there's a Realtor up there. Actually, it's your friend, Ms. Micelli."

"Lanie is upstairs?"

"Yeah. She's showing the apartment. Took a young couple up there right after Mr. Oliver left. Gee, I'm really sorry to see you go. You and Mr. Oliver are two of my favorite residents. Nicest couple in the building."

"Thanks, Henry."

I went into the lobby and stood awkwardly in front of the elevators, trying to decide if I should go upstairs and go home, or wait down here until

446

these intruders, and my best friend, vacated the premises. I knew Lanie was just trying to do her job, but it seemed a little macabre to me, like proposing to a widow during her husband's funeral.

After three minutes of loitering and indecision, I decided to go upstairs. After all, it was still my apartment. At least for now.

I pressed the up button and waited for the doors to open. When they did, Lanie was inside, flanked by a young couple in their early thirties. The woman looked very pregnant and very excited. Her husband looked excited too.

"It's perfect! I love everything about it!" she gushed as they stepped outside.

Lanie gave me a quick wink as she passed by with her clients. The elevator doors closed, and the car left without me.

"Three bedrooms!" the mother-to-be exclaimed. "Three! We'll have a separate room for the baby plus a guest room. My mother will be able to come from Michigan to visit!"

The husband pretended to frown. "Hmm . . . maybe we'd better rethink this."

"Very funny," his wife said, then turned back to Lanie. "So do you think they'll be willing to close quickly? I really want to move in before the baby is born."

"With the right offer," Lanie said confidently, "anything is possible. Matt? Are you as excited as Amy is? Ready to make an offer?"

"Definitely," he said, putting his arm around his bride. "Amy's right. It'll be perfect for us."

"Great!" Lanie enthused. "I've got to take a short meeting. You two go grab some lunch, then meet me back at the office." Lanie looked at her diamond-encrusted wristwatch. "Let's say one fifteen. Don't forget to bring your checkbook."

After escorting the young couple out of the building, Lanie turned around. "Did you see that? I just sold your apartment, probably for full price. Yes. I am *that* good!"

Grinning, she walked toward me with open arms. "Darling! It's so good to see you!" she exclaimed, giving me a hug. "You've lost weight, haven't you? You look great! See? There *is* an upside to divorce. But I thought you weren't coming back until tomorrow. I cleared my whole day so I could drive up and help you close the house. You didn't do it all by yourself, did you?"

"No, I'm putting that off for a couple of days. I came home to talk to Brian."

The bow of Lanie's lips flattened into a disapproving line. "Gayla. Darling. *Don't* debase yourself by trying to beg him. You've got to face facts. Your apartment just sold. It's over; Brian doesn't want you anymore. If you try to chase after him, you'll just end up looking pathetic."

"Thank you, Lanie, for that reminder."

"Hey!" she said, raising her hands. "Don't get mad at me. I'm on your side."

"Yeah? Well, sometimes you make it kind of hard to remember that."

Lanie scowled, her expression a mixture of anger and confusion. "That's not fair. What the hell is wrong with you anyway? I'm just trying to help."

"Are you? Then start by being a little more supportive. Not treating me like an idiot would be good too."

I didn't even mention the part about not being quite so gleeful about selling my home out from under me. She wouldn't have understood what I was talking about.

"I didn't come down here to chase after Brian," I said. "It's too late to salvage things; I know that. But I really wanted to talk to him before the lawyers start piling on and things get ugly. I wanted to tell him that I forgive him, once and for all and completely. And I wanted to ask him to forgive me for suspecting him even before I had proof."

"You can*not* be serious." Lanie threw out her hands in exasperation. "Did you talk to Libby about this? You can't have that conversation with Brian, Gayla. Not now. Trust me; that's the kind of thing he'll end up using against you. I know you're not over him yet, but you've got to start thinking of Brian as the enemy."

"Brian was *never* my enemy," I spat. "Divorce or no divorce, he never will be."

She rolled her eyes. "Okay, fine. He's not your enemy. And if you bare your soul to him, he won't think of using that against you. Because men *never* do that," she said in a drippingly sarcastic tone. "If you do this," she said, pointing a finger at my face, "you are going to end up looking like a fool."

"Maybe. And if that's true, so be it. But I'm not going to spend the rest of *my* life steeped in bitterness and anger, Lanie."

She pointed her finger at me again, stabbing it directly toward the bridge of my nose. "Stop it. I know you're upset, but I've had just about enough. I am *not* bitter—"

I talked right over her, ignoring her commentary. I really didn't care about Lanie's wounded pride, not at that moment. "And let me tell you something else, Lanie. If there was ever a man worth making a fool of yourself over, then Brian is that man."

"You're an idiot," she spat. "You always were. Even back in college. And I was an idiot for ever taking you on and trying to make something of you. Waste of time. Well," she said in a clipped tone, "I've learned my lesson. I'm done here, Gayla. Good-bye. And good luck."

She turned around and walked away, her heels echoing against the lobby's marble floors as she strode toward the glass doors. "You're going to need it," she called over her shoulder. "Let's just see how you do without any friends to help you."

Henry, who was standing out on the street, opened the door. Lanie marched through it and took a right turn down the sidewalk.

As I watched her disappear from sight, I was filled with relief but also with regret. I had known Lanie a long time, even longer than Brian. There was no way I wouldn't miss her, but she was wrong about me. I wouldn't be without friends. For the first time in my life, I understood what real friendship looked like.

Though it was still early afternoon, I decided not to drive back to New Bern that day. I'd sleep in my apartment that night. Who knew how many more opportunities I'd have to do so?

It was funny to be back home after so many weeks away. Everything was almost exactly as I'd left it. It felt like an exhibition in a museum dedicated to the life I used to live.

My desk was just as disorganized and messy as it had been on the day I'd fled the apartment in an anguished panic with nothing besides my keys, not realizing I'd be gone for nearly three months. In the bedroom, I found the clothes I'd folded on the morning of my departure still sitting on top of the dresser, waiting to be put away. The novel I'd been reading was still sitting on the night-stand, a dog-eared fold marking the place I'd left off, a pair of purple-rimmed reading glasses lying beside it.

Apparently it hadn't occurred to Brian, and obviously it hadn't stood in the way of incurring the sale, but if I'd been home and trying to show the apartment, there would have been vases of fresh flowers on the tables and a bowl of fruit on the kitchen counter. Every surface would have been cleared of clutter and the least indication that actual human beings occupied this space. I'd have tried to make it look like the world people imagine they'd like to inhabit, instead of the one they actually did.

Instead, the rooms looked completely authentic, almost painfully so. But walking through them didn't upset me as much as I had supposed it might. There were things that brought a smile to my face or made me feel wistful, pictures and little artifacts of our family history, items that I would want to take with me when I left. But I didn't feel as connected to the space as I once had. They were just rooms now, and the memories I had created there, the good and bad, would be boxed up and brought with me when I departed, the same way I would bring along the furniture and photos and bed linens.

This wasn't home to me, I realized. Not anymore. My heart belonged to a more northern latitude now. How odd.

I went back into the bedroom to put away

the stack of folded clothing. As I opened the drawer, I heard a noise coming from the living room.

"Brian?" I called. "Is that you?"

I walked through the bedroom door and met him coming down the hallway. Seeing my face, he did a double take.

"Gayla? What are you doing here?"

"I came to see you. There was something I wanted to tell you, but Henry said you'd left, carrying a couple of suitcases. Guess you're planning on being gone for a while." I swallowed and tried to force a smile. There was no point in giving in to tears.

"Well, yes. I had to run some errands, and then I was going to head out of town, but before I got to the bridge, I thought of one more place where I might have left my phone, so I decided to come back and take another look."

"Your phone?"

"I lost it a couple of days ago, looked everywhere for it. Or so I thought. Turns out it was right where I left it: in the freezer." He pulled his phone from his pants pocket. Sure enough, it was coated with a glaze of white and starting to drip. "I suspect it's a goner," he said.

Even in these circumstances, it was impossible to keep from chuckling a little. I mean, honestly. Who leaves their phone in the freezer?

"Brian, how did you ever think to . . . You know

what? Never mind," I said, realizing there were more important questions on my mind. "Did you get any of my phone messages?"

"I did, a couple of them. I'm sorry, Gayla. I should have called you back. I intended to, but there were some things I needed to attend to before I was ready to do that. As a matter of fact, I was on my way to New Bern when I remembered the phone and the freezer. I thought we should sit down and talk. It isn't the sort of thing you discuss on the phone."

He had planned to come up and see me face-to-face? That was decent of him.

"I know," I said. "You've listed the apartment and you need my signature on the paperwork. I think it sold already. The couple Lanie brought over loved it. They're probably in her office right now, writing up an offer."

"Really?" he asked, looking a bit shocked. "That was fast."

I nodded. "They're pushing for a quick occupancy. I'd planned on staying here for a few weeks to sort myself out, but maybe I'll have to check into a hotel. Unless I'm lucky enough to find a perfect apartment quickly. Doesn't seem likely, though. I just fired my Realtor. Or maybe she fired me. I'm not sure. It doesn't matter. . . ."

Brian shook his head back and forth violently, as if he was trying to clear water from his ears.

"I'm sorry, but . . . Gayla . . . what are you talking about?"

"About Lanie." I sighed. "We had a falling-out. I think the damage is beyond repair."

Brian screwed his eyes shut and held up his hand, as if trying to block out the sound of my voice. "No! Not that. I don't give a damn about Lanie. What was it you were saying about finding a new apartment?"

"Just that I'll need to do it soon. I've got to live someplace after the divorce."

His eyebrows shot up. "Do you think I'm filing for divorce?"

"Well, yes. Aren't you?"

"No. I don't want a divorce. Do you?"

My throat felt so tight that, for a moment, it was hard to speak. I shook my head. "No," I said. "I never did. Not really."

Brian took in a breath and let it out again, then smiled. "Good. I'm glad."

He opened his arms, and I fell into them. He held me tight, smoothing his hand over my hair as I blinked back tears of relief and happiness.

"But why were you coming to New Bern to see me?" I asked once I'd gotten hold of myself. "What was so important that you couldn't discuss it on the phone?"

"Right. I almost forgot. Come on," he said, taking my hand. "Let's find a place to sit down and talk."

We were nearest to the bedroom, so Brian led me through the door, and we both sat down on the bed, pulling up a leg so we could face each other. Then Brian started telling me his story.

"Today's trip to New Bern would have been my third this week," he said. "I've driven up twice to interview for a job."

"What kind of job could you find in New Bern?" I asked skeptically. "It's not exactly the commerce capital of the world."

"No, it's not," he said. "But I'm rather over commerce at this point, and as Mike Barrows made clear to me only days ago, the world of commerce seems to be over me as well. I'm looking for something a little calmer, something with a little less pressure that will allow me to spend a *lot* more time with you. And, just as importantly something I'll actually enjoy and feel good about."

I gave him a doubtful look. "And you think you'll be able to find something like that in New Bern."

"No," he said, looking just a teeny bit self-satisfied, "I *have* found something like that in New Bern, something exactly like that. You know the music store, the one on the highway?"

I nodded. "The one with the manager who talks like he's been to a few too many Grateful Dead concerts? Yes. What about it?"

"Well, it seems that the owner has decided to sell it. And I've decided to buy it. At least, I hope to, if it's all right with you. That's what I was driving up to discuss."

My jaw went slack; this was the last thing I'd been expecting. My former audio-industry-executive husband, who had traveled the world and pulled together mergers worth hundreds of millions of dollars, wanted to sell sheet music and harmonicas in Connecticut? The look on his face said that he did, that he was actually pretty excited about the prospect.

"Well," I said slowly, giving myself a chance to regain my mental equilibrium, "I guess so, sweetheart. If that's what you really want to do. But, Brian, does that store make any money? I never see anyone parked in front of it. Those strings I bought for my guitar had cobwebs on them, they'd been sitting on the shelf so long."

"It doesn't make a dime," he confirmed. "In fact, it loses money. But I've looked at the books, done a bit of research, and I think it has potential. Don't get me wrong—we'd never get rich owning that store—"

"That's okay." I shrugged. "I never wanted to be rich."

"That's good," he said, laughing, "because it's never going to happen. But I don't want to go broke either. So I've worked out a deal with the owner.

"He's going to hire me as the manager for one year. I'll have complete control over every-thing—inventory, advertising, lesson offerings, and schedules. I plan to teach the guitar classes myself. If, at the end of that year, I'm able to bring the business at least to the break-even point, then I'll buy it. There's no real risk for me. We've agreed upon a sale price and will put it in writing, so he won't be able to jack it up after I turn things around. I do have to put down a deposit of forty thousand earnest money that will be held in escrow. But, if I change my mind, I'll get it all back less twenty-five hundred. I can walk away free, more or less whole."

"And the owner has agreed to all this? He's willing to put it in writing? How were you able to get such good terms?"

"Number one, because he knows he'll never be able to sell the place. Who besides me would be interested? And number two, because your husband is a shrewd negotiator. Had to pick up something doing acquisitions for three years, didn't I?"

"Brian! That's brilliant!"

"Do you really think so?" he asked, a note of caution in his voice. "We'd have to sell the apartment to pull it off. The severance will make up for the loss of my income while I'm trying to bring the store into the black, but after that, we'll need money for the deposit, too, and some working capital. Selling the apartment would give us that, plus a bit of a financial cushion going forward. I didn't expect to get an offer on the apartment so soon, but we don't have to accept if you don't want to. I know you love this building and the neighborhood."

"What I'll love is being with you," I said, bending my head forward, touching my forehead to his. "And New Bern is a wonderful place to live. I love it there."

"But you love New York, too. And what about your business? And your clients?"

His concern for my happiness was genuine and so touching. I knew that he very much wanted to buy that store, but I also knew he wouldn't unless he was completely convinced that I was on board.

Was I? Apart from the pleasure of seeing Brian happy, was I truly ready for such a big change?

I put my hand to my mouth, gnawing on the edge of my thumbnail as I thought it through. "I do love New York," I mused. "There's no city quite like it. But I could come in on the train once a week or so to see people. Most of my client contact is on the phone anyway. I'm sure I can find new clients in New Bern too. I'd like to start working with kids from more modest financial circumstances, kids like Drew Kelleher, people who deserve a little help. I probably wouldn't be able to charge as much, but money isn't everything. There's a lot to be said for working where you're needed."

I took my hand from my mouth and placed it in Brian's. "I think you should do it," I said. "I think this is a really good idea—for both of us."

His face lit up. He looked so excited, like a boy who'd been handed his first set of car keys. "Do you? Oh, Gayla. That's wonderful!"

He lifted my hand to his lips and then lowered it and moved in to kiss me, but I pulled back.

"Just a minute, sweetheart. You got to tell me what was on your mind, but I didn't get to do the same, not really." Brian sat up and scooted back a little, indicating that he was ready to listen. "Before I drove down here, I had a talk with Philippa, the minister, about forgiveness. And what I wanted to say was—"

Brian lifted his hand and placed his fingers on my lips, ending my explanation. "Gayla, let's make a deal. Instead of going through yet another course of apologies, why don't we agree to wipe the slate clean, forgive each other for any of our past transgressions, be completely honest with each other from here on out, no matter what, and love each other madly until the day we die. Is that something you could live with? Because I think it would work for me."

I smiled. "You're a pretty tough negotiator. But I think I can manage that."

He leaned toward me, and this time, I let him kiss me. When we broke apart he said, "Are you hungry? I'll take you out to lunch, so we can seal the bargain."

"What if we seal the bargain right here instead?" I pulled him down on the bed with me and whispered in his ear, "Lanie says that makeup sex is amazing. Let's see if she's right."

⚜ 38 ⚜

Gayla

Labor Day was beautiful, bright and clear without a cloud in the sky. The last of my tomatoes were ripe on the vine, and the garden had never looked better. The heads of the hydrangea flowers were blushing pink now and so heavy that the branches holding them bowed toward the ground.

When I came out of the house, carrying a bowl of potato salad to go with the hamburgers and chicken, the children were playing hide-and-seek, the men were standing around the grill holding cans of cold beer, watching Brian turn over the meat, and the women, who had been sitting in lawn chairs under the shade of the biggest maple, talking and laughing while they stitched on their crazy quilts, were now on their feet, clustered around Ivy, chattering excitedly. I left the potato salad on the table and went to see what the commotion was about.

"Oh, it's lovely! I'm so glad you finally found one you liked," I said when Ivy showed me her ring, a white gold engagement ring crafted in a circular floral design with a round-cut diamond in the center and six smaller stones set into the surrounding leaves. "I've never seen anything quite like it. Where did you find it?"

"At Lipscomb's, the estate jewelry shop on Commerce," she answered. She rocked her hand so the sunlight filtering through the leaves caught in the facets of the diamonds, making them sparkle. "It's vintage. Mr. Lipscomb said that it had belonged to a woman who was married for seventy years. Her son didn't have any children to pass it on to, so he brought it into the shop and asked Mr. Lipscomb to sell it to a nice young couple and that he hoped whoever bought it would be as happy as his mom and dad had been."

Ivy looked up. Her face was glowing. "When I heard that, I knew this was the ring for me. I just love it."

Margot squeezed Ivy. "I'm so happy for you!" she exclaimed. "Have you picked a date yet?"

Ivy bobbed her head. "December twentieth. It's only five days after the end of classes, so I'll have to scramble a little to get everything ready in time, but we'll manage. It was either that or wait until school ends in May, and Dan didn't want to wait that long. Neither did I," she said with a smile. "It's not going to be a big ceremony, but you're all invited, so mark your calendars. Evelyn and Bethany will be bridesmaids, Drew and Bobby will be the best men—we decided to have two—and Philippa is going to officiate."

"That's right," she said. "I'm going to have some fancy new vestments for the occasion. Virginia is going to make me a quilted clerical stole."

"Be sure and let me know as soon as you pick your colors," Virginia said to Ivy. "I want Philippa's stole to match the flowers."

"Oooh!" Margot enthused, hugging Ivy again. "A Christmas wedding! How romantic. I hope it snows. That would be just beautiful."

"Where are you going on the honeymoon?" I asked.

"Disney World."

Abigail shot Ivy a disdainful look. "Disney World. Aren't you and Dan a bit old for that? Florida is very nice in winter, I'm sure, but why not Miami or West Palm? Or even St. Augustine?"

"We're taking the kids," Ivy explained. "After all, it'll be Christmas. We can't very well leave them home, and we wouldn't want to. Besides, I've never been to Disney World. It'll be fun."

"Very romantic, I'm sure," Abbie mumbled under her breath.

Evelyn, ever the diplomat, gave Abigail a nudge with her elbow and changed the subject.

"When are you and Brian leaving for Italy? It's coming up soon, isn't it?"

"On the fourteenth," I said. "I can't wait! We'll be gone for two weeks and come back at the end of the month. Brian's been going into the music store to train with the owner, but he won't really take over until we return. I've got a ton to do between now and then. I took on two new clients, both from New Bern, and I've got to plant all those bulbs I ordered. As usual," I said, giving Tessa a look, "I got a little carried away."

Tessa laughed. "Sister, you're singing my song."

"Oh!" Ivy exclaimed. "I've been meaning to ask you. Do you think Brian would be willing to play his guitar and sing at the wedding?"

"You'll have to ask him," I said, glancing toward Brian, who was frantically spraying water onto a flaming hamburger as Charlie looked on with alarm. "But I'm sure he'd love to. He's very talented."

With the burgers done—more like well-done—everyone gathered around the table and started filling their plates. Though I'd told them it wasn't necessary, the women had brought food anyway, so in addition to the burgers, chicken, potato salad, green salad, and strawberry shortcake, we had baked beans, corn salad, cucumber salad, carrot cake, and brownies. The table was positively groaning.

Though I waited until everyone else was served before getting a plate for myself, there was still enough food to feed a marine battalion. I'd just put a spoonful of corn salad onto my plate when I noticed someone was missing.

"Dan, where did Drew run off to? Isn't he hungry?"

"Drew is always hungry," he assured me as he shared a bite of brownie with Ivy. They were so adorable together. "He had to run back to the house and check something in his e-mail. Don't worry. He'll be back in a minute."

He was, emerging from the swath of trees that separated our two properties, now so thick you really couldn't see past them, and then loping across the lawn with an enormous grin on his face.

Dan twisted around in his lawn chair when he saw his son approaching. "Well? How were they?"

"Two hundred and thirty points better than last time," he reported with pride. "Mrs. Oliver, it looks like I owe you twenty dollars."

"Your SAT scores! Oh, Drew, that's wonderful! Congratulations!" I whooped and threw my arms around him. He blushed a bit but submitted to my embrace. Such a sweet kid.

"Can I pay you next week, Mrs. Oliver? I'm a little short right now."

"Oh, Drew. That bet was just a joke. You don't owe me anything."

"But I want to," he insisted.

"Tell you what," I said, handing him a paper plate and some silverware, "why don't we take it out in trade. Come over and weed the garden for me while we're in Italy. I don't want to come back and find it all overgrown."

"No problem," he said. "I'll stop by every day after school."

"Thanks, Drew. That'd be a big help."

People lingered through the afternoon, returning to the table again and again to refill their plates or take another can of beer or soda from the cooler, and then returning to the shade of the trees, choosing a different lawn chair, and sitting down next to someone new to catch up with an old friend or get to know a new one.

When the sun began to set and the crickets started to chirp and fireflies started to appear, skipping like fairies through the air, people packed up their loved ones and covered dishes, kissed and hugged, said their good-byes and reminded one another that quilt circle wasn't canceled just because it was a holiday week, then headed for home. Brian and I stood in the driveway, waving as the last set of taillights disappeared behind the privet hedge, then went back into the house to wrap the leftover food and wash the serving dishes that my friends had helped carry inside before departing.

Brian sat on his haunches in front of the open refrigerator, trying to find a space to stow the leftover baked beans. "That was a good party," he said. "Really good. Usually with a group that large, you're going to find at least two or three people you don't care for, but they were all very nice. Interesting too. Of course"—he chuckled—"Charlie gave me a bit of gas about burning the meat and being British. He said his blessed mother back in Ireland would turn in her grave if she knew he was consorting with an Englishman."

Brian shoved the bean bowl onto a shelf and closed the door quickly before it had a chance to fall. I rinsed soap off a platter and made a mental note to be very careful when opening the refrigerator door again.

"He's an odd duck," Brian continued, "but I like him. I like all of them."

"So do I. Sweetheart, could you go into the linen closet and get me some more dish towels? This one is so wet I think I'm just moving the water around."

"Sure. Be right back."

A minute later, I heard Brian calling me from the hallway but couldn't make out what he was saying.

"Can't you find them?" I shouted. "They're

on the right side of the shelf, next to my fabric. Do you see them?" I waited a moment, sighed, and wiped my hands on my jeans. "If it was a snake . . . ," I mumbled, walking across the kitchen.

He met me at the door, carrying two terry-cloth dish towels and the remains of my ravaged quilt top.

"What happened here?" he asked, holding up the quilt to display the enormous tear down the sashing and another along the border.

"Oh. That." I cleared my throat. "That happened a couple of weeks ago. It's supposed to be your birthday present, but I had a bit of a meltdown. I was out of teacups."

He frowned, giving me a quizzical look. I took the dish towels from his hand, draped the torn quilt over the back of a chair, and went back to the sink.

Brian walked over to the chair. "So it's ruined? That's too bad," he said, looking down at the ragged red edges. "I like these colors."

I smiled and wiped water from the platter. "Not ruined," I said. "It can be repaired."

"How?" he asked doubtfully, reaching out to touch the rent patches. "It's a mess."

I put the platter back in the cupboard and came up behind him, wrapping my arms around his waist and laying my head between his shoulders. "I know, but the tears are only along the seams.

The fabric itself is still strong. I can sew it together again. And by the time I'm finished, it'll be just as good as it was before, maybe even better."

Brian turned to face me, draping his arms over my shoulders.

"Are you sure?"

I rose on my toes, wrapped my arms around his neck, and kissed him.

"I'm sure," I said. "I'm absolutely sure."

Discussion Questions

1. When Gayla Oliver learns that her husband, Brian, has had an affair, she points out that when the gossip mills start churning in the wake of marital infidelity, someone always says, "Well, she *must* have known. Down deep, she had to have at least *suspected*." Do you agree with that statement? Do you believe people with cheating spouses actually know what is going on at some level but choose to look the other way? Or do you think, as Gayla does, this is something that people say to make themselves feel more secure in their own relationships? Or does the truth lie somewhere in between?

2. Gayla learns about Brian's affair and unhappiness in their marriage when she stumbles upon a memo he wrote to her but failed to send. Why do you think he did that? If he changed his mind about divorce and never intended for her to see the memo, why do you think he never deleted it? And why, if he was so unhappy, didn't he simply speak to her about their problems? Was the memo his way of sorting out his thoughts and desires? Or avoiding them?

3. Ivy Peterman is distressed when she learns that, according to the law, her abusive ex-husband, Hodge, who is soon to be released from prison, has a right to be reunited with his children. What do you think of these types of laws? Should parents with records of abuse be allowed contact with their children? Never? Sometimes? Only in certain circumstances? In these instances, should children have a right to refuse to see their parents? If so, at what age and under what circumstances?

4. In spite of an understandable wariness about entering into a new relationship, Ivy, after spending so many years alone, decides to give speed dating a try. If you've been married or in an exclusive relationship for a very long time, how do you think you'd feel about dating again? Do you think the process of meeting new romantic partners is something that would be fun? Anxiety producing? Something that you'd never do in a million years? If you're on the dating scene now or have been in the past couple of years, what do you think is the best way to meet new people? And for everyone, can you recall the best date you've ever been on? The worst?

5. Looking for a way to explain her sudden appearance in New Bern without giving away

too much about her personal life, Gayla tells Tessa and the other women of the Cobbled Court Quilt Circle that she is taking a "sabbatical" and using the time to try things she's always wanted to do but has never found the time for. What about you? If you could take a sabbatical from everyday life, what things would you want to try? Would you take up a new hobby or sport? Take an exotic vacation? Go back to school?

6. Think about the list you created in response to the previous question. Obviously, there may be financial, vocational, or lifestyle factors that would keep you from taking up some of those activities now, but can you also identify items on the list that you could try now or in the near future? What obstacles are standing in your way? Can you think of ways to overcome those obstacles? Are you ready to do so?

7. In the story, Gayla has to wrestle with a very fundamental question: Is it possible for a marriage to survive in the aftermath of infidelity? Gayla's friend Lanie says no, asserting that a man who cheats once will cheat again. Brian, Gayla's husband, says yes, believing that they can work through their problems and give the marriage a second

chance. Gayla isn't so sure. What do you think? In cases of infidelity, is divorce the best or only option? Why? Or do you believe that couples should stay together no matter what, even if one of them has been unfaithful? Or do you believe that, when somebody cheats, the couple should stay together only under certain conditions? What are they?

8. Overwhelmed by emotions she seems unable to control, Gayla stumbles upon an unusual but effective method for dealing with her anger—smashing dishes against a stone wall. What do you do when you're angry or frustrated? How is that working for you? Do you think there could be a more constructive way of handling your emotions?

9. Gayla and Brian originally bought the cottage in New Bern because they hoped it would give them a means of staying connected as a couple during a challenging season in their careers. While it didn't work out the way they'd hoped, at least not at first, it wasn't necessarily a bad idea. What about you? Do you and your spouse or partner have a special place you like to go together? Some place that helps you clear your heads and reconnect romantically?

10. When Brian suggests dating as a means of healing their broken relationship, Gayla is skeptical but grudgingly decides to go along with his plan, quickly realizing that she doesn't know her husband as well as she thought she did. If you've been married or in a relationship for a long time, what suggestions do you have for keeping the interest and romance alive for the long haul?

11. Gayla knows that if she hopes to repair her broken marriage, she has to find a way to forgive Brian, but it isn't easy. When someone we love hurts us deeply, it can be very hard to move past the hurt and truly forgive. Some people, like Lanie, would say it's impossible, even foolish, and that people who do so are just setting themselves up to be hurt again. On the other hand, Philippa believes forgiving is the only way to free ourselves from the worry and anxiety of past hurts, telling Gayla that, "every debt we choose to hold on to actually has a hold on us." What do you think? Do you agree with Lanie? Or with Philippa? This may not be an answer you wish to share with the group, but did reading the story remind you of any half-healed hurts in your own life? Is there some-one you need to forgive? What

difference would it make in your life if you were able to do that? Or perhaps you've realized that there is someone of whom you need to ask forgiveness. Are you ready to do so?

Dear Readers,

Greetings!

Allow me to begin this note by saying "thank you!" It is because of your ongoing support and encouragement and your love of these characters that the Cobbled Court Quilts books, which began with what I thought was a stand-alone story, have grown into a six-novel series. Six! When I say I could never have done it without you, I'm not exaggerating, just stating the facts. My readers are just the best!

In the digital age, there are more ways for you and me to keep in contact than ever before. You can follow me on Twitter, Pinterest, and Facebook. (If you're looking for me on Facebook, please "like" my fan page. I post there almost every day.) You can also contact me via e-mail; just go to www.mariebostwick.com and write to me via the contact form. And, of course, you can always pick up a pen and write to me via snail mail at . . .

Marie Bostwick
Box 488
Thomaston, CT 06787

It is such a joy for me to hear from you! Please know that I do read all my mail personally and that everyone who contacts me will receive a response.

The quilters among you will be happy to hear that, once again, my dear friend, partner in crime, and fellow fabric enabler, Deb Tucker, has created a beautiful companion quilt pattern for this book. This pattern, as well as the five patterns from previous books, are available as free downloads *only* to those who have registered on my Web site. If you haven't yet registered, just go to www.mariebostwick.com, click on the "Register/ Login" link in the upper-left-hand corner of the home page, and fill in and submit the registration form. Please know that we won't share your per-sonal information with anyone and that registered readers will receive my monthly newsletter.

Also, in addition to the free downloadable patterns, Deb Tucker has designed several full-sized companion patterns to go with my books—including "Deep in the Heart," from *Between Heaven and Texas*; "Garden Dance," from *Ties That Bind*; "Providence," from *Threading the Needle*; "Star-Crossed Love," from *A Thread So Thin*; and a new, as-yet-unnamed pattern from *Apart at the Seams*—which are available for purchase from Deb's Web site:

http://www.studio 180design.net.

Again, thank you so much for picking up this copy of *Apart at the Seams*. I hope you get as much pleasure from reading this book as I did from writing it. Maybe even more!

Blessings,

Marie Bostwick

Center Point Large Print
600 Brooks Road / PO Box 1
Thorndike ME 04986-0001 USA

(207) 568-3717

US & Canada:
1 800 929-9108
www.centerpointlargeprint.com

2 1982 02843 4821